The Osiris Revelations

AJ Marshall

MPress books

First published in 2005 by M*Press*

This edition first published in 2006 by M*Press*

British Library Cataloguing in Publication Data
A catalogue record for this book is available from the
British Library.

ISBN

0-9551886-0-1

978-0-9551886-0-2

Typeset in Minion
Origination by Core Creative,
Yeovil 01935 477453
Printed and bound in England by
J.H. Haynes & Co. Ltd, Sparkford

The Osiris
Revelations

Contents

Prologue

21st December 2049

'Admiral Ghent, excuse me, Sir, it is time!'

'The President?'

'Due to arrive in fifteen minutes, Sir; the helicopter will land directly outside the main facility.'

Admiral Gregory Ghent finished the sentence he was writing. Barely moving his head, he peered above frameless half-moon spectacles; taking time to focus on his Private Secretary, who stood, harassed and uncharacteristically dishevelled, some distance away in a large, ornate doorway. Despairingly, he placed an elbow on the cluttered desk and leaned forward to rest his wrinkled brow in his hand.

Admiral Ghent: military tactician, politician, patriot and former Director of the CIA, slowly massaged his temples, briefly closing his sore, reddened eyes. He was tired, so much so, that there was little contrast between his shock of white hair, bushy eyebrows and pallid complexion.

'Did you get any sleep, Sir?' Naval Captain Randle Myers enquired politely.

Admiral Ghent reread the closing paragraph of his letter; reflecting thoughtfully on his choice of words. 'The salvation of humanity . . . a discovery of truly universal proportions . . . the return to global stability . . . '

Placing both hands firmly on the desk, to steady himself, he rose wearily to his feet; struggling to support a much heavier burden. He looked again at Captain Myers.

'I haven't slept in days!' He replied, curtly.

Assuming his full stature and the ingrained, powerful demeanour of a national statesman, Admiral Ghent pulled the uniform jacket from the back of his chair and beckoned for Myers to follow him.

'Let's go then,' he said quietly, his voice humbled by unfolding events.

Walking purposefully, the two men passed several offices on their way to the lobby. As they did, three other high-ranking military officers joined them, closing in from different directions. They walked behind the Admiral and picked up the step. No one spoke.

Outside the air hung with dampness. Dark green mould advanced, covering the white Portland stone that formed the building's grand New England architecture. Dense, grey cloud subdued the midday light, as though the unseen winter sun had already begun to set.

Forgotten leaves, brown and contorted, blew across the broad steps. For a few moments they swirled, caught in a final excited flurry, before being doused; their brief bid for freedom overwhelmed and drowned in dark foreboding puddles. Resident crows, disturbed by the cavalcade, squawked hauntingly as they launched from perches in the portico.

Admiral Ghent, a tall, lean man, took his seat in the back of a waiting limousine. Myers walked behind the vehicle to join him, there was no cover and even before the door had closed, he was dripping wet. A second car arrived. They would be driven to the makeshift reception area, as the imposing building of red brick, discoloured by months of continuous rain, was a good deal further away than it appeared.

Both men looked on silently as they passed a huge white spherical construction, blotched and streaked by years of corrosive neglect. It was supported well clear of the ground by a number of giant stone columns, like monoliths supporting a decaying planet. They both read the large sign that hung, stark, from the towering security fence.

REACTOR THREE
DECOMMISIONED
UNAUTHORISED ADMITTANCE PROHIBITED

'Will it work, Randle?'
'Indications are that it will, Sir.'

'The British, and the others for that matter?'

'All standing by, Sir, it's a joint effort, all the way," Myers replied woodenly.

The Admiral nodded, still lost in his thoughts.

'It's an impossible job, this one,' he confided. 'Secretary of State for Energy, when there is no energy.'

Captain Myers could see the stress lines etched into the Admiral's face.

'The Federal Generating Bureau is standing by too, Sir,' he replied positively.

Admiral Ghent nodded again, slowly.

'Who will benefit first?'

'The north-eastern sector, and part of the mid-west, down as far as Ohio. When stabilised, the second facility will lock into the south-eastern sector. Good news for the East Coast I'd say; no more rationing, power, twenty-four, seven.'

'Are we not being a little over confident here, Randle? Perhaps state by state would have been more prudent.'

'I spoke to one of the scientists involved in the reinstatement programme yesterday, off the record. It is going to work, Admiral.'

Both cars stopped outside the main facility. There was a large group of people waiting, most beneath a sea of black umbrellas. Admiral Ghent looked across at the low wooden podium, vacant save for the stars and stripes draped limply over its railings. A pack of hungry PR

4

officials and reporters jostled for position.

'Then I hope, indeed, pray, that it does.'

CHAPTER 1

In the Beginning

Four months earlier

'Hello? Base Operations from Survey One, how do you read?'

'Come in, Richard, we read you five by five. Where are you?'

'Cross coordinate one, one, five, East Sector. I'm just starting the initial survey.'

'OK, Richard. Oxygen level eighty-seven percent, that gives you, hold on, yes, that gives you three hours and three minutes on task. Be cool out there, 'operations normal' calls every twenty minutes, please.'

'You got it. Survey One out.'

Richard James Reece replaced the small navigation handset into its pouch on his belt. Straightening his back and flexing his arms a little, he looked slowly left and right, scanning the distant horizon. Although Richard Reece, a British astronaut, had been a member of the Osiris base survey team for almost a year, the sights of the magnificent Mars landscape still astounded him. The planet surface seemed to glow; radiating colours between bright orange and blood red as the distant sun rose for the new day. In many ways, the landscape was very similar to that of the moon, a dusty surface about two, sometimes three, centimetres thick, with loose boulders of various sizes strewn all around. However, quite unlike the lunar landscape the colour was rich, incandescent. The atmosphere had an eerie glow about it, which, reflecting off the low mountain range to the right, radiated a deeper, almost condensed shade of red, its luminosity bursting over the surface of the crater in which he was standing. The towering rim of this vast depression, itself some sixty kilometres in diameter, was craggy and almost totally complete except for a wide breach on the far side. It looked somehow, nonsensically, as if the access had been driven through by a giant excavating machine, so abrupt was its architecture. More likely, though, it had been the work of a raging prehistoric river. Over tens of thousands of years its thunderous waters crashed down, wearing and eroding, eventually cascading down into the crater below, filling it like some vast inland sea.

A waterfall of those dimensions, thought Richard, it must have been an incredible sight, quite remarkable!

Of course, surface water had been proved to exist on

Mars several years earlier by the first landings, but the sheer quantities that would have filled these vast natural reservoirs always left him in awe.

Checking his suit integrity meter and oxygen level, now eighty-three percent, he moved away from the scout vehicle towards a rocky outcrop that seemed to reflect light back at him, like a mirror reflecting the early morning sun. As he walked towards the area, he began to see an abundance of small, transparent, fragmented rocks lying on the surface. Some large, some small, they averaged three or four centimetres in diameter and appeared to congregate around the entrance of a small, shadowy cave. Richard stared at the opening for several seconds.

Seems to have been formed by a minor meteorite impact, he thought. Bending equally at the knees and waist, he stepped inside, walking a few paces into the darkness; it was absolutely quiet, utterly still. Richard hesitated; it didn't feel right, not at all. He had visited a makeshift mortuary once, after a devastating earthquake back on earth, in the Middle East region, but that was years earlier! Why he remembered that, he was not sure.

Surely, it was that feeling he remembered. Feelings like no other place could evoke, feelings that had been locked away in his subconscious. Death, no what ifs or maybes: death, pure and simple.

Richard had no explanation and he was not ordinarily easily troubled. Instinctively he stepped back into the light.

He scanned the horizon nervously. At that moment, a rock specimen caught his eye. It was different from the others that lay scattered around his feet, although it was the same size. He bent down to pick it up. There were, he noticed, a few others, similar but smaller, approximately twenty millimetres square. Richard, almost mesmerised, counted nine in total. His hand, made clumsy by a thick glove, struggled to pick up a smaller example. Succeeding at last, he was perplexed by its weight. It was heavier, much more so, than he was expecting, and holding it up close to his visor, he could see to his surprise that it was, in fact, a crystal and not a rock at all.

With some unusually symmetrical facets, it almost looked like a large, partly-cut diamond. However, in addition to reflecting light with a sparkle, it also seemed to glow from within, with an opaque, hazy, white light. Richard studied the object intensely, along with the other specimens lying on the ground. Again, they appeared symmetrical for the most part, but each had a fractured or damaged face. He knelt on the red sand and peered closely at the largest one, captivated. Then, intrigued, he tried to 'fit' the other smaller examples to it, by repeatedly turning and offering, as one would when making up a jigsaw puzzle. To his surprise, each seemed to 'mate' quite convincingly.

Could these seemingly splintered crystals once have been one?

Forgetting his earlier anxiety, he turned his attention to

the myriad of fragments strewn around him. Transparent, glass-like, and displaying a subtle shade of green, they were different from the crystal he retained in his left hand. Many of these fragments had something in common, whatever their size: they all had at least one curved face. Richard could imagine them once making up a glass ball or sphere, and quite a large one. There were enough pieces shimmering and reflecting in the Martian sunlight for it to have been at least one metre in diameter.

Was that glass sphere a protective ball around a single large crystal?

His initial theory on the fragments being an exposed outcrop of a naturally occurring mineral, or even the splintered remains of a small meteorite, shattering on impact with the planet surface, dissolved instantly.

With the crystal resting on the open palm of his left hand, he noticed it was time for an 'operations normal' call, and Richard activated his radio headset with a switch on his belt.

'Base? Base? Hello, base? Survey One. Come in, please?' As he spoke, Richard became totally entranced.

'What the hell is going on here?' he muttered quietly.

Within seconds, his amazement turned to alarm.

The crystals were emitting a pulsing low-level glow, which, in turn, seemed to illuminate the glass fragments around him. As he stared, he felt a sharp pain in the centre of his palm. It was instantaneous; it gave him no time to react. Looking down at his hand, the small crystal he held was also glowing. Simultaneously, a tiny column of smoke appeared, as the crystal burnt through the heat-resistant outer layers of his glove and began to burn his skin.

'Shit!' he exclaimed, shaking his hand wildly as the crystal fell to the ground, still glowing uncannily. Shocked and staring wide-eyed at his palm, a small spout of condensing oxygen issued from a pinprick hole in the centre of his glove, and almost immediately a warning buzzer sounded from his suit's integrity unit.

'Warning. Warning. Suit Integrity Breached. Three Percent Pressure Drop. Warning. Warning.'

He pressed the flashing amber caution light on the control unit, which was also located on his belt, silencing the computer-generated feminine voice.

'Bloody hell! I'd better get back,' he said in an agitated voice.

Richard pulled the standby radio handset from his belt and gripped it tightly in his left hand, plugging the leak. Just then, base called.

'Richard?' the voice said anxiously, 'it's Jenny. My monitor is showing a problem with your life support systems, just a false reading, right?'

'Negative, Jenny, I've got a problem, but it's contained at the moment. I'm walking back to the buggy. I've got a leak in my suit.'

'But that's impossible!' she exclaimed.

'It's not impossible! My suit *is* breached, in the palm of my left hand.' His voice trailed away. To his dismay, he noticed that the nine crystals, which lay close to his feet, were being energised again and were glowing with an even brighter intensity. Stepping over each one carefully, as he made his way back quickly to the scout vehicle, he realised that intermittent periods of radio silence seemed to reduce the pulse of the crystals.

'They seem to glow and heat up when I transmit on the radio', he whispered, astonished.

With no time to waste, Richard quickened his pace, almost breaking into a run.

'Richard, come in please? What's happening out there?'

'It's OK. I'm just climbing into the buggy. Oxygen is at forty-two percent. It's an hour's drive!'

'Well, get back here fast, but be careful. I can see that you've stemmed the leak but you're still losing gas. You have an hour at most; it could be tight. We're sending someone out. Over?'

Richard didn't answer, but hurriedly strapped himself into the small, six-wheeled open cab scout vehicle, slammed it into gear and sped towards base camp, clouds of dust rising in plumes behind him. Once into sector forty-one, and the sites he had surveyed several months before, he knew the way by heart. By now a little less concerned, and still with twenty-eight percent oxygen, he thought about the crystals.

'Being radiated with high-frequency radio waves induced in that small crystal enough heat energy to burn through a samite-lined glove in a matter of seconds,' he said aloud. 'Nothing known to man can burn through samite!'

He pondered for a few more seconds before being snapped back to reality. Driving at full speed over the undulating surface made the vehicle unstable. It bounced violently. By now, he could see the dust being kicked up by the incoming rescue vehicle. The large alpha-type Personnel Transport and Service Vehicle was a very welcome sight as they intercepted each other on the high plain, some thirty kilometres from base camp. Richard's oxygen showed just nine percent.

The PTSV was a cylindrical tube on wheels; measuring twenty metres long and supported by twelve large, independently suspended 'bubble' tyres. It could support ten scientists in the remotest areas for anything up to a month. The cockpit windows, five of them, in the front face of the tube, incorporated deep blue filters and the backlit cockpit area made them gleam, like menacing eyes. Smaller circular windows, nine on either side, together with a multitude of aerials and microwave dishes, gave it the appearance of a giant, hairy caterpillar, but it was the row of large white oxygen cylinders, secured above the wheels, reminiscent of torpedo tubes, that Richard identified first.

The vehicle billowed huge clouds of dust in its wake. They trailed it for miles and tried to engulf it at every change of direction. The welcome sight brought a smile to Richard's face, as the vehicles closed on one another. At just the right moment, he released the throttle. His smile soon faded however, as the automatic Target Enhancement System rotated on top of the PTSV and turned towards him. The Cyan Magnetic Pulse Cannon was a close defence system. Although never used in anger, the sight of the three-metre long barrel pointing towards him was menacing enough. Even though he knew that the tracking system required fail-safe activation, it was always live. Having operated the cannon himself on irregular test firings, and while it was almost obsolete, it could still make a hell of a mess of anything within five or six kilometres.

The rescue vehicle slowly drew to a halt alongside Richard, its trailing plume of dust and surface debris, arriving moments later. The unwelcome deluge showered the scout vehicle like persistant heavy rain.

'Hey, careful!' Richard shouted, as the two vehicles slowly collided. 'That's quite close enough!'

The large circular door of the portal chamber opened with a metallic clunk, accompanied, momentarily, by the deafening hiss of venting gas. Keeping low to the ground, Richard climbed into the airlock and sat down on the nearest metal seat of a row of three, that were hinged on the right hand bulkhead.

'Richard, its Sean. Are you all right?'

A fierce blast of incoming gas all but drowned Richard's reply, as the airlock was pressurised with an atmospheric mixture.

'Yes, I think so. Thanks, thanks a lot, though that was possibly a little too close. Wouldn't you say?'

The inner door accessing the environmental chamber opened with less fuss. Standing up, Richard walked into the familiar surroundings to be greeted by several anxious faces, including Rachel's, his close friend and colleague. As the Mars base Chief Medical Officer, the CMO, Rachel knew only too well the excruciatingly painful results of a full, or even a partial suit depressurisation on the outside.

'Richard!' Her voice was stern, but as she looked him in the eyes, it softened, almost to a whisper. 'Why can't you be more careful?'

'I was. It wasn't like that.'

'We were worried sick; we thought we were going to lose you.'

The familiar sparkle in Rachel's alluring brown eyes was absent, dissolved in a watery film, as she blinked repeatedly, trying desperately to disperse the tears that threatened to spill out from the corners.

'Yes,' Richard said again, almost flippantly. 'Well, sorry about that but I've found something.'

Just then, Greg Searle, the Yorkshire-born Security Officer, stepped forward from behind Rachel.

'Well, it had better be good,' he warned. 'OK, everyone, that's it. Someone attach the scout vehicle and let's get back.' Looking over his shoulder at Richard, he scowled. 'Put a lid on it until the debrief. The commander wants you in the main theatre at fifteen hundred hours. Get a DP check in sickbay first.'

Greg Searle picked up Richard's burnt glove from

the adjacent bench. He looked at the tiny hole and then straight into Richard's eyes. Having an aggressive nature, he was not often lost for words, but on this occasion, whilst trying to push the tip of a fingernail through the perforation in the samite lining, he seemed speechless. Looking back at Richard, his eyes narrowed, and then he turned and stormed into the living chamber.

'Five minutes!' he snapped to the assembled group.

'What's his problem?' asked Richard.

'Just the usual,' replied Rachel.

Deciding to remain in the environmental chamber and avoid any further demonstrations of temper from Searle, the group sat down and strapped themselves into two rows of uncomfortably rigid seats for the twenty-minute drive back to Osiris.

Richard looked down, staring at the deck for several minutes, thinking. He eventually became aware of Rachel looking at him, and surprised her by asking, 'any abnormal signs, Doctor?' He looked up at her as she turned her head away; despite the company of friends, she felt a little embarrassed. For the remainder of the drive they sat in silence. Presently a voice came over the PA.

'Docking complete. Clear to disembark.'

'Come on, you. Sickbay for a complete check!' Rachel insisted.

The group laughed as Richard set off after her, looking back with a grin on his face. He followed her into the sickbay obediently.

'Ah, mission control,' Richard teased.

'Richard, be sensible, and for once just act your age, forty!' Rachel retorted.

'Sorry!' he replied, taken aback at the strict nature of her tone. 'Thought you might have been at least a little bit pleased to get me back in one piece?'

'Well, I am. OK, I really am pleased that you're back in one piece. No bodybag for you, eh, and anyway, what would you know about how I feel? Now get on the examination couch!'

Rachel was in no mood for playful banter and Richard could see it was time for him to stop. Not overly tall, but lean and muscular, he did as Rachel instructed.

'Right, of course,' he said in a serious tone. Head bowed, but still looking up at her with his mischievous blue eyes, he climbed onto the grey metal-framed bed that doubled as an operating table.

The sickbay was a large room by base standards, the best part of eight metres by eight metres, and in addition it benefited from two small offices on the far side, one of which was normally used as a treatment room. It was, for a self-contained mini hospital, a very pleasant room; light, airy and definitely not clinical. In many ways, it reflected Rachel's professional approach to her role. Indeed, even the odour of the place was not surgical spirit, but lightly fragrant and relaxing. The facility was a good deal better equipped than one would expect for an outpost around eighty million miles from earth, which was only restocked every six months.

Rachel Turner was both a General Practitioner and a surgeon, having specialised in space medicine during the latter years of her training. Although she was a classic English rose, most agreed that numerous Italian genes, having skipped enough generations to be unaccounted for, had resurfaced; as her striking features and almond shaped eyes hinted at her mediterranean ancestry, and the maturity of her early thirties only emphasised these features. Her professional team was composed of a junior house doctor, Bill Bates, and two nurses.

'So, Richard,' continued Rachel as she passed a hand-held scanner over his half-naked body. 'You nearly died out there, but your pulse is still only fifty-two; blood pressure still one hundred and ten over sixty; red blood cell count still four eighty eight to one; haemoglobin point eight eight, gamma count still six over fifty!' Rachel put her hands over her face for a moment then pulled a handkerchief from her white trouser pocket, stifling a sob. Immediately, Richard sat up and spun round on the couch, putting his legs astride her. Placing his hands tenderly on her shoulders, he looked kindly at her.

'Oh come on, Rachel, what's all this, then?' he said, half knowingly but not admitting as much.

'What do you think, Richard? I was beside myself out there. I thought that I was going to lose you and nearly did! Why don't you ever see the danger?' A single tear appeared in the corner of her eye. She quickly wiped it away.

'It wasn't that close,' replied Richard, nonchalantly.

'Oh, really!' snapped Rachel, 'three percent is OK, is it?'

'All right . . . all right,' Richard conceded. 'So it was a little tight.' He took the handkerchief from Rachel's hand and gently blotted the corners of her eyes. 'But we're onto something aren't we, big time?'

'I don't care about it,' Rachel sighed. 'I care about you. But you don't see it, or won't see it, probably don't want to see it! I don't mean anything to you, Richard. To you I am just another fanciful female on this god forsaken planet.'

'Oh, come on, that's not true and you know it!' Looking straight into her eyes, he gave her a hug and kissed her neck.

'Richard, you mean so much to me. I don't want to lose you.'

'And you won't. I'm not going anywhere,' he said reassuringly. 'It takes more than a hole in a samite glove to put me out of action!' He smiled at her and gave her another kiss. 'We shouldn't be doing this, you know the rules. Strictly no fraternisation between base members. Article 7, Paragraph 9,' Richard continued, playfully.

'Why won't you ever give me anything back Richard, anything?' Rachel continued, ignoring the last remark. 'Just say that you care, or something? It's like you open the door, just a little bit, and just as I get my hopes up, you shut it again!'

'OK. I'll let you into a secret. I'll tell you something

I've never spoken of, not to anyone.' Richard leant over to pick up his white t-shirt and slid it over his head. 'There was someone special. It was on moonbase, five, almost six years ago, on my second tour as a shuttle pilot. She was an American engineering student on placement.' He shrugged his shoulders. 'Funny, I seem to be a mug for the intelligent ones. We had plans. We made plans. God, she was beautiful. I loved her, too much. Then she left to go back to college for her specialist training; should have only been a year or so. We planned to get married after her finals. Yes, it was the real thing!' Richard sighed and looked up at the ceiling. 'But, of course, she never came back. She didn't want to know me, in fact, a shuttle pilot wasn't good enough; went off with another bloke almost straight away, some high flyer. Apparently did the same thing again, after she met an older, much richer man. He was a professor or something, a physicist. German, I think. They married and went to live in Berlin, or some bloody place. That was the last I heard of her. God, I loved her. She broke my heart, absolutely. It affected me for ages, a year or more. My career suffered for a while, too. I made a few mistakes flying the shuttle and ended up at a desk in moonbase operations for six months before I got it together again.' Richard stopped abruptly, and taking a deep breath, he looked back at Rachel. 'Stupid, eh? Not what you were expecting at all.'

'I'm so sorry, Richard, I had no idea.'

'Of course you didn't. First time I've mentioned it, and

it's confidential OK? A long time ago, and a long way away.' He touched her face with his fingertips. 'So,' he continued, 'couldn't stand that again, for the sake of my pride, nothing to do with my heart.' Richard stood up and handed back her rather damp handkerchief. 'But that's not to say that there's nothing going on in the latter, know what I mean?' He gave Rachel a big smile and as he did so a call came over the PA.

'Lieutenant Commander Reece to the briefing theatre, will Lieutenant Commander Reece please report to the briefing theatre, immediately?'

'Saved by the bell, don't you think?'

Richard grinned. Rachel's smile became a smirk as they looked at each other for a few moments.

CHAPTER 2

The Problem

As the door to the small theatre slid open, Richard was surprised to see the front two rows of seats full of people, almost all of whom turned to look at him as he entered. The Base Commander caught his eye, as did the five heads of department: Base Operations, Life Support, Scientific, Biological, and Research. Surrounding the Commander were several people Richard recognised but did not know.

'Come on, Richard, we have been waiting almost ten minutes,' snapped the familiar voice of Greg Searle.

This remark was greeted by a look of contempt from Richard, whose eyes passed back to the Commander. He stepped onto the low podium, walked a few paces to the lectern and stared out at the audience.

'Afternoon, Sir; everyone,' said Richard, a little embarrassed, which was quite unlike him. 'Sorry about the trouble.'

'Forget it, Richard,' said the Base Commander, Todd Miko, dismissing the apology. 'Now, what's this all about? I would like a full debrief on everything that happened out there this morning. Earth wants answers, too. They've heard, though God knows how, that a samite suit has been breached!'

The Commander's face tightened as he looked at Greg Searle. It was clear that he was not pleased with his security officer. Searle looked sheepish in response.

'Yes, Sir,' Richard replied, shedding his embarrassment in favour of his normal confident manner. Feeling a little proud of the impending calamity, he went on to describe the events of the day in full, much to the amazement of those gathered.

'So, that's it, Sir,' he said, finally. 'Are there any questions?'

Peter Mayhew, an American Professor of Thermal Dynamics and Head of Science, stood up. 'You know, Richard, that once the chemical reaction used in the manufacture of samite has taken place, nothing known to man, at least at present, can fracture the resulting adhesion. Those bonds are established within the materials' molecular matrix, at a sub-atomic level. In other words, nothing yet known can impact or penetrate that material?'

'I know that, Sir,' replied Richard, with an understanding nod of his head.

'Well, my people have run an initial scan on your glove,' Peter Mayhew went on, but now turning his attention to the Commander. 'To make that hole in Richard's glove we believe two processes must have occurred: firstly, extremely high temperatures, probably over four thousand degrees centigrade!' The audience gasped. 'Secondly, and perhaps more importantly, we believe some sort of atomic destabilisation effect has also taken place; something that has allowed the fundamental bonding of the materials' atomic structure, as we understand it, to be broken. If this is the case, the consequences of such a discovery to mankind are amazing. But, in the wrong hands, to say it could be seriously threatening would be an understatement!'

A sudden hush descended over the theatre until the deeply resonant voice of John Graysham, biologist and Head of Department, broke through it. He was a short man, in his late forties, overweight and red faced, but a veteran of space exploration, having been a member of the first moonbase team years earlier. Much respected, he pondered a moment as he stood up, his delivery calm and mellow.

'Richard, this is most important. Did you feel or see anything else, either from the crystal, or around you at the moment you felt the burning?'

Richard hesitated and looked around the audience as he thought back over the morning's events. 'Actually, no, Sir, I mean the surrounding crystals, as I said, glowed white, but also with a bluish hue. This created an eerie incandescence all around. The effect increased as I transmitted on my communicator, reduced slightly as I received transmission from base, and died when all transmissions stopped. I mean, we are talking a few seconds here, ten to fifteen at the most. Then there was a stabbing pain and then the breach in my suit.'

Turning to Rachel, who had entered the theatre a few minutes earlier, Graysham asked, 'what's his radiation count, Doctor?'

'Background level is slightly high, but that's normal for Richard, he spends most of his working life outside. Alpha, beta and gamma count up one or two percent perhaps, when compared to the average base member.'

'OK, thank you. That's all from me.'

Graysham, looking rather perplexed, sat down. His expression caused a variety of conversations, the volume of which belied the number of people in the theatre. In response, Todd Miko stood up, raising his arms, causing the commotion to subside.

'OK, everyone, listen carefully. What we have here has far-reaching consequences for all of us, but more importantly everyone back home. This discovery has the potential to solve the worsening energy crisis on earth and without the radiation hazards of conventional nuclear power. Which means, without the devastating by-products that have caused so much environmental damage to the earth's ecosystems. This could be the answer to our prayers. However, there's potential for World War Four here if it gets into the wrong hands.' He hesitated for a moment; one could almost feel his thought process. 'I want a lid on this, big time! Nothing gets out, and I mean nothing!' he urged, turning to the security officer.

'But earth's got a lead, Sir. What do I tell them?' asked Searle.

'Tell them anything. That there's been a mistake, that it was a joke, anything, but close it down!' Turning to the science officer he said, 'I want all of your resources on this; the full team and an outside working unit. I want containment of these crystals, and some kind of control system. I want a daily update and some hard results in two weeks, but do not bring any of those things onto the base until you are one hundred percent sure of containment and you have cleared the full quarantine process. No shortcuts, I don't want any accidents.' He turned again to Greg Searle. 'Do you understand my orders?'

'I understand, Sir,' replied Searle, who, trying to reassert himself, continued, 'I'll lead the outside team myself.'

'Negative!' the commander responded immediately. 'Richard is in charge of all external operations. He's got more outside hours than most of us put together. I need that experience where it counts. You deal with all security measures inside and off base.'

Richard and Greg Searle's eyes met; their mutual distrust plain to see. Commander Miko sensed the antagonism between the two men.

'I want round the clock effort with one hundred percent collaboration from all departments. All other projects take second shout. HODs meeting sometime tomorrow, late afternoon.' Commander Miko stepped onto the podium next to Richard. 'That's it everyone, carry on. Richard, my office please.'

'Yes, Sir,' Richard replied, looking again at Greg Searle as he turned to leave the theatre.

As the audience rose amid a multitude of conversations, Greg Searle, shouting above the cacophony of voices, was heard to say, 'security state remains green everyone, but communication state now red; all transmissions from the planet must first be cleared by my office, effective immediately.'

Richard woke the next morning feeling troubled. He checked the time, then lay back on his pillow with his hands behind his head to think. 'I've got thirty minutes,' he said to himself. He was lucky. His room, or cabin as he insisted on calling it, was one of the largest on the base. This was due to the amount of personal kit he had acquired as the survey team leader. He liked his space. Measuring about three and a half metres square, the room had a curved ceiling, a small shower, a washbasin and a bunk, all integral; being extruded from the cream coloured plastic wall lining. At one point eight metres long, the bunk was just a little short for his frame, and when he lay on his back, his feet hung over the end. Richard insisted on retaining his nautical roots, confusing most of his colleagues by using naval terminology: bulkhead, deck, overheads, bunk, going ashore, heads. It always brought smiles; indeed, he was popular, well respected by his colleagues and renowned for his calm and confident manner.

As he lay back, staring at a picture of Rachel which was stuck on the service pipes immediately above him, he recalled the events of the previous day. He pondered that shallow cave for several minutes. It was that which troubled him the most. He recalled that cold, uneasy feeling as he entered it and his subsequent relief to be back outside. It needed another look, a good look, he thought. 'But I'll keep quiet about it for now,' he said aloud.

'Keep quiet about what?' asked a familiar voice; it was Rachel. And it's the first sign of madness, you know, talking to yourself!'

Richard simultaneously leapt from his bunk and his thoughts. Wearing only his underpants, he stood, wide-eyed, looking at Rachel for a moment. Rachel smiled, looking him up and down.

'Wow,' she said teasingly. 'And what were you looking at above your bed, I mean, your bunk?'

Richard was desperate that she did not see the photograph. He quickly stepped towards the shower, and clumsily pulled a large, blue towel around his waist.

'In or out, but close the door!' he demanded, changing the subject.

Rachel looked at him playfully. 'Unfortunately, its out,' she sighed. 'Anyway, there's no time, the surface briefing starts in ten minutes. It's for you, of course!'

'What! But it's only . . .' Richard checked the wall clock,

zero eight twenty. 'Where did that half hour go?' He heard the door close gently. From behind it, Rachel shouted, 'nine minutes!'

Richard made it to the briefing room moments before Commander Miko. Taking a seat at the back of the room, he hoped to save himself from criticism for not shaving. Second Science Officer Michael Winters, a gangly man at two metres, took the podium.

'Lieutenant Commander Reece will commence today's survey at midday,' he said. 'The effects of solar flows Sierra Fox One Zero One and solar crescent Sierra Charlie Three Three Four of last week will give an increased gamma ray and background radiation count for the next three to four days. Therefore, surface time will be restricted to four and a half hours. At the moment background radiation is normal at twenty three point six microrads, but is expected to start rising by late afternoon. Other surface factors normal.'

Winters stood down, and was followed by Biological Officer John Graysham.

'Surface reads normal, Sir, but the team should be aware of the slightly higher surface temperatures for at least the next week.'

'Thank you, John. Security next, please,' said the Commander.

Greg Searle leapt to his feet and ran to the podium from the second row of seats, the epitome of obedience whenever the Base Commander was present. Smartly dressed in his grey and red uniform, he had short black hair, groomed with tonic, and a thin face. A prominent nose and chin emphasised his slightly sunken cheeks. Standing at around one point seven metres and fifty seven kilograms, he was of slight build. He looked at Richard for a moment, noting his uniform was non-standard, dressed as he was in an obsolete green navy flying suit and a white t-shirt. He knew why Richard was sitting as far away from the Commander as possible. Richard shifted a little nervously in his seat. It was not beyond Greg Searle to mention dress standards at morning briefing, this being his other hat.

'I have instigated all the security measures as detailed in your directive, Sir,' he said clearly, looking back at the Commander. 'All external communications are being routed through the secure network prior to transmission and a revised security code has been issued to the heads of department only. Long-range communication units have been disabled on all surface vehicles, and entry to the Accelercom Operations Centre restricted to essential personnel only. The station is fully established in communication state red and security state green.' Searle paused, waiting expectantly for a pat on the head by the Commander like some lap dog having performed a trick for its owner. It did not come. Coughing nervously into his fist he continued. 'Reece will be accompanied by NCO Preston of the Special Security Contingent today and for the rest of the week. He will provide additional scientific support but will mainly oversee the security of the crystals and any other materials collected for research. Searle looked at Richard. 'Whilst on survey, keep Mr Preston with you at all times. Keep him informed of any samples collected. Do not, I repeat, do not do your own thing out there, Reece. We expect a full report every twenty minutes.'

Richard seethed, but while several people in the theatre looked around at him following this remark, his expression remained fixed. He just shook his head slightly, registering his contempt.

'OK, that's all,' said the Commander, standing up and turning around to face everyone. 'HODs meeting time has changed; now in here at twenty hundred hours.' The Commander avoided looking at Richard as he turned and left the theatre. Richard, for his part, signed with relief, as it was unusual for him to break the dress code.

Searle, who could see what was going on, could not help remarking, ' a few minutes earlier out of bed would not go amiss, Reece.'

Richard ignored him as he made off eagerly for the canteen, and his breakfast.

CHAPTER 3

New Recruit

The two men sat next to each other in silence as the scout vehicle made its way across the central high plain towards the east sector, leaving the customary cloud of red dust behind it. Richard had no problem with Preston. He was a thirty-something Non Commissioned Officer of the Support Services Directorate and a security specialist. He was pleasant enough, although Richard didn't know him particularly well. Richard was, however, upset by the inevitable lack of freedom that the NCO's presence would dictate. Used to doing his own thing whilst on survey, he was not at all keen on this scenario.

Occasionally checking the navigation display, Richard steered through an area where larger and more frequently occurring surface boulders began to pepper the landscape. As they continued to press eastwards, Richard smiled to himself and decided to break the stony silence.

'Spent much time outside, Preston?' he asked.

'No, Sir, relatively little considering I've been here almost twelve months. I tend to handle the administrative side.'

'So why has Searle given you this job?'

'Well, I've always worked directly under Captain Searle, Sir, in the office. Although I am fully up-to-date with my safety drills and briefings and I have a current surface vehicle licence.'

Seems innocent enough, thought Richard as he negotiated the final one hundred metres or so of the plateau area.

'We leave the high plain now; do you see that breach in the mountains over there, like a pass?' Richard asked, pointing about twenty kilometres ahead on the horizon.

'Yes, Sir, I see it.'

'Well, that's where we're going, through that rift and into the Kalahari Crater. It's about another half an hour's drive, maybe forty minutes.'

Preston seemed impressed. 'Furthest I've ever been,' he said.

'Furthest anybody's ever been, Preston; on surface survey anyway.'

Richard paused. Then he enquired quietly, 'what do you know about Searle? I mean, where does he come from?'

The two men looked at each other briefly, distorted reflections of themselves and their surroundings on the broad visors preventing eye contact.

Preston's voice hardened slightly. 'He's a well-respected

officer, and runs an efficient department. A little hard at times, but always fair. An Honours Degree from Michigan University in Personnel Management, I understand and over six year's experience in base security, mainly on Andromeda. That's all I can say, really.'

'But what about his background, before the space programme?' Richard persisted.

'Can't say, Sir. Never asked.'

The men fell silent again as the buggy climbed the final few metres of the pass, which in turn, led up to the crater's edge; a huge shadow, cast by the high ridgeline and occasional isolated peaks causing a four-degree drop in surface temperature in as many minutes.

As the vehicle flipped awkwardly over the crest of the ridge, both men gasped; blinding, bright orange sunlight hit them full in the face; the fiery ball was hanging low in the sky even in the early afternoon. Preston flipped the integral sun visor down over his helmet and held his arm up to further shield his eyes.

'Oh, that's bright,' he cursed.

'Yes, sorry, I should have warned you about that, it's the contrast as much as anything. We have spent the last fifteen minutes in shadow. Look down for two or three minutes, allow your eyes to adjust to the light.'

Richard was already thinking ahead. How was he to survey the cave alone? Preston seemed all right, reliable, but there was no room for error.

'Base? Survey One. Come in?'

'Five by five, Richard, go ahead.'

'Cross coordinate one one five in ten minutes, all systems green. Ready to proceed.'

'OK, Richard, command approved. Your oxygen, seventy-nine percent and Preston's, eighty-two. You must be doing all the talking!'

Richard could hear laughter in the background. 'Oh, ha ha,' he retorted, with a smirk on his face. 'I'll be back !' he continued in a deep voice. He could hear Rachel join in the giggling back in the communication centre.

'Operations normal calls every twenty minutes, I know. Talk to you soon. Out.'

Richard brought the buggy to a halt about two hundred metres from the crystal site and well away from the small hillock, beneath which was the cave.

'Well, there they are,' he said, pointing for the benefit of his colleague. 'Listen Preston,' Richard paused, 'would you like me to call you by your first name?'

'No, Sir, Preston's fine, in fact everybody calls me that. My first name is, well, let's just say I don't use it much!'

Richard nodded and smiled. 'Preston it is then,' he agreed. 'Listen, Preston, I know the orders, but there's some work I'd like to do on my own. Do you have a problem with that?'

'Well, Sir,' came the awkward reply as the two men climbed out of their seats. 'We are supposed to stay together; my orders are clear on that point. I'm to stay with you at all times, direct orders from Captain Searle himself.' Preston's breathing rate quickened slightly, with apprehension, as he walked around the front of the vehicle to face Richard.

'Yes, I know that. But we can cover more ground if we split up?'

Walking together, the two men made their way towards the crystal site.

'Anyway, if we stay together, we are more likely to talk to each other,' Richard continued, 'and look what happens when we do.'

Richard pointed to the small group of crystals twenty or so metres away.

'Wow!' exclaimed Preston. 'They're glowing!'

'Exactly,' replied Richard, 'so keep communications to a minimum and whatever you do, don't pick up, touch or even kick one of those things.'

'Yes, Sir,' murmured Preston, still half mesmerised.

'Right,' ordered Richard. 'You can conduct the initial survey over there, there and there,' he said pointing to a one hundred and eighty degree sector to the west of the vehicle. 'I'll do this side. Check in every twenty minutes, but make it sound as if we are together, OK?' Richard hesitated for a moment while he waited to see if Preston would go along with the plan.

'Yes, OK, Sir, every twenty minutes,' he replied, still seemingly confused.

Not waiting for him to change his mind, Richard

walked off to the right and disappeared behind a low hillock. Doubling back on himself after a few minutes, he made his way back towards the cave. Strangely, with apprehension, he felt his heart rate quicken once again. What was it about this place?

Stepping over the large crystal and avoiding the others, he reached the shallow entrance and looked around to make sure that Preston was nowhere to be seen.

'Just what is this place?' he whispered. A bead of sweat ran down his left temple. Looking down, he checked the solar charged battery indicator on his flashlight. 'Fully charged. I'm going in!'

Walking down a shallow incline, he instantly sank up to his knees in the soft red sand. It had been blown into the mouth of the cave by thermal winds over what must have been hundreds of years. After ten to fifteen paces, the natural light disappeared. The beam from his small torch pierced the darkness, whilst the top of his helmet scraped the roof of the cave producing a ghostly, echoing screech. He stooped and despite the silence in the cave, he could hear the blood surging in his ears.

'What is this place?' he said again, quietly.

After a further ten paces or so the ground firmed up and the cave widened slightly. He noticed the dust covering the ground was a little thinner, maybe ten to fifteen millimetres, even less in some places. Just then, his foot caught something on the ground; losing balance, he stumbled forward, putting his hands out to break his fall, and each ploughed almost parallel grooves in the sediment as he hit the ground.

'Ugh!'

Richard lost a hold on his torch, it flew out of his hand, landing a metre or so away. Almost instantly, total darkness engulfed the cave, descending suddenly from above. He froze momentarily, but then there, to his right, he saw the dull, misty glow of the torch's restricted beam. The thick cloud of aggravated dust began to settle quickly. As the fading beam all but disappeared, Richard scrambled to his knees and snatched the precious tool from the sediment.

'God, be more careful!' he scolded himself.

Climbing to his feet, he turned to look at what had been the cause of his fall; the torch light illuminated, incredibly, a curved doorsill. As he moved towards it, something brushed against his left shoulder.

'What the?' he gasped.

Reacting instinctively with a violent movement of his arm, which, to his increasing alarm, became entangled in something wiry, he tried in vain to rid himself of the debilitating mass. Like dense, dangling tentacles of a poisonous jellyfish his attempts to break free only trapped him further. Heightened by the adrenaline pumping through his veins, he grasped the tangled mass with both hands and in the near darkness, pulled hard. What followed almost had him running back the way he had come, as a mass of debris dislodged above him and crashed, unexpectedly to the floor, sending yet more clouds of fine dust into the murky, shadowy atmosphere.

Richard stood his ground, motionless, almost waiting for the next instalment. A moment later, all was again silent, eerie.

The single beam of light slowly penetrated deeper and deeper into the murk as the heavier particles of dust drifted downwards to settle again. Taking a moment to collect his thoughts, he rotated the beam of light upwards.

'Arrrrgh!'

A sharp intake of breath followed his terrified gasp. A humanoid face stared at him through a hole in the roof.

His lungs were full, bursting, but there was no movement! He breathed out slowly, controlled and then straightened up, regaining his composure. He stared back at the face, it's features, its blank expression; torch light giving it a most haunting appearance. It was some sort of mask. Richard settled down and felt his heart rate drop.

'Just as well they can't monitor my vital functions down here,' he said quietly. He probed further with the torch beam. No more surprises please, he thought.

The mask had an almost human appearance; a large, slightly oval shape about the size of a human adult face, but with narrow slits for eye sockets. There were two side straps, which clamped it to the wearer's head and a full width curved glass visor that rotated upwards to clear the eye slits. Richard reached up and pulled the object down for a closer look. Still connected by a mass of what looked like wires to the ceiling of the cave, he shook it gently; a layer of very fine sediment became dislodged and floated away to reveal a black highly polished surface of what was most definitely some sort of electronic sensor or monitor screen. Grasping the screen, he gently pulled it downwards to cover the eye sockets. To his surprise and amazement, the screen rotated smoothly and clipped into position.

My God, this is a sensor mask, I'm sure of it! Like the type we wore on the Stratofighter. This screen must have provided navigation data or information of some kind to the wearer. This is a pilot's mask, no question.

Richard stood absolutely still, as if paralysed by the thoughts rushing through his mind.

If the being who wore this mask was a pilot, then this must be a ship!

He peered past the mask and into the darkness above his head, directing the beam of light into the area from which the debris had fallen. Once the object had been illuminated, it began to make more sense.

'Oh my God! It's a seat, it's a seat. It's definitely a seat!' he said aloud, forgetting himself.

Coming down from his tiptoes, and bending down onto one knee, Richard swung the torch beam forward at waist level, letting the mask hang gently on the attached wires. After a pause of what seemed like minutes to collect his thoughts, he took several paces forward. Clearly visible was a large semi-circular desk-like structure, which lay uprooted and resting on its side about a metre in front of three high backed chairs.

'This is a console, these guys were pilots and whoever sat in the chair up there was the captain, for sure!'

Richard relaxed his breathing, his eyes still straining to gather in as much of the dim light as possible. Reaching forward he wiped the dust off the face of a panel. A circular instrument with pictorial markings appeared beneath a transparent window.

'This is the flight deck of a spaceship. There is no doubt about it. It must have crashed onto the planet's surface, driving this forward section into the sand, the remainder disintegrating on impact.' Realising he was talking to himself, Richard thought of Rachel. 'First sign of madness,' he smiled to himself.

Standing up and checking his watch, Richard was surprised to see that he had been in the cave for twenty minutes already. He continued to walk in the direction he perceived to be the forward end of the structure. Now realising what he was seeing, he began to identify several smaller consoles on this lower level. Some of the seats had been ripped from their mountings by the force of impact, others were in place, but there were no signs or remains of its occupants at the time of the crash. Becoming more thorough in his examination of the forward area, Richard pulled out what appeared to be a book from an open shelf between two of the consoles. It was surprisingly light considering its thickness, about fifty millimetres. He wiped away the layer of dust and slowly opened it. The pages were made of some kind of metal; paper-thin but stiff like a sheet of card. Drawings and indecipherable text were etched onto the sheets, which reflected the light from his torch with a variety of colours, like a hologram. The text reminded him of writing he had seen during history lessons in his school days.

Pictorial letters and words? Richard cast his mind back. This looks like ancient Egyptian Hieroglyphics he thought, or maybe from the ancient civilisations of South America?

Interestingly, what occurred repeatedly, as he flicked through the undamaged pages of the book, was the pictorial representation of pyramid structures. He had flown over the pyramids of Egypt and Mexico a hundred times whilst serving, years earlier, in the orbiting space station Skyport. They were often clearly visible during low orbital manoeuvres. These drawings looked very familiar. As he turned the pages towards the back of the book, his torch beam flickered. Richard looked at its indicator.

'Eighteen percent; better get back,' he said quietly, subconsciously hoping not to further disturb any more of the hanging debris from above his head.

Then something he saw hit him, as if he had walked into a bulkhead.

'I know this,' he said, peering at a diagram. He turned several more pages quickly, excited like a small boy with a new storybook. He could not believe it, diagram after diagram, together with incomprehensible text. 'The engineering of this ship!' he said again in utter amazement.

'Its construction, its layout, propulsion, engineering. Wow, what a beauty she was!' Richard paused. 'This is the flight manual, absolutely, and the navigation directory and an engineering manual!'

The torch beam flickered and all but faded. Richard snapped to his senses. He turned and made his way to the entrance, stumbling several times in the poor light. Placing the find in his shoulder bag, he straightened up, wincing again as the bright orange and red sunlight of the Martian day caught him full in the face. Dropping the helmet visor, and walking clear of the site, he found Preston wandering aimlessly around the scout vehicle.

'Where have you been, Sir? It's been nearly forty minutes and we are due to make another operations normal call!' Preston exclaimed, exasperated.

Fortunately, their attention was diverted by the glowing, pulsating crystals, which, although some way off, were in clear view.

'Keep the chat to a minimum,' replied Richard, parrying the question. 'I'll do the call.'

'Base? Survey One. Operations normal Sector One One Five, how do you read?'

'Loud and clear, and right on time, Richard,' came the reply. 'The Commander has authorised you to place one small crystal into the Yearlman Cube and run a visual, and if it checks, retrieve it for analysis. Then it's time for your drive home. Over.'

'OK, understood,' said Richard. 'Maintain radio silence

until further notice. Over and out.'

The Yearlman Cube was a lead box with a hinged lid about three hundred millimetres in height and depth. It had been designed about twenty-five years earlier by Professor Yearlman of Harvard University, to transport small amounts of highly radioactive reactor grade plutonium to the early moonbase nuclear power module. That was before the development of the Quasar Solar Power System. In the early days, it wasn't known how some materials would behave in space, so the cube was designed to protect the contents from all types of electro-magnetic energy, but primarily gamma and x-rays. It was ideal for this current purpose, the lining material being a sandwich of lead, gold, iridium and a synthetic derivative of uranium, all dense, heavy materials, high in the periodic table. Mars base had retained an example of the cube on its inventory since the very beginning.

The two men struggled with the heavy box and placed it on the ground next to the group of crystals. Richard, looking up at Preston, put his right forefinger to his helmet visor, close to his lips indicating 'no talking'. Preston nodded, acknowledging that he understood and Richard, using plastic tongs, placed the specimen into the box, and secured the lid. Standing back, he flicked the radio switch on his belt.

'Base? From Survey One, it's in the bag. Two way radio check, please.'

Simultaneously, the remaining eight crystals, including

the largest of the group, glowed with the low-level pulsating effect now familiar to them both.

'Acknowledged, Richard; radio check, five, four, three, two, one, out.'

The crystals glowed again but with a reduced intensity. Richard looked again at Preston, indicating radio silence, and stepped forward to check the cube externally for any signs of heat damage or burning. Next, he opened the lid and checked inside; there were no signs of damage and the specimen appeared inert.

After the examination, Richard looked up, smiling, and then gave a thumbs up signal to Preston. 'Let's load it up and go home, my friend,' he said.

CHAPTER 4

Background Information

On returning to base, Richard somehow managed to get his shoulder bag through the decontamination bay without detection. Fortunately, Rachel was busy performing a minor operation in sickbay, as she surely would have had her suspicions aroused by his secretive behaviour. Walking as casually as he could down the thirty-metre corridor to the living quarters, Richard wondered if he was doing the right thing by keeping his discovery to himself. Nevertheless, he was running on a hunch and felt he had good reason for his clandestine behaviour.

Greg Searle rounded the corner at the far end of the accommodation corridor, just seconds after Richard had closed and locked his cabin door. Searle walked the corridor, stopping at Richard's door. He raised his hand to knock, hesitated for a moment and then looked at his watch. For a second or two he pondered, then changed his mind and continued down the corridor, his face displaying a humourless expression. A voice came over the PA system.

'Heads of department to the theatre please, HOD meeting in the theatre, thank you.'

Searle quickened his pace.

Richard hid the extraterrestrial flight manual under his mattress for want of a better place and quickly changed into a dress uniform, but of a working, less formal nature. The lightweight clothing consisted of pale grey trousers, with a pencil-thin royal blue strip down the outside seam, and a similarly grey, loose, long sleeved jacket with a raised, royal blue collar. This blue colour, together with two intricate stirling silver insignia worn on each side of his collar, was significant in indicating his maritime heritage. The tiny badges, composed of a pair of crossed anchors with the state crown above, also denoted his United Kingdom National Joint Forces parent service. Richard's badges of rank, worn on the shoulder, were of platinum silver colour; that of a Lieutenant Commander being two thick strips with a central thin stripe. Finally, Richard's uniform was completed with the addition of a carefully embroided badge in platinum and gold thread over his left breast pocket. The emblem, being standard issue and worn by all his colleagues, was of a pair of angel's wings encircling the planet earth. It signified that he was a member of the International Space and Science Federation, the ISSF. At that moment, the only thing non-standard about Richard was his customary white, long sleeved cotton t-shirt; long since past its sell by date. Fortunately, in this uniform, with its raised collar, it could not be seen; unfortunately, his light brown hair, always hovering on the regulation limit, could.

Richard left his cabin in a hurry, almost knocking over a nurse who was passing his door, carrying a rack of glass sample jars on a large tray.

'Hey! Careful, Richard. I'm sure you wouldn't want to clear up forty urine samples, would you?' she said, smiling.

'No, you're right there, Pam. Sorry, I'm in a bit of a hurry.'

'Oh, anybody I know?' The Latin American nurse continued down the corridor, laughing, as Richard broke into a brisk walk in the opposite direction, composing himself on his way to the theatre.

Richard need not have hurried; the Commander was absent anyway, held up for ten minutes or so with the Science Officer. Taking his seat, he noticed Greg Searle looking at him. Searle raised his voice, enough to be heard over several other conversations.

'How did it go out there today, Reece?'

'Actually, it went fine Greg,' Richard replied. He tried not to appear over-friendly. 'Preston's a good man. Competent, capable, you know, the usual.'

'Anything else to report?' Searle continued, suspiciously.

'No, all routine, Greg; just as briefed.'

Richard looked down, trying to disguise his nerves; he wasn't a good liar.

Searle's eyes narrowed, but he was distracted as Commander Miko entered the theatre with Peter Mayhew. Everyone in the theatre stood up.

'Thank you, ladies and gentlemen. Please sit down,' said Commander Miko as he took his own seat. 'Go ahead, Greg.'

'Yes, Sir, thank you.' Searle paused momentarily to gather his thoughts. 'I am pleased to report that the surface survey conducted today was a success. A single crystal has been retrieved for analysis. It is temporarily in Laboratory One, under tight security and will remain there until the permanent facility has been completed. The Yearlman Cube appears to be totally adequate for isolation, Sir. Engineering informs me that by midday Tuesday, the second laboratory will be converted to Yearlman standard and the crystal will be relocated there for continued experimentation.'

'Excellent,' interrupted Commander Miko as he turned in his seat to address Richard. 'Well done . . . good work!'

'Thank you, Sir,' Richard replied, a little surprised by the praise. The brief continued, but Richard's thoughts were elsewhere.

What if I could decipher the script, he thought, actually read the symbols in that manual. God, what a revelation: interstellar navigation, advanced engineering and propulsion, new forms of energy!

'Lieutenant Commander Reece, are you listening?'

Richard was wrested from his thoughts by John Graysham, who was standing on the podium. Irritated, he said again in a raised voice, 'are you interested?'

'Sorry, I was . . . sorry,' Richard replied, slightly embarrassed.

He looked around; almost everyone was staring at him. Just then, Rachel walked into the theatre.

'My apologies for being late, Sir,' she said, directing her remark to the Commander.

'No problem, I understand. How did it go?'

'Yes, Monaghan's fine, Commander, all sewn up. It was a nasty cut and he will be out of action for at least a week.'

The Commander acknowledged her with a nod, and returned his attention to John Graysham. He was still on the podium, halfway through his brief. Rachel's eyes met Richard's as she sat down. She smiled warmly.

'As I was saying,' continued Graysham. 'Surface radiation across the entire spectrum, but particularly the gamma count, appears to be more intense than we had predicted. This increase is due to the sun's present instability and the unusually prominent solar activity that was discussed yesterday. Consequently, I recommend that further surface surveys are postponed for at least two or three days until radiation levels fall back into the safety zone. In addition, I recommend Richard and NCO Preston have a gamma screen today sometime, just to be on the safe side.'

'Agreed, make it so,' said Commander Miko. 'Anything else?'

'As you know, we are flat out on the second laboratory, Sir. It should be ready as detailed, by Tuesday evening at the latest. We are using the shielding from the remote communications boosting station south side, so, can I just remind everyone that the building is now out of bounds until further notice? That's it from me.' Graysham stepped down from the podium.

The Commander turned to face the audience as he stood up. 'OK, thank you everyone. Same time tomorrow please. Oh, and good work, all departments.'

Greg Searle approached the commander as the audience left the theatre. 'I've prepared the coded message to Admiral Ghent in Washington, Sir,' he said quietly, almost whispering, 'ready to transmit on your order.'

'Thank you Greg, go ahead please. Hard copy the reply directly to me please. No emails, dictions or data files.'

'Understood, Sir,' replied Searle.

As the Commander left the theatre, Searle looked around to see Richard and Rachel in a quiet tête-à-tête. 'If there is anything else you would like to report, my door is always open,' he said, looking directly at the couple.

Neither of them responded, before the door closed gently behind him.

'What did he mean by that?' asked Rachel.

'If I tell you, I'll have to kill you,' replied Richard, playfully.

'Oh, very funny. Who do you think you are, 007? Come on, its sickbay for you and these gamma counts!'

CHAPTER 5

Previous Writings

With a few days free from survey work, a mixed blessing in his view, Richard spent that entire afternoon and much of the evening in his cabin. He had taken the unusual precaution of locking his door, so he could study the alien flight manual.

About the cover size of a magazine, there were at least three hundred aluminium-coloured pages; giving it a thickness inappropriate for its weight. Although paper-thin, flexible and somehow welded at the spine like a conventional book, the material was amazingly tough. Richard could not bend, crease, tear, or damage the pages in any way. Apparently etched without colour, the pages of script and diagrams, when turned, diffracted, then reflected primary colours, just as a prism would: almost as if light itself had been encapsulated within the material.

As he slowly turned the pages subtle shades of red,

yellow and blue danced on the walls and ceiling of his cabin. However, Richard, understandably, was more interested in the book's contents than the light display.

He had studied aeronautical engineering before his flying career, and, latterly, materials science after becoming survey team leader. He had a good science background and an analytical mind, but now, he could hardly believe what he was seeing. Although he could make no sense of the text, which he termed hierographics, because of their pictorial nature, the diagrams, drawings and sections of the large spacecraft were plain to see. The interstellar projections in the navigation section were, of course, unrecognisable, but the size of the section in relation to the manual itself, indicated to Richard that large tracts of this, and probably several other galaxies must have been charted. The whole thing was just incredible. Then, suddenly, one page caught his eye. One projection appeared remarkably like the constellation Orion when viewed from earth. Moreover, the following page, an expansion, looked remarkably like the Crab Nebular, which lies central to that constellation. In particular, the text highlighted a bright star in the midst of that nebular; it caused Richard to ponder the theory that possibly it was the home solar system of the space travellers. Travellers, whose disintegrated ship, had become a lasting, though lost, memorial.

Wherever they had originated from, it was obvious that they were highly advanced technically; civilized and similar, it seemed, to humankind in many ways. There were no pictures of the alien beings in the manual; Richard had been thorough in his study. However, the seats and consoles on the ship's flight deck were laid out in a half-circle and what appeared to be a command or master console, was raised to a higher level, overlooking the others. This corroborated what Richard had seen in the ship itself. Further, he concluded that a command structure or hierarchy had existed within the vessel: similar to that which had been employed by humans since the earliest civilizations and indeed still was. The contents of the manual appeared highly comprehensive, truly amazing and beyond words.

'I've got to try and decipher this text,' he murmured quietly, almost spellbound by what he was seeing. Suddenly, someone turning the handle of his door shattered the silence in the room. The handle rattled for a few moments.

'Richard, it's Rachel. Are you in there?'

Richard leapt to his feet, hid the book under the mattress again, and cautiously opened the door.

'Are you OK?' Rachel asked, concerned. "It's eight thirty and dinner is almost over!'

'Is it that time already?' Richard replied, looking at his watch.

'You never lock your door, Richard, and you rarely miss dinner!' Rachel continued, 'so what's going on?'

Richard paused for a moment, considering the implications of telling Rachel what he had found.

'Oh, I just felt a bit tired and needed some rest,' he said, gently touching her elbow. 'Have you eaten yet?'

'Actually, no. I've been waiting for you in the restaurant,' Rachel said, starting to look a little suspicious.

'So, let's go. I'm starving.'

Richard closed the door behind him and locked it, Rachel looking at him, puzzled.

'What's going on? First Greg in the theatre, now there is all this cloak and dagger stuff? I know something is going on, I know you too well.'

Richard turned and looked Rachel directly in the eyes and then he hesitated. He tried to imagine all the consequences of telling her. He wanted to research this himself, for a while at least.

His face softened, and with a smile he replied softly. 'Look, Rachel, I'm pursuing some personal research, it's of no consequence. Just some work that I would like to keep to myself for the moment. I would like to ask you for some help in the coming days or weeks, but it is confidential. I don't want to raise any suspicions and I definitely don't want Searle on my back.'

'Is it to do with the crystals?'

'No, well, not exactly. At the moment, it's a theory, that's all, OK? So, no more questions, just be normal, routine, you know.' He gave her a kiss on the forehead. 'Come on, let's make dinner before it's all finished.'

He put his arm gently around Rachel's waist for a few

moments as they walked along the corridor. After letting her go first through an emergency airlock hatch, he looked at the long, dark-brown hair over her shoulders and her tall, slim body, emphasised by her white figure-hugging medical suit.

She is beautiful and she deserves more, he thought.

Osiris's main dining hall was, in reality, more like a canteen than a restaurant: and it was affectionately known as 'Stargazers' by base personnel. An enormous square structure almost thirty metres across, its wide blended corners gave the open planned communal area a circular feel; an impression reinforced by the high curved ceiling, which resembled the vaulted ceiling of a cathedral. Supporting this entire structure was an elaborate and intricate framework of tubes, brackets and bracing sockets.

A dark grey, almost black coloured carbon-resin composite encased the myriad of titanium-alloy components and associated structural engineering. This, in turn, contrasted vividly with the pale blue tint of the covering material. On first sight, this impressive structure gave the appearance of a perfect spider's web, blown into a crescent shape by a strong breeze.

The material used for the dome covering was also quite remarkable. Multi-layered, yet nearly transparent, its composition of protective, insulative and, of course, airtight materials, produced a barrier some two hundred millimetres thick. Light in weight yet immensely strong, design criteria would enable the material to self-seal following penetration of a meteorite, up to half a metre in diameter; allowing only minimal pressure loss. It also allowed the beautiful red and orange hues of the Martian atmosphere to filter through, allowing this tantalising, flickering light to dance on the floors and walls of the hall. It reminded many of the northern lights seen regularly at high latitudes back on earth. In the evening, subtle, low-level electric lights created the atmosphere of an intimate, quiet, even romantic restaurant: provided one ignored the bright over-lighting of the self-service counter. The kitchen, positioned immediately behind this service bar, could adequately cater for the entire base company, which numbered a little over one hundred and twenty personnel, although usually, in two sittings.

Osiris, the first and only permanently manned Mars base, consisted primarily of this large central dome and eleven other smaller satellite domes. Completed around ten years earlier, initial construction included the central and first five satellite domes; a further three years being required to complete construction of the six second-phase domes. Positioned symmetrically in two concentric circles around the central dome and linked by transparent, semi rigid, air-inflated walkways, the eleven sub-domes provided the majority of the living quarters. Nevertheless, some subterranean accommodation, albeit limited, remained an important aspect of contingency planning in the event of an emergency. Known as fallout shelters, there were five underground facilities, excavated over a period of six years, each positioned below the five inner domes, providing full facility shelters for up to twenty-five people. Twenty metres below ground level, they could withstand major meteorite damage and, in addition, provide safe accommodation at times of excessive radiation bombardment from space.

Currently underway, the third and final phase of the planned Osiris base expansion programme, involves the construction of a further six sub-domes together with a more complex network of interconnecting walkways. Although work is expected to take another two years, a monorail system, including a single carriage for eight people, is already up and running. This system will eventually circumnavigate the whole base, but at present links only the first four domes of the phase three expansion.

The central dome houses the restaurant, an emergency electrical generating plant, the library, and also some private accommodation. Two out of the second ring of domes are biodomes growing fruit and vegetables. Two further domes contain scientific laboratories, and the theatre, whilst the fifth is for accommodation. All of these structures have two floors, except for the central dome, collectively known as the Space Centre, which is predominantly open-planned. Upper floors are devoted almost entirely to unisex accommodation.

Garaging and servicing for the surface vehicles,

decontamination, base maintenance, and the survey department are housed in two of the latest three-quarter-hemispherical outer ring domes. Each has a radius of about twenty metres, and the third outer ring dome, commissioned the previous year, is now the life services centre. Here, water, drawn from three kilometres beneath the Martian surface is cracked into its component atoms, providing oxygen for atmospherics, and hydrogen for the electrical generation plant. Carbon dioxide and nitrogen for the breathing mixture is extracted from the biodomes and the recycling plant respectively.

With Osiris base expanding in terms of both real estate and personnel, electrical consumption is high. Transparent solar panels, covering about sixty percent of the combined surface areas of the domes contribute some thirty percent of the daily requirement, but can, when combined with a network of subterranean electrolytic batteries, supply the entire base in emergencies. However, this arrangement requires careful management and is for limited periods, as solar charging is diurnal and the naturally occurring underground reservoirs of dilute sulphuric acid, quickly lose potential.

Contributing considerably to the success of the Osiris base expansion programme is the ingenious electrical distribution system. Designed initially in the first few years of the new millennium, skeletal distribution saves on time, weight and literally miles of traditional electrical cable. The primary component of the system is the Picotube.

These microscopic hollow tubes formed into honeycomb-shaped walls, give immense strength at a molecular level. The walls of these tubes are composed of two or more layers of linked carbon atoms, resulting in long cylindrical structures with a diameter thousands of times smaller than a human hair and a strength-weight ratio hundreds of times greater than the equivalent titanium alloy strands. In addition, Picotubes have amazingly low electrical resistance and are able to conduct electricity better even than copperlithium wire. Heat resistant paint, a material composed for the most part of Picotubes suspended in a metallic emulsion, covers almost the entire Osiris base. This coating, permanently electrolysed, gives unique benefits. Supply of electrical power, anywhere in the base, requires just a distribution socket bonded onto the inner skin. Within the socket, integral terminals penetrate the skin to make contact with the outer electrolysed coating. This process saved transporting hundreds of tons of cable from earth and hastened the development and expansion of both the moon base, Andromeda, and Osiris.

An unexpected benefit also comes in the form of solar ray filtration. The electrification of the domes produces an electro-magnetic flux, a kind of force field, around each dome, which helps to absorb or reflect harmful solar radiation. Unlike the earth's atmosphere, which contains ozone, a naturally occurring barrier to radiation, Mars has only a very thin and unstable atmosphere and this offers minimal protection against radiation, with its complex wavelengths. When it was discovered that this radiation, particularly in the gamma ray spectrum, is considerably lessened within the domes, the use of costly shielding materials largely became redundant.

Permanently occupied for the last nine years, Osiris is home to over one hundred technical, scientific, medical and administrative personnel from at least twenty different countries, and possibly the same number of religions. At forty-eight, Base Commander Todd Miko is the longest serving and oldest member of its complement. With a little less than two years to retirement, his career has been divided between Mars, the moon, and several space stations. The youngest is undergraduate Gillian Dean, just twenty-one. She has served for just eight months and three weeks, having successfully applied to the Combined Northern Universities Board of Scotland to study astrophysics and astronomy. After an academic field year on Mars, Dean is due to return to earth on the next manned shuttle.

Osiris has several specialist scientific departments. Research and development into a variety of high profile projects is ongoing: the Institute for Space Sciences funds most of them. Occasionally, however, private enterprise funds the research. For example, PORAPEP the giant cosmetics conglomerate generated billions in profits by using the reduced gravity of Mars to develop the pioneering anti-ageing treatment, Dermavail. This treatment involves ion absorption and skin elasticity improvement in a zero weight chamber, and has become the essential weekly therapy for the fashion conscious, middle-aged women (who can afford it) back on earth.

Other high profile projects involve alternative energy source development for earth. There, traditional carbon-based fossil fuel suppliers are particularly hard pressed as the remaining known and accessible subterranean deposits are finally drying up after decades of over production and wastage. A more recent, and spectacular success, applauded by the whole interplanetary science community, has come from the small space telescope group, STG, which forms part of Osiris's Space Science Department. Last year, the optical telescope, Vision, in high orbit above Mars, with an unprecedented and unobstructed view of the galaxy, managed to track an extraterrestrial satellite. Thought at first to be a tiny comet as it entered the solar system from behind the planet Pluto, the satellite passed quickly through the solar system, and within ten thousand miles of earth. Then, accelerating by using an excessively close orbit around the sun to move at almost the speed of light, it continued on its journey back into the cosmos almost on an exact reciprocal track. Travelling too fast to be intercepted, even by an earth-based fighter on its initial pass, and at a ludicrous speed on its return, the telescope took scores of photographic images of the satellite, many of astounding clarity. To great excitement, it revealed the satellite to be a large construction, although it was probably unmanned. By emitting and receiving electro-magnetic energy by radio telescopes situated on Mars and earth, the satellite was documented to be the first sensory probe from another galaxy. Sadly, the transmission spectrum was not compatible with current technology and, with its passing being less than a few hours, adjustments were not possible. The consensus of opinion was that the vehicle had been sent specifically to take a close look at earth, possibly for a return visit. From the evidence, there was no other logical reason for such a close encounter.

As Osiris was immensely important to the science community and the space programme generally, and with international funding set to continue, Commander Miko was confident of seeing his time out there.

When Rachel and Richard arrived in the restaurant, the kitchen had just closed.

'Disaster,' he said. 'I'll see what I can do, just hang on.'

Rachel looked disappointed as Richard disappeared through the double doors to the kitchen. A few moments later, his face appeared around the door, sporting a broad grin.

'Amanda's the chef this evening, so what would you like?'

There was no doubt that Richard had a way with the fairer sex. Indeed, the majority of women on Osiris considered him to be naturally charming. Anyway, it generally worked both ways and favours were always repaid. Amanda, one of the five chefs, was also a geologist, and Richard frequently found interesting specimens for her collection.

'That's great,' replied Rachel, lightening up a little. 'I'll have a tuna salad.'

Richard's head disappeared behind the door. Moments later he reappeared again, and walking towards one of the corner tables, gestured to Rachel.

'Shall we?' he asked, pulling out a chair for her.

'How do you do it, Richard? You're impossible!' Rachel said as she sat down.

'Just my way with women,' he beamed, adjusting the condiments.

Ten minutes later Amanda appeared with two large tuna salads. The vegetables came from Osiris's biodomes; only the tuna steak was synthetic, made from rehydrated soya protein with tuna flavouring.

'You're a star,' said Richard, putting his hand on Amanda's shoulder. 'This is very much appreciated, I must say.'

Amanda looked at Rachel and raised an eyebrow. 'What do you do with him?'

'Ignore him as much as possible,' Rachel replied. They both laughed.

'Oh look! There's Bill Bradley. I must catch him before he goes,' said Richard, sensing impending harassment from the two women. 'I'll be two minutes, maximum.'

Richard caught Bill Bradley at the restaurant doors. 'Hey Bill! Got a minute?'

'Richard, my dear chap. So, you're the one responsible for all this extra work on my desk? You've caused a huge stir with these crystals you know.'

'Yes, sorry about that. Listen, Bill, I need your help.'

'Really, that's unusual. How can I be of service?'

'I need access to the education centre computer,' Richard continued in a hushed voice. 'Mainly out of hours, I've got a personal project to get started and I need access to the linguistics database.'

Bradley threw his head back and laughed loudly. 'You're going to learn a language?' he snorted, with a confused expression of surprise and amusement.

Richard waved his hands in an effort to suppress Bill Bradley's laughter.

'Well, not exactly, but it's confidential.'

'OK, Richard, I get the picture. I can lend you a key. The centre usually closes around seven o'clock.'

'Cheers, Bill. Does the programme include hieroglyphics?'

'Hieroglyphics?' said Bradley, incredulously.

'Shhh! Yes, and ancient Greek and Mayan and any other ancient languages that use pictorial text,' said Richard almost in a whisper, in order to emphasise the secret nature of his request.

'No! The linguistic programme doesn't include ancient languages at all; only current ones.'

'Well, can you get a programme that does?'

Bradley thought for a moment. 'I'll have to request it from earth and all routine communications are restricted. As you know, anything that does go out has to be cleared by security.'

'Yes, and that's bound to raise suspicion?'

'Well, you have to admit, it's a bit of an odd request Richard.'

'Is there anyway you can help me with this? It's important.'

'Well, there is one way, but if Searle hears about it there will be problems, serious problems, so it had better be worth it.'

'It is. What's the time scale?'

'There's a secure communication file planned for transmission at eight tomorrow morning, I can clip an e-diction on the side tone. A friend of mine will open it and respond. I do it sometimes, it's risky, but normally foolproof.'

Richard looked Bill in the eyes; he was surprised to say the least. Bill Bradley was a good friend. Of similar height to Richard, but somewhat overweight, he had a rounded face with a red complexion and a thick neck. He was also of a similar age: but a receding hairline and greying temples, together with his heavy frame, combined to add around ten years to his appearance.

Nonetheless, as far as Richard was concerned, Bill was totally dependable. As a senior communications engineer, he had unlimited access to the accelercom operations centre and supervised the databank storage facilities for almost the entire computer network on Osiris.

'Have a response by midday, I would think. I'll condense all the loose files, plus any ancillary information into a single programme and transfer it to a health chip. That way you can keep it on you between sessions.'

Richard nodded, impressed. 'Thanks Bill, much appreciated, see you tomorrow then, about twelve? Mum's the word,' said Richard, tapping his nose with his finger. 'Got to go . . . dinner with Rachel.'

Bill Bradley was true to his word and provided Richard with a Series 2 health monitor chip, a powerful microprocessor and memory chip, approximately ten-millimetres square and three thick; with its programming containing all known ancient languages with their written word as pictorial text. Richard noted that they were all dated to before year zero on the Gregorian calendar. Placing the chip into his combined electronic identity tag and vital functions monitor, Richard knew that it would be well concealed. He had decided not to question Bill further on why he should continue to communicate with earth, despite the ban. Perhaps more to the point, why he should use such a secretive method. He was just grateful for the help.

CHAPTER 6

Toil and Trouble

With three further days confined to base due to the high gamma count, Richard's intention was to use this unexpected down time productively in his quest to decipher the alien text. He used his personal key, acquired from Bill Bradley, to enter the education centre later that evening, having first ensured that all staff members and other users had left for the day.

Richard sat at a computer terminal on the far side of the room, one that was concealed from view, particularly from the main doors, by an opaque plastic dividing screen. He removed the modified health chip from his electronic ID locket and after inserting it into the machine's HC drive, entered, twice, a new security code. It was one he had conceived earlier that day, and one he felt was rather appropriate.

The leader page of the programme appeared on screen

as he pulled the alien flight manual from his bag. First up was ancient Egyptian. Richard skipped the history lesson and moved straight onto the written word section. Confronted with the ancient Egyptian alphabet and their numerals, he continued to scroll through page after page of deciphered text. These apparently, were planned exercises for the advanced student to practice sight-reading. Richard considered it too dangerous to engage the audio teach facility, for fear of someone over-hearing his efforts.

Frustrated, he moved forward to the other three principal ancient languages that had been selected on his behalf, by a professor of linguistics at Oxford University. The professor, as luck would have it, was an old college friend of Bill Bradley's.

Phoenician, Mesopotamian and Northern Semitic or Sumarian all featured. Unfortunately, the study format was the same. Here though, Richard found a note. 'Try also Ancient Greek and Ancient Chinese: the former derived from Mesopotamian with cuneiform script, the latter based on pictograms.'

'That's not much help, and what is cuneiform script anyway?' Richard whispered.

Realising that this was going to take a little longer and be a little more involved than he had first expected, Richard went back to the contents page of the Egyptian section. Scrolling through he stopped at section two, the Egyptian Alphabet.

'Section two,' he said quietly. The computer responded

with the contents page of section two. 'Select chapter one, English Transcriptions, and raise volume to level two.'

'Chapter one,' responded the machine, in a woman's voice remarkably similar to Rachel's. 'The Basic Alphabet.'

The screen changed to a block layout of the Egyptian alphabet. Beside each figure was its English counterpart; and numbers were at the bottom of the page, one to a hundred. Richard quickly opened the flight manual to the first full page of text. He scanned the text slowly, as he had done several times before, in order to refresh his memory, then he turned his attention to the screen.

Moving between the two texts, he immediately saw a similarity between several of the characters. A bird, standing, drawn facing to the left; that was similar to the figure depicting U. A hawk, facing left but looking at the reader; that was almost the same as the M figure! Then that one . . . the top half of a circle, its translation was exactly a T! Richard, beginning to get excited, propped up the manual next to the screen, his head and eyes moving between the two like a spectator in the front row of a tennis tournament.

'Look at that! he exclaimed, leaning back excitedly in the swivel chair.

'I'm sorry, Richard, I do not understand the directive,' responded the computer.

Richard looked around nervously before resuming his semi-crouched position.

'Expand letter M, full screen.'

'Letter M, the pictorial representation is of a small hawk. Believed to date from the earliest period of Egyptian writings, this letter has sacred connotations relating to ...'

'Stop audio,' said Richard suddenly, cutting short the description.

He peered intently at the screen. 'It's exactly the same, exactly the bloody same!' His jaw dropped open, with sheer amazement.

'Try U. I mean, expand the figure depicting U!'

The computer responded by filling the screen with the picture of a standing bird. It had two clearly defined legs and small wings, like a chicken, or a waterfowl. The cancelled audio narrative now appeared as text at the bottom of the screen.

'Again, from the earliest writings ...' said Richard, in a hypnotic whisper. 'Seen in script carbon-dated to the First Dynasty; over four thousand years before Christ!'

Scanning the flight manual, he counted the number of times the M picture occurred.

Six, seven, eight. Only eight times, in a whole page of text, he thought. Therefore, M isn't that common. What about T? He checked twice. There were thirteen, so T is more common than M ... pretty much the same as in English. 'Which has both Latin and Germanic derivatives?' Richard concluded aloud.

Leaning back in his chair again, Richard looked across towards the main doors of the education centre.

'This is going to be easier than I thought, almost a direct

translation. Surely not!'

He counted the pictorial representations which were identical, then those less so and finally those which had some common features.

'Six definites, four probables and five maybes,' he whispered. 'Fifteen characters from an English alphabet of twenty-six, plus nine numbers and a zero, thirty six digits in total, that's a forty percent hit!'

'Programme. How many letters and numbers in the ancient Egyptian, Greek, Roman, Mayan, Inca and, well, the ancient Hebrew alphabet, if there is such a thing? Audio on.'

The sophisticated machine hummed for a few moments before replying. 'Richard, the ancient Egyptian alphabet had a basic thirty written characters, numbers were in addition. Greek, has a basic twenty-four characters, again numbers are in addition. Hebrew however, is more difficult, as there is no agreement over the use of a single transliteration system in this case. The equivalents given in the library files are widely used, but several other possibilities can be found. As a result, we retain very little information on Hebrew. The Romans used . . .'

'OK, OK, stop now!'

The information was coming too fast to correlate, and anyway, Richard was not sure if it had any relevance.

'Just out of interest,' he asked again, 'what about the Maya and Inca languages?'

'The Mayan and Inca civilisations were totally

independent societies, separated both by time, several thousand years in this case, and geography. The Mayan civilization was very advanced and had a sophisticated written language, again based on pictograms. However, the Inca did not have a coherent written language,' the computer responded.

Richard thought more about Hebrew. Despite its current use, he also knew that it was a very ancient language, almost unchanged or diluted over the millennia.

'Programme, display the ancient Hebrew alphabet,' Richard demanded.

'I am sorry, but in this instance I am not able to present details of the Jewish language, ancient or modern!'

'Why not, programme?'

'Hebrew, and all references to it, were removed from my database prior to formatting, Richard.'

'Why, and by whom programme?'

The computer fell silent.

'Answer programme, immediately!'

'I am not at liberty to say, Richard, this function was prohibited.'

'Who compiled your database? Respond!" said Richard, becoming irritated.

'Mandy Wheeler, operative 0044242 of the National Linguistic Library Oxford University, United Kingdom.'

'And why did she delete those files?'

'I am not at liberty to say, Richard.'

'Right' said Richard, suppressing the need to raise his

voice in frustration. 'Was your database complete when you left the NLL?'

'Yes Richard, it was.'

Taking a deep breath, Richard lay back in his chair and studied the ceiling, his euphoria evaporating swiftly.

'Shut down, programme. Save to health chip memory and eject. Do not save, repeat, do not save in any other mode.'

There was a whirring noise from the terminal. The computer's main voice, a synthetic neutral voice, somewhere between male and female, responded.

'Linguistic programme shutdown Lieutenant Commander Reece, health chip ejected, Sir.'

Richard removed the chip from the computer, shut down the system and left the education centre deep in thought. Troubled, with a dozen questions nagging in his mind, he stepped out briskly along the walkway leading towards space centre, his head down. Suddenly he stopped in his tracks.

'Blast! I've forgotten to lock the education centre!' he lamented, shaking his head.

Turning on his heels, he quickly retraced his steps. Rounding the final corner, which led to the main door of the centre, he paused momentarily. He thought he heard the quiet thud of a sliding door closing; but there was no movement. The education centre's east door was at the bottom of a cul-de-sac, there were no other doors, and, of course, no one had passed him. He looked at the small square electronic panel on the left side of the door, about half-way up the frame. The red light was on, indicating that the door was locked.

Had he locked it without thinking, and not recalled his actions? He passed his health chip over the sensor panel. The red light extinguished, there was a clunk as the magnetic locks retracted, then the green light illuminated. The door slid quietly open from left to right. He pressed the little-used light switch selecting manual or automatic lighting to manual, and stepped into the dark room. The door closed behind him.

'Who's there? I know someone's there, I'm not security and it's not a problem to me.'

Richard fumbled unsuccessfully for the manual light switch with his left hand. The silence became almost deafening and his eyes strained to become accustomed to the darkness. There, towards the far left-hand corner of the room, he could see the misty glow of a monitor screen: and over the silence, there was the barely audible hum of a computer system in operation.

Senses heightened, with his pupils dilated in order to steal what little light there was in the room, Richard subconsciously held his breath. He could feel someone was in the room. Barely able to see the gaps between desks and modules, Richard walked slowly towards the monitor. He sensed the slightest hint of perfume in the air.

'I know you're there, believe me it's not a problem, its me, Richard Reece. I'm not one for calling security, but I will if I need to.'

He paused, his heart racing.

'What the?' Raising his fists instinctively, Richard stepped back a pace.

A figure lunged out from between two filing cabinets, almost standing on his toes. He could feel the adrenalin flowing through his veins.

'No, Richard. It's me!'

Seeing Richard's clenched fist held high, the figure stumbled backwards, tripped over a chair and landed clumsily: accompanying the mayhem was the clatter of a plastic tray and its contents of stationery. The subdued light of the monitor cast a shadow over the face of this unlikely impostor.

'Rachel! What the hell? Are you all right?'

Richard stepped forward quickly, reaching out to her with both hands.

'Ow! That hurt!'

Rachel grasped the outstretched hands. Richard pulled her up gently.

'Sorry about that. Are you OK?'

'Yes, I think so . . . just! But why were you so threatening?'

Richard's pulse rate began to settle.

'Well, I didn't know who was there, did I? Could have been anyone. Anyway, Rachel, sweetheart, what on earth are you doing here at this time of night?'

'Actually, I came to consult the CMO database, I've got

a small operation coming up in a few days and I needed to remind myself of the procedure.'

Rachel looked down at the floor, avoiding eye contact with Richard.

'What, at this time of night?' said Richard, a little aggravated.

'Well, I don't have a great deal of spare time during normal hours these days, do I?'

Richard breathed out loudly, shaking his head; his sigh like one instigated by sad news. 'If I didn't know better?'

He put his hand under Rachel's chin, lifted her head gently and looked into her eyes. The delicate, barely perceptible, but all too familiar perfume softened his resolve.

'Something's going on here, Rachel. It's bigger than both of us and it's going to get messy, I can feel it. You know something I don't; I can feel that too. I'm onto something at least as big as the earth-saving potential of those damn crystals, but you and I, Rachel, us, we are going to suffer if we are not one hundred percent honest with each other. That is if you're bothered about us?'

'I am bothered about us, Richard, and you know it. Anyway, you're the one being secretive. I have no idea what you are talking about. Look.' Rachel pointed at the monitor screen. 'Basic surgical procedures for melanoma removal, all right?'

Richard stared at the screen for several seconds and then looked up again. 'OK, Rachel. I understand, and I apologise, OK?'

'And so you should Richard, you know that we have had an increase in the rate of skin cancer over the last six months and it's me who has to provide the care, and the reports, and the statistics. It's a lot of work, you know. How you manage to stay clear, I just don't know. Even with the increased sun spot and solar flare activity we have seen over these last few months, you still seem to be totally immune.'

'Well, its genetic, isn't it?'

'I suppose it must be, Richard, anyway, let's get out of here, it's late and I'm tired.'

'Yes, I suppose it is,' agreed Richard, as he shut down the computer system. 'Is there time for a little glass of wine? I've got a bottle started,' he asked, half expecting a firm rejection.

'Yes! Why not?'

Richard, eyebrows raised to smooth his frown, smiled.

'My place then?'

'Yes, your place, but just one," said Rachel softly.

'One's enough!' replied Richard mischievously, breaking into a broad grin.

'You're incorrigible, you really are!'

CHAPTER 7

Secret Enemy

Richard could not believe it. Sitting back, shaking his head then pinching the bridge of his nose between his thumb and forefinger, he looked up, bleary eyed, at the green digital chronometer on the far wall of the now very familiar education centre. It had looked so easy at first.

'It's just not working, six nights and stalemate. No progress at all,' he sighed.

The clock read zero four ten MCT as he stood up, arching his back to reverse a prolonged hunch that had developed after hours in front of the computer screen. Richard's computer skills were good but not good enough for this work.

'I think I'm going to need some help on this,' he admitted to himself quietly, looking again at the clock to verify the early hour. 'Better go, I've got a briefing tomorrow and I had better stop talking to myself. It's becoming a habit!'

He looked around the dimly lit education centre, as if to check that no one else was party to his murmurings. Then, as he looked down at the keyboard to close the programme, he noticed out of the corner of his eye, in the bottom right hand corner of the screen, a row of four or five digits. They appeared briefly and then they were gone.

'What's this then?' he whispered, suddenly snapping out of his sleepless haze and sitting down again. He pressed auto on the keyboard, knowing his computer skills were not good enough to freeze-frame and recall the previous picture.

'Main programme, come up, volume one!'

'Yes, Richard. You are working late again tonight, I see. How can I help you?'

'Firstly, you don't see!' snapped Richard uneasily. 'I require you to freeze frame and recall, second by second, the previous five minutes of display time on monitor three.'

There was silence.

'Do it now programme!'

'That is a simple function you can perform yourself on the keyboard, Richard. Please refer to the help menu, section four, subsection four.'

'Damn it, computer. Do it now!'

Silence followed; the machine's procrastination inappropriate and insubordinate.

'Very well, Richard,' replied the main programme

eventually, its patronizing, almost condescending tone, unfamiliar to Richard.

The screen began to flicker, one frame per second passed; they came and went monotonously. After two minutes and thirty-five seconds, the digits appeared.

'Stop!' ordered Richard. 'Freeze the screen now!'

The frame stopped at two minutes and thirty-nine seconds. He peered closely at five small digits in the bottom right hand corner.

'Enlarge the five digits, bottom right.' Almost reluctantly, the computer responded.

'Alpha, Romeo, Zero, Zero, Zero. Now what's that?' he asked. 'Programme. What's the nature of these digits? Is it a code?'

'I have no idea Richard. I do not recognise the two letters and three numbers as a code.'

Richard felt the hairs on the back of his neck prickle.

'Someone's accessing my work. Programme, come up security.'

The computer voice changed to a deep male voice.

'Main security programme, Richard. How can I help?'

'Do you have a free terminus or are you restricted? Answer!'

'I have restrictions in Level 2, Communications; Level 4, Power and Life Support, and your personal clearance level also restricts Level 7, Base Personnel and Medical Records. That's all Richard.'

'OK, access my personal health chip programme. It's

running now, language study.'

'It is done Richard, an ancient language study course, interesting. But I see you are also working in other areas, and not completing the study course in the correct chronological order.'

'Yes, that's right. Now listen to my instructions. On my screen, monitor number three, I have freeze framed a real time image that occurred about ten minutes ago. Can you access this?'

'Yes, of course.'

'Right. There are five small digits in the bottom right hand corner. They appeared for a second or two, by mistake I believe. What are these digits?'

The computer responded instantly. 'It is an access code Richard, but I do not recognise it. Alpha, Romeo, Zero, Zero, Zero. It's not one allocated to any Mars based personnel.'

'How is that possible? Communications are restricted between earth and Mars.'

'I do not know Richard. Apart from your first session on the seventeenth, every minute of logged-on time has been accessed in real time.'

'So who's downloading my work? Where is it going?'

'I am unable to answer that question Richard. However, to access a personal health chip, Level 7 security is required. Only three people on Mars have that level of security: the Base Commander, The Chief Medical Officer, and the Medical Officer.'

'Legally, that is!' said Richard, becoming increasingly agitated. 'So, after access, what happens then?'

'It is quite simple. After access, one requires only a datalink to pass and store the information. I reiterate Richard, there are no files, in any system in Osiris, active or dormant, listing Alpha Romeo Zero, Zero, Zero. It is possible that the information is being passed back to earth during one of the routine communication parcels.'

Richard stared blankly at the screen for a second or two, mesmerised by the enlarged code.

'There's a lot more to this than meets the eye, and I don't like it, not at all.'

'Can I be of any further help Richard?' the main security programme enquired after a delay of several seconds. 'My services have been requested at another terminal.'

Richard checked his watch. 'Be available tonight programme, twenty two hundred. I'm going to log on at the normal time. I want to trace this access code, find out who the hell's looking over my shoulder.'

'I understand, Richard. I'll see you then.'

The comment passed Richard by as he shut down the terminal. 'I need a few hour's sleep,' he muttered.

Two gentle taps on Richard's cabin door later that morning got no response. The following three, more energetic, had the desired effect however and Richard awoke abruptly from a deep sleep. The door opened gently, just enough for Rachel to squeeze her head through; she looked down at the pile of clothes covering Richard.

'Wow, Richard, you're slacking. You left your door open. Unlike you these days,' she commented sarcastically, displaying a broad, sweet, butter wouldn't melt kind of smile. 'Come on,' she continued, 'its nine o'clock. Surveys start again tomorrow, holiday's over.'

'I know, I know.'

'God, Richard, you look terrible. I think you would benefit from a few early nights. I've got to pass you fit at this afternoon's briefing and . . .'

'Don't say it! I know, you've got to be one hundred and one percent sure.'

'Correct! Now I'm going to breakfast and I expect to see you there in fifteen minutes,' ordered Rachel, closing the door slowly.

'Oh really? So I take orders from you now, do I?'

'It's for your own good.'

'How could I forget to lock the door?' said Richard. His words were wasted; Rachel had already gone.

Richard placed his congested red plastic breakfast tray down on Rachel's table and pulled up a chair. He scrutinized attentively, his two large bowls of wheatflake cereal, three thick slices of toast, a small pot of traditional seville orange marmalade, a depleted glass of fruit juice and his favourite cup of English breakfast tea. He was definitely looking better. Shaven, hair combed, a clean white t-shirt, but still bleary eyed. Three mouthfuls into his first bowl of cereal before he looked up, Rachel knew that nagging him was pointless.

'You know the importance of a good night's sleep, Richard! You've used it as an excuse on several occasions. You know, priorities!'

'Oh ha ha.'

'OK, I'm sorry, but look at you. I'm worried about you. You know more than anyone that your judgement must be one hundred percent when you're outside and on two or three hours sleep a night, for I don't know how many nights, frankly I'm not sure that it is!'

'Oh really, and how do you know I'm only getting two or three hour's sleep a night?'

'Richard!' Rachel exclaimed before checking herself. 'The medical programme monitors your health chip continuously as you well know. I can access the records and get a printout of your biorhythms and cerebral state at any time. It's my job apart from anything else.'

'Oh yes? And what other programmes of mine are you accessing?' asked Richard, looking directly into Rachel's eyes.

'What do you mean?' Rachel pushed her coffee cup to one side, squaring up for a showdown.

'Oh nothing. Nothing at all.' Richard's spoon hovered over his second bowl.

'No, come on Richard, it's time we had this out. You have locked me out of your life since that night in the education centre and you're putting in more after hours work than a regular night watchman. So I need to know if your medical capacity's in doubt.'

Richard's spoon dropped into the bowl of cereals, splashing long-life milk over his toast. He paused, knowing full well that Rachel could, and would, ground him if required. He also knew that it was time to navigate a different course if he was to achieve his goal of deciphering the flight manual of the Ark, the name he had given to the spaceship. He looked at Rachel, beautiful even at that time of the morning, with her hair pulled back tightly into a neat chignon, emphasising her elegant neck.

'Rachel, I know that you have an open, practical and logical mind,' he said, trying not to sound condescending, 'and all the other qualities that make you a great CMO, but how open are you to, well, extraterrestrials?'

'Oh come on, Richard, we all know that aliens exist. It's been proven beyond doubt. The sighting in 2009 for example and the evidence on the moon. It's overwhelming! Of course I believe in life outside the galaxy.' Rachel looked at Richard, a little confused.

'OK, what about hard evidence? Evidence so categorical and with such potential, that it completely rewrites the history books, accelerates the colonisation of other planets by humans, accelerates technical development and possibly lends a hand in solving the energy crisis back home? What would you say to that?'

'My first reaction would be, are you serious? But I can see that you are. Richard, I know you have found something on survey, probably in or around the Kalahari site. It's since then that you've been acting so strangely. Locking your door, studying all hours, cloak and dagger behaviour, but you know the rules as well as I do. Anything unusual you find on the surface is documented and then only retrieved to base on express approval of the Base Commander.'

'Yes, I know, but this is different.'

Richard shifted slightly nervously in his chair and looked around to see if anyone was within earshot. His eyes widened slightly, surprised that despite his best efforts, he appeared so transparent to Rachel. Late into breakfast, the restaurant had all but cleared; nevertheless, since the computer programme hacking incident, he had become cautious, very cautious.

'Look Rachel, I've got something to tell you. Maybe I should have let you in earlier, but more to the point, I need your help. You've been patient with me, I know. I thought long and hard about it and without you, I don't think that I can achieve a result. Having said that, and despite my feelings for you, I think that there's more to you than you're letting on.'

Rachel paused mid-breath. Shocked, perplexed, and trying her best not to show it, she sat back in her chair and crossed her arms defensively, but at that instant and perhaps for the first time, it was clear to both of them that their feelings for each other were beginning to mean more than their vocations. She instinctively put her hands on Richard's, momentarily avoiding his eye contact.

Then, looking up at him, she said, 'You know I love you, Richard, don't you? But you just won't go there. If my job had been simple and straightforward I would have wanted more from you, pursued you even.' She smiled. 'I've tried to understand your reluctance, but life's moving on. For a start, I've only six or seven months to complete in this appointment and then, God knows where I'll be? Probably, I should say, back to earth. It's been a tightrope for me these last twelve months: your bravado, my feelings locked away as a result, my work, your carefree attitude to everything. I've wanted to tell you, but . . .'

Richard opened his mouth to say something in his defence.

'You don't need to explain,' Rachel continued, cutting him short. 'But things are complicated, more than you think, and some serious problems are simmering just below the surface.' She looked at her watch, relieved to have spoken honestly and frankly after so long, but visibly disappointed at the lateness of the hour. 'The time, Richard! Twenty minutes to brief and then back to work for you, the holiday's over, I'm afraid.'

If Richard had had something to say he was unable to find the words, rather he sat there, somewhat stunned and suddenly defenceless. For a brief moment and after so long, Rachel glimpsed in his eyes the spark she had wished and hoped for. Indeed, if anyone else had been present, the open expression on Richard's face would have conveyed it all plainly enough.

'Hey, you two! Don't you have jobs to go to? Breakfast is over.'

The voice broke through the atmosphere like a knife through butter, but the chef's remark, typical of Craig Jones, revived reality from a momentary arrest. Enough had been said, however, or perhaps, not said, to have shifted the orbit of Mars, as far as the two of them were concerned. Richard stood up, his left index finger pointing at Craig and his thumb cocked; like a boy with a make-believe pistol. Trying not to smile, he playfully pulled the pin out of an imaginary stun grenade with his teeth and tossed it into the canteen. Craig, in turn, bounced it on his left knee, then his right, setting up a left-footed volley back to Richard, who avoided the invisible projectile with a duck. Laughing as he grasped Rachel's hand, Richard pulled her through the doorway into the corridor. The door closed behind them. Richard's infectious laughter spread to Rachel who shrieked with delight as she was dragged away from space centre.

As the pair neared the theatre, still laughing, Greg Searle crossed the corridor in front of them. Striding purposefully from right to left, whilst diligently carrying an armful of files, he was obviously on his way to prepare his briefing. Deep in thought, he paid little attention to his surroundings. Richard pulled up short and dropped his hand from the small of Rachel's back. Normally not at all concerned by Greg Searle, or his position, he looked, on this occasion, a little nervous, as he straightened his collar and closed a pocket on his flying suit.

'That was close! Searle is suspicious enough without him seeing us together like this.'

'Like what?' Rachel responded immediately, laughing. 'We're allowed to laugh you know!'

'You know what I mean.'

'Actually, Richard, I don't, and you are becoming paranoid! Shall we continue this conversation tonight, after dinner? Nine o'clock in the sick bay.'

'The sick bay,' repeated Richard slowly, his thoughts in all directions.

'Actually, you're right, probably the most secure area and certainly better than my cabin, considering someone could be listening!'

Rachel frowned and looked at Richard in disbelief, but she realised somehow, or was beginning to at least, that he was very serious.

'I'll see you at the briefing, ten minutes,' she said with a smile. "I've got a general Med-dec to post.'

The unusually large and prolonged solar crescent Sierra Charlie Three Three Four and its associated sunspot had resulted in a sustained gamma ray bombardment of the thin Martian atmosphere at levels not recorded for at least twenty years. Rachel's emailed General Medical Declaration 'posted' to every base member's individual health-chip, explained the results. For most, it would mean a twenty-three day reduction in the average assigned three-year posting to Mars.

Being the first surface briefing for almost ten days, Greg Searle's opening report was long winded, even by his standards. He liked the sound of his own voice and the feeling of self-importance he got from his position as briefing coordinator.

'Earth's been kept fully informed of all developments, Sir; as you directed. Communications status remains red and the Accelercom transmitter is now established as a strictly off-limits area to all non-essential personnel. The protected walkway linking it to the science sector is just about finished. We expect to leak check and pressurise the section later today, or tomorrow morning at the latest. When that's complete, armed security will be in position twenty-four hours a day.'

A murmuring spread around the twenty or so personnel attending the briefing. Richard looked across at Rachel, who looked as surprised as everyone else. Bill Bates raised his hand.

'Yes Mr Bates. You have a question?' said Searle.

'Armed security? Bit over the top wouldn't you say? I've been here almost three years; most of that time in charge of life support, and to my knowledge there has never been a requirement for armed security.'

'Can't be too careful, there's a lot at stake.'

Searle looked at Commander Miko for backup. Commander Miko turned to the audience.

'It's a directive from earth, Bill. I informed the Secretary of State for Energy several days ago; that is my directive regarding the chain of command. His office subsequently decided to release information on the discovery. It is their prerogative. As a result, the crystals are causing quite a flurry amongst the political and scientific communities close to the President, who no doubt fully recognise their potential. To my knowledge only the United Kingdom has been a party to the briefings and security has been set at the highest level.'

'I see. Thank you, Sir.'

'Carry on with the brief, please.'

Searle continued. 'As you are aware, Sir, from the interim report, converting Laboratory Two to a Yearlman standard proved more of a challenge than was first thought. During testing, the electromagnetic leakage rate exceeded safety limits and was therefore unacceptable. The engineering department immediately set about devising a more practical containment device for the crystals and I am pleased to say that this has now been completed. I have taken the liberty of having it moved into the Accelercom building, which, as previously briefed, now has our highest security classification. Basically, the new device is a large container that better utilises the materials available. Approximately one metre in height and depth, the container exceeds the Yearlman standard by fourteen percent. Tests have proved entirely satisfactory. I reiterate that it's the best the engineers can do with the materials available, Sir. They expect it to provide more than adequate shielding.

Incidentally, security around Laboratory Two will remain in place, as the facility is still useful for some experimental work.' Searle paused, to lay weight on his next statement. 'So, the purpose of tomorrow's mission is for Lieutenant Commander Reece to retrieve an additional consignment of the crystals. Now, over to science.'

Peter Meyhew stood up and took the podium.

'Thank you, Greg. As far as we are able to calculate, Commander, the new containment device will be safe for specimens with a combined mass of approximately three kilograms. I reiterate, this is total mass. To remain within this parameter, we expect Richard to select and retrieve a further five smaller specimens. Of course, at the moment, we still know very little about these things, only what they can do when radiated with electro-magnetic energy in the radio-wave spectrum, that is wavelengths above ten centimetres, and quite honestly, their potential is awesome. Using the crystal specimen we have, and by subjecting it to extremely short bursts of energy, we have isolated the frequency spectrum that instigates the heating effect. Incidentally, we have called this extreme heating 'boil-off'. We have found that this 'boil-off' only occurs when the crystals are exposed to radio waves between the frequencies one hundred and twenty kilohertz and two hundred and fifty kilohertz. You may recall that this is the lower VHF to the upper UHF frequency range. Amazingly, these frequency ranges are now only employed by the older line-of-sight communication devices, such as the type utilised for communication with the survey team. Apart from those systems, all our current equipment uses the microwave spectrum, which has much shorter wavelengths. Indeed, if Richard hadn't doggedly hung onto his antiquated radio communicators, as opposed to the current V and W band voice-activated sets that we have been unsuccessfully encouraging him to use, he may never have discovered this awesome and quite unique phenomenon.'

Most of the audience looked at Richard, who shrugged his shoulders.

'Fame at last, Richard!' came a remark.

'So what does this do for us?' questioned Commander Miko.

'Well, Sir, basically, as far as we can deduce, provided the crystals are shielded from these frequencies, there is no reaction and they appear to be quite safe; however, if they are exposed and without some form of foolproof containment, a situation similar to an uncontrolled reactor meltdown will occur. We believe that this situation would be similar to the catastrophic meltdown process experienced in a few of the old nuclear reactors back on earth, in short, the 'China Syndrome'.

'For the uninitiated, Peter, what threat would the China Syndrome pose for Osiris?' enquired the Commander.

'It's quite straightforward. In layman's terms, after prolonged exposure, and we are working on that time frame, the supra heated crystal, reaching we calculate, temperatures only found in the heart of a nuclear reaction, or on the surface of the sun, would quite simply keep going down. It would burn a hole, albeit small, first through the base structure, then through the outer crust of the planet's surface. Exposed to water molecules, this would without doubt generate spontaneous atomic fusion, a self-perpetuating hydrogen bomb no less. Our supposition is that this would destabilise the tectonic plates in this area causing Marsquakes. Worse still, unabated, it could tear the planet apart. Oblivion within, say, ten to fifteen minutes of release.'

'I see, thank you,' continued the Commander with a surprisingly blank expression. 'Two things puzzle me. Firstly why this has not happened before? They have already been energised on the surface?'

'Don't know the answer to that one at the moment, Sir, but we have considered it. We believe that where the crystals lay, there may be either a layer of resistant strata beneath the sand, or, more likely, that there is some sort of filtering or energy absorbing material in the immediate vicinity.

Richard, who was listening carefully, immediately considered the numerous green, glass-like crystals that lay, apparently haphazardly, around the site. Perhaps I was right after all, he thought. Those glass fragments are part of a containment device and they still influence the crystals?

Commander Miko nodded slowly, not entirely

convinced. 'I see. And why do you think these crystals are, where they are? I mean, would you say that they are a naturally occurring mineral, or did they fall from space, as something like a meteorite? Alternatively, could they have been left here by someone or something in the past? It's an open question. Theories anyone?'

There was a murmuring in the theatre and a scratching of heads, as the question had, so far, not really crossed the minds of the audience; save for Richard, who shifted a little uneasily in his seat.

'It's a good point, Sir,' interjected Greg Searle, capitalising on the moment. He sensed a chance to put Richard on the spot. 'Richard. You are probably the most qualified to answer the Commander's question, for obvious reasons. What's your view on the origin of the crystals?'

Richard pondered momentarily. Did Searle know something, or was he just doing his normal thing of trying to discredit people in front of the Commanding Officer? Searle was suspicious about something, Richard was sure of that!

'You're right Greg, it is a good question and one which will need to be resolved sooner rather than later, in order to fully understand the chemistry of the crystals. I mean, discovering their origin will be of fundamental importance I imagine.' Richard looked directly at Searle; he was not happy about the predicament.

'Yes, that's obvious Richard, but do you have a comment relevant to the Commander's question?'

Richard, normally so cool, tingled with aggravation. Rachel, who had moved across to sit next to him in the back row during the previous brief, quietly put her hand on his knee.

'At the moment, Greg, I can't say that I've given the matter much thought. They could be the result of a meteorite impact, but if that were the case, I would expect a wider spread. As the spread is quite small, it's more plausible that they form the head of a mineral outcrop or something like that. Not much help, sorry!" Richard winced.

'I see,' replied Searle condescendingly. 'Perhaps, while on the survey you could take some linear photographs and a seismic overlay of the site? Pass them on to geology, who in turn could do some work on the topography.'

Searle looked at Stephen Myers, head of the geology department. Myers, a popular American scientist in his late thirties, nodded in response. He was not keen on taking orders from Greg Searle either, but it was a logical request. Searle's subsequent, emaciated smile had that irritating self-gratifying look only he could conjure.

'Can we have the specifics for tomorrow's surface survey, please Greg? Time's getting on,' reminded the Commander.

'Yes, of course, Sir,' replied Searle. He walked back to the lectern and checked his notes. 'Tomorrow's survey will commence at zero eight hundred hours and is planned to terminate here four hours and fifty minutes later. Mission directive is the Northeast Sector, covering cross coordinates one fifty through to one seventy-five. It's a three-man team, with the addition of Peter Yung from my department for security and Jennifer Middleton from science.'

Richard's look of surprise was plain to see. Jennifer was a fairly experienced surveyor, having logged around eighty surface hours; but she had been suspended from outside work a few months earlier, following a panic attack close to the West Sector boundary. It had almost cost her her life. Only Richard's prompt actions, which included introducing a phial of Nuromild sedative gas into her helmet via the condensation discharge port, had saved her. The gas calmed her sufficiently for Richard to get her into the buggy and back home, and this only minutes before hyperventilation had exhausted her oxygen supply.

Later, she said that she had seen two humanoid figures standing together, arms raised with fingers pointing at her. They stood inside the mouth of a small shelter created by overhanging rocks. This sighting had subsequently been attributed to hallucinations caused by oxygen starvation. The eerie presences had caused her to confuse her position. She had, apparently, run back and forth within several steep-sided ravines before being found in a state of near hysteria by Richard, and this, only after the medical monitoring team in base operations had alerted him.

Richard's actions, although totally non-standard, had saved her life. Subsequently, Rachel had recommended six months of light station duties for Jennifer, before any thoughts of a case review. Further, a brief investigation had diagnosed the images she had seen as being illusions attributable to a low blood sugar level count, mistakenly overlooked during pre-med.

For these and several other reasons that came to mind, Richard was baffled why Jennifer should be recalled for survey duties within two months of the incident and without a case review. This was not at all the usual routine. Richard turned to look at Rachel; she was impassive. He stared at her momentarily but she was oblivious. He just could not make out if Rachel had a hand in this. Why Jennifer? There were other qualified, although not regular, survey assistants available in science, including Rufus Plant, who would have been a much better and safer choice.

Greg Searle continued. 'In accordance with the current security procedures and amendments due to this rather unique situation, all surface parties will be escorted by an armed security guard. Peter Yung has Class 3 experience and will monitor all surveys for the remainder of this month.'

With this, Richard just had to say something. 'You mention armed security. Just what arms do you have in mind, if I may ask?'

'You may indeed Richard,' replied Searle smarmily. 'I've agreed with Commander Miko that a Mk11 stun pistol, a quasar rod and possibly one or two type twelve low key ionising grenades will be sufficient.'

'Sufficient for what?' demanded Richard. 'What are you

expecting out there? Those weapons are close quarter anti-personnel weapons. Just who do you think the enemy is?'

'Let's not overreact here, Richard. A high level of security is necessary, considering the situation. We can't have these things falling into the wrong hands can we? Over adequate security means an under achieving threat, right?'

Richard sat back in his seat, barely concealing his contempt. He knew if he made too much of this situation it would appear that he had something to hide, but most could see that he was not at all happy with Yung's potentially lethal mini arsenal.

Greg Searle continued with the remainder of the survey details, failing to see Richard's blatant inattention. Leaning over to Rachel, he whispered into her ear.

'What's the deal with Jennifer? I thought that she was out for the duration.'

Rachel was wearing her usual white, two-piece suit and a cream lightweight polo neck . In this, she always turned heads, although, strangely, more attention than this was rare. Perhaps people were aware of her attachment to Richard. On occasion, even he could be thrown off course by her looks. He waited for Rachel's reply, still close enough to her to sense the subtle tones of her perfume. Here was a relevant question and it needed an adequate answer. Interestingly, it was one of those disparate moments, when Rachel could say just about anything and Richard would, in the end, condone her actions.

'She retook the de-sensitising and the psychological

build-up modules and passed them with flying colours; in fact her results were better than her initial course, so what more could I say? Anyway, who's to say that she didn't see anything out there? Maybe she did. Paranormal, spirits, ghosts, who knows?'

Richard could barely believe what he was hearing.

'Ghosts?' he whispered in total bewilderment.

The two people sitting in the next row of seats were within earshot of Richard's inexplicable outburst, and equally bewildered, they turned to look at him.

'Sorry,' he ventured and then shook his head to dismiss Rachel's explanation.

Richard knew full well that ISSF procedures required a full rehabilitation course after a surface incident such as the one Jennifer had barely survived. Normally taken part time, a few hours every week in between other duties, the full course would take a minimum of three months. Adrenaline induced 'fight or flight' attacks as they were called, were not common among such highly trained personnel, but they did still happen, although normally on the moon and in the early stages of training. The rehabilitation procedures were proven and well documented, so, with the de-sensitising and psychology courses taking an additional four weeks minimum, Richard's suspicions were well founded.

Rachel had nothing else to say on the matter and would not be drawn into conversation, despite Richard's disapproving stare. Eventually, he accepted the situation with an appraising nod and an uncomfortable half-smile. His attention refocused on Greg Searle as the brief was concluded.

'One final point, ladies and gentlemen. Please be aware that the PTSV will also be conducting some test firings of the Cyan cannon between ten hundred hours and twelve hundred hours tomorrow. The pulse cannon has only been used, according to the records anyway, five or six times since the initial proving tests post construction and that is well over nine years ago. It is an old system and, apparently, it does make a bit of a racket, but as the main offensive and defence weapon on the vehicle, it's time to bring the system up to full operational efficiency. Two further points regarding this matter. Firstly, as of today, the PTSV will be held at Alert 5 status, that is five minutes from standby to dispatch, the entire period that a survey team is on surface duty. That means fully staffed, continuously. Finally, a decontamination cell has been set up in docking bay four. All survey team members will pass through the cell without exception. We cannot afford for even a speck of these crystals to enter the base area. That completes the briefing. Do you have any comments, Sir?'

Commander Miko shook his head. 'No, nothing specific, but I will say one thing and it's directed at everyone. Things are beginning to get a little complicated, both outside and internally. Do not push it, be critical of your own and everyone else's performance, all departments. Any problems report them. OK, that's it. Greg, plan the debrief for tomorrow evening, sometime convenient to the HODs.'

'Any other points or questions? No? Then brief complete, tomorrow's time will be promulgated,' concluded Searle.

Richard began to feel isolated. He understood the requirement for decontamination, but why only for those actually handling the crystals? Specifically, that would mean him. With armed security accompanying every survey, it didn't take a blind man to see just who potential suspect number one was.

Rachel, ruffling his hair, snapped Richard out of his thoughts.

'Come on, you have something to tell me remember? It's an hour before daily surgery, so how about a coffee in sickbay?'

Most of the theatre had cleared, with just the final few people filing out of the main door when Richard stood up and smoothed his hair down. He frowned disapprovingly at Rachel.

Greg Searle was collecting papers together on the podium. 'I hope the message has got through to you, Reece. You cannot bring anything into Osiris without express command approval. It's an offence under Section 4, as I am sure you are aware.'

Searle looked across at Rachel. He liked her, as most people did, but he also resented her disinterest in him. To Richard, it was plain to see, Rachel, perhaps, preferred not to notice.

'Isn't it about time you two grew up?' he said, visibly aggravated, but passing the comment flippantly as he left the theatre.

CHAPTER 8

A Friend in Need

Richard was in the survey preparation room before seven the following morning. He had several pieces of equipment to check in his inventory, including the current W band communicator. As head of the survey department, he was his own boss. Domestically, he had only himself to worry about and often had a good deal of free time, which he normally put to good use keeping up his flying skills in the fixed base S1 flight simulator, a generic simulator with up to date visuals, but no motion simulation.

Apart from his full time materials assistant, Stores Accountant Miles Perry, additional personnel, supplied on an opportunity basis from other departments, would complement the survey team. Mainly scientists or geologists, all have full time jobs in their respective departments. Normally, around a dozen men and women maintain the relevant qualifications, including emergency drills and procedures, and in a regular month, surface duties would occur two or three times. Usually volunteers, and normally in their late thirties or older, due to unpredictable effects of solar radiation on the human chromosome, they either already had their own families, or alternatively, had no plans to start one. The arrangement was perfect for Richard. He enjoyed working with a variety of people, but had none of the administration, welfare, or general headaches associated with the position of departmental head. On top of that, his salary was in line with his HOD colleagues.

Disappointingly, with his renowned flying abilities and broad experience, Richard would have expected a squadron command a year or two earlier, but the trouble on Andromeda, combined with a temporary loss of his SA1 medical category, scuppered normal promotion prospects. Having said that, three years on Mars suited him well and in this quiet and supposedly low profile appointment, he had gained a good deal of experience and made many friends.

It had also allowed him to regain his self-esteem amongst other things. He had not however, bargained on Rachel. Having kept her at arm's length since their first meeting, his initial surface medical, over a year previously, he was aware of the make or break situation coming his way at Mach ten! Being honest with himself, he also knew that he would not be able to leave in a different direction to her, when that fateful day finally arrived.

The conversation, which they were due to have had the previous day, had not happened. Rachel had been called away during the first few minutes of their coffee break and he had not had time to tell her the full story; maybe he would have an opportunity in the next day or two. Anyway, progress on deciphering the flight manual had practically stopped over the proceeding week and any doubts about asking Rachel for technical assistance had disappeared.

Richard was loading the last few items of equipment onto the buggy when he heard the motors of the PTSV gun turret running up for tests in the adjacent bay. He felt uneasy about live ammunition being carried on board the vehicle. It wasn't necessary and he was very suspicious about Searle's motives in pushing for armed security in general. Richard's train of thought was broken as Miles Perry walked in pushing a trolley with the original Yearlman cube strapped on top. Miles was a Londoner, born and bread in Hackney. He was several centimetres taller than Richard, but with a much slimmer, gangly build, and unlike Richard, he was already thinning on top, despite being in his late twenties. Richard liked Miles very much and not just because of his competence and efficiency in running the section. He was a genuinely nice chap and their common naval background served only to cement their mutual respect and friendship.

'This one has had some minor modifications, boss. Additional shielding in the form of another lead case and two extra brackets for securing it to the buggy, but watch it, it's heavy, damned heavy!'

'OK, thanks Miles. That's the last piece of inventory for today. I'll give you a hand to get it in place.'

The two men struggled to slide the larger cube into position on the rear platform of the scout vehicle; the extra space required being at the expense of the satellite navigation and Stellar Positioning System. Navigation would therefore be back to basics, with a survey chart and frequent position checks passed by radio from operations. Richard knew the survey area quite well, except perhaps for the 'one seventies', which to some extent would be virgin territory.

Richard had also strapped his rigid helmet box onto the overflowing stores platform. Miles caught sight of it. Without speaking, he pointed to the green plastic-coated box, looked at Richard and shrugged his shoulders. Richard just nodded and changed the subject.

'Now listen, Miles. As we discussed yesterday, I've still got my old VHF communicator. I'm not supposed to take it as you know, but I am, as back up so to speak. So keep an open channel. Seven will be fine and don't mention it to a soul. Not even the Doctor!'

'I understand, boss. I'll monitor it continuously whilst you're outside. I'll use 'ear select', no one will know, even if they're talking to me directly. Oh, and by the way, I know that you're a bit concerned about things at the moment, so I, er, shall we say I permanently borrowed this little baby from the security section.'

Miles pulled out a standard Mk11 stun pistol. It was the same as the one Yung would be carrying on survey duties. The Mk11 was small, palm shaped, about fifteen centimetres long, and seven wide. On full power, it packed a plasma charge that would stop an elephant at twenty metres! Normally though, the weapon was pre-locked at forty percent of its maximum charge, setting two of five, where it would render a man unconscious when used at close quarters. A command security code was required to increase its power beyond forty percent.

'Is it coded?' Richard asked with just a hint of a smile.

'I'm afraid so, Sir, but I'm working on it.'

'Well done, Miles. Makes me feel a little less naked, if you get my drift, but keep working on that code all the same.'

'I'm being as charming as I possibly can be, without going over the top. You know what I mean, Sir. Nearly there though.'

Richard knew Miles was referring to a girlfriend of his in security, but did not enquire further.

Yung was OK, a good man, capable and disciplined. He would have preferred Preston, if just for some continuity, but Richard had worked with Yung in the past and was happy to have him along. What he was not happy about however, were the weapons strapped to his belt.

As Yung climbed into the single rear seat of the buggy Richard said, 'You haven't been out for a while have you?'

'No, Sir. It's been a couple of months, my other duties keep me busy, but I'm looking forward to being involved in the programme again.'

'Look, Yung,' replied Richard sharply. 'I'll be perfectly honest with you. I'm pleased to have you along, although I personally do not see the requirement for security on survey duties, but orders are orders and that's fine. What I don't agree with, however, is that weaponry strapped to your belt. I cannot condone it. I mean, who do they think we are going to meet out there?'

'Major Searle has his reasons, Sir. I'm not party to them. I'm just doing my job.'

'Well, that's fine, you do that. But out there, I'm in charge. You do what I say, and so we both understand each other, you don't release the safety catch on those things unless I say so, OK?'

Yung looked him in the eye and nodded. Richard was usually blunt, but even Miles was a little surprised at his authoritarian manner.

'Here's Lieutenant Middleton, Sir,' he said, breaking the frosty atmosphere between the two men.

Jennifer walked confidently towards the buggy and scanned the equipment. 'Morning, Richard,' she said politely, 'and how are you this morning?'

'Morning, Jennifer. Good thanks and yourself?' Richard replied, lightening up a little.

'Yes, fine. Excited about outside duties at last.'

'You're back earlier than expected, Jennifer. You're

happy about that and your rehabilitation?'

'Yes, I'm fine, really, one hundred percent. You don't need to worry about me, Richard!'

'OK, if you say so, that's good enough for me.' Richard stepped towards Jennifer and lightly gripped her forearm, looking at her with a concerned expression. 'Stay a little closer to me than you're used to. If you're worried about anything, let me know early. Agreed?'

'Agreed, Richard,' Jennifer replied smiling. 'Oh, one small problem. My helmet is still in maintenance, waiting for a new condensation valve no less and no spares apparently, until the next shuttle. So I'll need the spare if that's OK?'

'Well it would be OK if we had one. We are generally short on a number of things and Peter here has taken the last remaining in service spare. I'll tell you what, you use mine. It's over there on my locker. I'll go and get my personal spare from my cabin. But be aware that you will be wearing the team leader logo on the back of your helmet, Jennifer.' Richard looked over to Yung, 'You're happy about that?'

'Quite happy, no problem to me. Presumably your replacement helmet is unmarked, Sir?'

'That's right, it's a new one. Still in the box so to speak, I haven't needed to mark it up yet, but I've tested it. It's good, so problem solved. If you two wouldn't mind finishing up the preparations with Miles, I'll be back in a jiffy.'

With that, Richard turned to his assistant. 'Don't forget

our conversation,' he said, and walked towards the door.

'Under control, Sir,' replied Miles Perry, with a nod and a wink.

Richard returned to the survey section with his helmet tucked under his arm and was pleased to find the buggy fully loaded and ready to go. He was keen to get out and do some work: cramped up in the base for so many days had made him irritable. He climbed into the left hand of the front two seats to take control, although with the controls on a central panel, the machine was drivable from either side. Peter Yung and Jennifer had changed seats. Yung climbed in by Richard's side, whilst Jennifer felt more comfortable in the rear seat. Richard switched on his cross band communicator.

'Base ops? This is Survey One. How do you read?'

'Reading you five by five, nice and clear. How me?'

'Yes, loud and clear also thanks. All seated and strapped in. Final systems check, please, and then we can get on with it.'

'All systems in the green, Richard, have a nice one. Time check, zero seven fifty nine, opening up.'

The broad main door of the survey section, crescent shaped to match exactly the contours of the dome itself, rolled upwards in front of them, clattering as it went. Seconds after the seal broke, the cathedral-quiet void reverberated, as a mixture of dust, sand and condensing water vapour filled the air. Like a giant vacuum cleaner, the

Martian atmosphere sucked out the suspension of particles with a deafening whoosh. As the polished aluminium door rose further, glinting and gleaming in the probing sunlight, the resplendence of a new day presented itself. Yung, startled, sat up nervously in his seat and shielded his eyes. Jennifer knew better, focusing for those first few seconds on her feet. Richard gently shook his head from side to side.

'Yes, I know, never fails to catch someone. One day they'll manage to get it right,' commented Richard, pressing the accelerator.

Yung felt his 'street cred' dissolve as Richard looked over his shoulder at Jennifer, smiling.

'No worries, there's worse to come,' he said reassuringly to Yung.

Richard turned the buggy onto a westerly heading and sped off at maximum speed, causing it to bounce every now and then over the uneven terrain.

It was a beautiful morning. The sun, a huge red ball, seemed almost to hang, pendant like, above the horizon, as it cast its familiar, almost molten hue over the vast landscape. Richard breathed in deeply though his nose and scanned from left to right.

'Magnificent, every time,' he said. 'Nice to have a bit of space, don't you think?'

'Yes, it is,' replied Jennifer, 'quite a sight, Richard. Do you intend collecting the samples on the way to Sector one seventy, or on our return?'

'On our return, definitely. The less time we have those things on board, the better.'

Richard began to think of the Ark as he pressed the speed hold facility on the dash. Was there anything to be gained by a visit to the ship, or was it better to keep away from the entrance altogether? He looked across at a more relaxed Yung. No, I had better stay clear, he thought, but it is going to be difficult.

He also had to be sure to orientate his linear camera carefully, and scan each side of the opening, lest someone identify it for further scrutiny. The scout vehicle struggled as it climbed the steep eastern ridge of the Ascension Crater. Richard floored the accelerator almost to no effect. The electric drives, already moaning at him, whined with disapproval.

'Not used to three people and a shed load of stores,' he said, feeling the need to defend the buggy's diminishing performance.

'We'll have to get out and push soon,' replied Yung smiling sarcastically.

Richard forced an agreeing nod. 'Hasn't let me down yet,' he countered.

Avoiding some large, black, circular boulders, Richard steered the vehicle the remaining one hundred metres to the crest of the ridge, and onto an area of level ground, which was comfortably wide enough for the buggy's two-metre track. Teasingly, he took a sharp ninety-degree right turn just before the precipice of the crater rim.

'Wow, that was close,' he joked, as Yung gripped his seat in panic, peering down at the abyss.

'It's quite young you know, relatively speaking,' Richard continued reassuringly. 'In geological terms the meteorite that formed this one impacted yesterday!'

'By that he means at least a quarter of a million years ago,' interjected Jennifer, unimpressed by Richard's boyish antics. 'And the crater is the size of the Isle of Wight.'

'Ha, you've been reading my script then, Jennifer,' said Richard, before being interrupted.

'Survey One? This is Base Ops. How do you read?'

'Yes, loud and clear,' replied Richard.

'Come on, Richard, its thirty five minutes. Where are you?'

'Sorry, Giles. Time goes so fast when you are enjoying yourself! We are negotiating the Ascension ridge line, approaching the half-way point.'

'OK, understood. Be aware that the PTSV is also on station, in line with the new security procedures.'

'Roger, copied, where is it now?'

'Well, its directive is to remain within thirty minutes of you, terrain permitting. It left about twenty-five minutes ago, but it's too big for the Ascension Pass, so it will head your way via West Sectors one twenty, one thirty and the Monument. Oh, and by the way, they are reporting a tracking system malfunction, so they will call in due course for an ADF signal.'

'Roger, that's understood. Listening out! What a waste of resources,' snarled Richard, shaking his head.

'Well, you can understand it,' replied Jennifer, quietly. 'I mean, the potential of these crystals is just amazing and they have to protect them!'

'Yes, but from who? We are quite a long way from home to say the least.'

'Well, you never know, do you?'

With that remark, Richard turned to look at Jennifer; but the expression on his face was all but lost behind his polished, reflective visor.

It took almost twenty minutes to drive to the opposite side of the crater, circumnavigating its rim, despite Richard flooring the accelerator for most of the way. After Ascension, the terrain was almost entirely uncharted. He had spent five ISAPS, about twelve days, in the area over the previous four months; yet he had barely covered twenty percent of the mountainous terrain between the main ridgeline and the wide plain, stretching as it did to the west, as far as the eye could see.

Interestingly, in this area, the wild atmospheric storms so common-place to most of the planet, occurred only infrequently; a phenomena Richard attributed to the topography. As a result, there was little in the way of 'weather' to disturb the surface covering of fine sand and dust. Successive track marks, left by the buggy as it travelled backwards and forwards on regular journeys around the ridge, created the impression of a busy road. Indeed, humouring himself, Richard had nicknamed this sector of the rim Route 66.

The view from the ridge, towering some four thousand feet above the surrounding landscape was monumental, particularly into the crater itself. Richard stopped the buggy and pointed east, towards a tiny glint of light. There was a metallic reflection, almost in the middle of the crater.

'There's the Hydrosysmic equipment I installed in April. The results are very promising, amazing actually,' he said.

Jennifer squinted against the sun, which was now in its full glory above the ridgeline on the opposite side of the crater; its effect was to cast a broad, progressive shadow onto the crater floor. Like a menacing, multi-fingered hand, the dark shadow completely engulfed the area beneath the majestic cliffs. Penetrating this blackness, a thousand feet above the crater floor was a bright, highly contrasting, but narrow vein of yellow coloured rock. Dividing the strata of the cliff face in two, the geology was luminous against the foreboding background.

'What are those amazing yellow streaks?' enquired Yung, pointing in their general direction.

'It's sulphur,' answered Richard. 'It's a substrata, the layer is almost pure, and about eight hundred feet wide. It is normally about a mile beneath the surface. When this meteorite hit, it deformed the crust, rupturing the layer. What we are seeing is where the layer has become exposed.'

Richard turned to the west. 'This mountainous terrain is also a result of the impact. Some of those peaks are almost five thousand feet above the plain. You can see how they radiate out from the main crater, like ripples on a pond after throwing a stone.'

'Wow, must have been some show,' exclaimed Yung, mesmerised.

'I should say so,' replied Richard equally impressed. 'We calculate that the meteorite was at least fifteen kilometres in diameter and impacted at an angle of around thirty degrees: coming in from slightly south of east. It impacted the surface forming this crater, over a mile and a half deep and the seismic disturbance pushed these ranges of mountains up. You can see that they gradually run out of steam to the west some seventy to eighty kilometres away.' Richard pointed to the distant plain. 'We've nicknamed that vast area the Pacific Plain; it's easier than using its correct name, *Isidis Planitia*'.

'I can understand that,' replied Yung, turning to look eastwards again, 'and that huge mountain on the distant horizon?'

'That's a volcano, its called *Elysium Mons*: extinct for over two hundred million years fortunately and over twice the height of Everest. Mars was a very different place when that baby was smoking!'

'So why isn't the place strewn with debris? I mean a meteorite fifteen kilometres in diameter, that would weigh millions of tonnes!' asked Yung, genuinely interested.

'Well, that was the lucky part. Because of the shallow angle of impact, the meteorite literally bounced off the surface and ricocheted back into space. It probably lost about thirty percent of its kinetic energy in the impact. The factor that really saved the planet was its orbital position around the sun.' Richard pointed again. 'It was over there, somewhere. A strange place, due to Mar's eccentricity of orbit. The meteorite was accelerating under the influence of the sun's gravitational pull, Mars got in the way; its own gravity pulling in the ancient slab of ice and rock like a magnet. Fortunately, with the sun's enormous gravitational influence still in the direction of travel, the ball bounced back into space and carried on towards the sun. Incidentally, they estimate that it missed the earth by a mere seventy thousand kilometres. Believe me, in the scale of things, that's nothing, a hair's breadth.' Richard looked at his watch. 'Standby,' he ordered.

'Base Ops? Survey One. Come in.'

'Yes, Richard, strength four. How me?'

'Yes, five by five, thanks. Leaving Route 66 for survey sites fourteen and fifteen. What's the status on the kit?'

'Working normally. The Hydrosysmagragh at West 14 shows photocell number two down to eleven percent, so replace that as planned. The Biorecall at West 15 is just about capacity, so replace the tray and retrieve as briefed. By the way, a request from geology: the water table is indicating unusually close to the surface around fourteen, thirty metres or less, sounds incredible, but they have asked you to keep your eyes open for surface traces!'

'Really?' responded Richard. 'Amazing, surface water. First time in, what? Two hundred and fifty thousand years? Sounds like I'm going to get my feet wet!'

'Well, not quite Richard. Rest of the team OK, I presume?'

'Yes of course, everybody's fine ... just finishing a history lesson. We will be at fourteen in about twenty minutes.'

'Copied. Talk to you then, stay cool.'

'Oh, there is one thing.' Richard stopped short. 'No forget it, it's nothing.'

'Forgotten. Over and out.'

Richard was still concerned about the PTSV's position and status, but had initially forgotten to enquire. He paused momentarily, as he and the crew climbed back into the buggy.

'The PTSV, where the hell is it? We have heard nothing?'

'Probably broken down somewhere,' replied Jennifer.

The gradient steepened as they closed the crater floor and from thereon Richard became a little more delicate with the decelerator drive. He carefully negotiated the twisting track, minimising the sideways skidding for fear of overturning the vehicle.

'About ten minutes to go. I suggest it's a good time to turn on your pre-warmers, people,' he said. 'Once we get into shadow the temperature drops very quickly as you know.'

Jennifer responded first. 'They're on Richard, thank you.'

'I'll leave mine on automatic if it's OK with you. Save a bit of power.'

'That's fine with me, Peter,' replied Richard, looking across at his co-driver, 'but don't forget that the suit sensor is reactive and not proactive. Bit like offering Jennifer a drink at the club bar after she has just bought one. You. might end up getting the cold shoulder for a while, that's all!' Richard smiled.

'One other question, Sir,' responded Peter Yung, ignoring Richard's thinly-disguised gibe. 'The water question, these vast basins and this rock erosion. Just how much water was here?'

'Well, it is an interesting question,' replied Richard, distracted for a moment as he narrowly missed a large outcrop of quartz-encrusted granite. 'The current theory is that Mars was forty to fifty percent ocean at one time. Not as much coverage as the earth, in percentage terms, but substantial none the less. It was a long time ago, when the climate was thought to be much milder, and it wasn't just water. Actually, it would have been highly acidic in some places, almost dilute sulphuric acid, and highly alkaline in others, depending on the underlying rock strata. In either case, corrosive enough to have taken the rubber soles off your boots. It's also believed that areas existed where mixing took place, giving an almost neutral pH and it is in these areas where we have found some high bio-counts. Not just primitive amoebas either, but evidence of complex multicellular organisms. West 15 is one of these sites. They're finding an abundance of dormant plant-like spores, as well as the remains of primitive animal cells.'

'So what happened to all the water?'

'You explain, Jennifer,' responded Richard. 'You know more about it than me.'

'Hey, I'm very impressed with your knowledge. Not just a driver, but a tour guide as well!'

'Well, thank you!' said Richard. 'But it's your turn now.'

'You've seen the satellite pictures of the surface, haven't you, Peter?'

Yung nodded.

'You know the three big craters?'

'Yes, Kalahari, Ascension and Christmas.'

'That's right. The local names anyway. All huge craters, all the result of meteorite or asteroid impact and all now calculated to be within a few thousand years of each other. The impacts created and released vast amounts of heat. Billions of tons of water evaporated, just vaporised, but the majority of it, we think, simply drained away, lost down vast chasms, literally splits in the planet's crust. Atmospheric dust and debris reflected the sun's energy for thousands of years, subsequently, the planet's surface entered an ice age. Atmospheric water condensed and froze, mainly at the poles, as we see today, and that, as Richard said, was between four hundred and fifty thousand years ago and two hundred and fifty thousand years ago. Relatively recent in the scale of things. As the dust settled, the sun's energy pushed through and warmed the place up, much more so in fact due to the absence of water, and that's where we are today. As for the water question, that is, how, in the future, we will be able to truly colonise this planet, tapping the vast underground seas. The rest you know.'

'That's pretty amazing. So 2021, when they were discovered, was a pretty important year?'

'It certainly was, and now it's time for some work,' said Richard. 'Base Ops? Survey One, come in.'

'Ops. Survey One. How do you read?'

The radio crackled.

'Only background interference?' Jennifer said.

'Base? Survey One, come in please.'

Richard paused for a few moments, but there was no reply. He looked at his watch, then up at the reddish, darkened sky. He could see one or two of the brightest stars.

'It's to be expected, behind this ridge you can't get direct communications. We still have another ten to fifteen minutes before the next satellite comes over the horizon. OK, not to worry, West 14 is coming up, so we will do the necessary there first.'

Jennifer nodded in agreement. At that moment there was a breakthrough over Richard's communicator.

'Survey One? This is Support One. Are you reading us?'

'What the hell do they want?' Richard rebuked on intercom only. 'Affirmative, strength three with light background interference. How me?' Richard replied.

'Strength three to four,' came the reply. 'Where are you?'

'Just arriving site West 14. We have a few minutes work then onto West 15, over.'

'Understood. When do you estimate the Kalahari site?'

'Around midday,' said Richard, 'not before. Anyway, why aren't you tracking us?' Richard turned to Yung, shaking his head. 'What's the point of their so-called support if they don't even know where we are?'

Yung agreed.

'We have a partial computer failure and it's affecting all our tracking facilities.'

'Understood,' replied Richard impatiently. 'I expect to arrive at the Silent Falls on the west side of the Kalahari basin in about one hour. See you there. Out!'

Richard selected standby mode on his communicator.

'If they can find it?' he concluded, forcing a smile at Jennifer.

Richard brought the buggy to rest just short of the Hydroseismic equipment. It was not a large piece of machinery; a box about half a metre in height and depth, supported about a metre off the surface on a tripod of three titanium alloy legs.

The instrument was primarily a dual monitoring device, part of an extensive network of similar devices used for detecting and recording surface and sub-surface seismic disturbances, and detecting changes in the level and volume of the subterranean seas. Mars-based geologists had previously confirmed that continuous changes in subterranean water levels were entirely normal and believed them to be due to interplanetary gravitational forces including those of the two moons, Phobos and Deimos: their combined influence keeping these vast seas constantly moving. Yung watched Richard intently, as he exchanged the small, depleted nickel-cadmium battery for a new one.

'Why should the water suddenly come to the surface?' he enquired.

'The shifting of the subterranean seas is believed to be influenced by the rotation and axis tilt of the planet and where it actually is placed, in its orbit around the sun,' explained Richard, checking the output voltage of the battery with a small instrument. 'Pretty much what generates the tides on earth. OK, that's it, onto 15,' he said.

Jennifer, who had not left her seat in the buggy, asked, 'if the PTSV has a system malfunction, why doesn't it return to base and have it repaired? I mean, what's the point?'

'Yes,' agreed Richard. 'What's the point in the first place?'

After a brief visit to the second site to retrieve and replace the biopod's organics tray, the buggy started the hour-long drive to the Kalahari crater, some sixty-five kilometres to the north. The mountainous terrain north of Ascension eventually softened into the broad flat Pacific Plain, where the going was easier. As the surface covering of dust became thicker, an ever-growing plume of dust began to track the vehicle. Yung broke almost forty minutes of thoughtful silence.

'You're right,' he said. 'The more I look at it, the more I can see that this was definitely the sea bed.'

Richard looked across at Yung, a little surprised by his remark, and then back at Jennifer. 'We'll make a geologist out of him yet!'

They all laughed.

Richard had contacted base operations several times during the previous hour. His first call, made promptly after satellite Galliano IV's orbit had lifted it above the horizon, enquired as to the position of the PTSV. Neither Richard, nor base operation, as it transpired, had heard anything from its crew since their last distorted communication and a normal operations call was well overdue. Although it was probably returning home with electrical problems, a sensor-less PTSV roaming the area, particularly with a charged Cyan cannon, made him feel noticeably uneasy. As they began to negotiate the soaring ridgeline of the Kalahari crater, Jennifer voiced similar thoughts.

'I suppose the support vehicle has returned to base, seeing as we haven't heard anything from them for over an hour?'

'Yes, I think you're probably right, Jennifer,' replied

Richard, focusing his attention on steering the buggy along a particularly narrow section of track. 'Complete waste of resources. Anyway, they wouldn't need a tracking device to see us up here. With this dust plume they could see us coming for miles.'

Presently, Richard negotiated the buggy into an area that allowed a little lateral leeway and stopped at an impressive vantage point. Remaining seated, he pointed down into the vast, gaping hole and directed his colleagues' attention towards an area where the bedrock had rippled, forming low craggy undulations, upsetting the seemingly endless flatland.

'Presumably the crystal site, Richard?' Jennifer observed.

'Yep, you got it. To the left of that small outcrop, but we are not going to drive directly to it because of our communicators.'

'But we are using W band and apparently that frequency spectrum has no effect on the crystals?' Jennifer countered.

'Yes, I expect you're right, but you never know. Better safe than sorry. We will stop some four hundred metres short, behind the outcrop itself. I'd like you two to survey a very interesting area, while I go and pick up the specimens.'

'But that's not the brief, as you well know, Richard. Aren't we supposed to do this together?'

'I'm quite capable of picking up a few crystals, Jennifer. Anyway, the other site has indicated an incredibly high carbon count and I would like you to take a look.' Richard winced at his unconvincing argument.

Jennifer paused for thought. 'OK,' she agreed, reluctantly. 'I didn't realise there was a second site.'

'Potentially,' assured Richard. 'Peter, obviously you will accompany Jennifer. I shouldn't be more than ten minutes.'

Richard fell silent; he wondered how long he could keep up this cat and mouse diversion. It was only a matter of time before someone else discovered the entrance to the Ark.

It took Richard another twenty minutes to drive down the winding, uncomfortable and, often dangerous, downward incline, which he had marked with yellow dye, several months earlier. From the top of the ridgeline and even down the shallower incline to the wide breech, the track, full of hairpin bends, looked like an enormous snake. As the buggy negotiated the final few hundred metres and moved onto the broad, flat, central plain of the crater itself, Yung broke the silence, pointing to the top of the towering cliff face, some distance around to their left.

'Look there! I think I saw the PTSV.'

Richard scanned the area. 'I don't think so. The ridgeline is not generally accessible for a vehicle that size, too rocky and too narrow for the most part. Anyway, I can't see anything.'

'I'm sure I saw something moving, up there.'

'It's possible, I suppose, but not likely,' replied Richard, straining his neck to look almost vertically upwards. 'Apart from anything else, it's recognised as an out of bounds area for the PTSV and base would have notified us of its position.'

'They would have, if they could,' answered Yung. 'We've been out of radio contact again, at least for the last fifteen minutes, and there's going to be another delay until the next meteosat comes around.'

'Well, you've got a good point, that's the problem with being in these damn holes.' Richard for some unexplained reason felt the hairs on the back of his neck prickle. It was another three kilometres to the Kalahari site and in order to avoid any complications, he gave it a wide berth.

Yet he definitely had a feeling of being watched. As he was driving, the feeling grew stronger. It was instinctive, something he had developed during his combat pilot days. His neck hairs prickled again. He looked up repeatedly towards the pinnacles; but it was impossible that someone or something was behind them.

Presently the buggy arrived at the site Richard had mentally earmarked as a safe area from which to direct the survey. The crystal site was around five hundred metres to the north, but a localised outcrop of rock, mainly pink basalt, rising some twenty metres or so above the ground, effectively obstructed any direct view; so Richard could collect his samples unobserved. There was already a

Biopod in place from a previous visit, so the situation was ideal and avoided further, difficult questions.

As Richard climbed out of the vehicle, he pointed to a small canyon, barely three metres wide, over to the right, which, surrounded on three sides by vertical faces of craggy pink rock of various shades, had a fairytale feel about it.

'That's your area, Jennifer. Two bioscans have identified it as one with an unusually high level of remnant organics. You know what you have to do. Yung will help you with the sampling equipment. The biograph is in the green container and there's also a replacement organics tray.' Richard tapped his hand on the large green box marked 'Fragile', which was strapped to anti- vibration mounts on the baggage platform.

'OK, Richard, understood,' replied Jennifer, totally oblivious to his growing unease. Yung on the other hand was not. His experience gave him some intuition in body language and he could sense Richard's more authoritarian manner.

'You're thinking we may have visitors?' he enquired quietly.

Richard who had been using his binoculars to inspect the horizon, turned to look at Jennifer, who, on hearing the comment, promptly stepped out of her seat.

'To be honest, I don't know,' Richard conceded. If the PTSV is around, why would the crew conceal it? At this range, they could call us direct, no problem. So, there can't be any visitors, it's impossible. All the same, I have a niggling feeling that we're being watched.' Richard checked his watch. 'OK, let's get moving. Time waits for no man.'

'Or woman,' said Jennifer quickly, 'sexual equality, please!'

'Indeed,' said Richard, 'or woman. So please, unload what you need and I'll take the buggy to the crystal site. I will be gone for fifteen minutes maximum, don't forget the brief. Radio silence from now on, until I give you the all clear. I'll bag the crystals and be back as soon as possible. Any questions?'

'No questions, Sir.'

Jennifer and Peter Yung unloaded the two green canisters and stood back fanning the air, as dust flew out from beneath the buggy's wheels, following Richard's over-zealous use of the throttle. Moments later, he was out of sight.

The two surveyors carried the first box between them into the narrow canyon. The tone on Jennifer's hand-held 'carbon element' detector rose quickly, almost to a constant screech.

'Wow,' she commented. 'This is the highest residual carbon reading I've seen on Mars. It's the sort of reading you would expect back on earth.'

Yung did not answer. He was already on his way back for the second canister, keen to get the job done and 'move out'.

Richard parked the buggy as close as was prudent to the deposits of crystals and used his sonic key to open the security lock on the heavy lid of the Yearlman Cube. With a final check that all communication devices were off, he walked towards the group of smaller crystals just a few metres to the left of the vehicle.

The surrounding area was clear as far as he could see, with the high ridgeline being a particular focus for his nervous attention. Despite his nagging feelings of unease, there was nothing: no movement, no dust trails, just a desolate silence.

'That will do nicely,' he said to himself quietly, reaching down with his tongs to grasp the first small specimen, then selecting four others of a similar size.

At that moment, he heard a loud explosion, like an artillery shell. It was close, very close. Spinning round instinctively, he looked back towards the survey site. The sky was filling with thick dust and debris; it began to rise in a billowing column. There were flashes of bright blue light, which danced like lightening on the rocks that formed the escarpment.

'What the hell was that?' he called out. Forgetting the final specimen, he dropped the fourth one, tongs as well, into the container and slammed the lid shut. Within seconds, he was speeding back the way he had come. Pieces of rock and debris fell from the sky, bouncing on the ground around him, each raising a ball of dust and sand, like heavy rain dousing a pond.

Arriving at the survey site, Richard was completely unprepared for what he found. There was utter destruction. He rounded the final corner that led to the entrance of the canyon. The heavy tripod base of the biometer was still standing; arcing neon-coloured sparks ran up and down its metallic legs. The instrument however, was gone; ripped off and blown away by the explosion.

'Jennifer! Yung! Where are you?' Realising that he was not transmitting, Richard switched on the W band communicators on both his suit and the buggy. 'Jennifer! Yung! Come in! Where are you?'

Slowly the dust began to settle. A large boulder tumbled from a ledge above him, he leapt backwards, startled, it crashed to the ground, raising yet more dust into the choking atmosphere. As he ran into the open, Richard tripped and fell to his knees. Looking back, he saw a large red stain in the sand, lying next to it was a limb. He looked closer, in disbelief. It was a leg, severed below the hip.

'Oh my God!'

Ten metres to his right was the torso. He stumbled over to it, and rolled over the limp, bloodstained remains. He looked into the shattered helmet visor. It was Yung. Half of his face was missing; he could do nothing but lay the twisted corpse gently back onto the sand. Richard transmitted again, this time in desperation.

'Jennifer? Jennifer, can you hear me?' A blue plasma streak discharged weakly on the canyon wall behind him. 'This was a Cyan cannon blast, no question,' he said aloud.

Standing up, Richard looked around blankly, feeling utter dismay. The dust-laden atmosphere had all but cleared. Twenty metres further into the canyon lay what was left of the survey equipment canisters and there, close by, was Jennifer. She was lying face down in the sand. Running to her, the reality of the situation struck him like a thunderbolt. The large orange circle painted on the back of her helmet, his helmet, denoting survey commander. . . the cannon blast had been meant for him!

A jagged fracture on the right side of Jennifer's helmet oozed shiny crimson fluid. Richard knew she was dead as he lifted her upper body and turned it gently inwards, his body cradling her contorted helmet. Explosive decompression of her suit through the fracture had literally coated the inside of the helmet with blood. Richard could not see her face; probably just as well. Dazed for several seconds, he tried to comprehend the scale of the explosion, and the loss of two colleagues.

'Mayday! Mayday! Survey One to base, come in!'

Silence.

The range of the W band communicators was too limiting, particularly surrounded by the high outcrops of rock. Richard ran to the buggy and drove three hundred metres into a clearing. The more powerful radio on the buggy crackled into life.

'Affirmative, base, that is affirmative. We have had an accidental discharge of the Cyan cannon. We are not sure if it has caused any damage. Over.'

'Transmissions from the PTSV,' Richard confirmed aloud.

He could not hear the reply from base operations due to the extreme range, and the next meteosat was not due above the ridge for several minutes. Nevertheless, by receiving transmissions from the PTSV, he knew they were close and he was not going to give his position away by calling them.

He had an idea, his VHF radio; he knew Miles would be listening on the pre-arranged frequency in the survey department.

'Miles? Miles, this is Richard on Channel 8, do you read?' He selected full volume and turned noise suppression off.

'Yes boss, barely, strength one. What's happening out there?'

'It's serious, Miles. My team members are dead. I cannot explain how. Have you any information? I can't get hold of operations, I'm out of range. This bloody useless W band communicator.'

'Apparently it's bedlam in the operations room. The PTSV has reported a tracking failure and accidental discharge of the Cyan cannon in the Kalahari area. God alone knows how that could have happened. I have been trying to raise you on the distress channel for the last ten or fifteen minutes. They're waiting for the meteosat to rise in the next few minutes.'

Richard strained to hear against the background interference. 'OK, understood. Who is the commander of the PTSV?'

'Standby, I'll check.' A few seconds later Miles returned. 'Peculiar I know, but the crew log has been withdrawn. It's just saying it's classified. I cannot get into the system even from this terminal, but I know Renton Dubrovnic is on board. I met him in the Survival Equipment Centre picking up a pool suit; his own was in for repairs.'

'Listen Miles, I'm going to make my own way back, avoiding the PTSV if I can, but I'm running out of oxygen. Do not mention this to anyone, but try and find out the PTSV crew names before they disembark. Do you copy?'

'Yes, I understand boss,' replied Miles, barely audible. 'I'll do my best, the only way is for me to get into the surface transport section, so I'll be closing down this frequency for a while.'

'That's understood. It will take me an hour at least to get back, maybe a little more. I am comfortable with life support if I leave now. Open the channel in thirty minutes precisely, over and out.'

Richard floored the accelerator and took a detour from the established route between the Kalahari crater and Osiris in order to avoid being tracked by the PTSV. Crossing the broad, flat, crater surface, with a plume of dust behind him, he would be an easy target should the PTSV try the same thing again.

They had raised the stakes and they were onto him; whoever they were. Was it for the crystals, or, because of his attempts to decipher the Ark's flight log? Maybe even both. In either case, it was now a killing game.

The crater was several kilometres behind him when Richard thought it was safe enough to answer the persistent calls from operations on his main radio. The meteosat, having risen some twenty-five minutes earlier was providing clear, direct contact, Richard however, had ignored the often-desperate calls until he was sure that the PTSV was returning using the less direct, but easier northern route. That meant they were at least thirty kilometres apart and out of tracking range for the Cyan cannon. During that time, he had listened carefully to the conversations between the senior operations controller and the PTSV.

They had given a lame excuse for the tracking failure: excessive electronic interference, caused by moisture in the field computer circuits. This had rendered the system effectively out of control for an hour or so, until evaporation had dried out the circuits. Somehow, the system had locked onto low-grade radio transmissions, intercom transmissions, between the survey party and an automatic firing sequence had started unbeknown to the crew.

Richard considered the implications. He knew full well that several red warning lights on the operator's firing panel, as well as the commander's master display clearly indicated a discharge sequence. There was no way that the crew would have been unaware of a countdown, not unless they were walking around with their eyes shut. Moreover, there was the audio warning tone during the final thirty-second engagement lock-down. At any time, the firing could have been aborted by simply cancelling the sequence. No, this was no accident. His two colleagues are dead and the Commander, if not all the crew of the PTSV had a hand in it!

There was no doubt in Richard's mind that a twist of fate had saved his life, and by the same count, Jennifer and Yung were dead. His train of thought was broken.

'Is that you, Richard? Base operations calling.'

'Yes, I can hear you, but who is that?" Richard demanded, trying his best to suppress latent anger.

'Its Giles, and I have Commander Miko right behind me. What the hell's going on out there?'

Richard paused for a moment to control his emotions; his answer was short and to the point.

'I'm approaching from the eastern boundary of sections ninety through one ten. You will see me on the radar in about fifteen minutes. I am on my own. Jennifer Middleton and Peter Yung are dead, killed by a direct hit from the Cyan cannon. I've left them at the survey site, or what's left of them more to the point!'

There was a stunned silence.

'Confirm Middleton and Yung are dead?'

'Confirmed." His tone left no one in doubt. 'Where is the PTSV at the moment?'

'Hold on,' said Giles, checking his sensor screen.

His voice trembled. 'I can see it. The PTSV is about ten minutes ahead of you, quite a way to the north. We have it on surface sensor, but not you. You're low on life support, keep your foot down.'

Richard did not answer. Instead, he glanced down at his bio-indicator. It was true. He had failed to notice that his oxygen level had fallen into the amber sector.

'I've got enough.' he responded after several seconds. Barely, he was thinking.

A few minutes later, the silence was broken. The commander of the PTSV called for docking clearance. Richard did not recognise the voice at all.

'Docking approved, gate two. Check and confirm all systems in docking state green.'

'Confirmed, docking state green.'

So, the PTSV is back, thought Richard. 'Oh shit!' he cursed aloud, realising that he had turned the volume down on his VHF communicator during his conversation with base operations. He increased it to ten; full volume.

'Miles? Are you there? Are you receiving me?'

'Yes Sir! Loud and clear. I've tried to call, several times, but no joy!'

'Sorry. I'd turned the bloody volume down.'

'There's four crew members on board boss. Renton Dubrovnic is definitely the systems coordinator. Alice Meriton is life support and medic; I know her, she is good, I'm sure of it! Beriton Brown is pilot, that's routine, but get this! Bill Bradley is the commander! Be aware that the names of the crew have been censored, I had to use a few favours.'

Richard lifted his right foot off the throttle in shock and was jerked forward on his straps by the resulting deceleration. Dazed momentarily, he slammed his foot back down. There was no time to waste; his oxygen indicator was moving into the red.

'Copied that, and well done Miles,' he said. 'Listen. I have a situation developing here. My oxygen . . . it's going to be close. Appreciate if you could be waiting in the bay . . . get me home, so to speak?'

'Standing by, Sir,' came the closing transmission.

Negotiating the final few kilometres to Osiris, Richard's thoughts were not on his worsening predicament, but what, if anything, he could do to lay the responsibility for this so-called accident directly onto the shoulders of the PTSV commander. If it was Bradley, and Richard had no reason to doubt Miles's source, then at worst he and his crew should be arrested, confined to quarters, and returned to earth as soon as possible for court martial. At best, they could be tried for murder. In Richard's mind, the latter was the only course of action, but of all the people . . . he still could not believe it.

Bill Bradley was a good friend; Richard had known him since their academy days. Bradley had not made the grade for pilot; either in fighters or the freighter fleets, but they had always kept in touch, although Richard had at times sensed his ongoing grievance with the system. Bradley had confided in him once, a long time ago; he felt he had not been given a fair chance, but he had done well in his alternative career. He had chosen systems engineering, had been promoted and was due to go even further, so why this?

Osiris finally came into view. First the bristling aerials, then the main dome with its gentle orange glow, as if it were itself a living entity.

'Survey One. Five minutes,' snapped Richard.

'We have you visual, Richard. How's it going?'

'Fine!'

'We are showing life support zero, Richard. Be specific, how's it going please?'

'I said fi . . . ssh, sssh . . . .'

The oxygen regulator in Richard's helmet started to squeak as he tried to suck in the gas that was normally delivered under pressure. He was out of oxygen. His system was empty. Almost at once the red warning lights on his life support controller flashed.

'Life support. Life support,' came the synthetic voice in a menacing monotone. Richard cancelled it. That's the last thing I need, he thought.

He held his breath. He knew that there was about a minute of breathable air in the helmet itself.

'Open up! Two minutes!' he barked.

He sped at full tilt towards the smaller left-hand dome. After a minute or so, with possibly five hundred metres to go, he could just see the door opening to the survey bay. He breathed out slowly and sucked the last breath of air from inside his helmet. He felt dizzy. Controlled to the last, he knew this was the effect of carbon dioxide poisoning.

At twenty metres from the entrance, Richard raised his right foot off the floor, releasing the throttle, and stamped it hard on the brake pedal. The six wheels were locked and skidding as he screeched into the bay amid a cloud of dust and debris. Pulling the wheel hard to the right, full lock, the vehicle responded with a one hundred and eighty degree skidding turn, before the rear of the buggy crashed into the back wall of the survey bay. There was a loud bang and an instantaneous whoosh as the heavy roller door closed behind him and the room pressurised.

Richard fumbled instinctively for his helmet clips. One, two, where was the third? His head began to spin. Disorientated, he pulled hard on the restraint lugs. The last clip sprang open. Losing consciousness, his helmet rotated.

CHAPTER 9

Two Ends Meet

'My head! I've got the mother of all headaches!'

'You bloody fool!'

Richard opened his eyes and then, instinctively, with his hands, shielded them from the bright lights above the operating table. Realising where he was, he sat up with a jolt.

'My head,' he said again, both hands rubbing his temples.

'Does it hurt?'

'You bet it hurts.'

'Good!'

An oxygen mask that lay on Richard's chest fell to the floor.

'Please be careful, Richard. That's irreplaceable at the moment.'

'Sorry about that, Rachel,' replied Richard, hauling the

mask up by its yellow rubber hose.

'Seems to go from bad to worse, doesn't it? Here, drink this, it's aspiritine; it will clear your head. Something needs to!'

Richard knocked the small tumbler of clear liquid back in one gulp, and spun around to put his shoeless feet on the ground. He was still in his flying suit.

'How long have I been out?' he asked.

Rachel looked at her wristwatch. 'Oh, not long, an hour, or maybe a little more. You fell unconscious just as the bay was repressurising. Miles had your helmet off within seconds. You owe him.'

'Really? I remember doing that myself.'

'Even you need help sometimes Richard,' retorted Rachel, 'and I think you're going to need all the help you can get explaining what happened out there today. Poor Jennifer, she was a good friend. What a terrible accident.'

'It was no accident Rachel, no way.' Richard sprang to his feet and clipped the oxygen mask onto a stainless steel hook beside the operating table. 'That crew knew what they were doing, and what's more, I was the intended victim. By some quirk of fate, Jennifer had my helmet on. That plasma blast was meant for me.'

'That's ridiculous, how could that happen and, more to the point, why?'

'I know how Rachel, that's easy enough, but I don't know why, and I intend to find out.'

Rachel walked over to Richard and put her arms around

him. It was a completely open show of emotion, and a rare one, especially while at work. Richard could see that she was upset, but sensed that she was also frightened. He gave her a hug in return, and looked into her eyes.

'You remember several days ago I was going to tell you something, a secret, and I was going to need your help? In the end, something came up and we didn't talk. Since then I haven't progressed with the project, lack of secure computing power for one thing. I put it on the back burner so to speak. I've put off telling you, particularly with all this going on, about the crystals. Well, I was wrong. I should have told you then, about everything. We have to talk. I trust you implicitly, Rachel, you know that, but I really need to know who else I can trust around here.'

'OK,' said Rachel. 'Maybe tonight, after the debrief, it's Code 1, twenty hundred. You had better have a good story ready. With what you are saying, I get the feeling that the truth may not be entirely prudent at the moment. Oh, and thanks for the hug. I needed it.'

Richard gave Rachel a kiss on the forehead and turned for the door.

'Don't forget your boots, Richard. I'll sign you off as fit, but take it easy for a day or two, OK?'

Richard nodded. 'Of course, and thanks, lots.'

By eight twenty-five that evening, Richard, who was first to speak, had debriefed Commander Miko, the assembled HODs and several other personnel who had all been sitting sullen faced in the theatre. He had stopped short of condemning Bradley, the PTSV Commander, of gross negligence. That would be for a Court Marshall to decide, but he made his feelings plain enough, particularly where he thought the blame lay for the deaths of Jennifer and Peter Yung.

These were the first fatalities on Mars for almost four years; not since the explosion in the second-phase power generation dome had killed four engineers, had such a loss been felt. As with any small community, everyone felt it, everyone had a memory. Richard was no exception, but he had no intention of spending the rest of his appointment on Osiris looking over his shoulder. He looked Searle straight in the eyes as he gave his reasons why it was impossible for a plasma cannon to discharge without the knowledge or control of its crew. It was a powerful argument, as Richard was also a PTSV commander and probably had more experience on the machine than anyone in the logistics group.

Commander Miko was well aware of Richard's thoughts, and, in military judicial terms, that he was sailing very close to the wind with his thinly disguised condemnation. He also knew that Richard was right.

'I therefore respectfully suggest, Sir, that Bradley and his crew are confined to quarters pending completion of the enquiry,' said Richard, concluding his debrief.

Commander Miko stood up. 'That's not for you to decide, Lieutenant Commander Reece. I hear your argument, but the initial enquiry will make its recommendations. Until then, there will be nothing else said publicly on this matter. The PTSV crew will be on limited duties but not confined to quarters until I say so, if at all.'

Richard knew that Commander Miko's hands were tied. By virtually arresting them, it would automatically imply professional misconduct, but by limiting their professional responsibility until the results of the enquiry, he was seen to be impartial; 'innocent until proven guilty'. None the less, Richard seethed.

'Ladies and gentlemen, any further questions for Lieutenant Commander Reece?' asked Commander Miko.

Doctor David Trafford, a civilian scientist and head of Life Support raised his hand. As a Grade 1 Civil Servant, he had an equivalent military rank of Commander.

'Yes?'

'Richard, you stated in your debrief that you were placing the fourth specimen, a crystal approximately four centimetres by two centimetres, and weighing approximately two hundred grams, in the Yearlman Cube before you were distracted by the plasma blast. Do you remember closing the cover plate and securing it?'

Richard thought for a moment. 'Yes, that's correct, Sir, and yes I am sure I closed the cover plate, although, to be honest, I can't recall activating the magnetic lock! Anyway, as you know, even if I didn't secure it, an acceleration of nought point six 'g' automatically activates the system to prevent the cover opening during transit.'

'Of course,' said Trafford. 'So how hard did you accelerate the buggy after stowing that sample?'

'The maximum,' replied Richard confidently, 'and several times too!'

'I see. So several times to one point two 'g'?'

'Yes, that's correct." Richard was a little surprised that the head of the Life Support department knew this technical data about the buggy.

'I see, so it's reasonable to assume that the cover plate was magnetically locked before you arrived at the blast scene?'

'Almost definitely,' replied Richard.

'Commander Miko', said Trafford, standing up. 'You have been informed about the crystals, correct?'

'Yes. Greg informed me about an hour ago. No samples were retrieved on this occasion. We will have to repeat the mission.'

'Commander, one of my people and one of Greg's accompanied the geology team to the survey bay. The container was empty; but the lock was set. It required a full magnetic deactivation. I believe that there were specimens in the container when the scout vehicle returned to base, albeit surrounded by pandemonium. I believe that they are now unaccounted for!'

The theatre hushed. One could have heard a pin drop.

'Any ideas on this matter, Richard?' Commander Miko demanded.

The look of surprise on Richard's face was plain to see. David Trafford chose to ignore it.

'I think that it is you, Lieutenant Commander Reece, who should be confined to quarters; for theft of ISSA property!'

'That's ridiculous!' Richard protested. 'I was unconscious by the time the outer door shut. Anyone with access to the survey bay could have taken those crystals.'

'How so? Only a handful of people know the matrix combination required to release a Yearlman lock. The coded sequence is highly confidential; but you know it, don't you?'

'Of course I know it! I need to. It's part of my job.'

'So, you could have stopped at any time and removed the crystals, any time between the crystal site and Osiris. God damn it, man, you even diverted from the established return route from the East Sector!'

'Think carefully, Richard,' said Commander Miko sternly. 'Think what you did before leaving the crystal site.'

'To be honest, Sir, I don't recall closing the lid to the container, or setting the lock. I was placing the second to last crystal in the container when I heard the explosion. I looked up immediately to see a cloud of dust and some plasma arcs above the organics site. After that, I was in the buggy and gone. It's possible that the crystals bounced out of the container due to the movement of the vehicle. It's possible that I didn't close the lid securely,' said Richard cautiously.

'You disobeyed orders, man,' interrupted Trafford, almost shouting. 'You split your team. Jennifer Middleton and Peter Yung to this other site, which was not specified in the brief and you to the crystal site. Why?'

Miles Trafford was a complex character. He was British but spoke fluent German and Dutch, having lived for many years in Maastricht. As a Grade 1 officer of the European Space and Science Agency he should have been a departmental head by this point in his career, he certainly had the experience. However, as the life support section was part of the much larger science department, which in turn was run by Peter Meyhew, Trafford was regarded as a lower grade officer. Moreover, Richard surveyed a good deal of the bases external defects; particularly any atmospheric problems or leaks and was indirectly instrumental in the life support department's impressive atmospheric integrity record. As a result, Trafford was basically beholden to the survey team for his professional standing. That said, they had always maintained a reasonably good working relationship, Richard regarding his role as 'just part of the job'. Fairly astute about people's feelings, and not short of human resource experience himself, Richard often felt that it was this pseudo-dependency on the survey department that contributed heavily to Trafford's often frosty attitude in their dealings, but Richard couldn't understand the rational behind Trafford's aggressive stance, this was a new direction and there must be a motive.

Richard looked directly at his accuser. 'Likely or not, I

collected four specimens, one short of the number I was briefed, and placed them in the container. That much I know. After that, I can't account for them. If I had them on my person when I was carried out of the survey department to sickbay, the dense electromagnetic environment we live in here on Mars base would have activated them for sure. I do not have them and I do not know where they are. In my view, they didn't even make the return journey; otherwise we would have some indication of their presence.'

'I'm inclined to agree,' said Commander Miko, breaking the frigid stare between the two men. 'If a crystal had been removed from the Yearlman Cube within the confines, or even in the immediate area of this station, we would possibly have suffered some fairly disastrous consequences to say the least: having said that we can't take any chances.' Commander Miko turned to Greg Searle. 'Raise a Category 5 security report to include a full debrief of all personnel in the survey department and docking portal: everyone who had access. I want it on my desk by nineteen hundred hours tomorrow. Until then Richard, you are confined to your quarters, understand?'

Trafford raised an infuriating wry smile, and even Searle took pleasure in that directive. Richard knew better than to protest. Anyway, it was standard procedure: confinement until close of enquiry. Miko was a good Commander, knowledgeable, capable, experienced and also rather shrewd. He was not blind to the antagonism between certain members of his staff and although not party to all their reasons, he had a fair idea of his best men.

Turning again to Searle, Commander Miko said, 'all interned personnel and that includes the entire PTSV crew, will take their meals in their quarters until further notice.'

'Yes, Sir, of course,' replied Greg Searle.

Richard was escorted to his cabin by NCO Jeremy Preston, who was a little embarrassed to do so. Rachel caught up with them both just before entering Richard's accommodation dome.

'Preston,' explained Rachel, 'I need to talk to Richard for a few minutes privately.'

'That's not possible M'am, you know the rules. He has to be interviewed by a minimum of two people for the report, then, until the completion of the enquiry, he can have visitors only after approval from the Base Commander.'

'Yes, I know all that, but it's important, very important. Richard's career is at stake here.'

Preston looked at Rachel uneasily; he hesitated for a few moments. 'Look, I've got the rest of the afternoon watch, that's forty minutes,' he said. 'You've got thirty, maximum! More than that and I'm dead.'

Approaching the door to Richard's cabin, Rachel nodded in agreement and then stepped inside as Richard held it open.

Raising his arm, Richard patted Preston's shoulder. 'Thanks, I owe you one,' he said.

'I'll knock three times when it's clear; four if I have a problem?'

'Agreed,' replied Richard, closing the door and setting the lock.

Rachel sat on the bed. 'I think you'd better tell me exactly what's been going on in your life for the past few weeks,' she said.

Pushing her legs gently aside, Richard reached into the untidy cupboard under his bed and retrieved a green canvas bag. It was well worn, with tatty, frayed corners. Richard's initials, RJR and the old Royal Navy insignia painted on one side were all but erased: a combination of age and use. Unzipping it, he pulled out a plastic box file and from there he carefully withdrew the shiny, densely bound flight manual.

'Come on, Richard, we don't have much time,' said Rachel impatiently.

Richard passed the manual to her. Instinctively, she knew what to expect with a volume that size and grasped it with in both hands. To her amazement, it weighed almost nothing.

'What's this?' she whispered placing it on her lap. The manual flopped open, revealing the bright metallic leaves.

'Rachel,' Richard said looking directly into her eyes. 'This is the flight manual from an alien space craft, the remains of which are buried in the ground near the crystal deposits.'

Rachel began to speak. Richard stopped her by placing

a finger gently on her lips. 'The drawings and technical diagrams I can relate to, I mean, they are not unlike the systems diagrams we find in our own flight or engineering manuals and I've actually interpreted a number of them. But the text, look at it, it's so similar to that of our own ancient civilisations.'

'Egyptian hieroglyphics?' Rachel murmured, mesmerised.

'Exactly, and there's more.' He pointed to some other characters. 'These belong to the Sumarians and these to the Assyrians; their writings predate the Egyptians and even Hebrew. These other examples have similarities to Mayan and these from the very earliest writings discovered on the Indian continent, all these cultures, the very earliest in the sense of the word, from the very beginnings. Do you see, the dawn of civilisation as we know it, one of the very first things that defined the human as the dominant species on earth? Language, and the written word, it's here. These symbols, there is so much commonality, it can't be a coincidence.'

Rachel looked up from the manual, her eyes wide. 'What are you saying, Richard?'

'I don't know what I'm saying, not yet anyway, but I have a theory and one that would blow apart all our established beliefs and knowledge about the origins of civilized man. Right to the very beginning, forget evolution, I mean.'

'What about the crystals?' enquired Rachel retrieving her senses. 'Where do they come into all of this?'

'Well, I don't know for sure about those, either.' Richard

sat back in his chair. 'But I think they were the power source for the craft, some sort of central power core. The diagrams point towards it. I think that when the craft collided with the surface, however long ago, the front section, the bridge, or the cockpit if you like, penetrated the sand. Look, this section.' Richard confidently flipped over a few of the pages and pointed on a clear diagram of the whole craft. 'This section, being in front of the main bulk of the craft, penetrated the sand and was preserved. That's where I've been, where I found this. The remainder of the ship just disintegrated, exploded and caught fire, maybe just corroded away with time, or more likely a combination of them all, who knows? Anyway, there is no trace of it now, but the crystals, I believe they originally formed one large central crystal, here in the middle of what looks like a reactor. It provided the power for the ship, but fragmented on impact. Whilst the material of the craft itself has disappeared for whatever reason, these have remained. Like a diamond, they are resistant to fire, corrosion, erosion, this acidic atmosphere, everything. Whether they occur naturally somewhere in the galaxy or are synthetic, who can say?' Richard continued eager to unfold the full results of his previous work.

Rachel interrupted. 'Listen Richard, this is pretty amazing to say the least, but I can't get my head around it right now. I'm still thinking of poor Jennifer and Peter Yung. I have an autopsy to do for my report and I'm a bit rusty on those, to say the least.'

'Well there's not much doubt about the cause of death is there?'

'Perhaps not, but there's a lot of speculation about motives. My report will just confirm cause of death and I think it needs to be foolproof, one hundred percent accurate.'

'What do you mean, motives?' asked Richard.

'Well,' Rachel sighed. 'In truth, Jennifer wasn't a particularly close friend, but we did talk, often, initially in my capacity as her doctor, but later as a friend, a confident. I have that relationship with many of the women. No one knows this, I shouldn't really be telling you, but I'll have to put it in my report in case there is a follow up back on earth.'

Richard closed the flight manual and put it on the table behind his chair. 'Go on.'

'Jennifer was three months pregnant, contrary to all base orders and disciplinary codes. It goes on of course; we all know that, but she made a mistake, mixed her dates up and then, subsequently, mistimed her cyclex tablet, the monthly cycle suppresser. She came to me about three weeks ago worried sick. I tested her, there was no doubt. You know as well as I do that's a career stopper.'

'Who was the father?' asked Richard.

'To be honest, Richard, I don't know for sure. She wouldn't say outright, for obvious reasons. But I'm pretty sure it was Renton Dublovnic.'

'Herman Grafts' replacement?'

'Yes, I think so. Captain Grafts' appointment terminates on the next shuttle changeover. Renton Dublovnic is due to be promoted into the position. He's young, very young in fact for the promotion and he's ambitious, almost single minded. Jennifer was petrified that if he knew, or worse, if ever it got out, it would be him on the next shuttle to earth not Graft.'

'I can understand that. He's a bit intimidating at the best of times, what you see is what you get. He's not popular in the physics department, I know that!'

'Well, there's more!' continued Rachel. 'Dublovnic was one of the crew members of the PTSV.'

'What?' spluttered Richard, having his reasons not to disclose to Rachel that he already knew the contents of the crew list.

'Shhhh! For God's sake, Richard! I shouldn't even be here, let alone be telling you this!'

'Sorry,' whispered Richard. 'I can't believe it. So he was the fourth crew member?'

'I don't know about the others,' continued Rachel, 'but it's possible that your theory, of the plasma blast being meant for you, isn't true at all. What if Dublovnic, knowing Jennifer's predicament, decided to get rid of her, what if that happened? He murdered her?'

'God what a mess.' Richard leaned forward and put his hands on Rachel's knees. Looking justifiably concerned, he continued. 'Listen Rachel you cannot mention Jennifer's pregnancy in your report. The first thing the authorities will ask is 'who is the father?' If Dublovnic is that desperate, you may be putting your own life at risk. No, just ignore that and destroy any notes you have relating to the tests. Trust me on this.'

Rachel looked frightened. 'But what if they find out in a subsequent autopsy? It won't look good for me.'

'You could just say that you decided not to carry out any tests which might report a pregnancy, because in your view they weren't necessary, it's your professional judgement, they can't question that. Anyway, a slap on the wrist is infinitely better than looking over your shoulder for the rest of this God damned appointment!'

Richard was interrupted by the PA. 'CMO to sickbay, please. Doctor Turner report to sickbay, please.'

Rachel stood up and walked toward the door. 'That's the PTSV returning, they've retrieved the bodies. After decontamination they'll be taken to the operating theatre.'

'All right Rachel, stay cool and be careful what you say to people, for your own good, eh?'

Rachel nodded and forced a smile. She knocked three times on the door. There was a pause, the door opened and Preston's face appeared in the gap.

'OK, it's clear M'am, quickly,' he whispered.

'Rachel, I need a laptop, with at least a thousand gigabite memory capacity and a scart lead, please, ASAP.'

Rachel nodded. The door closed behind her.

Three, maybe four hours later, there was a quiet tap on the door. Richard, in his confinement, had been pondering, speculating and analysing the events of the previous forty-eight hours. He had been convinced that the plasma munition had been meant for him and his so-called friend Bill Bradley had delivered it, but the pregnancy thing had thrown him into doubt. Dublovnic, as the systems coordinator and science officer would have been at the firing console. Bradley, barely qualified as a PTSV Commander and certainly out of recent currency, basically out on a jolly, may not have realised what the warning lights on his panel meant until it was too late, especially if Dublovnic had distracted his attention at the critical moment. Would he give him the benefit of the doubt, or was that just too dangerous? Richard broke from his thoughts and responded to the second, more earnest tap on his cabin door. He sprang up and opened it gingerly.

'It's Preston, Sir. I've got something for you.'

The door was pushed open a little further and an OROMAR CT400 lap top computer with the word 'Sick Bay' engraved in white on the lid was thrust in. Richard took it, along with the scart lead that was dangling from the machine and closed the door. He tapped twice, then three times, on the back of the door. If he was to be confined to his quarters for any length of time then he was going to make good use of the time.

Sitting at his desk with the computer lid open, he

pushed the end of the computer scart lead into the wall terminal. Rachel's personal laptop was perfect for his work. By nature, all medical documents, personnel files, and anything of a welfare nature were highly confidential. Only one person, apart from the Chief Medical Officer could access the entire medical library and that was the Base Commander. Even then, it would be irregular for him to do so without consulting Rachel. Richard inserted his pseudo health chip into the socket and switched on the machine.

'Good evening, Lieutenant Commander Reece, it's been some time since you logged onto the central data system. I see you have accessed via the CMO porticel. Are you authorised?'

Richard said nothing but typed in a seven-digit number which he had found written on a piece of paper and sealed in an envelope when he initially opened the lid of the laptop.

'I see,' responded the computer, 'system ready.'

'Run the programme and open all memory files listed on my health chip. Transfer nothing out. Transfer nothing in. Restrict all access from other users below Medical in Confidence. Acknowledge?'

'Acknowledged,' responded the computer again. With only the Base Commander listed above that category, Richard felt confident to work, but first he had something to check.

'Engage Main Security Programme,'

The computer voice changed. 'Security, how can I help?'

'Its Lieutenant Commander Reece, we spoke a few days ago regarding a security breach.'

'Yes, you missed the planned rendezvous. I see you have Level 7 access, Lieutenant Commander. That is highly irregular.'

'I have an authorisation code, you can check it later. Now listen carefully. My personal language course has been engaged, but two-way transfer is closed at the facility access. When I give the command, lift the 'gate' and monitor closely for any access junctions. If any engage, track them, understand?'

'I understand; your authorisation code is ratified, standing by!'

'Now, do it now.'

There was a pause of a few seconds. Richard watched the screen closely.

'We have one access request, Lieutenant Commander Reece.'

'Lock it!'

'I have complied.'

'Track it, quickly.'

'Completed.'

'Close the gate.'

'I have complied.'

'Present on screen and review.'

'Processing.'

Richard watched for the access code to appear on his screen. Then, after a short pause, there it was, 'Alfa Romeo Zero Zero Zero'.

'Yes, now I have you!' he said gleefully. 'Review.'

'This is very interesting' commented the security programme. 'I can verify that this code is not one allocated from the Osiris register. It also has a complicated route network; I am still running the trace, a further four billion route options to track. This will take two minutes and eleven seconds.'

Richard watched the screen patiently; the word 'tracking' appeared mid-screen.

Presently, the computer programme responded. 'Completed, and we have a serious security breech,' it said.

'Specify.'

'The coded access digits that we have isolated are in fact the shrouded identifiers of a synthetic virus. The virus has a direct link with a terminal facility on earth using a route structure so complicated that it would have been impossible to track unless we had achieved the 'lock'. It attaches to the side tone of an Accelercom transmission and in so doing, breaks the communication curfew. I shall have to report this breech to the security department.'

'Bill Bradley!' Richard paused for several seconds, coming to terms with the unexpected and disappointing news. 'Very well, do it,' he responded, 'but remember that your source is Level 7 protected and therefore cannot be disclosed to anyone but the Base Commander and the CMO. Confirm?'

'Confirmed; will you require my services any longer Lieutenant Commander Reece?'

'Negative, you can close down.'

Richard was both relieved and happy with his day's work. Now he could get on with deciphering the manual without sharing his findings. He leant back in his chair and stared at the screen, rather more concerned than he had been previously.

'Bill Bradley, Dublovnic, what the hell is going on?' he said to himself, quietly.

Richard reviewed the files he had previously worked on, as it had been several days since the incident in the education centre. Since then, his suspicions had prevented him from working on the project using the central computer system, and his own personal laptop, with only one hundred gigabytes of memory, was hopelessly inadequate. He had eventually identified seventeen letters and four numbers directly from the Ark's flight manual. Eight were direct translations from Egyptian hieroglyphics, five directly from Mayan text, five, apparently from ancient Babylonian writing and the final four from the little known southern Indian civilization of the Mohenjo Daro.

Unfortunately, the latter four characters were of little use as the written language of this civilisation had never been deciphered, and again, sadly, of the seventeen letters, the six he had identified were duplicated in each of the ancient alphabets. Therefore, in fact, he clearly had only eleven letters of the twenty-six required for the English alphabet. He knew that he had exhausted the painfully slow process of analysing each symbol of the alien text and comparing it, like for like, with the old writings of long-since disappeared civilizations. Superimposing symbols onto each other by using the computer programme had yielded some additional results over plain observation, but by giving himself a free artistic license with a few of the interpretations, he wasn't that confident with at least four of his b-list translations.

Richard worked until three the following morning. No one had troubled him with an evening meal and being completely immersed in the work, he hadn't even thought about it until too late. Closing down the programme, he decided to get a few hours' sleep. On reflection, he had concluded several important facts: for one thing, the alien text seemed to be the common base or basic building block for the other languages. Also the commonalties between the ancient writings, despite being from vastly different areas of the planet, were plain to see, and further independent adaptations or 'progressive evolution' had caused changes, both obvious and subtle, to the written word and presumably, therefore, the spoken word as well.

Richard got his head down for a couple of hours but couldn't sleep. He was on the cusp of discovering something amazing and his mind would not settle. By seven thirty, he was at the keyboard again. Whilst browsing the Egyptian course, he read how, during the last century, some progress had been made in deciphering the long forgotten inscriptions of the ancient Egyptians. However, it was not until the discovery of the famous Rosetta Stone in Egypt, which had a trilingual inscription in Egyptian hieroglyphics, ancient Greek and demotic, that a full transcription was finally possible, bringing enlightenment to both individuals and the scientific community alike. It opened up the world of one of the first great civilisations, just like a book. That's what he needed, a key. He knew with some help, namely Rachel's computer skills, that transcription of a few more letters of the alphabet was possible, but, staring blankly at the screen for a moment, he sensed that there was something missing, a vital element, a Rosetta Stone if you like.

'Hebrew,' he said aloud. 'Ancient Hebrew, that's it!' He snapped out of his semi-coma and looked at the clock. Just gone eleven. Dialling one seven one one on his intercom he recalled that the Hebrew course had been denied to him for some unknown reason on his initial request.

'CMO.'

'Rachel, its Richard. How's it going?'

'Hello Richard,' she replied, sounding rather depressed. 'Oh, I've had better days.'

'What's going on?'

'Well I'm just finalising the post mortem reports. What a mess, it's so sad. I can't believe she went like that.'

'Yes, one way or another I intend finding out who is responsible. They need locking up and the key thrown away,' responded Richard. 'Listen Rachel, can I talk to you about something else?'

'Go on.'

'I need your help with my project. An hour would help.'

'Well, you're due a daily medical visit. I could do it myself I suppose.'

'When?'

'Well, not until later I'm afraid. I need few more hours to finish here, then I'll come round.'

'OK, that's fine, thanks, see you later then. Oh, by the way, mention to the canteen will you that I haven't eaten for a day.'

'Richard, you should have said something earlier!' Rachel scolded.

Richard closed the channel and decided to give it a go. He had not tried, to date, to input his known English alphabetical characters onto a page of text, and now was the time. Opening the flight manual at the first page, he placed it on his scanner, closed the lid as much as possible over the binder and scanned it into his programme. Then, using the basic Egyptian teaching programme, he replaced the characters of the Egyptian alphabet, where possible, with his deciphered symbols and left blanks where a translation wasn't known against the English alphabetical character. Next, he transferred the scanned page of text into his teaching programme and pressed the 'translate' icon. The programme ran for a while, seemingly baffled by the request, but then, to his delight, a page of partly translated text appeared on the screen.

'YES!' he cried out loud, throwing himself back in the chair. His euphoria was, however, short lived. The page, understandably, was full of blanks. Several words were missing altogether and most had missing characters, thus making the text, at this stage anyway, impossible to read. Nevertheless, on closer scrutiny, it became obvious that, a few of the words were recognisable.

Richard smiled to himself with satisfaction. Partial success and, incredible as it may seem, before him was something written by an intelligent life form probably thousands of light years away and many thousands of years ago. Richard focused on the main heading: _ ta_ o_ Ho_ _. 'Now, do I read that left to right, or right to left?' he whispered. Just then, there was a tap on the door and the handle moved downwards. Richard covered the computer with a hand towel and sprang up to unlock the door. He opened it to find Rachel carrying an afternoon tea tray, complete with a selection of cakes. Looking at the security guard who nodded his approval, Richard opened the door wide enough for her to negotiate the opening with the tray. Then he closed and locked it behind her. He walked directly over to the desk and removed the towel.

'Look, reading left to right, or right to left, but not apparently, up or down!'

Rachel was plainly impressed. 'Is this ?'

'Yes, it is,' replied Richard, taking the tray from her. 'Thanks for this.' Rachel sat on the chair, staring at the screen.

'Page one of the Ark's flight manual,' he continued.

'The Ark?' questioned Rachel.

'The Ark is what I've called the ship, or what's left of it at any rate. I've got a funny feeling it was an ark of some description,' he said reflectively.

'Were there any remains of the crew, you know, the aliens in the craft?'

'No, nothing, not that I saw anyway. Having said that, the flight deck was in relatively good shape. I mean the consoles were all in place, and the seats. There was some debris hanging from the ceiling but it looked remarkably intact. I think it made a reasonable touchdown, perhaps skidding for a while before colliding with the basalt outcrops in that part of the crater floor. Against all odds, the flight deck penetrated an area of soft sand maybe between two outcrops.'

'That means that there may have been survivors?'

'I think actually that there were; those who were on the flight deck, or the bridge. At any rate, if that portion of the ship had been covered in sand, it would have benefited from a protective layer, a buffer, shielding the structure from any subsequent explosions or fire. Sadly, I don't think the survivors lasted long. The organics site I surveyed a month or so ago, in a sheltered area close to a small canyon and within half a kilometre of the crystal site, where Jennifer and Yung died. It's there that the carbon count is abnormally high, I think it may have been where the survivors took refuge, that is until their life support systems were exhausted. Not a nice way to go, but it would explain the carbon count. Jennifer was going to conduct a scan, which may have told us how many there were and provide a carbon date.'

'It's an amazing discovery, Richard, but don't you think you should make it known?'

'Of course I should and I will, but not now. There are problems here. I don't mean the Jennifer thing, it's to do with the crystals. There's so much energy locked up inside them, they could provide a long-term power source for the earth, one to replace the exhausted carbon based fuels. Even if they lasted a few decades, they would offer a breathing space. In that respect, they are priceless. I mean, who could put a figure on what they are worth? Knowledge is power Rachel, with power comes control, and in the wrong hands it could be exploitation on a scale never seen before. If you want my opinion there's already a conspiracy underway.'

'Oh, don't be ridiculous Richard, how can that be?'

'It can be, Rachel, because all my work has been monitored. I'm always looking over my shoulder, because of Jennifer, because of Peter Yung, because of the missing samples.'

'Greg Searle's security report concludes that the samples

were lost in transit. I've seen the draft,' said Rachel. 'It's on the Commander's desk now, along with mine.'

'Oh really, and what did yours say? Accidental death, I suppose!'

'Richard,' Rachel replied coldly, 'my report deals with the probable cause of death, as you know. It's not a coroner's verdict. But you're right; it probably will be accidental death.'

'I knew it!' Richard slammed his fist on the desk beside the computer, causing the screen to flicker for an instant. 'That was no accident and whoever is responsible has demonstrated that they will not allow anybody else to get in the way, and that basically means me!'

'Well, I hope you're wrong Richard, I really do.' Rachel's voice softened, she was too fond of Richard to argue. 'I'll give you my thoughts on it another time, not right now. So how can I help?'

Richard pulled up a chair and beckoned Rachel to sit beside him at the desk. 'I need your help with this programme. I've spent hours, days in fact, isolating these characters from the text and transcribing them into the English alphabet.'

'I see what you're doing! These characters, you have identified them mainly by observation, right?'

'Correct.'

'OK, let's take this logically. Take that text character there. 'Rachel highlighted a letter on the screen using the integral mouse. 'A direct and definite copy of the Egyptian hieroglyphic, agreed?'

'Agreed,' replied Richard leaning forward and peering at the screen.

'And a character which equates to H in the English alphabet?'

'Yes, but that's an H as in hat. See that character? Apparently that's also an H, but as in itch.' said Richard. 'And another example, those two are almost identical, but that means S as in saw and that one Z as in zebra. I've identified seventeen, but several I'm not entirely convinced about.'

'That's my point. Mathematically that definite would carry high odds, say one thousand to one. However, take this character from the text; it is basically similar to A as in water, in hieroglyphics. Look, a bird, but the horizontal line is missing, so you are not considering it a successful translation, but it is close. Therefore, the odds in this case are lower, say ten to one for argument's sake. It is possible, if your theory is correct, that the alphabet used in the text writings formed the foundation of these ancient languages. Then, over time, some marks may have been dropped for ease of writing, or, altered slightly from transcription to transcription by subsequent writers. They might not look quite the same, but the computer can identify the similarities more accurately than you can, depending on the latitude you give it. By that I mean dictating the odds.'

Rachel scanned into her laptop the first five pages of the flight manual.

'By using the first five pages of the text, the odds are high that every letter of their alphabet will have been used.' Rachel's hands flew over the keyboard like a touch typist's in full swing. 'I'll amalgamate the characters of the four ancient languages you're using: Phoenician, Mesopotamian, Northern Semitic and Sumerian, plus also the two derivatives you have identified; ancient Egyptian and Mayan. I'll isolate using thousand to one odds first and, hey presto!'

Rachel pressed the 'enter' key. Within a few seconds the 'task complete' icon appeared. Rachel pulled up the first pages of text. Richard studied it closely.

'That's the same as I achieved earlier,' he said, slightly disappointed.

'Yes, I know. That's because we are using your odds, the statistically certain 'one thousand to one'. Now, if I start to reduce those odds, allow for some artistic license so to speak, you know, let the computer speculate a little.'

'Well, go on then!' encouraged Richard, impatiently.

'Let's try one hundred to one.'

Richard agreed while Rachel pressed the necessary keys. He had given up trying to follow her fingers.

'Now the first page again,' she said.

The translation appeared on the screen with a few more characters.

'Look, we've got another one in the title,' he said, 'the middle word is 'of', something of something. It's the name of the ship, I'm sure of it.'

'Let's cut the odds, say fifty to one,' Rachel offered.

'Why don't you just use, say, two to one, or five to one?' Richard suggested.

Rachel explained. 'As we reduce the odds, the accuracy decreases. The programme will pick up on anything, however remote, and we will end up with mumbo jumbo. There's an optimum. It's just a case of finding out what it is.'

Richard nodded, slightly confused, but trying not to show it.

'Wait a minute. I've got an idea,' she said, her hands dancing over the keyboard again. When Rachel pressed the final key of an impressive flurry with gusto, a number popped up on the screen.

'Seventeen point eight eight recurring, what does that mean?' Richard asked.

'It's our optimum, the best odds for success with our known characters,' replied Rachel.

'Go on, then. Do it!'

Rachel pressed a few more keys. 'It's done,' she said, leaning back in the chair.

The complex programme ran for several seconds before responding.

'God, it's slow!' said Richard, slapping his knees in frustration.

'It's not slow, Richard. It's a powerful programme and it's performing literally millions of computations,' retorted Rachel defensively.

They both stared at the screen in anticipation. The few seconds seemed like eternity. Finally, the icon appeared. Rachel displayed the first page of the manual again.

Richard's jaw fell open. Normally so composed he could not conceal his absolute amazement. There were still several blanks in the text, missing characters and the occasional word.

'Star of Hope,' he murmured.

Rachel was not listening. She had spotted a few words where a missing character was obvious and was busy filling in the blanks. 'That's got to be a T, LEF blank, RIGH blank, Left and right, just like a cross word,' she said, pressing further keys which paired the characters she had deduced against the appropriate text character in Richard's initial file. With that task complete, she contemplated the results.

'Strange,' she said, 'so near, and yet, so far. It's probable that with a little more work the computer can fill in the remainder of the text, certainly enough to allow reading, but it's as if something is missing; characters that have been lost, or at least don't appear in our ancient alphabets.'

'Hebrew,' said Richard bluntly, 'one of the first great written languages of mankind. A language over five thousand years old and still, if I remember from my history lessons, one which has barely changed over the millennia.'

Rachel stopped pushing keys and looked at him perplexed. "Why Hebrew?'

'It's a long story but it fits, it's the only other written

language known to historians from that period. Apparently, the very earliest written words originate from between five and six thousand years ago. First, there was nothing and then there was the written word. Just like that, overnight.'

'What are you saying, Richard?'

'Something that would make me very unpopular with the religious communities back home.'

'Oh, come on, Richard. Was God an alien? has been topical for years.'

'Yes, you're right, it has, but never taken seriously; except by a few. Listen Rachel, they proved conclusively at the beginning of the century that our DNA molecule, that of the *Homo sapiens*, and the language gene particularly, was far too complex to have evolved naturally in the relatively short period between neolithic man and modern man. The first evidence of writing itself dates back only about seven thousand years. That scale of genetic evolution would have taken hundreds of millions of years. First nothing; then language, in the blink of an eye.'

'So?'

'So, this may be the elusive evidence that our ancestors were in fact from another planet. Science was right after all!'

'Richard,' said Rachel, almost flippantly, 'this ship crashed on Mars, not earth.'

'Star of Hope,' Richard paused. 'I think this ship left earth on a mission; maybe to get help, sometime between five and ten thousand years ago. But for one reason or another it didn't get very far.'

'That's total speculation, and you know it, Richard. Look, it's a fantastic discovery, amazing, but let's not go too far!'

Richard shrugged his shoulders, thought for a moment and said, 'OK. Hey, listen. It's time for a break. Can you save it? I'll get into it later.'

Rachel was dubious of Richard's thoughts, but did as he asked. After shutting down the machine, she spun round on her chair to find Richard already tucking into a toasted teacake. Before he had time to finish the first half, there was a determined knock on the door.

'Lieutenant Commander Reece, it's security. I need to talk to you now, Sir.'

Richard and Rachel's eyes met. For a few moments, they were anxious.

'It's OK; I'm giving you your medical examination, remember?' she said.

Richard sprang up and opened the door. It was Preston.

'Sir, Commander Miko wants to see you in his office right away.' He caught sight of Rachel who was pretending to write at Richard's desk. 'Pardon me M'am, you as well.'

'What's it about?' asked Richard, sternly.

'I don't know, Sir, but its causing some hassle in my department.'

'So, I'm released from my quarters?'

'Guess so, Sir. My orders are to escort both you, and the

doctor, to the Commander's office, immediately.'

'Give me one minute,' Richard said, almost closing the door. He turned to Rachel. 'What's this all about then? Where are my shoes?'

'Under the table, look, there,' replied Rachel, slightly bewildered by the rapidly changing events. 'Anyway, you're fit for duty, agreed?'

'Agreed.'

Richard and Rachel, with Preston following a few paces behind, strode purposefully through the restaurant, taking a short cut to the administration dome. A few base personnel were sitting at a table to their left taking coffee.

'Hey Richard! You OK?' one of them shouted.

Richard looked over his shoulder; it was Jeff Waters, one of the engineers who maintained the surface vehicles, or more particularly, the buggy.

'Jeff! Fine, thanks for asking. Repaired my wheels yet?'

Richard barely heard the reply as the three of them left the restaurant by the opposite door to which they had entered.

CHAPTER 10

Forgotten Skills

There was a commotion going on outside the Commander's door. A gaggle of security personnel, in uniform, engaged each other in heated discussion. Two women from the secretariat, wearing their customary pale blue tunics and white trousers, milled around aimlessly. Each one grasped a number of thin plastic files with both hands, protectively hugging them to their chests. In addition, there was Peter Mayhew, head of science, talking to Roland Pier. Pier, as head of communications was Bill Bradley's boss.

As if on cue, the Base Commander's office door opened as Rachel and Richard arrived; surrounding dialogue ceased mid-sentence. To greet them was Greg Searle. He sized up the pair, his face conjuring a customary scowl, before dismissing Preston with an authoritative nod.

'Strange you two arriving together, again!' he snapped.

'I was conducting a routine medical if you don't mind, when we were summoned,' replied Rachel defensively.

Richard put his hand on her shoulder. 'Rachel, don't bother,' he said, returning Searle's unfriendly gesture with interest.

'Follow me,' Searle continued, turning and walking back into the office.

'Gallant as always,' Richard replied under his breath, allowing Rachel to enter first.

Mayhew and Pier followed them in. Commander Miko, standing quite still, stared out through a large circular porthole-type window as if hypnotized. His view of the Martian sunset was uninterrupted and quite magnificent. The planet surface looking west, with the escarpment of Syrtis Major and Galliao Mons rising dramatically in the far distance against the setting sun. With a planetary rotation speed greater than that of the earth, the distant fiery-red ball slipped quickly behind the craggy peak of the towering volcano, its light splintered into a multitude of familiar red and bright orange hues.

Inevitably, the darkening lid of night closed; subduing the final remnants of the day into submission. Strangely, those who were gathered seemed to respect the impromptu spectacle with a moment of silence. Finally, as total darkness claimed its victory, Commander Miko turned and beckoned for the assembled to sit. No one spoke, not even a comment; a visual feast for the privileged, adjectives such as amazing would be barely descriptive, and extraordinary, well short of the mark.

Commander Miko remained standing for a few moments; he looked drained.

'This meeting is private,' he began. 'We have had a serious breach of security. I don't like what's happening here.' He turned and sat down behind his desk looking directly at Richard. 'Lieutenant Commander Reece, you are off the hook. You are no longer confined to quarters.'

'Thank you, Sir,' replied Richard warily.

The Commander placed his forearms on his desk and leaned forward purposefully.

'At eighteen hundred hours this evening the Accelercom was initialised in order to send a routine, albeit restricted, communication to earth. Within seconds the system registered a malfunction due to an intra-casing overheat situation. The main electrical supply was isolated in accordance with fire prevention procedures and auxiliary power retained. Promptly dispatched to the communications dome, engineering were unable to find the cause of the problem, until one of the team found a small hole, about ten millimetres in diameter, through the upper radiation screen of the centre core. That, in itself, is impossible, as the casing is a sandwich of samite, basalt fibre and titanium. The engineer considered switching off auxiliary power to investigate further. Fortunately he didn't, and kept the magnetic flux generator running while he called science and security.'

Commander Miko raised his left fist and dropped it

aggressively onto a pile of papers on his desk.

'This is the official report into the events of two days ago. I had already signed it. It notes that, in the absence of evidence to the contrary, the four crystals collected by Richard whilst on that fateful survey were lost at some time during his dash back to base. Further, it contains recommendations to the coroner on earth, that the cause of death of Jennifer Middleton and Peter Yung was accidental.'

The Commander paused for a few moments, staring at the papers. Slowly, he continued.

'However, when engineering used a cathode boroscope to investigate the hole in the Accelercom casing, they found, ladies and gentlemen, one of the missing crystals. Yes, suspended fortunately, in the dense magnetic flux-field of the Accelercom core. That field effectively cocooned the crystal, shielding it from further influences of radio waves. We have concluded that someone was either disturbed and subsequently fled the scene, inadvertently leaving the crystal on top of the machine, or, more likely, that it was a deliberate act of sabotage. Subsequent initialisation of the Accelercom to send the communication resulted in the crystal's exposure to the secondary aura and a mutative frequency spectrum. It reacted by super heating; then burnt its way down into the core, creating a finger-sized hole through the casing material. It dropped apparently, like a hot skewer through butter and that is where it is right now, seemingly safely insulated. I dread to think what would have happened had the engineer shut down the auxiliary power to the core magnetrons.'

The room fell silent. If anyone was breathing, it was imperceptible. Searle began to fidget.

The Commander elaborated. 'So, we have some good news and some bad. The bad news is that we can assume that the remaining three crystals retrieved by Richard are now in the hands of someone who should not have them. We obviously have the fourth under tight security. The good news is that, by accident, the problem of effective containment, which has totally baffled the science department since Richard first discovered these damn things, may have been solved!'

'What about the two deaths?' Richard questioned.

Commander Miko picked up the pile of biodegradable synthetic paper under his left hand, which composed the entire, but now redundant report and dropped it into the waste bin by his chair marked 'recycling'.

'We must now treat their deaths as suspicious.'

Searle's fidgeting attracted the Commander's attention.

'Instigate security code red. All non-essential personnel will perform secondary role security duties. Issue stun weapons to your 'Class A' personnel only. Start a systematic search of the entire station. We need to find those crystals quickly. The consequences of not finding them, doesn't bear thinking about.'

The strain on the Commander's face made Greg Searle cringe.

'Do it now, please,' he ordered firmly.

'Yes, Sir,' replied Searle, standing to leave the room.

'Rachel, you can stand-down now as well. Remain medical state 3 until further notice.'

'Of course, Commander,' she replied and then left the room behind Searle.

Commander Miko turned his attention to Richard. He was just about to speak when there was a knock on his door. 'Come in, please,' he responded.

It was Lieutenant Carol Murray, an American electronic and communications engineer and deputy head of the communications research department. Having hurried to relay her information she was out of breath.

'Sorry to disturb you, Sir, but I have some important news regarding the crystal.'

She looked over at her departmental head, giving him a nervous smile.

'OK, come in, close the door and sit down,' replied Miko.

She did so, looking next at Richard as she sat down beside him.

'Hi, Richard,' she said warmly.

'Hello Carol,' Richard replied, in a matter of fact tone.

'What's the situation?' Commander Miko enquired.

'As you know, Sir, we have been conducting some experiments with the damaged Accelercom. We have found that the crystal remains physically suspended in the magnetic field down to a flux density of eighty-two point two percent. That is a little over four hundred and twenty machroteslas. Below that, Sir, the crystal begins to fall though the field. However, at and above that level, the crystal appears to be completely insulated from any external electro-magnetic influences. It's completely contained!'

Commander Miko nodded his approval.

'But the real breakthrough is in control, Sir,' she continued, her excitement obvious. 'We have found that, by manipulating the control fields, we can generate a tiny corridor to the crystal. Within this corridor, the density of the magnetic field is reduced. We utilised the hole in the casing, burnt by the crystal as it fell into the chamber, to create a wormhole, if you like, about the diameter of a pencil. Then we directed a low-grade radio signal down the hole, directly at the crystal. It began to react immediately, giving off omni-directional plasma spouts of super-heated gas.'

Carol, barely pausing to take a breath, and obviously very excited, was interrupted by Commander Miko. He had suddenly become quite concerned.

'No accidents, I hope?' he enquired.

'No, Sir, not at all, on the contrary. I quickly increased the field density again, closing the wormhole. It screened the plasma bubble immediately and completely. There were no leaks, nothing!'

She could barely control her emotions.

'That's it, Sir,' she gushed again. 'We can control it, and

what's more, the thermal potential is incredible. I exposed the crystal to a medium wavelength radio wave with a frequency of four hundred hertz, for three hundredths of a second. Subsequently, within two further seconds the plasma effluence passed six hundred degrees celsius. I closed the hole after no more than three seconds, by which time we recorded a temperature inside the chamber of one thousand and sixty-nine degrees. Based on those measurements, the computer simulation gives us an exponential plasma temperature of *over* seven thousand degrees, totally controllable. Ultimately, we don't know how hot the crystal will go, but it's surely well beyond our materials technology.'

Having said her piece, Carol fell back in the chair almost exhausted.

'This is what we have dared to hope for,' said Commander Miko, standing again to look out of the window and into a dark night sky now punctured by countless shiny stars. 'This could be what earth needs.' He stopped suddenly and turned to look at Carol. 'What was the radiation level in the Accelercom dome?'

'Normal, Sir, completely normal,' Carol replied, wide-eyed.

'So, it's clean,' he mused, looking again out of his window. 'We must give earth a full report as soon as possible and prepare the crystals for transportation.' He turned again to Lieutenant Murray.

'How long to correlate your report and prepare it for

coded transmission? We will have to use the old system, the Accelercom is obviously out of commission until further notice.'

'I'll have it ready by zero eight hundred, Sir.'

'Very good, please go and make a start. Oh, and by the way,' he said, smiling, 'damned good work, well done!'

Commander Miko opened the door for Carol to leave, and then addressed the remaining officers.

'Meeting over, gentleman. Standard briefing twenty hundred hours tomorrow, please.'

The three men stood up to leave.

'Richard, hang on for a bit will you? I'd like to have a few words in confidence.'

'Yes, Sir,' Richard replied.

Once they were alone the two men sat down again. They faced each other over Commander Miko's large office desk and he opened their private conversation in a far more sombre tone.

'NASA has brought the shuttle forward. They launch in a little over three weeks and they're using the S3.'

'The Enigma!' Richard interrupted, surprised. 'I didn't think she was ready, Sir, not by a long shot!'

'She's not. Less than half way through the initial flight test programme. However, command cannot, or more to the point, will not, wait the fourteen maybe fifteen weeks it takes for an S2 to arrive here, then of course the same to return. Apparently, although top secret, I can tell you that the S3 has exceeded all expectations. They estimate a flight time of five or six days each way, a twelve day round trip!'

Richard's eyes widened in amazement, 'wow, that's incredible.'

'Yes it is, to say the least. Consequently, if everything goes to plan, she should arrive on the thirty-first, this month, twenty-nine days from now. Commander Miko paused and looked questioningly at Richard. 'Richard, I need your help. We must find out who has the other crystals before the Enigma arrives. If we don't, if this gets out, not only will the whole Mars programme be in jeopardy, but also the lives of everyone here.'

'Of course, Sir, no question.'

Commander Miko nodded with approval. 'OK, in my view, whoever has the crystals probably had a hand in the deaths of Middleton and Yung. That rather narrows the field of suspects to the PTSV crew, and probably an accomplice in the base somewhere. Keep a low profile Richard, find out what you can and run a check to see who is keen to get back to earth on the next shuttle; mystery illness, compassionate grounds, that sort of thing. Report to me daily, and by the way, you have my authority to draw out a personal weapon. Use code fourteen fourteen. Be careful, there's a lot at stake.'

Commander Miko paused again momentarily, as if considering avoiding the forthcoming subject altogether. 'Listen, there is one other thing I would like you to consider.'

Richard raised his eyebrows expectantly.

'The Enigma is not clean, not yet anyway. There is a polarising and particle filtration system called, apparently, a zantum sieve. It isn't ready and won't be for the foreseeable future, therefore will not be fitted for this mission. As a result, the Enigma's propulsion stream is seriously radioactive. It cannot be discharged in a proximity-orbit for fear of irreparable damage to the Van Allen belt and unacceptable pollution to earth's atmosphere. The ship therefore, will be lifted into an extremity orbit by Skyport 2, which is already undergoing modifications. It will then use a minimal emission discharge to blast clear of the earth. Somewhere between the earth and Spartacus, Enigma will utilise its full potential. Similarly, it cannot land here on Mars, but will remain in a seventy percent elliptic orbit. This will minimise pollution. Essential personnel and all the crystals, I hope, will be transferred by Columbus.'

'The Columbus hasn't flown for, well, five years, Sir!' Richard burst out, taken aback at what he was hearing.

'I know, but it's been kept in a constant state of readiness, and has been fully maintained for that period, so I see no reason for it not to.'

'I understand, Sir, but there's also the problem of fuel. Osiris stores enough liquid oxygen and hydrogen for one emergency flight to earth and that is it. Consequently, the old fuel cells have either been capped, or have fallen into disrepair. We never expected to produce any more of that obsolete fuel!' Richard's expression of astonishment turned to concern. 'We have enough fuel for probably two flights at seventy percent. That will leave enough for a landing back on Mars, or to complete an extended transit to earth, probably about six and a half months. There's no more, Sir! Osiris will loose it's albeit limited emergency escape system and, as you are aware, Sir, that will make most base personnel very nervous. Although never thinking it would actually be required, they have always felt, well, secure knowing that it is there.'

Commander Miko nodded and sighed, straightening up his chair. 'I know that too Richard, only too well, but the S3, apart from the pollution issue, isn't kitted up for an interplanetary landing. God damn it, I hear almost thirty percent of its systems are not functioning at all?'

Commander Miko's voice trailed off, he continued almost in a whisper. 'Command need those crystals, Richard, and we need those two flights to seventy percent: the first to pick up the containment device, and the second to deliver the crystals back to Enigma. I tell you this in confidence: the earth's dying Richard, the one we remember anyway. Humankind is killing it. These crystals represent a clean power source, and they are apparently inexhaustible. They're our only hope, a ray of light on the horizon, and at all costs we must get those crystals back to earth.'

Richard was speechless. The two men looked at each other in silence for a few seconds.

'So what is it you would like me to do, Sir?'

'When was the last time you flew an S1?' enquired the Commander.

Richard hesitated. 'Six years ago, maybe more.'

'But you had a lot of experience on it, right?'

'Well, yes. I suppose so. I flew one between earth and Andromeda for a few years, and I was on Andromeda Wing when it was superseded by the S2. I flew both types for about a year until the S1 was decommissioned.'

'Then perhaps more importantly, when was the last time you had a flight simulator session?'

With that question, the Commander leaned forward, as if to emphasise the importance of Richard's answer. Richard breathed out hard through his nose, almost in exasperation. He could see where Commander Miko was going with his line of questioning.

'When I first arrived on Osiris, Sir, I tried to keep some regular sessions going, but Witherspoon wasn't keen. He always said he needed the hours for the dedicated flight crew, and they only do the minimum six monthly checks these days!' Richard scratched his head as Miko looked him in the eye, pursuing a more accurate answer. 'Well, I can check,' he continued warily, 'but I suppose eight or nine months ago.'

'Oh, I see.'

Commander Miko looked down at the papers on his desk seemingly disappointed. Without looking up, he asked Richard the inevitable question.

'Are you confident to pilot the Columbus to a free

orbital docking with the S3?'

Their eyes met again. Miko could sense Richard's next question, but without giving him time to ask it, the Commander pressed his case.

'Rightly or wrongly, I have to be very careful who I trust at the moment. There can be no room for error. Unscrupulous people want control of these crystals as much as we do. I don't know Morgan or Horowitz very well. They are good pilots on the face of it, and their reports reflect that, but I just cannot afford to trust them. You are a very good pilot, one of the best, most people here think.'

'Was!' exclaimed Richard; momentarily, reflecting on his lost career.

Richard had a great deal of respect for the Commander. With his short white hair and close-cropped white beard, he exuded experience and maturity. Immaculately dressed, as usual, in his trademark white cotton polo neck sweater and a smart black tunic with three gold bands on each shoulder, he was a veteran pilot himself, albeit of a bygone era. Miko knew exactly what he was asking of Richard.

'Listen, Richard, I don't know exactly what happened to you during your last appointment on Andromeda. I heard about it, but have never bothered to read the file, I'm not interested. When you joined Osiris, I took you at face value, and it proved the right thing to do. You have enjoyed considerable autonomy, quite rightly; you are one of my best officers. I trust you, as I think you know, and I need you to do this job.'

Richard nodded, 'thank you, Sir. I'll do my best of course.'

'OK. That's good enough for me,' concluded the Commander. 'Now, I'd like you to visit the Columbus as often as you can over the next three weeks. There will be no simulator practice I'm afraid, that might arouse suspicion. Re-familiarise yourself with the systems, the flight deck, fly some profiles on your personal terminal. Prepare yourself as much as you can.'

'Yes, Sir,' answered Richard, 'I know just where to start.'

'Very well, thank you Richard, you're dismissed.'

'Thank you, Sir.'

Immersed in his thoughts as he walked back to his cabin, Richard was surprised at the progress of the S3 programme. Its propulsion system was unique: utilising breakthrough technology similarly employed in the 'bond-splitter' that provided Osiris with power and oxygen. Whereas on Mars, the molecular structure of water was broken, split into two atoms of hydrogen for energy, and one of oxygen for atmospherics, with the Enigma, the process utilised molecular remnants as a propulsive matter stream. Richard had made a point of keeping abreast of the science involved, despite his relatively isolated outpost. That system, he recalled, utilised five massive cylindrical chambers, in which the atomic structure of a heavy metal isotope was broken, split into its component parts: electrons, protons, and neutrons. In reaction to this rearward stream of dense atomic matter, the ship would be propelled forward at hitherto unheard of speeds. With the five propulsion chambers set in a circle, directional control, theoretically, is achieved by increasing and blending the matter stream on the opposite side of the required turn. The practicalities of directional control however, had frustrated the programme's advancement for the last decade, not to mention those of navigation. Surely, he would have heard if another such important breakthrough had been achieved? Travel at light related speeds had been anticipated using the ARPS design, but not for several years yet! Richard broke from his thoughts as he arrived at his door. Thankfully, the security guards had been reassigned. Now he had investigations to pursue.

CHAPTER 11

Building a Picture

Rachel started work early that morning. She had several reports to complete, including the post mortem on the remains of Jennifer Middleton and Peter Yung. It was a sad time, particularly as the majority of the staff had not experienced a fatality and certainly not since Rachel had taken over as base CMO. It was almost as if a veil of unease had fallen over its people, heightening subconscious feelings of isolation. Several female staff had already confided feelings of anxiety to Rachel, and she knew that if unchecked, irrational behaviour could occur. Morale generally was lower than she could ever recall.

Coincidentally, the biannual freighter from earth was expected to dock in the early hours of Tuesday morning, in three days time. The remains of the two bodies would be frozen and returned home on the next leg of the ship's endless cycle. To this end, Rachel was keeping an eye on her junior doctor via the video link. Doctor Bill Bates, twenty-nine and still relatively inexperienced in space medicine, had completed his work and was zipping up the black plastic body bag when Rachel next looked at her monitor.

'All complete, then?' she asked, leaning over to speak into the microphone at the base of the monitor screen.

Bill Bates looked up at the wide-angle camera, which made the tiny white mortuary look much bigger than it actually was.

'Yes, M'am. I'll preserve at minus twenty-five degrees celsius and then they are ready for shipment.'

'You mean transporting, or returning, or even transferring, but *not* shipment. They're human bodies, not engineering parts!'

Bates, a little surprised, but also embarrassed by Rachel's response, replied. 'Yes, sorry M'am,' and then turned away from the camera. Rachel shook her head and switched off the monitor screen. Irritated, perplexed, even apprehensive she chewed her pen top, absorbed in thought.

Of the seventeen S1 interplanetary craft originally built in the twenties and thirties, only three remained in flight-worthy condition following the introduction of the superior S2. The S1, developed from the successful space shuttle of the early twenty-first century, was similarly powered by two conventional liquid hydrogen rocket motors. However, as with its predecessor, fuel capacity for this basic propulsion system proved highly limiting, and the four to five month transit between earth and Mars in the first years of exploration created more problems than the establishment of the Mars base itself.

Columbus, named after several famous predecessors, had been assigned to Osiris as an emergency escape vehicle. Its capacity for the transit to earth was nineteen people, including the crew of four; whilst the forecast base population was cited to grow to almost one hundred and ninety people in the coming few years. The remaining two ships: Quest and Spirit of Humanity, had been converted to crew-less freighters. They 'sailed' continuously backward and forwards between the earth and Mars carrying low priority provisions: clothing, spare parts, medical equipment and so forth and would cross twice yearly, approximately half way between the two planets.

NASA had requested a quick turnaround for the Quest and she was expected to be on Mars for two or three days at most. Rachel, along with several other heads of department, was under pressure to complete all outstanding projects, administration and packaging, in order to comply with a tight schedule and the timely relaying of all exports to the freight terminal.

Richard had asked Miles to pack several routine rock samples for the passage back to earth, while he had remained glued to his personal computer terminal, flying S1 profiles over and over again. By mid afternoon his eyes were stinging, as was his back, from hunching over the small screen, and he decided to give it a rest. He sent an e-diction to Rachel.

Fancy a coffee?

Hi Richard, thanks for the e-dit, would be nice but can't until at least 6, came a prompt reply.

'That's it, then,' he groaned. Punching four four two into his intercom, he opened a channel to Flight Operations.

'Lieutenant Commander Macmillan speaking?'

'Adam, its Richard, how's it going?'

'Busy, busy,' came the reply.

'What time does the Quest arrive?'

'At the moment it's giving zero one fifteen, a very unsocial hour on Tuesday morning.'

'Mind if I come over for the landing, sit at the console and watch the automatics?'

'No problem at all, very welcome, I'll need someone to talk to at that time of night.'

'Cheers, Adam, see you later then.'

He leant back in his chair. Time for some more work on the Ark's log.

Richard lifted the thin synthetic mattress off his bunk and pulled back the moisture recycling cover with his other hand, taking care not to damage the connecting pipework. Hidden by a support bracket was a plastic lid about twelve centimetres square, covering a neatly cut hole in the bed base. He slid his hand inside and retrieved a metal box; long and thin, and because of it's matt, light-grey sheen, evidently made of titanium and bearing the initials N.R. Norman Reece, his father. Inside the box, amongst other things, was his 'alternative' health chip. As he lifted it from the box, a small, three-dimensional digital photograph that had stuck to the moisture on his finger, fluttered to the ground and landed with the image face up. It was of a young woman: her face radiant and engaging. Recalling and reflecting on forgotten memories, it caused Richard to hesitate for several seconds. Eventually he replaced it in the box and returned them both to their secret home.

Sitting back at his desk and inserting the chip into his laptop, Richard wrestled with his thoughts for a while longer before concentrating on the job in hand. Rachel's idea of scanning each and every page of the flight log into the computer, then transferring the data to his health chip's memory, was a good one and he had stayed up late the night before, certainly well after Rachel had retired, in order to complete the task. Now, the manual itself could remain well and truly hidden in his cabin. Further, Rachel's analytical skills had enabled her to decode another three symbols into corresponding letters of the English alphabet; the exceptional probability had surprised Richard. Nevertheless, several frustrating hours of work and manipulation had revealed symbols with more than one meaning, sometimes even several. This had confused and complicated matters somewhat.

Although in most cases the grammatical construction and phraseology of the writings was close enough to read 'straight off', a few areas of text had probability factors low enough as to make them almost incomprehensible. Rachel's unexpectedly dedicated work the previous evening, performed whilst Richard had 'flown' S1 emergency profiles on the adjacent terminal, would inevitably pay dividends, and at this moment, he was keen to incorporate any additional progress or discoveries she had made into practical reading opportunities.

With the almost continuous amazement and excitement that the identifying of individual symbols had generated, particularly over the last two weeks, now beginning to wane, Rachel and Richard agreed that the modified language programme had enough information to begin deciphering the manual, and he was keen to get started. For several reasons Richard was very serious about the task and had arranged in his mind the order of chapters he would concentrate on. However, the 'missing link' element still made him sceptical about recent progress, and so convinced was he that ancient Hebrew held the key, that he had sought some advice from the base librarian, regardless of her department's surprise at their new anthropologist.

Richard commenced the morning's work by opening a covering e-diction from Rachel.

That's the best I can do Richard, it read. Any words or phrases that the computer cannot recognise, after referring to each of the four ancient languages and any other stored symbologies, it will automatically re-characterise (based on falling probability rates) then translate back into

English again. By the way, dear heart, I did some research into the 'origin of languages' from the attached historical files. Your theory about ancient Hebrew is, in my opinion, ill founded. Why? Because I found that all the alphabets in use around the world (I mean the earth) can be traced back to a 'Northern Semitic' alphabet, from which Hebrew, Phoenician and Arabic developed. Apparently, the hieroglyphics or pictographs (as they are also called) from Mesopotamia and Ancient Egypt predate these written languages by quite some time, maybe a thousand years or more. The history files are talking about the earliest of these dating from around four to five thousand years BC. Moreover, and this is interesting, apparently the first evidence of a true spoken language, something called Proto-Indo-European, is also from about the same time, or just a little earlier. Who knows, maybe this was when your visitors arrived, seems quite coincidental I have to say? Anyway Richard, I think you have enough to make a qualified start, so get to it and happy reading!

Richard closed the diction then thought on it for a while. After some time, he reopened and erased it. He knew there was more to it than that.

Seems to fall rather conveniently into place, he thought. Perhaps a little too conveniently, but on the other hand, if I'm wrong, if my conspiracy theory is ill-founded, then I haven't done myself any favours by asking outwardly for information from Steffe Hoffman. Richard smiled and scratched his head, all the same, thanks Rachel, good work, just the job.

Using the integral hemispherical mouse, he flipped through several pages on the screen before arriving at what appeared to be the largest section in the manual. It began with eighty or so images of the heavens, impressively high in resolution; indeed, as good as, if not better than the digital mapping photographs taken by NAVSATS 'Microrad' radiation cameras.

The images plotted the galaxy, or possibly many galaxies, highlighting particular stars as apparent navigational aids. Several of the stars had symbols set adjacent to them. Richard flipped through the images, stopping at one, second to last, which he seemed almost to recognise. He looked closely and studied it meticulously.

'That's it, I'm sure of it. Definitely.'

In his excitement, he could not help talking to himself.

'It's our solar system orientated towards the sun, taken further out than Mars but closer than Saturn, and that's the earth, there we are!'

Richard's suspicion that these pages were in fact navigation charts, seemed to be confirmed. He flipped the page to the last image.

Why didn't I spot this before? he thought.

The image showed the earth and moon as large, bright spherical objects, a kind of close up, taken this time, evidently, not far from Mars. He knew therefore that, had he the patience, magnifying the earth would reveal the continents. Additionally and of greater interest, there were these four thin white lines, like arrows pointing at the earth from different directions, each with adjacent writings. Richard quickly moved his cursor to the decode icon and selected it impatiently. The programme paused for a second or two, and then the image reappeared with the text in English, and it was complete!

'Yes, yes,' he enthused, feeling both startled and elated. Oh my God, look at this!'

Richard read the text adjacent to each white line, which in turn pointed directly to a particular area on earth. Then the penny dropped. They were approach vectors; approach corridors from space, to positions on earth, and not just positions, but cities!

ATLANTIS, ZERO FOUR FIVE
TE AGI WAKHAN, TWO FIVE FIVE
ERIDU, ZERO NINE ZERO
MOHENJO DARO, ONE SEVEN SIX

Richard breathed out loudly; almost sighing with incredulity. He was speechless. The fabled Lost City of Atlantis he knew about, as did most. History or legend has it that this great, ancient city had prospered, sheltering a thriving population several thousand years before Christ. Only to be completely lost, without warning, beneath a huge tsunami generated by a sudden severe earthquake. Archaeologists had even agreed on the site, the Island of

Theira, now known as Santorini. Richard enhanced the area where the white line terminated, magnifying it by ten. It was the eastern Mediterranean.

'So it was true? Atlantis had existed, and what's more, it had a spaceport.' Richard moved his cursor to the 'Te Agi Wakhan' symbol and enhanced. 'Mexico,' he whispered. He thought about the name for a few minutes. This was the vast city of the Mayan civilization, thousands of years before even the Incas. Apparently, its people just walked away, for no apparent reason at all. The city, reclaimed by the jungle, was rediscovered almost intact last century. 'God, this is incredible!'

Next Richard focused on Eridu and enhanced manually by factor twelve.

'The Holy Land, of course, the oldest city,' Richard continued, his trailing whisper now barely audible. 'Where modern science believes it all started. Mesopotamia and later Sumaria, the Sumarians?'

Richard shook his head. He remembered them as an ancient and advanced civilization, but he knew nothing more.

'And the last one, Mohenjo Daro, India. Never heard of it!' he exclaimed. Richard sat back in his chair and swivelled gently left and right, his thoughts divergent and his imagination fired.

If this section was anything like our own flight manuals, the next logical progression would be landing information; he thought and then turned to the next page, of which half was occupied by a strangely familiar diagram, the remainder being text. Richard fumbled for the decode key. The machine took a little longer this time, as if initially baffled, then the results appeared.

'Atlantis incoming, Britannia Bridge' read the title. Richard leant forward again, peering wide-eyed at the screen. He deleted the machine's interpretation for the word 'incoming', replacing it with 'arrival' and saved it once again.

'Just like ours,' he whispered. 'The trajectory, the descent angle, the inbound vector, the check heights and the speed check.'

However, the system used for positioning and its associated units of measurement were not as recognisable. Richard paused for a moment.

'Fifty one ten, zero one, forty-nine, Stellites, Stellites, Stellites,' he repeated several times. 'Stella, Stella. Maybe, just maybe.'

Richard studied the diagram closely. The Britannia Bridge was a checkpoint. A navigational fix to check speed and height against recommended parameters. Richard looked at the text lower down the page and read off the associated coordinates.

'Well, our system came from somewhere?' he speculated, justifying an unlikely theory that the coordinates would read like standard latitudes and longitudes.

Riding his castored chair across the room towards a plastic cabinet with a generously sized top draw, Richard, impatiently pulled it open and began rummaging through a lifetime's worth of odd bits and pieces. He delved enthusiastically into the array of mementoes and old flying knick-knacks, several items falling onto the floor as a result. He was looking for something specific.

'Ah, there it is, my old GPS,' he blurted, a grin appearing on his unshaven face.

The palm-sized Global Positioning System was an instrument used for navigation back on earth in the early days, and was long since obsolete. To his pleasant surprise, its nickel-cadmium battery was still functional and the small liquid crystal display lit up when Richard switched it on. He fumbled with excited anticipation as he punched in the navigational coordinates from the text; then selected the 'details' key.

N051 010.6' W001 049.5' - STONEHENGE
SALISBURY PLAIN   UNITED KINGDOM

Richard's birthplace was a small, traditional and picture pretty hamlet in the county of Wiltshire called South Lavington. He had spent a good deal of his childhood there before his parents had moved further west to Somerset, in a desperate bid to distance themselves from the relentless growth of London's conurbation. The hamlet's geographical proximity to the ancient monument meant that Richard knew it well. Indeed, for those early years the prominent ring of stones had literally been on his doorstep.

He knew something of its origins, or thought he did, and also how historians had speculated over its position and purpose for centuries.

The diagram occupying the lower half of the page that Richard was studying detailed a shallow dish, like a saucer, facing skywards. Much larger than the famous ring of stones on which it rested, the saucer was, without doubt, an antenna or a transmitter. It directed, or possibly reflected, a signal of some kind vertically upwards. The spacecraft, Richard pondered, would, on its final approach course, fly through the signal, which was possibly a beam of light, or a radio wave, or some kind of electrical or magnetic signal, and then adjust to the perameters on the chart.

'It's what we've been doing for years,' he reiterated aloud, oblivious to his solitude.

Richard recalled his early science lessons at school in Wiltshire. He remembered vividly his teacher, Mr Bartholomew, speaking of the reported publicity and general hype associated with the stone circle when it was discovered, back in 2009, that the monument lay within a few miles of one of the earth's most significant magnetic hot spots, one of only nine discovered on the entire earth's surface and fifth in relative magnetic density and stratospheric penetration. He recalled also that scientists, knowing precisely the drift rate of the earth's magnetic core, had calculated that for almost one thousand years this hot spot, the result of a magnetic leak through the earth's mantle, was directly beneath the ring of stones and that the resulting 'polarised flux spout' as it was termed, radiated at times, deep into space. The spout had been designated 'Garwin 3', after the scientist who had discovered the phenomena.

Perhaps it was the granite, the rock that composed the stone circle, quarried hundreds of miles away in North Wales, with its extraordinarily high iron content; perhaps they used the circle to channel, magnify and then direct the magnetic spout? Instead of speculating further, Richard decided to call a friend. 'Whatever the reason, they had an incredible understanding of magnetism,' he whispered to himself again and then punched three numbers on his intercom panel.

'Yes? Ramir Pushtarbi, robomotives.'

'Ramir, its Richard Reece. How's it going?'

'Ah, Richard Reece, a friend of unlimited enterprise, creating all this additional work, then nonchalantly calling to say 'how's it going'! What do you have to say for yourself my friend?'

'Come on, Ramir, you know it's not all my fault. Anyway, sorry, how's that?'

'Ha, you'll have to do better than that. Nevertheless, it concentrates the mind, quite a relief in my tiny world. So, Richard. How can I help?'

'Garwin 3, Ramir. What do you know about it?'

'I know a great many things Richard, do not forget that I am a scientist foremost and a mechanic to robots . . .'

'Yes, sorry Ramir, I didn't mean to question that. Listen,

this is important, more than I can say at the moment. A question. When did the Garwin 3 spout align co-axially with the circle of Stonehenge? What era, you know, through the middle. It was calculated.'

'Your questions never cease to amaze me, Richard. The findings were of great interest as I recall. The magnetic core of the earth stalled, its position fixed for almost a thousand years, and for no apparent reason. Most said that this was a physical impossibility, the fundamental laws of the universe such as gravity, inertia, fluid dynamics, all ignored; discounted. But the calculations proved it happened. Between approximately 4900 and 3800 BC, the Garwin 3 spout radiated directly through the centre of that prehistoric monument.

Ramil paused, 'How much do you want to know?' he asked Richard.

'What next? What happened next, Ramil? Why did the spout begin to move again?' Richard demanded.

'Then, the tectonic plates shifted with great power, an immense release of pent-up energy; earthquakes, tsunamis, again unexplained. Some calculated the North Atlantic tsunamis to have been over one hundred metres high. Apparently, it funnelled through the Straits of Gibraltar and into the Mediterranean, growing to twice that height. The entire region from the Atlas Mountains to the Alps was flooded, and remained so for many months, perhaps even years. Far to the east in Palestine, the vast canyon of the river Jordan filled to produce the Dead Sea and the

Sea of Galilee. Did you know that the story of the biblical character, Noah, dates from the same period, Richard? Perhaps that story was true, eh?'

'They lost control,' interjected Richard. 'They lost control and were instrumental in their own destruction.'

'My dear fellow. Who lost control?' Ramir asked, intrigued.

'It doesn't matter. Look Ramir, thanks for your help, I owe you, really.'

Richard closed the intercom channel without waiting for Ramir's response; he was desperate to decipher more of the text. He recalled another, less well-known ring of stones in Cornwall. He tapped his fingers on the desktop.

'Yes, the Merry Widows, near the Lizard peninsula,' he continued and typed the name into his GPS.

The resulting coordinates he then compared to the list. About halfway down he found the entry, and in comparison, they were only very slightly inaccurate, but that may have been because the machine had used the nearby village coordinates and not the monument itself.

Nevertheless, there was no doubt. He had discovered why these ancient monuments had been built, and by whom. However, the annotated speed, measured at the check fix, continued to puzzle him. The time unit seemed, incredibly, to be common: the second. It almost translated directly from the word 'secondi' in the text.

'I always thought Britannia was the Roman word for Britain,' he mumbled, 'but apparently it goes back a lot further.'

From Stonehenge to Atlantis on the Island of Theira, the chart gave two hundred and sixty five secondis or seconds.

He used his GPS to calculate the great circle distance using the text coordinates. 'One thousand four hundred and fifty miles…so, it's elementary. Distance over time gives speed in nautical miles per second, times three thousand six hundred. That's nineteen thousand seven hundred knots!'

Richard performed a second calculation, to confirm his results, and using the GPS, he calculated a distance of one thousand five hundred and seventy miles between the Lizard peninsular and Theira.

'Wow! That's upwards of twenty two thousand miles an hour and that is on final approach. Almost three times faster than the tropospheric top speed of an S2, impressive!' he nodded in approval. 'What about this final fix, much closer to Atlantis, Hagar Qim, seems to be on an island to the south west?'

Richard loaded the coordinates into his GPS, and within seconds he had an answer. 'Malta. Yes, much closer. Only five hundred and forty miles from Theira and the final check fix for an inbound ship with ten seconds to run.

He performed the final speed calculation, and concluded that it was just short of one thousand six hundred miles per hour. This was definitely a final fixing point and a speed check; airliners back on earth still use the same system!

At that moment, the intercom provided an unwelcome interruption.

CHAPTER 12

Double Cross

'Lieutenant Commander Reece, Sir? Are you there?' It was the voice of Miles Perry in a forced whisper.

Richard replied at a similar volume, 'yes, Miles, listening.'

'I'm in the workshop, boss. I've found them!'

'Found what?' asked Richard, turning up the volume on the intercom panel.

'In the place where no one would think to look, hidden in the Yearlman Cube, in the container on the back of the buggy,' Miles continued.

'The crystals? You've found the other crystals?'

'Yes, quite by accident! I was doing some repair work on the buggy; I'd postponed it, waiting for spares and a routine inspection, you know, the 'once over'. I found a sheet of Yearlman material, boss, left lying on one of the front seats. It's square, heavy, the dimensions of the cube, maybe a little smaller, with corner extensions, kind of supports. I think it formed a shelf, a sort of false base inside the cube. I checked the matrix combination, it was neutered, so I looked inside and there they were, all three of them! Thought you had better know first boss, what with the other one and all. By the way, I've managed to get your stun gun modified. Wait, the light's gone out! There's somebody in here! Who's there?'

Richard heard Miles shout loudly. He was challenging the unseen intruder. Then he heard a weapon firing, the unmistakable crack of a sonic discharge, followed quickly by numerous bangs and crashes, then another discharge?

'I'm hit!' Miles groaned. That was his final communication.

Richard immediately closed the lid of his laptop, stuffed it under his mattress, locked the door to his cabin and ran towards the transport dome. As he passed the sickbay, he narrowly avoided knocking Rachel and a female patient for six.

'Careful,' Rachel warned. 'What's happening?' she asked after Richard, who was already around the corner and out of sight.

'Trouble,' came the reply. 'You had better follow me.'

Richard arrived at the transport dome and pulled up sharp. He walked, gingerly, the final few metres to the door of the servicing department. It was half open. He peered inside. Although the overhead lighting was off, some ambient luminosity filtered through the roof louvres as the Martian day drew to a close. The room was quiet.

Richard was just about to step inside when Rachel arrived with a security guard.

'Is that wise?' she said, clutching Richard's arm to hold him back.

'Miles Perry is in there, I think he's hurt.'

Richard looked at the security guard. 'You go right, I'll go left. Don't shoot unless you're challenged and have a clear target.'

The guard nodded. Once inside, Richard skirted the wall, avoiding a bench and some equipment on the floor. He quickly lost sight of the guard in the shadows on the other side of the servicing bay. Keeping his head down, he crept slowly towards the buggy, which was almost at the far end of the bay. Even in the gloom, as he drew closer, Richard could see that the vehicle was still supported about a half metre above the floor, by four magnetic jacks. The little light there was, began to fade.

'Ow, that's me,' blurted Miles, as Richard accidentally kicked him in the thigh. Miles was lying on the floor, almost underneath the buggy. Without hesitation, Richard grabbed him under the arms and pulled him clear. Miles moaned in pain.

'Where are you hit?' Richard enquired in a strained whisper.

'Left leg and it hurts like hell!'

Just then, the security guard shouted from the other side of the bay. 'I've found someone, he's dead!'

Richard could not see his precise position, so kept his

head down; but he did hear a commotion start up outside, followed a few moments later by the two main doors bursting open, and the overhead lights exploding into life. Richard squinted, blinded temporarily by the bright light; for a few seconds he saw stars. As he focused, he saw it was Greg Searle. He was armed and demonstrating some sort of killer pose in front of a SWAT team of five officers. It obviously rubbed off, for they also, with their rigid outstretched arms adopted similar static examples, their weapons pointing in all directions.

Everyone paused for a few seconds, not quite knowing what to expect. Rachel, peering around from behind the body of men saw Richard crouching with Miles's head in his hands, and with the lights on, his injury was immediately apparent; his right thigh was split open down to the bone. As if that was not enough, the surrounding tissue was blackened and burned. His trouser leg was tattered and shredded, and blood stained the floor. She rushed over, medical bag in hand.

'Did I get them both?' Miles asked, wincing from the pain.

Richard looked at him, nodding slowly. 'You got one of them, mate. No sign of anyone else.'

'There was two of them, boss,' Miles continued, 'couldn't recognise the second one, it was too dark. The first I did though, he was a PTSV crew member for sure.' Miles squirmed as Rachel dabbed a sterile dressing on his wound.

'Don't worry, we'll talk about that later. You're in good hands now,' Richard said reassuringly as he looked up at Rachel, her white suit blotched and smudged by blood. Rachel did not respond, but summoned two orderlies, who lifted Miles gently onto a microfibre stretcher.

Richard indicated to Greg Searle to look inside the cube on the back of the buggy. He did so, slamming the lid closed immediately.

'There are three!' he blurted, visibly perspiring.

'Sickbay. Quickly please,' ordered Rachel, who then ran over to the other casualty still slumped over a box of mechanical components. She put two fingers on the inside of his wrist for a few seconds, then changed position to the man's neck. 'Nothing,' she concurred. 'He's gone.'

With due haste, Miles was carried out of the bay. Richard, watching him go, walked over to the dead man. He crouched down and looked up at his partly concealed face. It was Bill Bradley. Richard was stunned. Bradley had taken a Level 4 discharge just below his larynx. Most of his neck was missing. Richard felt someone behind him and looked up. It was Searle and he was not happy.

'Two unauthorised personnel with sonic pistols, both tampered with and illegally coded above Level 3. Now, how has that happened?' With his tone of voice, Searle may as well have been pointing a finger at Richard, who subsequently stood up, making it Searle's turn to look up.

'I accept full responsibility for the weapon,' Richard said. 'It's been cleared by the CO.'

'Really? Then you're culpable. Dereliction of duty, I would say, wouldn't you?'

Rachel ignored Searle's pathetic remark and looked directly at Richard. Her expression was troubled, as if Richard had failed to share some emotional secret with her. She turned and left quickly for the sickbay, without saying another word.

Searle smirked and continued. 'I'll take that weapon, thank you.'

'Negative,' replied Richard ready for a stand off. 'It's authorised, as I said!'

Searle looked around at the other men. 'Dismissed!' he barked, then turned slowly, almost dramatically, back to look Richard in the eyes. 'There will be charges to answer,' he said with a callous grin. 'Be prepared and make yourself available within the next day or two.' Then he turned to leave.

'Don't forget the crystals, Searle,' Richard replied, equally sourly. 'I suggest you get your men back.'

Searle squirmed; visibly embarrassed, he stopped short of the open doors. Still facing them as he spoke, the tone of his voice was one of barely contained frustration.

'I'm fully aware that the crystals are my responsibility and I don't need you to remind me of my job!' He found and then spoke into his communicator. 'Warrant Officer Machin, return to the transport dome immediately!'

Richard left the bay, shaking his head.

CHAPTER 13

Lost Wisdom

A little less than two hours later, with Richard drinking a blend of coffee made primarily from the ground shells of homegrown Brazil nuts, and staring blankly at his cabin wall, Rachel paged him.

'Richard, are you there?'

'Yes, I am.'

' Listen, I have some bad news I'm afraid.'

'Go on?'

'It's about Miles, Richard, I'm so sorry. He's passed away.'

'What? How can that be? He was fine.' Richard leapt to his feet.

'He looked fine, I agree,' said Rachel softly. 'I'm still trying to find out exactly what has happened. He was stabilised and sedated, sleeping. He didn't feel anything, I'm sure.'

'Oh, come on, Rachel,' retorted Richard, growing angry and upset. 'Miles would not have just died in his sleep. He, I, I mean I knew him too well. He wouldn't have.'

Sensing that Richard needed some additional information, Rachel continued. 'I think a blood clot from his wound became detached and lodged in his heart. I think he had a thrombosis, Richard. But I won't know for sure until I have done an autopsy.'

Richard sat down, shocked. He could not believe it.

'Are you all right, Richard?' Rachel enquired sympathetically.

'Yes, I'll talk to you later.' Richard turned off the intercom. After a few moments, he realised that he was sitting on his laptop, which was still concealed under his mattress. He stood up, checking for damage and placed it back on his desk.

'Lucky,' he said, opening the cover.

For some reason he thought about the other man that Miles had recognised, the accomplice; obviously directly involved in Jennifer Middleton's death and probably the theft of the crystals, to boot.

'Was it Renton Dublovnic? It had to be! Who else could it be, unless there was another person involved? Did Dublovnic fire the fatal shot at Miles? Moreover, what of Bill Bradley, my old friend from way back, dead! Why had he become involved, surely not for money?'

Saddened, Richard reached across to Rachel's call button, and then paused, having had second thoughts.

There was no point in asking Rachel; Miles would not have mentioned it, he knew that.

Richard sat for almost an hour, thinking. He knew Commander Miko would be calling for a report on the day's tragic outcome, and any updated espionage theories, and he would want it pronto. Searle would no doubt take full credit for recovering the crystals; it just wasn't worth going there, he concluded. Miles had not married and he knew his nominated next of kin was his mother, who lived near Manchester. Commander Miko would no doubt write to her in due course. Richard was not in the right frame of mind for an interview with Searle, or the Commander for that matter, so typed a brief e-diction and mailed it to them both, hoping it would buy him a few days to get his thoughts together.

Unusually, Rachel had not called; so by nine, having missed dinner, he decided to take his mind off things, and do some more work on the log. Unable to concentrate, however, he flipped through the reflective pages almost aimlessly. What caught his eye though, were the last few pages. They were a different format, a different typeface, informal. Richard opened his laptop and scrolled through the pages on the screen until he identified the same in his programme; then, selecting decode, he waited.

What appeared on the screen was nothing short of dynamite. At any other time, in any other place, the revelations that unfolded in front of him would have heralded a new chapter in human history. Indeed, one so earth shattering that it would split the established evolutionary, anthropological and religious communities into as many parts, as the years that their beliefs had been held.

Richard began to read, got halfway down the page, and stopped.

This script, these writings, they would stop an entire army of sceptics, he thought.

The two pages of text were the informal writings of the Ark's captain: an unofficial account of his people's history, written, it appeared, on a final voyage. Awe-struck, Richard went back to the beginning and started again.

Diary of Admirel Dirkot Urket

On the eve of this final journey, I scribe these thoughts. Mostly for thyself, as I know many in kinship do likewise, but also for diarist, as destiny may this voyage foretell its course for my kind. This quest, at the least doomed, at most the destiny of our souls, but as wanting as the light of a coming dawn. I am I yearn with the heaviness of heart that weighs with bidding forever farewell to my brethren, but blessed too with the smile of hope and gaiety of spirit that we may yet bring salvation to our creed. The history of my kind who abided on Homer, a fair body in the heavens of Zodiac, arises from the dusk of our mother place, the curtain of its lifelessness falling many myriad distant. Of all those that joyed on that most beau of celests only four vessels set forth. Two from the land of Sapia, five score and ten from the north, fair of skin and fair of pride yet fierce that none would cross. So too a dozen less a century from the south, white of hair and blue for seeing. From Meh Hecoe fortune bestowed a full century and four score, their kind dark of skin with hair black as night. Graced the last to account their lives from the consuming fire, but two score and a dozen less one from Mohenjo, thin of eye and yellow their look. These four chariots of kind sought the heavens, only these from so many, their beginnings no more a place. Many suns passed by and as many bodies. Monumental some, meagre others, until after a full celestial epoch the fairest place was behold and it was bequest them. In time, great places arose and prospered. The Sapiens of the north in Eridu, of the south in Atlantis. In Te Agi Wakhan the Mayans and in Mohenjo Daro the Harappas, all fairly multiplied. Ordained for two millennia all prospered, their numbers spreading the land until in much less time fortune changed. Great movements begot Eridu and later vast waters to eclipse Atlantis, of Mohenjo Daro a mountain of fire scorched so naught remained. But of Te Agi Wakhan the stone of light snuffed, its civil just to disperse. Of the stone that lit Eridu, two fragments were redeemed. One used thereafter to light Babylon, its great gardens a millennia to keep homage to those the lost. The other protected by a sacred casket, looked upon by angels until graced by understanding. Low, over the annals of time the stone that gave Babylon life has too waned. So be it to those here gathered, entrusted by our brethren the remaining, to breathe life into this our last hope, The Star. Should we be able to seek our kind and others for salvation. May Astrolias be with us, for in faith we will find the course.

'My God,' said Richard, mesmerised, if not hypnotised, by the text, which he read again, several times, until the flashing red light on his intercom panel caught his eye. Richard deselected the privacy function, surprised by the late hour. The message key indicated that he had been called; it was Rachel.

'Richard it's me, are you OK? I've called you several times, I'm waiting. Call me back.'

As it was almost midnight he hesitated, but Rachel wouldn't be asleep, Richard thought.

'You awake?' he said softly into the microphone.

After some delay, Rachel answered. 'Just out of the shower, it's been a long day. How are you feeling?'

'Shell-shocked to be honest. Sad for Miles, he was a good man and a good friend.'

'Yes, I know Richard. Life on Mars appears to be losing

its simple appeal.'

'Rachel, you know the boss has asked me to find out who's behind all this trouble?'

'Er, yes. I got that impression.'

'So I need to find the identity of the other man involved in the shoot out, for want of a better expression. Do you have any ideas, suspicions, anything?'

'No, I don't. Not a clue.'

'I see,' Richard hesitated. 'You know there's only one thing worse than an enemy, and that's an unknown enemy. Anyway, I have something else to talk to you about, regarding the other thing. Have you got any spare time tomorrow?'

'Yes. I can meet you for lunch in the restaurant, say twelve thirty?'

'OK, twelve thirty it is. Look forward to it. Have a good rest.'

'And you Richard.'

CHAPTER 14

Special Delivery

It had been two days since his lunch date with Rachel and he had not seen her since; but Richard was still a little troubled by their conversation. Having spent a good deal of time detailing the text he had discovered and how it proved, unequivocally, that the human race, *Homo sapiens*, were after all, seeded by visitors from another planet, Rachel just had not seemed moved.

He was still surprised and disappointed; after all, the ramifications of such revelations would be far reaching to say the least. Instead, she had seemed much more interested in The Star, its log and how the crystals fitted into the scheme of things.

Richard leaned back in his chair and rubbed his eyes. His cabin, lit only by the glow of his computer screen, and the small shaving light above the washbasin, looked as if a bomb had hit it. This, in itself, was unusual for Richard, who normally had a place for everything. At almost two in the morning, he had been at his desk for the best part of twenty hours, save for a few 'natural' breaks. During their discussion, Rachel had enquired, quite out of character he had noted, as to how the crystals had been harnessed, in order to power the space ship. At the time, he didn't know; but he did now, to some extent anyway.

Richard reselected a page from the log that he had referred to several times over the past few hours. It was an overview of the ship's primary power system and the schematic reminded him of drawings he had studied years earlier during his engineering training. The system appeared strikingly similar to that of the obsolete nuclear reactor plants of the 1960s, a generation of low efficiency reactors which ran on for more than fifty years, and in some countries of the world, even longer. However, in this case, at the heart of the 'reactor' was the crystal, clearly shown as a complete sphere. The accompanying script was equally explanatory. The crystal was also shown to be encased, protected, by a much larger sphere of a transparent material labelled 'glasifate'. His theory about the glass fragments was, after all, correct.

At first he had seemed surprised, amazed even, at how close these words appeared to be to recognisable English words. However, English he knew, a good deal of it anyway, had been derived from Latin and other indo-European vocabularies, and these languages had much earlier roots. Considering it further, it seemed logical. These people had brought their language with them, and as their descendants had become the dominant species on earth, their language would form the basis of future derivatives.

Richard worked diligently gathering an understanding of The Star's systems and made a few notes on his computer scratch pad. He studied the 'core' diagram again and identified an intricate series of 'conduits' that stippled the heavy jacket shrouding the glasifate sphere. Labelled 'magnetronic ducts', they ran rearwards towards the exhaust nozzles. Surrounding this jacket was an intricate cooling system.

'The glass was a protective barrier, an insulator in this installation,' he thoughtfully considered. 'So it can still be now, I've already found that out in part. What's more, The Star left earth with an incomplete crystal, part of one, that's clear from the diary entry; and apparently, it was nearly exhausted by thousands of years of previous use. No wonder the ship didn't get far! What were they thinking? Why launch a one-way mission; it was suicide! Why were they so desperate?'

Richard's thoughts digressed; he looked at a reference book lying on his desk. It had been leant to him by Mary Ann from geology, more as a joke than anything else, after she had heard about his visit to the library. Mary was an archaeologist by trade.

'Would she be impressed by this?' he whispered to himself, smiling.

Richard stared at the books cover and its bold title

The Origins of Mankind, for several seconds, and then focused on the thought provoking colour photograph. It was an old book, well-thumbed, and the picture of a semi-crouching primate, complete with man-like features, seemed somehow quite plausible, despite areas of his body being completely erased.

'Hidden, like the truth!' he whispered again, absorbed in his thoughts.

The book was first published in 1986, but as Mary had explained, it was still a leading reference work on the subject. Richard had barely started it, only the first few chapters.

'No wonder a genetic chasm exists between Neanderthal man and *Homo sapiens.* All that time looking for the 'missing link'. It was never found, because it never existed. The Yeti and the others for that matter, a load of rubbish. We didn't evolve from the primates at all. Neanderthals and their like walked a one way street, tens of thousands of years earlier; to a dead end, literally!'

With that, Richard shut down the computer, closed the lid and removed the health chip. He had developed a sullen expression, as if weighed down by the implications of his discovery. He looked at the time, two thirty and hesitated momentarily. He had a letter to write, to his mother; one was overdue anyway. He had best do it now!

Levels View Cottage
Chalice End
Buckersmead
Nr Martock
Somerset
United Kingdom

Dear Mother,

I hope this letter finds you well and as I write, enjoying the last weeks of your English summer. You always love them, don't you? All things being equal, you should be reading this sometime in early February, sadly with last summer's memories long since forgotten. For me, its mid August, the fourteenth to be precise, although the time of year makes very little difference here. I understand from Laura that you have had more than your fair share of rain over the last few weeks and the 'levels' are already overflowing. Very unusual for the time of year I must say, but then, you have said for years that the seasons were becoming disorientated. Anyway, I trust you can still make it through to Muchelney Ham, as I know how much you hate driving all the way round when visiting Aunt Pamela.

Listen Mum, I am not going to say too much because it will be old news and irrelevant by the time you receive this note and the accompanying parcel. The contents of the box you have unwrapped are very, very, special; more so than I can say at this point in time. It is not too heavy and I would like you to store it for me. Somewhere 'out of sight and out of mind' so to speak, but definitely as far away from the house as possible. If it's not full of water, possibly the car pit in Dad's old workshop, then covered by the wooden sleepers? Please don't ask anyone to help and DO NOT tell anyone about it, even Rebecca. Handle it carefully Mum. If it sounds as if it is full of broken glass, don't worry; it is, amongst other things!

Now this is the important part. If I haven't called you by the 16th, please carefully place the parcel in another larger box with plenty of foam packaging. Seal it and have it collected by Royal Distribution, guaranteed secure delivery.

Address it as follows -

Doctor DN Marsh

Department of Physics and Astropropulsion

St. Mary's College

Bristol University

Somerset

Oh and don't worry, there is a note of explanation inside for the Doc.

Keep well Mum, I'll be in touch and thanks,

Love Richard

P.S. Not Laura and definitely not Rebecca!!!

The following morning Richard made his way

cautiously to the Flight Control Centre carrying his suitably packaged helmet box under one arm. In an effort to avoid embarrassing questions or arouse any suspicions, he went the long way round, through the biodome and the oxygen recycling plant, which bypassed the busy areas. Outside the large swing-doors of the dispatch section stood two security guards, one of whom he knew.

'Morning, David,' he said nonchalantly. 'Routine samples for the shuttle, sadly a little late!'

Sergeant David Norman looked both surprised and perplexed. 'You know the rules, Sir!' he said. 'All freight for earth is screened first by J Section, decontaminated and then tagged. It arrives in dispatch by departmental container, not by hand!'

'Yes, I know David, but the geology container has already been processed and is being loaded this morning,' Richard replied.

With round the clock security cover, he knew he was going to have a job getting past, so he changed his tack a little.

'I appreciate your problem, Sir, but this is highly irregular, maybe I should call my supervisor?'

'Look, David,' said Richard, shaking his head to indicate that that wouldn't be necessary. 'I'll nip down to J Section, get the thing processed and tagged, they're only rock samples for God's sake, then I'll come back. How does that sound?' Richard looked at his watch, pressing for a decision.

At that moment, as if by design, the PA sounded.

'Lieutenant Commander Reece to sickbay please, Lieutenant Commander Reece to sickbay.'

Pressing his point, Richard continued, 'look David, I'm in a bit of a hurry, what do you say?'

'Um, well, er, OK, Sir, I guess that will be acceptable.'

Richard did not hesitate, but made his way quickly to J Section. Leaving the box outside he walked into the cluttered, busy room. Sandra Powell, apparently the only operative on duty, looked up.

'Good morning, Richard,' she said, smiling at her visitor, 'checking on your container?'

'Er, yes, as a matter of fact I am, and good morning to you, too.'

'Well it's gone through, no problems, but it's absolutely full and a few kilograms overweight, so forget anything else! There is nothing else, right?'

'Nothing at all,' replied Richard, looking around at the desks and packing tables. 'Just thought I would check on its progress, you know, part of the job, that sort of thing,' he continued, smiling back at Sandra.

'Fortunately I have some spare capacity in the engineering consignment, so there is no weight problem this time.'

Richard smiled again, nodding his approval. He could see a reel of red release tags on the table close to Sandra.

'Good, thanks, much appreciated,' he said, walking over to her. 'Been busy?' he continued casually.

'Actually yes,' replied Sandra impatiently. A laboratory technician by trade, Scottish, medium height, a pretty brunette with fair skin and attractive green eyes; she normally exhibited a very congenial personality. However, being seconded to J Section for the week, particularly the one prior to the shuttle's return flight, had obviously stressed her.

'So you managed to get it all in?'

'Yes,' Sandra replied again, her brow furrowed.

'Then I owe you!'

She laughed, 'Ha! You've said that before, I know.'

Richard looked hurt.

Sandra finished packing a small box, tagged it and then walked over to the tetralene-fibre conveyor belt, which rumbled gently on aluminium rollers, before disappearing through a flapping rubber skirt into the dispatch section. Richard saw his chance and peeled off a tag, placing the reel back on the counter just as Sandra turned.

'Is there anything else, Richard? I'm beginning to think this is a social call!'

'No, no, that's it, just to say thanks.' Richard winced and wasted no time in making for the door. 'See you later then,' he said without turning.

Sandra had no cause to answer; she had obviously heard that line before!

Outside Richard quickly checked in each direction and then stuck the red release tag onto the lid of his parcel. He made his way quickly back to dispatch.

'There you go, David,' he said confidently. 'Checked, scanned, decontaminated and tagged, as required.'

The security guard hesitated, looking at his companion for a moment, who offered no help in making the decision.

'Um, OK Sir.' He paused, 'I'll feel better if I take it from here, Sir, you know, security?'

'Fully understand, David,' replied Richard, thrusting the box into the security guard's hands. 'That's fine by me, place it with the engineering consignment. Apparently, geology is full. Oh, and be careful not to shake it,' he concluded, forcing a smile.

David Norman looked at him with an apprehensive almost anxious expression, whilst Richard, trying to maintain his composure, suspected that he might have gone just a little too far with that last remark.

'Just joking,' he said quickly, spinning on his heels. 'Thanks very much David, appreciate your help. Must get down to sickbay, I'm running late.'

As he turned the corner at the end of the corridor, Richard looked back to see Norman returning through the main doors, empty handed.

'Helpful,' he said to himself, 'a bit of luck in life.'

CHAPTER 15

Mother Earth

Moon Shuttle ISS Nexus eventually broke through the seemingly endless layers of thick black cloud, about two hundred feet above Cape Canaveral's northern landing platform, coded November One. Intense white light from the sodium illumination system, positioned circumferentially around the elliptical landing platform, cut through the dense, murky drizzle; powerful spotlights piercing a darkened sky, yet visibility was still abysmal. It was eleven am unified time.

'Nexus, this is terminal control. You are clear to land.'

'Roger control, we're coming down.'

The International Space Shuttle Nexus was one of the current generation of shuttle operating the four-day round trip between earth and the moon base Andromeda. The large S series of craft, commencing with the original S1s, had flown the service for the past twenty years, ever since the permanent international base had been established. Two round trips to the American space terminal in Florida and one to the European Terminal in Strasbourg per week, was the normal schedule. Nexus, second of the three S2 shuttles capable of the Mars transit, landed amid clouds of steam as its six cryogenic retro rockets vaporised standing water on the platform.

'Nexus closing down. Nice weather?' came the unusually flippant remark over the control frequency.

'Platform secured,' replied the controller. 'Yeah, sorry about that, hasn't let up for a month or more.' The two crew members wasted no time in closing down the shuttle's integrated flight systems and made their way to the terminal for a much-needed coffee. A while later, with an appointment to make, the shuttle commander Major Tom Race stepped through the sliding portal door from the crew lounge and walked quickly the hundred metres or so to the main entrance of the terminal. Stepping outside, grim faced, he looked up at the dark forbidding sky. Several spots of rain splashed on him in quick succession, leaving dirty circular marks on his smart cream coloured flight suit. He tried to brush them off as if they were insects, but only succeeded in smudging the marks into unsightly streaks. Holding the door open for a greying, late fifties, United States Airforce Force officer in dress uniform, they both quickly stepped inside.

' Sir, how long has it been like this?' he asked of Colonel

Roper, the Terminal Director.

'When was your last visit?' enquired the Colonel.

'Well, I haven't been down for, um, it's got to be three months.'

'Yep, that's about right. It started with a deep meteorological depression, way up to the north; caused extensive and unusually thick cloud cover. After three or four weeks, sufficient pollution was trapped beneath and in the clouds to lower the surface temperature by an average ten degrees celsius. That had the effect of creating more cloud, increasing the pollution count to a record 'six-eighty' and it hasn't stopped raining, well, for at least two months. The phenomenon is self-perpetuating, Tom. It's colder so everybody's burning more fossil fuel in their homes, at work and in industry; more pollution, more micro particles for water condensation, therefore more cloud and so it goes on.' Colonel Roper looked out at the bleak scene through the large, copper tinted windows.

'They've tried everything possible, even detonating a twelve kiloton tactical nuclear weapon in Arizona; about a hundred feet above the desert surface, in an attempt to heat up the atmosphere and create a window to the sun, but the cloud's too thick and getting worse every day. Even Colorado and Texas are recording record lows for this time of year, down to daytime temperatures of five degrees and more rain than they can handle.'

'Gee,' replied Tom Race, 'sounds pretty well hopeless. We can see the extent of the cloud cover on monitors in

Andromeda. It's also covering most of Europe and Asia. Even so, most of the moonbase staff aren't aware of the situation, that it's so bad. Nobody is!'

'Well, that's because the State Department are playing it down at the moment. It'll cause widespread panic if the real situation gets out. And there's more,' Colonel Roper paused to look at his watch, 'but that'll have to wait until the brief and its time for that right now. We had better go!'

Tom Race signalled to his co-pilot who was talking to some other airforce pilots as he and the Colonel marched across the open reception area. Tom pointed at his watch and held up three fingers indicating three hours. Lieutenant Chan Sung acknowledged with a nod and a relaxed salute. Striding purposefully through a side door, then down the broad steps in front of the space terminal, Tom struggled to keep up with the Colonel.

'So what's this other matter, Colonel; some discovery on Mars?'

'You'll hear all about it in due course,' Colonel Roper replied coldly. 'Which reminds me, did your President's Level Class 1 Security Clearance come through?'

'Er, yes Sir.' Tom responded. 'Last week, I'm up to speed.'

'Good, the system works,' said the Colonel with a smile. 'Nobody under President's Level will make this brief.'

The two men climbed into a large black limousine, which was waiting in the covered VIP parking area.

'Morning Sergeant, HQ please, as quickly as possible.'

'Yes, Colonel, right away, Sir,' replied the Airforce driver.

The operations building was only about fifteen minutes drive down towards the old launch sites of the Saturn rocket programme. It was a particularly tall building for the area, being some fifty storeys high and sheathed almost entirely in glass. It was not however, as impressive as it should have been, the blue green panels looking blemished and discoloured by black clouds and persistent acid rain. As Tom was to find out, the most impressive part of the building was underground. Nothing was said during the uneventful drive and the two men subsequently stepped from the car into a large underground parking area.

'We shall be a good three hours,' remarked Roper to his driver. 'Get a coffee or something.'

'Yes, Sir,' replied the driver looking slightly agitated at the three closed circuit TV cameras watching his every move.

The two men strode purposefully up the stairs to the main doors and had their ID cards checked by a number of uniformed and armed security officers. Once inside and walking past the reception desk, Colonel Roper caught the eye of a female Non Commissioned Officer. 'Has it started yet?' he asked impatiently.

'Morning Colonel,' she replied. 'The President arrived fifteen minutes early, Sir, so it's probably just getting under way. Security's waiting; take lift number two, Sir, down the corridor and to your right.'

Shaking his head in disbelief that the briefing might have started early, Roper's rejoinder was curt.

'Call down to Harrison. Tell him to stall it, we'll be there in ten minutes.'

'I'll do that, Sir,' came the reply.

Pacing off toward the lift, Roper turned to Tom.

'What do you know about the Accelercom, son?'

'Well Sir, it revolutionised interplanetary communications from its introduction some five years ago,' replied Tom, somewhat startled by the question.

'OK and what about the physics?'

'Well, the system is still top secret, but basically speech from a microphone is digitised into electromagnetic pulses, in the ultra violet frequency range, if I recall. These pulses are then fired into a spiral acceleration device, which uses the 'push pull' effects of fixed magnets around the circumference. Switching of the magnetic polarities first to provide a pulling force and then a pushing effect as the pulse passes, was the breakthrough. I understand that a nano second interchange is now possible. The pulses are accelerated to around twice the speed of visible light and then fired into space to a receiver. As I understand it; the receiver unit decelerates the pulses in a dense magnetic flux chamber which then converts them back to audible sound.'

'OK, you've got it. So what was the benefit and who invented it?' continued Roper as the lift door shut behind them.

'Well, the main benefit is that it reduced the twenty minute or so communication delay between earth and Mars to just a few seconds, almost real time, no delay, no echo. With regards earth to moon communications, well it's like talking to someone across the street. As for the inventor, Sir, NASA has kept that under wraps.' The lift passed subterranean level seventeen, still going down.

'The inventor was one of our top brains,' explained Roper. 'Professor Sidney J Sanders, originally from England but naturalised several years ago. He was with NASA for more than twenty years and he went missing about five weeks ago under suspicious and as yet unsolved circumstances. There had been no trace of him until five days ago.' Roper paused. 'Subterranean level thirty four,' the lift's synthetic voice announced as the doors opened. The two men stepped out, with Major Race looking slightly in awe of the surroundings.

Roper continued. 'His body turned up in the Everglades, half eaten by alligators; it was identified by the one remaining plastic filled wisdom tooth. Everything else was beyond recognition. We believe that he was murdered. His left hand was gone, missing, clean off; we believe that it had been surgically removed, as had his right eye.'

The two men reached the security point at the end of a one hundred metre long straight corridor; they passed no doors or branching corridors, just polished floors and remote cameras. Roper looked directly at Tom. 'The security measures in place here at that time, and for several years prior, had been a dual left hand finger print and palm scan and a right eye retina scan. We are ninety nine percent sure that an intruder with a transplanted left hand and right eye made it through the check point, and with the security codes extracted prior to Sander's death, gained access to the most secret files in the country, probably even the world.'

'Saliva on here, Sir, and first booth on the left for a urine sample,' said a man's voice in a matter of fact manner.

'Major Race, Sir,' said the voice again. Tom was jolted from his thoughts. 'I'm sorry,' he said, startled.

'Saliva on here, Sir, and first booth on the left for a urine sample,' repeated the Afro American security guard.

'It's the new procedure since the security breech,' explained Colonel Roper. 'The samples have to be within point eight of a degree of body temperature, thirty eight point four degrees. That's a maximum of twenty seconds between passing and analysis.'

'But you have nothing to compare the data with,' said Tom.

'Your last routine medical, Tom,' replied the Colonel. 'We have the DNA breakdown of everyone who is in the programme above classified level.'

Tom nervously spat onto the glass slide, which then drew back into a small glass-fronted chamber in the wall, and was scanned by an orange beam of light from the chamber' s ceiling. Then, stepping into the booth, he passed a small sample of urine into a test tube, which he placed into a rack that again withdrew into a glass-fronted chamber for analysis. After scanning had taken place the contents of the tube was discharged into a hole in the side of the chamber. Seconds later, two green lights appeared above his head accompanied by two simultaneous tones.

'Very clinical,' said Tom.

The heavy security doors in front of him opened automatically and he stepped through, to be met by Colonel Roper who had successfully passed through the right hand channel. Both men continued to walk towards the two main doors of the theatre complex. Above the doors, an illuminated sign read 'Brief in Progress, Security PL1'. Roper paused momentarily outside the doors and turned to Tom.

'What you are about to hear has the highest security rating in the United States. In Europe, only the UK is already party to it; elsewhere in the world, no one else knows. We are briefing the top Europeans now, including François Margot the European President; Prime Minister Pushtan of Great Britain; Chancellor Heist of Germany and President Nokilstovic of Russia. Tomorrow it's the turn of China, Scandinavia and the Pacific Rim Federation. It's now a matter of necessity. Intelligence have confirmed the evidence, it's unequivocal. The intruder secured eighty to eighty five percent of the information about to be disclosed a little less than one month ago. We know certain organisations are now preparing to use it. Listen carefully.'

The two men walked quietly into the briefing theatre and took up their seats in the second row from the front. The brief was already under way. The President of the United States turned briefly to acknowledge Colonel Roper with a gesture of his head. Roper responded similarly. The brief continued. General Sherman Collins took the podium.

'Ladies and gentlemen, now that the introductions and formalities have been completed I'd like to get down to business. The brief you are about to hear is United States Security Classification President's Level 1 and European Top Secret Level 5. Shortly you will hear why these security measures are in place. The brief will last approximately one hour.' Major Race sat back in his seat and relaxed a little for the first time that day.

'As you may be aware, the latest figures on global cooling have identified the earth's atmosphere as being in a catastrophic, self perpetuating situation we have called the 'cold soak' syndrome. The scientific community responsible for forecasting the current climatic trends has been alarmed at the rate at which the earth is losing its heat, subsequent to the YASBAT effect. It is estimated that, with the present atmospheric pollution levels, the remaining three thousand square miles of clear sky, giving uninterrupted solar heating, which is centred over Mauritius, a small group of islands in the mid-Indian Ocean, will close in six months. This projection does not include an estimated three percent increase in present levels of carbonic pollution, month-on-month, as the

Pacific Rim area experiences an acceleration of the cooling process. Similar to that seen over Central Europe earlier this year. Ladies and gentlemen, the average temperature of the earth's surface is now seven degrees celsius. By December, it is likely to be minus one degree. I am aware that most of the audience here today does not have a scientific background. Therefore, in order for these people to fully understand the implications of what has been called an environmental 'catch twenty two' situation I will at this time cover some of the background.

As you are aware, the World Environmental Organisation, probably the most powerful global multinational organisation, voted to ban all nuclear power stations back in 2014. This followed the Hingsae Nuclear Reactor meltdown in China in 2008, and the similar but averted meltdown of the Risbek reactor in Israel in 2013. Despite the decommissioning of all remaining nuclear power stations by 2016, radioactive pollutants in the atmosphere are today still present at levels ranging from seven to eleven percent, and this some forty years after the Hingsae incident.

We all remember I'm sure, OPEC ceasing exports of crude oil from the Gulf region in February 2039. This was in response to its depleted reserves falling to an estimated four point five percent and as a result, oil prices rose at that time by almost nine hundred percent. Although we did not fully realise it at the time, that point was pivotal for the problems we have today. People throughout the world returned to burning the primary carbonics for energy; coal and coke where it was available, but wood where it was not. Worldwide, over the last ten years, monitored atmospheric carbon dioxide and microscopic pollutants have steadily risen by nine percent and thirty-seven percent respectively, based on reference data from the year 2007. As of last year, there are no weather significant rain forest regions remaining anywhere on the surface of the planet. Latest indications are that the Siberian oil reserves are also presently less than four percent and the South American fields are all but exhausted due to the insatiable demand from its own population, and that of North America. Indeed, globally, it is predicted less than nine months reserves remain at present usage. The adverse weather systems in the Polar regions are making exploration and extraction of known reserves pretty much impossible. It is therefore estimated, that Europe and Asia will exhaust their remaining oil and gas supplies, including their entire reserves, in ten to twelve months from now. As for the Americas and Pacific Rim regions, twelve to fifteen months from now. Concerning national coal reserves, that is a little more difficult to predict as most producers, principally in China and the US, are keeping what they have for contingency measures.

Ladies and gentlemen, that pretty much sums up the energy situation, or should I say lack of it. Now, before I brief you on what we understand of the current global weather systems, are there any questions?'

For several seconds a stunned silence pervaded the theatre. Eventually a representative of the European Democratic Republic enquired in a French accent.

'What, Sir, is the USA's stance on the question of the remaining gas and oil reserves in the North Sea, following NAO's backing of the United Kingdom?'

The general coughed into his fist and glanced quickly at the President. 'Well,' he continued somewhat hesitantly. 'That is a political issue for you people in Europe, but as a member of the North Atlantic Organisation, America must stand with the UK on that one. Quite honestly, Sir, we can see Britain's argument in withholding her remaining reserves from the EDR. After all, it was France and Germany who voted the UK, and, for that matter Spain and Holland, out of the old European Union, thereafter forming the European Democratic Union in its place with only selected members. And don't forget, if I may also point out, that it was France who undermined the stability of the old union on its fiftieth anniversary by refusing to accept the otherwise unanimous decision of that union to universally adopt English as the official European language. So, quite frankly, Sir, what do you expect?' The general's attention was momentarily diverted as he listened intently to a message through his discrete earpiece. 'I am instructed, however, to reiterate that this question is not an issue at this briefing. Thank you.' The Frenchman returned to his seat, visibly disgruntled. Another member of the audience rose to question the speaker.

'Why, Sir, does America expect over a year's reserves when most other countries will run out in the coming months?' Again this was a somewhat difficult if not embarrassing question for the General, who hesitated momentarily.

'Um, the United States capped most of its wells several years ago, as I'm sure you know. Since 2039 we have bought almost entirely from South America, progressively opening up our own wells to make up any deficit. Now that our prime supplier is empty, we will be feeding ourselves!' He paused again briefly to regain his momentum. 'Now I would like to continue with the brief.' He moved back towards his lectern and, taking up his position behind it, generated a three dimensional image of a slowly rotating planet earth on the large central screen. 'As many of you will know, coal powered generating stations now produce approximately seventy three percent of the world's electricity. NAO members Norway, Holland and the UK, have some limited natural gas supplies for vehicles and domestic use, and some hydro-electric power. However, as with other countries, such as Canada, this represents less than ten percent of total requirement. Asia and South America are now relying almost totally on wood and are rapidly approaching total deforestation. As a direct result of these processes, our latest figures indicate a global cloud coverage of ninety three percent, the average thickness now being close to three miles. In some areas it is almost twice that. The thickness is increasing daily as carbonic contaminants provide microscopic coalescent nuclei for further water droplet formation.' The General dwelt on that point for a second or two and then reiterated it. 'Basically more contamination, more cloud. This brings me back to this position.' He used a laser pointer to indicate a clear area over the Indian Ocean. 'Three thousand square miles of clear sky and closing rapidly!'

He paused again in order that the enormity of the statement should become painfully apparent. Then he looked straight at the audience focusing on several individual faces as he scanned the rows. He again reiterated the stark facts. 'Seven degrees celsius is currently the average global surface temperature. Six, maybe seven months from now, when this baby closes, it will be minus seven degrees and there will be no carbon-based fuels remaining anywhere in the world. Ladies and gentlemen, we have a very serious problem and it is not going to go away!'

The theatre was large and tiered. At least a hundred people attended the briefing, mainly in the centre section. Nevertheless, after the General's last statement you could have heard a pin drop. The General looked at the US President as if for permission to continue. The President gave a barely perceptible nod.

'Ladies and gentlemen; your attention please. A little under five weeks ago a discovery was made on Mars which has the potential to save mankind from this dilemma. We have discovered a source of energy. In its raw state this energy seems boundless to such an extent that our people are experiencing problems with containment. Since the initial discovery, work has been continuing twenty four seven on Mars and a breakthrough has been achieved; rumour has it, quite by chance. The energy source takes the form of crystals. These were discovered in the Kalahari Basin region, which is a large impact crater and actually on the surface, but I hasten to add, it appears in a very limited quantity.' He briefly referred to his notes and then continued. 'In a little over two weeks from today an unscheduled supply shuttle, using the new S3 system will leave earth's orbit. This new shuttle reduces transit time, incredible as it may seem, to a little over six days and with the new miniaturised Accelercom system we anticipate real time communications all the way. In addition, by this time, the science department assures me that Mars will have safe containment of the so-called Kalahari crystals. Bluntly, ladies and gentlemen, these crystals are 'hot' in more than one sense of the word!' A wry smile surfaced before being stifled. 'At least as hot as the core of a nuclear reactor if not more so, maybe even the surface of the sun itself, but, and this is the critical factor; with no detectable radioactivity. Clean, acceptable and limitless energy; green as grass.' The General paused again, his face relaxing, even smiling, with the delivery of good news.

"Knowledge is power, ladies and gentlemen. We have kept the wraps on this so tight that not even Congress knew about it. Security on Mars is such that not even a microbe can escape that station. Sadly however, having said that, we believe that a security breach has taken place here on earth. You will recall the sudden and unexplained disappearance of Professor Sidney J Sanders, the eminent scientist and inventor of the Accelercom. The recent grim discovery of his half-eaten and mutilated remains in the Everglades indicates intruder access at the highest security level.' The General walked across the stage to the lectern and pressed a button. Projected onto the screen were a series of images; he looked up at them. 'We are concerned about this.' His laser pointer projected an arrow onto the screen. 'We have been monitoring three massive construction sites for a little less than fifteen months. Each site covers at least fifty hectares. One here in Brazil, South America, one here in the Yangsei Delta region of China and one here in the Black Forest region of Germany. In two to three months, our intelligence sources estimate the buildings on these three sites will be operational. The construction effort is immense. They resemble the old nuclear reactor powered electrical generating stations of the type used extensively in the fifty years preceding the Risbec protocol. As I am sure you all recall, subsequent to that catastrophic problem, the protocol both banned and required the global dismantling of all nuclear power stations, commissioned or not. These buildings, however, are on a scale much larger than anything previously built on the surface of this planet.' The image changed to a satellite photograph of one of the sites. 'The electrical terminals being constructed here, here and here, are indeed on such a scale that our calculations indicate that these three stations alone could produce approximately forty percent of the entire electrical demand of South America, China and Europe respectively. In addition, we have evidence of a fourth site, of similar size, being cleared in the Congo Basin region of central Africa. Again, only a massive nuclear reactor, of enormous potential, could hope to produce the water vapour required to turn these babies.' His laser pointed to several rectangular buildings, each the size of a large aircraft carrier and each with giant semi-circular extensions to the roof. 'These, ladies and gentlemen, are multiple steam turbine systems, and they are, well, pretty impressive to say the least. Our science people tell us that the generating potential of these sites could be over a billion kilowatts, each! Incidentally, the common players relating to each of these sites are the world's greatest rivers!' The General paused again and briefly sipped from his glass. 'So, no shortage of water! Initially, our intelligence indicated that these stations were to be powered by massive nuclear reactors, probably fission type, these of course being universally banned by the international community. However, recent shifts in construction activity and material orders are beginning to indicate otherwise. Ladies and gentlemen,' the General stepped from behind the lectern and scanned the darkened theatre. 'We believe that the untried, untested and at the moment, barely controllable Kalahari crystals will form the heart of these generators.' There was a collective murmur from the auditorium. The General's face tightened slightly as he raised his arms for silence. 'Normally, I would be embarrassed to tell you that, despite the Risbec treaty, America retained a few of it's older nuclear power stations, as did the UK and Japan; possibly Russia did the same. Although,' he added swiftly, 'they were fully decommissioned. Work began in earnest on these sites a few weeks ago, again, twenty four seven. The mission? To modify and re-commission these stations and prepare them for the installation next month of the first shipment, perhaps the only shipment, of the Kalahari crystals. That is as little as four weeks from now if the Enigma lives up to NASA's predictions. However, by necessity, we are talking a much smaller scale: research, development, no accidents and no promises, just hope!' The General relaxed visibly as he took a deep breath and then concluded. 'There will be a more detailed brief for technical and scientific delegates later today. The final part of this brief will include the personal details of the team selected to retrieve the first crystals from Mars. Are there any questions at this stage?' A quickly fired question came from the audience.

'Who owns, or more to the point, who is funding these large power houses, General?'

The General found it impossible to pick out the questioner in the poor light and therefore addressed the audience generally. 'It's a good question and pertinent, but if you don't mind I won't go there today, Sir. In the cold light of day, we just do not have sufficient proof at this stage: just unconfirmed intelligence and theories regarding a whole lot of industrial espionage and a whole lot of money. What I can tell you, however, is that the three largest industrial conglomerates in the world: Spheron based in Strasbourg, Tongsei Heavy Industries based in Shanghai and Epsilon Rio based in Brazil are all registered owners of the land. The past record of these companies appears to be one of forced acquisitions, greed, corruption, and complete disregard for our environment. The Burspar disaster for instance; that resulted in sixteen hundred miles of highly radioactive coastal wasteland, and a significant proportion of the remaining cold ocean plankton decimated, for a thousand years or more! No clean up and no apology. I could go on but I am sure that you take my point. It does not take a genius to realise that if these corporations generate and control the world's energy supply, or just half of it for that matter,' he stopped suddenly and looked for a moment at the President before continuing. 'Well, that's one hell of a bargaining position. One more question, please.' It came from the front row.

'General, how many crystals are there and how long will they last?'

General Collins hesitated. 'The bottom line is we don't know. At the moment five have been reported: there maybe more, maybe not. Osiris has had problems with retrieval. We are hoping that they are some form of naturally occurring mineral, possibly an exposed seam or something. It may even be possible to synthesize them! I say again, we just don't know. If the numbers are limited we are going to be very disappointed.'

Another questioner shouted from the back. 'What kind of problems on Mars, General?' The General became visibly defensive in his demeanour. 'That's all from me, ladies and gentlemen, that's all we have time for. May I thank you for your attention. There will be a few minutes break, and then Colonel Todd Wilson of the National Aeronautics and Space Administration will complete the brief.'

The theatre fell silent for a moment, and then erupted with voices as a hundred conversations resonated around the cavernous room. The revelations induced a mixture of shock, surprise and disbelief in most of the officials. Several members of the audience, obviously secretaries, shuttled between senior officers, diplomats and parliamentary figures, taking notes and keying information into laptops. Tom Race could hardly believe his ears as he looked around at the bedlam of people. Several were now recognisable as Heads of State and senior government members now that the lights had been turned on. Roper, seeing Tom's expression, leaned towards him. 'Listen up son, the best is yet to come.'

At that moment, Colonel Todd Wilson in a United States Airforce uniform took the podium. The theatre, by now reaching a crescendo, hushed in anticipation. Wilson was a tall, stocky, smart looking man in his early fifties, with short, spiky fair hair. He was a veteran fighter pilot of the third middle-east conflict and an early generation shuttle pilot.

'Ladies and gentlemen,' he began. 'The United States Government has put together a team of the highest order. These men and women are to be entrusted with bringing safely back to earth the first shipment of crystals. These men and women are the best we've got. They are highly trained, highly experienced and highly motivated. They are drawn from several countries. The retrieval flight will be dangerous due to the hazardous nature of the cargo and a lack of knowledge of how these things will travel. I do not have to tell you how important it is for these crystals, all of them, to reach the proper authorities here in America, from where they will be distributed throughout the world. We expect the total shipment to weigh less than two kilograms. At all costs, they must not fall into the wrong hands. In order for national governments to be fully aware of and totally confident with the international team, I am now going to brief you on our selection.'

With these words, Colonel Wilson made a selection on the computer keyboard and as he did so, the large screen illuminated.

'The Commander of the mission will be Major T. J. Race, United States Air Force.' A photograph of Tom filled the screen. Tom immediately slid down in his seat and his eyes widened as he recognised it as one taken earlier in the year on moonbase.

Roper leant over and whispered, 'We're counting on

you Major, the decision was unanimous.'

'Major T.J Race,' Wilson continued. 'Joined the air force aged eighteen, now thirty-five. Joined NASA astronaut core 2035, graduated top of flight. Selected special duties 2038. Development test pilot XT44 Multi-role Interplanetary Shuttle and more recently the D Class Close Support Fighter. Orbital Pilot for the second manned Mars landing followed by various appointments. Promoted Executive Officer Moonbase Shuttle Wing December 2047. Qualifications: Masters Degree Propulsion Engineering. Status: Single. Relatives: Mother Irene alive lives in Connecticut. Father: The late Harrison Race, former senator. Security Code: Presidents Level 1 and ISSA Top Secret Class 5.'

Tom's jaw dropped open in stunned surprise.

'Relationships: currently none on record.'

He winced with embarrassment, looked down at his feet and muttered, 'what the hell difference does that make!'

Colonel Wilson continued. 'Second in Command; Commander Ronald Sampleman European Space and Science Agency. Joined United Kingdom Combined Services 2039 aged twenty-seven, now thirty-seven. Educated Oxford University, England. Winner of the Internationally acclaimed Wallrock Engineering prize for his pioneering work on magnetism. Commander Sampleman will be in charge of the engineering department and all aspects so related. Qualifications: Doctorate Fluid and Magnetic Engineering. Status: Single. Relatives: Father, currently living in London. Security Code: ISSA Top Secret Class 5 and US Presidents Level 1. Relationships: None on record.'

Wilson paused, allowing the information to be digested by his audience.

'First Pilot and Helmsman, Major Sam Brennan, United States Navy.'

This name immediately attracted Tom's attention. Looking up at the screen, he recognised the face by sight, but they had never met.

'Joined United States Navy aged 19, now thirty-three. Presently an instructor pilot serving in the National Space Administration Astronaut Academy where he originally graduated in 2035. Awarded Medal of Honour for his services during the Galileo Space Station incident three years later.'

Tom remembered the incident. Docking a shuttle during the space station break-up and rescuing a crew of fourteen called for superb handling skills. It made Brennan a national hero overnight. Tom was happy with this selection.

'Qualifications: Aerodynamics and Astrophysics Degree. Status: Widower. Relatives: Mother and father alive and living in Pittsburgh. Security Code: ISSA Top Secret Class 5, pending US President's Level 1.'

Just then, a security guard tapped Tom on the shoulder, 'Excuse me, Sir, could you pass this message to the Colonel?'

'Sure, Sergeant, no problem, thanks.'

Tom passed the white envelope to Colonel Roper who

quickly read the message. He leant forwards and whispered into the President's ear. The President nodded without turning his head. Roper looked at Tom and patting him gently on the shoulder said, 'We've got to go, son, they need your shuttle back at Andromeda with parts for the Enigma programme and a line of modifications as soon as possible.'

The pair stood up and walked between the seat rows towards the door through which they had entered. Noticing the two men leaving, but unperturbed, Colonel Wilson continued.

'Bridge Engineering Officer, Doctor Nicola Lynch. American.'

Tom stopped abruptly at the end of the isle and looked back at the screen. It was Nicola, beautiful as ever.

'Physics Graduate; 1st Class, Cambridge University England. Doctorate in Electro-physics Harvard University USA'. Tom gazed a little blankly at the screen.

'Major, Major,' said Roper in a forced whisper, as he stood at the open doorway, 'Let's go.'

Tom came to his senses and quickly made his way to the door. He glanced over his shoulder as he went through it.

'Age: 36. Currently heading the department of Electromagnetic Research, European Space and Science Agency. Doctor Lynch is on secondment to the International Space and Science Federation for this mission. Relationships . . .'

Tom strained to hear but the soundproof theatre door

gently closed behind the two men as they made their way to the lifts.

'You'll get the full crew brief from the operations department on Andromeda. It will be waiting with the rest of your paperwork when you get back to base. I'll be in touch in the next few days.' said Colonel Roper.

'Yes Sir.' Tom replied, but his thoughts were elsewhere.

'Shuttle Nexus, you have take off clearance, Platform One,' said the space terminal control officer. 'Initial vector one four five degrees; keep the speed below Mach three until clear of the corridor.'

'Cleared for take off, November One,' Chan Sung replied.

'OK, here we go; three, two, one, ignition on main engines,' said Tom Race, as he monitored the rising temperature indication of the shuttle's cryogenic propulsion system. He pulled back slightly on the pistol-shaped grip in his left hand and the six retrorockets lifted Nexus clear of the platform amid clouds of billowing steam and gas.

'Increasing thirty percent,' he continued, pushing the main thrust control lever forward with his right hand. The shuttle shuddered slightly as the main engines accelerated the vehicle, which promptly exceeded Mach one. 'No passengers, no freight,' said Tom with a big grin on his face, 'the only way to fly.' He banked the craft steeply to the right. 'Sixty percent, perfect,' he continued. A green light on the navigation display indicated that they were clear of the departure corridor as the airspeed indicator registered Mach three and rising quickly.

Chan Sung in the right hand co-pilot's seat looked across at Tom.

'Sounds like you'll be glad to get home, I mean back to Andromeda,' he said.

'Right first time, Chan,' Tom replied. 'Ninety percent, stabilising Mach nine,' he continued, then aggressively snatched the handgrip to the right.

The shuttle instantaneously performed a three hundred and sixty degree roll. 'That feels better.' He looked across to his colleague. 'It may not be home exactly, but I certainly feel more comfortable there than I do on earth these days. Engage auto pilot please.'

'Auto pilot engaged,' Chan Sung replied. 'All systems green.'

Tom leant forward and released the two shoulder straps of his five point seat harness. He pressed a button, which moved his seat backward eighty centimetres or so. As he reclined his seat into a more relaxed position, he put his hands behind his head.

'There's something going down, Chan; it's pretty big I can tell you. Can't say too much I'm afraid, it's President's level, you understand.'

'You're President's Level?' Chan commented, noticeably surprised.

'You bet!' replied Tom offhandedly. 'It's to do with the

next Mars shuttle and it's not routine.'

'Oh really? The Base Commander's number one on that flight, and I'm his co-pilot. He's been waiting a long time for it.'

'Yeh, I know, but he'll be waiting a little longer, as I'm afraid will you, Chan. The team's changed. It's all new and I'm the number one!'

'You!' exclaimed Chan Sung, visibly annoyed. He swiftly stifled his obvious disapproval. 'Mmm,' he continued, 'then congratulations are in order.'

'Well, not so fast,' Tom replied. 'As I say, it's not routine, not at all. Some very special freight and I hear they mean to break the current round trip record. That's why this baby is in for modifications; they need it to piggy-back some equipment to Spaceport. Equipment bound for the S3 programme and, in just a few days from now. Gee, things could get exciting around here for once! I expect to get a full brief in the next day or two.'

'The S3!' Chan replied, suppressing his astonishment.

Tom eyed his colleague again, this time a little more thoughtfully. He had known Chan Sung for three years. They had joined Andromeda wing together, trained together, partied, and got drunk together; nevertheless, he often felt that he didn't really know him. Chan was always vague about his past. Sensing that he had said too much already, he looked forward. Changing the subject he said quietly, 'never fails to impress, the sight of the moon, just coming right at us.'

The landing at moonbase Andromeda was uneventful. As the two men climbed from their seats, Tom leaned forwards and offered his hand. 'Thanks for the flight, Chan, always a pleasure to fly with you. Don't forget that this baby's in maintenance for the next few days, so pull the Flight Log please and pass it to operations.'

'Yes, will do; see you later,' replied Chan, with just the hint of a frown.

CHAPTER 16

A New Frontier

The following morning Tom reported to his commanding officer's private quarters. It was early; zero seven hundred corrected lunar time. He did not know quite what to expect, as a private briefing was unusual. The Base Commander, Adrian Moseley, was, at fifty-one, quite long in the tooth for space duties, having had his retirement postponed for two years until his fifty second birthday. A short gruff man, an engineer by profession, but a competent pilot, he expected to complete fourteen years in space, and five as Base Commander by his retirement: an exceptional achievement by any standard.

Tom knocked twice on the door and stood back. After some delay, it opened.

'Come in, Tom,' said Commander Moseley, who was making a pot of coffee on a small cabinet positioned in the far corner of the room. The Commander's day room was spacious, easily seven metres square. Dimly lit, it had a comfortable and lived in feel about it. Despite his long service in Andromeda, Tom had never visited the Commander's quarters and he couldn't help but notice the large framed photograph hanging on the grey wall to his left. It was the lift off of a Saturn V rocket.

Commander Moseley looked up to see Tom staring at the picture. 'Impressive isn't it? Lift off, Apollo Eleven, July 1969. Signed by Buzz Aldrin himself and given personally to my father, who was part of the mission control team.'

Tom looked at the Commander and then back at the photograph. He felt a little humbled. 'Sure is, Sir, history in the making,' he replied eventually.

'There's some more history to make Tom, and you're going to be a part of it, if you agree. Please sit down.' The Commander offered Tom the large dark blue couch near the coffee machine. As Tom stepped forward, the door closed behind him.

Commander Moseley continued, 'Have you met Professor Jason Nieve?'

Tom had not noticed the tall thin man who was standing behind him. Dressed in a worn dark blue suit, he had pale skin but cheeks that were healthily rosy. A shock of unkempt silvery white hair, seemingly out of control, emphasised the man's large head. Tom stepped back in surprise. 'Er, no, Sir. I haven't had the pleasure,' he answered, hesitantly. 'Morning, Professor. Tom Race, Andromeda Wing, real pleasure, Sir.'

'Morning to you, young man,' replied the Professor in a low, resonant voice, obviously very English.

The three men sat down: the Commander behind his desk; the Professor in a black leather, high-backed swivel chair and Tom, somewhat nervously, on the edge of the couch, resisting the tendency to fall back into the large squashy cushions.

'Professor Nieve is the senior design engineer of the Enigma programme, Tom. He's going to brief you on the forthcoming Mars mission; code named 'Saviour.'

Tom turned slightly to face the Professor. He wondered if the professor had put his head out of a viewing port during his flight from earth; as it appeared to be the only way he could have achieved such a 'vibrant' hairstyle. Trying desperately to hold a straight face, Tom focused on the scientist's pale blue eyes and listened intently.

Professor Nieve spoke quietly and seriously, almost aware of Tom's somewhat flippant thoughts, but choosing to ignore them.

'As you know, son, the Enigma programme is by no means ready. You have obviously seen the ship's construction progressing over the last eighteen months and no doubt been aware of Spaceport 2's increasing orbit, which has been necessary, as critical mass has increased. But that's probably as far as it goes?'

Tom agreed. 'That's right, Sir. We hear a few buzzes from time to time, you know, rumours, but as the programme is top secret, nobody really asks too many questions.'

'Um, well, you know, I'm sure, about the concept of the propulsion system?'

'Yes, Sir, just the theory!'

'I can tell you that the system is basically complete, as is the ship herself. We are just completing functional checks on all her ancillary systems and actually, the results are quite encouraging. However, no functional checks have been carried out on the propulsion system to date, only extensive simulations. We had a further eighteen months allocated for this and the flight test programme. So, NASA's request for the ship to be made available for this mission is somewhat premature to say the least.'

Tom nodded as the Professor continued, beginning to sense the enormity of the situation.

'We have designed and built the flight deck of the Enigma with some commonality to the S2. So much time and resources went into the ergonomics of the S2, that we felt we could not better it. So why try? You will recognise several fixtures and fittings, so to speak.'

Tom was a little surprised, 'such as what, Sir?' he asked.

'The tectronic seats, some of the consoles, the helmsman's flight display, that sort of thing.'

Tom nodded, 'I see.'

'However, the two propulsion systems are, as you know, totally different. The Enigma is revolutionary, unique and so is its control. On the Enigma, there is a dedicated control station. It is on the flight deck of course, but remote from the pilots' positions. We have a dedicated control engineer, a specialist who has been involved since the early simulations. She will be your flight engineer.'

'*My* flight engineer?' he said, eyes wide.

The Professor looked at Commander Moseley. 'He doesn't know?'

The Commander coughed into his fist and addressed Tom directly. 'Tom, I can't order you to do this, but you are the number one choice, unanimously!'

Tom recalled what the Colonel had said the previous day during the briefing; things began to fall into place. Commander Moseley continued. 'We want you to command the first flight of the Enigma. As you are already aware Tom, it's a very, very, important mission. Indeed, it is critical!'

'But I don't know anything about the Enigma, Sir. It's systems, navigation, engineering, anything!'

'The flight deck of the Enigma is basically the same as the S2,' said Professor Nieve matter of factly. 'A little bigger and substantially stronger, but by design, almost identical. The mid-section of the ship, housing the accommodation, and the rear section housing the propulsion tubes and neptunium chambers differ considerably, I agree. For one thing, they are substantially larger than anything you have previously seen; in space anyway,' continued the Professor. 'The five tubes, their concentric particle stream ports and the continuous annular accelerator increase the diameter of the rear section of the ship by a factor of ten, when compared to the S2, and the total mass is of course greater, nearly twenty times actually, due to the extensive strengthening.'

Tom frowned, not convinced. There were, in fact, few similarities, he thought.

Professor Nieve continued unabated. 'The philosophy of the flight deck has changed a little as well, I'm afraid. Nevertheless, you will become accustomed to it very quickly I'm sure. We have moved away from the two pilot concept and back to the bridge scenario of, say, an ocean going surface ship. We have a helmsman and a navigation officer sitting together in the forward flight deck area, which is similar to the S2. However, in addition, we have a propulsion engineer, a support systems officer, a communications officer and one or two other control stations. The Commander's station is in a central position with a semi-circular status panel set immediately in front. So you see, my boy, it is not technical knowledge or piloting skills that we want from you. Specialist officers that are already involved in the programme will supply those qualities; it's your command skills that we want.' The Commander concurred by nodding.

'Well, thank you, Sir,' replied Tom, stopping short of protesting, 'but any Commander must have an extensive knowledge of his ship, right?'

'Right, Tom,' said the Commander, reassuringly. 'And you will have an intensive nine day course which will give you everything you need to know.'

Tom's jaw dropped. 'Nine days!'

'You will learn the procedures,' continued the Professor, 'that's all. It's a straightforward flight regime, Major. Because of the speed, it is almost a straight line to Mars: a progressive acceleration over twenty hours; a cruise phase for only twelve seconds; then four days to decelerate. The ship's programming will put you in a high Martian orbit.'

Tom should have been speechless, but he managed to respond with the results of his simple but startling calculation. 'Five days to Mars! May I ask what speed will we achieve?'

The Professor leaned forward in his seat and peered intently at Tom, his eyes twinkled. 'For a few seconds, my boy, you will achieve forty-seven percent of the speed of light; some eighty eight thousand miles per second. At that speed, the mass of Enigma will increase by twofold. But the ship is capable of much, much more.'

With this remark, Tom really was speechless.

'The Enigma is the culmination of almost thirty five years of work by the best physicists, engineers and medical brains on earth. The programme has accumulated more simulator time than all previous space programmes combined. We are confident that the ship will perform as expected.'

Tom looked at the Commander, stunned. 'As expected then,' he said as if repeating an order for clarity.

'Tom,' responded the Commander, 'the nature of the cargo is such that it could reprieve the earth and mankind from the precarious position we now face. We simply cannot afford to wait seven or even six months for an S2 to make the return trip. By that time, the earth's ecosystems may have passed the point of no return. It's a tall order Tom, I know. There's so much riding on a successful outcome, but you are the man for the job and you have a very strong team, the best available.'

The Commander handed Tom a thin file, and beckoned Tom to look inside. Tom scanned the first page headed 'Mission Saviour, Presidential Level, Operational Profile.' Tom turned to the second page entitled 'Crew List'.

He scanned the first few names, stopping at Nicola Lynch, Propulsion Engineer.

'Unusually, Tom, for the aviation community anyway, you won't have seen or heard of these people for at least the last two years,' continued the Commander. 'It's because they have been quarantined, wrapped up in the Enigma project, so to speak.'

'So why hasn't a Commander been trained?' enquired Tom finally.

'It's a good question,' answered Professor Nieve, 'and particularly relevant. We have never trained a Commander for the programme, Major, because we came to the conclusion, sometime ago, that when we needed one, we would select an officer current in space operations and space flight. Not one who has sat in a simulator or a classroom for the last couple of years. No Major, the next generation of starship Commanders will be operational managers, not pilots.'

Tom nodded, satisfied with the answer.

'So, what do you say?' enquired Commander Moseley.

Tom paused and reflected briefly on the meeting. 'I'd say I'm honoured to be selected for this mission, Sir, and privileged to be the first Commander of the Enigma. You can count on me, Sir.'

'Thank you, Tom,' said the Commander. 'I knew I could.'

Commander Moseley looked at his watch and then at the Professor. Hastily he continued. 'The cargo is a batch of five small crystals, they were found a little over a month ago, on the surface of Mars. Apparently, under certain conditions, they have an amazing energy potential. Once in orbit, Osiris will dispatch an orbital system to dock with the Enigma, you in turn, will dispatch a small team to the surface. With them will be a specialised case, a holding and shielding device, designed and built to parameters supplied by Osiris's science department. The crystals are to be retrieved in this device and will remain secured in it, during the return passage to earth. The device apparently looks like a regular briefcase; there is also a spare. Professor Nieve assures me that they will both be ready in time for departure.'

'What system will Mars use to deliver these crystals, Sir?'

'The Columbus, Tom!' replied Moseley, almost embarrassed.

'An S1? But that system hasn't flown for God knows

how many years?' Tom replied, startled.

'That's all they've got,' sighed the Commander, 'and there is something else of a security nature I need to tell you. Please listen carefully to this. It's ears only, you won't find it written in the brief.'

Tom turned to face the Commander squarely.

'There's been trouble on Mars: deaths; possibly murders; the crystals went missing for several days. Fortunately, we now hear that they have been recovered. In addition, there is a communication problem and we are getting conflicting information.' The Commander's face tightened. 'I've known Commander Miko for years; he's an old friend. I trust him unequivocally. He is saying that he has a number of suspects under investigation and he has a trusted officer flying the S1 to the rendezvous. Unbeknown to Miko, however, the Security Departmental Head, a guy called Searle, is sending encrypted messages under the Rogue Command protocol, saying that his prime suspect is the one and same pilot flying the rendezvous! So what's really going on out there is unclear. But what is clear, is an immediate and ongoing threat of theft of the crystals.'

'May I ask the name of the S1 pilot , Sir?'

'He's a British officer: Lieutenant Commander Richard James Reece. He has a good record and renown as a quality officer and pilot. But he also had some emotional problems here on Andromeda; a few years ago and that fact is worrying Central Intelligence.'

Tom acknowledged the name, 'I knew of him, Sir,

but I never met the guy. He had just left for a spell of compassionate leave when I joined Andromeda Wing.'

'Yes, well, the full story of that saga is staff confidential. I am not party to it. But what isn't confidential is the threat to the mission. Please read the security brief carefully. Be fully aware of the situation. You will get a daily report from today.'

'OK Sir, I understand.'

'Now, Professor Nieve would like to start your training, Tom. So get to it and good luck.'

With that, the meeting broke up. Commander Moseley, totally out of character, warmly shook Tom's hand and patted him on the back as he left the room saying, 'we're depending on you, son.'

Tom nodded and raised a half-hearted smile. That's the second time I've heard that in as many days, he thought.

CHAPTER 17

Time Machine

Tom was already seated, albeit a little pensively, in briefing room three when Professor Nieve arrived. They were both several minutes early on the programmed start time of zero nine thirty. The Professor, still finding his way around Andromeda, seemed relieved to see Tom as he walked past the open door.

'Ah,' he said, 'eventually found the right place. It's like a rabbit warren around here.'

'Yes, Sir,' agreed Tom. 'It can be a bit confusing, until you've got the first few weeks under your belt, then life's a lot easier.'

'Not like I imagined. Expected it to be smaller, I suppose.'

'It's getting bigger all the time,' Tom added. 'Six percent extra real estate last year and the same planned for this year I hear.'

The Professor nodded, half smiled, and then gave Tom a sheet of A4 size paper. Tom was a little surprised.

'Wow! Paper!' he said, 'don't see much of this up here.'

'Yes, I know," agreed the Professor. 'I'm still behind the times, I'm afraid. But nothing quite like a hard copy, don't you think?'

Tom grinned, 'I didn't think there were any trees left to make this stuff.'

'There aren't,' commented Nieve, 'and when my stock runs out I'll have to join you in the twenty-first century!'

'Yes, Sir, I expect you will.' The two men laughed, relaxing the atmosphere.

Professor Nieve continued, 'this is your programme, Major. As you can see we have an initial brief this morning; any burning questions you may have, I'll take this session. Subsequently, this afternoon and for the next four days you are to complete a highly specialised and specifically compiled course detailing concepts, system design, operation and some limitations. Thursday, it's the morning shuttle back to earth, followed by intensive procedures and simulator training; after that its scenarios until the nineteenth.' The Professor paused to take a breath.

Tom's eyes widened, unable to conceal his well-justified anxiety. The Professor, clearly ignoring Tom's perplexed expression, continued unabated.

'On the twentieth, you will join Enigma, which should by that time have fully completed the shake-down phase and early on the twenty-second you go!' The Professor lowered his head and looked over his half moon spectacles sighting Tom squarely in the eyes. 'What are your thoughts, Major?'

Tom paused, reflecting on the programme presented to him. 'If you want the truth, Sir, Mission Impossible,' his matter-of-fact tone belying the situation.

'Um, of course, I'm not surprised you feel that way, Major. It's a tall order, a tall order indeed, but it is doable.' The Professor sat, perched on the edge of the table in front of Tom. 'System by system, this ship is the most advanced space craft ever constructed. The level of automation is quite simply staggering. It is by nature a very, very, clever machine. The central computer is, without doubt, one of the most sophisticated ever conceived, let alone built. The ship will do a lot for you, most things, if you let it, with very little external influence. In other words, you, or to be more precise your crew, direct it and it will do the rest. It is the beginning of a new era in space travel and exploration. To coin an old cliché it will enable us to boldly go where no man has gone before,' Tom smirked as he knew the phrase.

'How much autonomy do we allow the ship, Sir, if you know what I mean?'

'I know exactly what you mean, Major. By the way, do you mind if I call you Tom? Seems a little formal, this preoccupation the military has with rank,' replied the Professor.

Tom nodded and smiled, 'privileged, Sir,' he answered.

'To answer your question; sadly a lot less than we had originally planned. We are constrained by the New Geneva Convention. No, you and your crew retain full control of the ship and all her systems. It will be like that for some time to come I think.'

'I understand,' Tom nodded, not quite party to the full meaning of the Professor's answer, but letting it go at that. 'And just how fast will she go, Professor?'

'Metaphysical simulations show that Enigma is capable of over ninety percent of the speed of light; point nine two to be precise. Above that, the laws of physics become prohibitive. Hayden's theory of light speed travel appears to be entirely accurate. I'm sure that you are familiar with it?'

Tom's brow wrinkled. He looked down, slightly embarrassed, in order to avoid the Professor's penetrating gaze. 'Well, I, er, I'm not entirely up to speed with it I have to say, but . . .'

'Don't worry, Tom; you will be, soon enough.'

Tom changed the subject. 'Sir, when do I get the full crew list, and more importantly, when do I meet them?'

The Professor pulled a Septronic data Corum from his jacket pocket and handed it to Tom. It was cyan in colour indicating a top-secret security level status.

'You will need access to the Corinthian terminal in the Commander's synopsis room to read this file, Tom. He has cleared it. We have kept it simple. Just open it with your name backwards. There is a lot of information for you to digest, including the seven principal officers that will operate the Enigma under your command. As for your meeting; that's planned for the sixteenth at the Cape.'

Tom nodded, picking up the Corum. For a moment, his thoughts wandered. Five days, Nicola.

Professor Nieve stood up. 'Well, my boy, if you have any other questions, now's the time. You have a sixteen-hour day programmed and the same for the rest of the week, no let up until the twentieth.'

'I have one question, Sir. I'll find out in due course I know, but I'd like it from you.'

'Go on.'

'How do we navigate, or should I say, how does the Enigma navigate at these incredible speeds? I've always understood that this was one of the fundamental problems with light speed travel.'

'You're right, and to be honest we still have a very long way to go on this subject. After some twenty years of intensive research on a variety of systems, we settled some time ago for a stellar alignment comparison system coded Nebula. The concept is simple, the maths complex, but the computer power required really is staggering. At any instant during flight, Nebula will probably occupy some sixty percent of the main computer's attention.'

Tom looked suitably impressed and listened intently.

'You will recall the European Space Agency's Rosetta spacecraft and the lander, Philae?'

Tom nodded, 'Yes Sir, the first successful landing on a

comet; must be well over thirty years ago.'

'Precisely! The comet was coded '67 Papa' and called Churyumov-Gerasimenko, the year, to be precise, 2014 and the purpose to piggy-back the comet on its journey through this galaxy. Over a period of many years, using highly sophisticated instruments on Philae and a variety of others, including the long-range ARAMAR telescopes, here on Andromeda and the deep space Pathfinder satellite programme, we have precisely mapped the layout of our galaxy; out to a distance of approximately nine light months. Believe me, the databank required to hold this information is quite extraordinary. On top of that, the movement of every single stellar body in 'the picture', is being continuously predicted and its position precisely plotted in order to maintain a 'moving map', if you like, of the galaxy. Even now, as we speak, the Enigma's navigation computer is doing this; so, as the Enigma moves through space, the changing aspects of every star, every planet, asteroid, moon or comet is measured and then compared to the predicted model. It is then basic geometry to calculate the ship's position. The system samples at an incredible rate, once every one hundred and fifty billionth of a second; it has to, because of the incredible distance covered in a second, even at half the speed of light. As a result, my boy, you do not need to worry about navigation; the Enigma is continuously aware of its exact position, down to the metre.'

'Thank you, very impressive,' concluded Tom. 'But, um,

I understand the concept, Sir, but nine light months isn't going to get us very far; not even the nearest neighbouring solar system.'

The Professor shrugged his shoulders. 'You're right, doesn't sound very far, I know, considering Alfa Centauri, our closest star is some four point two light years away. Nevertheless, it has taken almost five years to build the map we have. This element is going to severely restrict travel at these speeds for many years to come.' Putting his hands in his pockets, he smiled. 'Don't happen to know anyone with a book of stellar charts we can beg, borrow or even steal do you?'

Tom smiled back, 'ha, not at the moment, Sir.'

'No, if only," sighed the Professor. "Anyway, you had better get on, young man. You have a great deal of work to do and I wish you the very best of luck.'

Tom stood up to shake the large hand offered by the Professor; they left the room in silence, turning in different directions.

'See you on earth in a few days,' closed the Professor.

'You bet, Professor,' replied Tom.

CHAPTER 18

A Strong Team

For the next four and a half days, Tom left Andromeda's learning centre only to sleep and with a sixteen-hour daily schedule, divided into three parts, there was precious little of that. Instruction was computer based; audio-visual, interactive, and pheromonal corroborated. The Pheromone Learning System had been a remarkable success, ever since the military first introduced it in the early twenties. Nostrum, the original, most successful and preferred production company incorporated a sophisticated computer, pheromone synthesizer and a simple delivery wisp in their system. Memory absorption, layering and capacity all benefited from the techniques, which involved allocating a particular synthetically generated 'smell' during the learning process. With literally millions of animal and plant pheromones available, the allocation of an individual odour to an important fact, figure, code, system operating method, or indeed almost anything that required committal to memory, allowed subconscious passage to the often-untapped deep memory. Interestingly, by design, human pheromones are often reserved for classified or secret information, because of primordial conditioning. Reviewing material, whilst simultaneously reintroducing the associated pheromone, enhances the process and once learned, retrieval rate and accuracy is dramatically enhanced. Indeed, so successful had the system become in corporate applications, that senior citizens, normally retiring at the age of seventy-five, were often able to completely change their career path and learn entirely new skills.

Tom was well used to the process; he had used it several times during his career and, as with many military pilots, had a NOSP, a Pheromone Allocation Record, in the shape of a computer memory chip, which prevented duplication and retrieval confusion. By close of play on the fifth day, he had a firm grounding in all of Enigma's systems; and impressive they were too.

The extent of classified research and development work that had taken place over the years on the Enigma project was, Tom realised, astounding to say the least. Although he was unable to understand the theory behind several of the more complicated and convoluted systems, the course gave him the knowledge to operate them effectively.

On the eve of his shuttle flight to the Cape, Tom was

summoned to Commander Moseley's office. 'You've done remarkably well, son,' he gushed, beckoning Tom to sit down. From behind his desk, the Commander reviewed the course results. 'Modules range between ninty-two percent and ninety-seven percent, with a ninety-four percent average for the course. Earth is very pleased with these results, and so am I.'

'Er, thank you, Sir,' replied Tom, still slightly comatosed.

'Right, now they're feeling a little more relaxed about your selection and the time scales involved. So go down there and do a good job in the simulator. Your bus leaves at zero eight hundred.' The Commander paused. 'Why don't you take my advice son and get an early night? You look as though you need it; your eyes are like two piss holes in the snow!' the Commander laughed.

He always does at his own jokes, thought Tom, who joined him by raising a polite, half-hearted smile.

It was rare for Tom to sit in the back of a shuttle. Indeed, try as he might, he could not remember the last time he had arrived on earth as a passenger. Nevertheless, it was a smooth flight and, looking towards the cockpit as he left the S2, he gave Lieutenant Rory Phillips an appreciative salute. There was no one to meet him at the shuttle terminal, just a limousine and its chauffeur to drive the five or so miles to NASA headquarters. Already feeling depressed, he surveyed the dull, miserable cityscape and grim, ever darkening sky, from the relative comfort of the automobile's rear seat.

'Probably all waiting for me in the lion's den?' he said suddenly.

'Excuse me, Sir?' came the surprised reply from the driver.

'Nothing Sergeant, forget it.'

Tom's thoughts drifted to the Enigma's crew again, or more precisely Nicola. He had not bothered to look at the crew list. For one thing, he had not had the time, but perhaps more to the point he did not want to read a lot of personal information about her. None the less, for a moment or two, he thought about their time together.

'We're 'ere, Sir, we're here!'

Tom recoiled from his daydream.

"We're 'ere, Sir, you know, the lion's den,' the driver smiled.

'Where are you from, Sergeant?' Tom asked, straightening his uniform tie.

'London, Sir, London, England and quite honestly, I wish I was back there. Know what I mean, Sir?'

'Yep, I know exactly what you mean.' Tom climbed out of the car. 'So long, Sergeant.'

'Goodbye, Sir. Oh, and good luck.'

Tom looked back. 'Thanks, I've got a feeling I'm going to need it!'

This time there was a welcoming committee, albeit

a small one: a gaggle of four or five military officers. Then Tom recognised Colonel Roper, who had begun to negotiate the twenty or so grand steps, which swept down to the pavement from the towering entrance of the main building. Large umbrella in hand, he approached Tom, leaving the remaining officers cowering from the persistent, discoloured drizzle under a hopelessly inadequate model.

'Good to see you, Major. Gee, you look like shit,' he said offering his hand, then pulling Tom under the temporary shelter.

'Thank you, Sir,' replied Tom with a smile, 'had a few late nights!'

'Well, I'm afraid we have a few more planned,' continued the Colonel. 'But first you will meet the team. They are assembled in the John Glenn suite, this way, Major.'

The two men climbed the remainder of the steps together, to be joined by the other, rather bedraggled, United States Air Force officers as they entered the headquarters building. Several armed military policemen, in smart attire, acknowledged Colonel Roper as his group entered the main foyer. They turned left, down a wide internal boulevard, floored in glossy black and grey marble. The towering surroundings had the men looking and feeling like dwarves, as they walked, unencumbered, between two rows of impressive stone columns. At the base of each column, facing inward, stood a soldier in full dress uniform; each wore spotless white gloves to grasp a ceremonial rifle and each snapped to attention to 'present arms', as the group passed by. Tom knew that this level of ceremony was reserved for the most senior of office. He could hear the noisy reception at least fifty yards before they arrived at a pair of large, engraved glass doors, the left one of which was open. The decoration on the door caught his eye; it exhibited a symbolised atmospheric re-entry of the old Gemini capsule with the words 'John Glenn 1962' beneath. The room fell silent as they entered. Tom was last, having politely allowed the other officers, all senior to him, to pass in front.

There were at least fifty people gathered and at that moment, many, who were standing, took their seats. Tom recognised the Vice President and Chuck Monroe, Governor of the State of Florida. The Colonel indicated Tom's position, next to his on the main dais.

'Mr Vice President, Governor, ladies and gentlemen,' the Colonel spoke directly and confidently into the single, pencil-thin microphone rising from the podium. 'This short, classified briefing is to introduce you all, at last, to the first crew of the international spaceship Enigma. Many of you, I know, have had the chance to meet some of these officers individually, but this is the first time the entire team will be together.' The Colonel nodded to a steward standing at the back of the room. Subsequently, there was a shuffling by the main door. Tom looked to his right to see what was happening. A line of officers in uniforms he did not recognise, almost paraded into the room. They looked relaxed and Tom had to admit smart, very smart. He barely had time to admire the deep violet-blue, almost indigo tunics when Nicola walked in, the seventh of eight officers. A few seconds later, two non-commissioned officers followed. Tom's attention became fixated on Nicola; he couldn't help it. It was the first time he had seen her in almost six years. She had changed, was older, but somehow, had not aged. Mature, still beautiful, perhaps more so. Tom felt himself staring. The officers and NCOs negotiated the three steps and formed a line standing side-by-side behind the Colonel. Tom acknowledged one or two with a friendly smile. Nicola looked forward into the room; she stood rigidly to attention, chin high, hands behind her back, her bright blue eyes clear and focused, even a little cold. The Colonel raised his hand to adjust the position of the microphone, the rather exaggerated, almost flamboyant movement serving its purpose of attracting Tom's attention. The Colonel raised his eyebrows to form a disapproving frown. Tom acknowledged, nodding subserviently, as if accepting the chastisement, then also looked forward. It seemed odd, almost awkward, to have Nicola standing so close without any emotion. They had shared so much?

'Ladies and gentlemen,' Colonel Roper continued. 'This is the team. The finest we have, assembled for an historic mission, one of crucial importance to us all.'

Several flashbulbs fired, like a volley from a line of infantrymen, their intense light ricocheting around the room as photographers took advantage of the moment.

'There will be time for images later, please,' he said, holding up his hands as if attempting to stop the oncoming barrage.

'First the introductions, if I may. To my right is Major Tom Race, United States Air Force; as of today, promoted acting Commander International Space Federation, the first Commander of the Enigma.'

Tom was flabbergasted; he had known nothing of the impending promotion. Trying not to show any emotion, he acknowledged the introduction by standing to attention.

Colonel Roper looked over his left shoulder. 'From left to right,' he continued, 'Commander Ronald Sampleman, European Space and Science Agency, second in command, Head of Engineering and Propulsion. Lieutenant Commander Sam Brennan, United States Navy, Helmsman. Captain Ishhi Chez Tsou, Asian Space Federation, Communications Officer. Major Moira Fairmont, NASA, Space and Science Officer. Captain Arno Raoul, Canadian Space Cooperative, Principal Medical Officer. Lieutenant Benjamin Bagley ESSA, Navigation Officer. Nicola Lynch, ESSA, Deputy Head Engineering and Propulsion. Major John Berrovich United States Air Force and Staff Sergeants Ike Freeman and Buzz Bateman, all on secondment from the Presidential Protectorate and dealing with all aspects of containment and security for the mission.'

Each member followed Tom's lead and stood to attention

upon introduction. The Colonel turned, smiling.

'We are justifiably proud of you all, please stand at ease. In addition to these fine officers, we have a further eleven service and four civilian crew members, all specifically selected from the international space and science communities to complete the team; in total, twenty-three highly competent men and women. Now, as you know, this programme is twenty-four seven, no let up. Due therefore, to mission commitments, these other crew members are, sadly, unable to be with us today. However, we congratulate them all on their selection and dedication.'

Tom felt a little uneasy at this remark. Amidst the applause, he knew the majority of the crew had been training for two, possibly three years to reach this point, whereas he had stepped into their midst literally in the last few days and, no doubt, at the expense of one of their colleagues. He knew he was going to have to earn their respect.

The applause subsided at the request of the Colonel, who concluded, 'if there are any questions, I will take them now.'

The first came quickly from the left-hand side of the audience, at the back.

'Morning Colonel Roper, Pent Santos, *New York Times*.'

'Ha, Mr Santos,' replied the Colonel light-heartedly. 'You appear to be following me round the country!' There were a few laughs.

'That's because I'm trying to nail you on this story. But you're very evasive, Colonel.'

The Colonel laughed loudly. 'What's the question, Mr Santos?'

'You keep telling us how critical this mission is and it's no secret that the Enigma is not fully tested. So why is the ISF pressing ahead with a manned flight to Mars at such short notice, way ahead of Enigma's first planned flight? And why aren't you using robotics if the programme is so 'sensitive', or maybe I should translate that as dangerous?'

'OK, they're good questions. The last part first, if I may. Some selected and highly specialised cybernaut systems could, theoretically, be employed on the Enigma; that is true. However, by nature, this would create several problems, the main one being that the anticipated programming would require memory capacity in excess of that agreed and clearly stipulated in the International Robots Resolution of 2018. If you recall the Skyport accident, that was caused when three HU40 Humotron cybersystems received plateau seven programming, making them, for the first time, self-aware. It didn't take them long to decide that they weren't going to do as they were told anymore. As a direct result of that tragic loss of life, all plateau six and above cybersystems were shut down or reduced below plateau five. In addition, the revised Geneva Convention of 2019 banned all cybersystems in military use above level four. With regard to the Enigma: her requirements are unique and so complex, that plateau seven, or I believe even eight, are necessary. We have that technology, but we are not allowed to use it. Frankly, I agree with the resolution. The dangers of this level of programming in a cybernaut far outweigh the advantages. My view is that you will never beat an astronaut up there in the hot seat. It's been proven time and time again over the years.'

'But what about the central computer, Colonel?' enquired Santos again, 'by all accounts it has a mind-boggling capacity. Why is that system above the law?'

'You're remarkably well informed, Mr Santos and you are right, the central computer is a magnificent achievement; indeed, a feat of computer technology and electronic engineering. Its capacity far outstrips anything previously built, and that includes all active and dormant global systems using the Rockwell Illinois Plateau Unit of measurement and reference. However, you cannot compare this system to the Humotron models, or anything else for that matter. The Enigma's central computer is code-named Emily. It is a static system. It is an integral part of the ship itself. It literally does not have any moving parts! Having said that, the computer boffs have learned their lesson here and installed numerous fail-safe inter-nodes. Emily has very limited autonomy and severely restricted direct inputs into the ships systems; we don't expect any problems!'

'I see, thank you, Sir,' came the reply from the *Times* correspondent.

Tom had listened intently to the Colonel. The sheer scale of his responsibilities was beginning to dawn on him.

The Colonel glanced at the free air projected clock face by his left shoulder. 'Mr Vice President, Governor, ladies and gentlemen, it is time for me to bring this briefing to a close, these good people have work to do. To remind you: the Enigma will break from Skyport 2 at zero one hundred hours on the twenty-second, and there is plenty to do in the five days remaining. We wish the crew good luck and a fair course. Thank you all.'

CHAPTER 19

Dangerous Liaisons

By the third day of simulator training, Tom was feeling more confident. His systems knowledge and handling were coming together and the flight profiles, or, as they were now called, 'stellar sequences' began to fall into place. The superbly trained crew went a long way to relieving him of the initial stress of command training.

The evening of eighteenth found him revising emergency procedures ready for the following day's test scenario. He still found it difficult to delegate decision parameters to the other bridge officers, having only flown single or two crew operations for his entire career. Nevertheless, it was happening. 'Stellar sequences' and procedures needed to be word perfect; indeed, second nature, if he was to develop spare capacity for the unexpected.

By eleven o'clock, he was beat, absolutely, so he closed down the emergency sequence programme he was running and leant back in his chair, rubbing his sore eyes. He was happy enough. The crew were friendly, conscientious and extremely professional and had openly accepted him as the Commanding Officer. Additionally, Tom sensed that he, Ronald Sampleman and Sam Brennan would become good friends; sharing from the outset a good deal of mutual respect. However, it was his relationship with Nicola that he could not understand. Tom looked at the group photograph temporarily housed in a black plastic frame, which he had carefully placed in a central, prominent position on his desk. He focused more intently on Nicola, leaning forward to scrutinise her features.

She had barely said a word to him outside the professional theatre and curtly closed any conversations he had tried to open during breaks in training. Strangely, he wasn't perturbed, although he had to admit he was a little disappointed; considering they had been engaged for almost a year and had spent some time planning their wedding. His thoughts drifted back to that time: six years earlier, both studying for a Masters in propulsion engineering and sharing most things in their lives, living accommodation being one of them. Even now, all these years later, he couldn't quite understand how, after recently graduating and having accepted his proposal of marriage, she had upped and left almost without a word, and certainly without explanation. After that, she wouldn't take his calls, reply to his e-dictions, nothing. Just cut the relationship dead. What had he done? he pondered in his daydream. It was almost two years later that he eventually secured his preferred appointment to Andromeda's Shuttle Wing, the first of two; only then, through a mutual friend, did he learn that she had married unexpectedly and been appointed to ESSA. That was the last he had heard of her, save rumours of her marriage to a prominent German scientist being in difficulty, and their subsequent split a few years later.

Tom stared at the photograph, systematically studying her face, every detail, as if he was trying to find a clue. Interesting, he thought; not relaxed and smiling like her colleagues, but without emotion. Was she focused and unswervingly professional; or tense, nervous, even protective? He looked at her eyes, as clear and bright as he remembered, but he couldn't fathom her out. He didn't know her well enough anymore, not after all this time. How did he feel? Something and nothing; interested but not interested; forgiving and not forgiving. Anyway, he was well over it; especially having been engaged again.

Yes, and what of Christine? The separation caused by his second two-year appointment to Andromeda had put paid to that relationship. No, there was little room in his timetable for recycling old emotions about Nicola, or Christine for that matter. With that thought, he called it a day and made for his bed.

Tom felt that he had barely switched the lights off and closed his eyes when the alarm call sounded. It pervaded his subconscious uninvited; then wrestled it back to reality, erasing the memory of his dream on the way. 'Six o'clock already,' he said, rubbing eyes still reddened from the previous day.

He had allocated a generous portion of adrenaline to the day's proceedings and it began to kick in early. By seven o'clock, he was in the officer's restaurant enjoying two large waffles with lashings of acacia honey and strong, black, American coffee. Halfway through his second cup, Ronald Sampleman joined him. Sampleman was a large man, perhaps a little overweight at two hundred pounds, but at six foot four, it didn't show. In his early forties, but looking a little older, he was typical of the European male contingent; usually wearing their hair a little more relaxed than the short crops or even shaved heads of their American colleagues. Whilst generous splashes of greying hair to his temples added to Sampleman's air of confident experience; it was, in fact, his manner that Tom had warmed to first. An abbreviation of his first and surname, he was simply known as Ross to his friends.

'How're you feeling, Tom?' he enquired, his strong Irish accent still unfamiliar to Tom.

'Fine thanks, Ross. Yes, hanging in there I guess.' Tom replied, happy to have the company of his new friend.

'You ready for the big one?'

'Ready as I'll ever be.'

Ross poured himself a coffee and topped up Tom's.

'How long you been in the programme, Ross?' Tom

asked, taking a mouthful of his rejuvenated coffee.

'Since the outset pretty much,' half answered Ross, looking around for something to eat. 'I mean the outset of the CCI programme.'

'CCI?'

'Crew Concepts and Initiatives, Tom; kicked off a little over five years ago. There were many ergonomic and physiological problems to overcome. Initially I was recruited as a design engineer looking at the effects of socio-human dynamics. You know, effects of high-speed travel, accelerations and decelerations to and from light speed, gravity concepts, that sort of thing. I was a member of the design team that created the Magnagrav magnetic deck system. It's used on the Enigma, you'll experience it in a few days; works well, if I say so myself. Once that and a great many other design projects were finalised, I moved to propulsion. Subsequently, they needed someone to start operating the simulator; that's how I got involved in crewing. Then, about two years ago I was asked if I would be interested in heading the flight engineering department and recruiting the team, jumped at the opportunity!'

'So, you recruited the people?'

'Several, but not all; but I sat on the selection board for the whole process.'

'What about Nicola, Ross? How long has she been involved?'

Ross paused, giving Tom his full attention. 'Nicola's interesting,' he said slowly. 'She joined twenty-two months ago, give or take a week or two. Came from ESSA's laboratories in Strasbourg, she was one I did not recruit; brought directly into the programme by Professor Nieve.'

'Ah, the Professor, I've met him,' interrupted Tom, nodding his approval.

'She's good at her job, Tom. Knows her stuff I have to say, very cool and collected. Doesn't socialise though; almost never anyway. You will see her at the official functions, that sort of thing; apart from that, she doesn't appear interested. Definitely not a 'group hug' type of person!' Ross laughed.

Tom smiled, almost agreeing. 'Is she liked?'

'Um, respected more than liked, I'd say. Never lets her hair down, always the professional, but I can depend on her fully; knows some of the systems better than I do, but I didn't say that, OK?'

Tom laughed this time, before taking the last mouthful of his waffle. Ross's bacon and eggs finally arrived and the two men enjoyed the forty or so minutes remaining before report time.

CHAPTER 20

Testing Time

Not entirely unexpected, Professor Nieve arrived early for the final simulator session. In fact, there were several people in the remote viewing facility that Tom recognised, as well as several that he did not. Even Colonel Roper was present, eager to witness this final test of the crew's abilities.

At exactly ten hundred hours, eastern time, the main door to the flight module was closed and the full complement of twenty-three men and women took to their respective stations. Only the security trio, with little to do but their initial equipment checks, seemed happy to be there. A piercing, intermittent alarm sounded in the module bay as the large canister-like capsule detached from its mechanical locks, and rose slowly on an intricate system of electro-hydraulic jacks. This computer-controlled system would relay realistic motion simulations to the capsule occupants, ranging from massive accelerations to relative weightlessness and pretty much everything in between.

'This is simulation control; all personnel to flight stations, standby for commencement of Phase 5 operations. This is a test scenario. Repeat, this is a test scenario.'

The alarm in the module bay sounded for another ten seconds whilst in the remote viewing room, the VIP party, numbering at least twenty, took their seats in front of a large viewing screen. Several continuous operation digital cameras positioned in the capsule's three main compartments: the bridge, engineering control room and propulsion control room, would provide an 'up close and personal' perspective on every angle of crew performance. First pictures to reach the viewing screen were from the bridge, with Commander Race seated in his central, slightly elevated position and the six other bridge officers at their respective terminals. A little way in front of Tom were five curved liquid crystal displays, together they formed a semi-circle, with each about forty centimetres high. With a control panel mounted on the left armrest of his seat, Tom would be able to select almost any system detail he wished and the display to view it. In addition, he could communicate directly with any control station in the ship utilising a digital video pick-up system. Above the five display screens, he had a clear view of the bridge and thereafter, an impressive uninterrupted view of the heavens through the one hundred and fifty degree panoramic viewing portals.

The sight was inspiring and the visual simulations generated by the control system were unprecedented in their accuracy. With Enigma still docked in Spaceport 2, control was handed over to its crew.

'Commander Race, this is simulation control. You have the ship.'

'I have the ship,' Tom replied. Despite his cool demeanour, Tom felt his heart rate quicken, as much with excitement as with restrained anxiety at what they would throw at him this time. He was confident though; his surroundings felt right. Ergonomically precise in its design, the cream interior of the spacious bridge contrasted favourably with the light blue seats and trim, and deep violet-blue uniforms of the crew. For a fleeting moment, he felt proud to be wearing the three striped, platinum shoulder boards of command; a fleeting moment, just an instant, was all he had.

'This is Skyport 2, control, you are clear to break lock,' came a voice over the PA.

'Roger, clear to break lock,' replied Tom. 'Confirm deflectors in position?'

'Deflectors green,' came the reply.

'Helm, standby for manoeuvre thrust.'

'Yes Sir,' answered Sam Brennan.

A high grade but low-density steam of nuclear particles, primarily 'light weight' electrons provided Enigma's manoeuvring and low speed propulsion. Siphoned from the tightly coiled 'particle accelerator' before entry into the main thrust chambers, the stream's relatively low atomic mass was more than compensated by its incredible velocity. With precise control of these two parameters and therefore the resulting reactive force, the Helmsman had uncompromised steerage and speed control.

'Twenty percent manoeuvre thrust please, Mr Brennan,' requested Tom.

'Twenty percent, Sir.'

As the potent particle stream was fired rearwards from a single omni-directional nozzle mounted central to the five main thrust chambers, Tom sensed the craft move. The visuals appeared totally realistic as Skyport 2 began to edge backwards in the screens.

Even though Skyport 2 had lifted Enigma into a suitably high orbit, a stream of electrons of such potency, if misdirected, would quickly cut a hole through earth's delicate stratosphere. Like a pin pricking a tiny hole in the skin of an orange and the subsequent seepage of juice, such penetrating damage to the atmosphere would result in the loss of ozone and other precious gasses, already depleted by record carbon dioxide levels. To avoid this problem, specially designed and positioned deflectors mounted on Skyport 2 would, in reality, direct the sub-atomic stream harmlessly into space. In addition, the Enigma will position at least fifty thousand miles from earth before engaging her main thrust chambers.

'Left five degrees, reduce thrust to ten percent, Sam, let's make it a clean break from Skyport.'

'Commander, I have a thrust control failure, no steerage,' said Sam earnestly.

'Engage standby systems,' replied Tom immediately.

'No response, Sir, on this heading we will collide with Skyport's outer gantry.'

'Take it manually, Sam, give me five degrees left, no delay!'

'No response in manual either, Sir, the nozzle control is jammed. Twenty five seconds to impact.'

Tom paused for thought, momentarily, then turned to Nicola who was seated at the engineering console to his right.

'Main thrust status?' he demanded.

'Green, Sir,' she replied.

'Helm, one percent, main thrust tube number two. Emergency cut-off, manoeuvre thrust.'

'We are too close to earth for main thrust, Sir,' interjected Nicola.

'Make that one and a half percent Mr Brennan, as quickly as you can please.'

Sam Brennan's fingers pushed several keys in quick succession on his control panel. Tom selected a pictorial schematic of the main thrust output on his number one screen. Number two main chamber began to show a green indication.

'One and a half percent, Sir, you have it.'

The off-centre thrust from chamber two began to swing the nose of Enigma to the left. Two large steel access gantries protruding from Skyport 2 came into view through the main viewing portals.

'Ten seconds to impact, Sir.'

Tom watched the course change carefully, mindful of the obstructions on the other side of Skyport's docking bay.

'Shut down MTT Two, Sam.'

'Aye Sir, thrust zero, number two.'

Subconsciously, for those seconds, Tom sensed everyone on the bridge brace themselves; even he gripped the arms of his chair. Nicola held her breath. There was silence. The seconds passed. The two gantry arms slid slowly out of view on the right side, missing the ships hull by mere centimetres. Tom assessed the inertia of his ship; it was enough to clear Skyport.

'Engineering,' he said, 'status?'

'Control failure, Commander, manoeuvring nozzle, tracing system fault now,' replied Nicola.

Tom pushed a button his armrest, selecting the video pickup for engineering control. Ross Sampleman appeared on his central screen.

'Can you fix it, Ross?' Tom enquired, with controlled concern.

'It's the nozzle initiator, Commander, total power loss,' replied Ross. 'I'm re-routing the supply at the moment, almost there.' He looked down at his control console.

Standby, standby, now, re-routing complete, you have it, power restored.'

'Thanks, good work.'

Tom looked across at Nicola for a few seconds, their eyes met.

'Thank you for the warning,' he said with a blank expression. Nicola nodded, 'that's my job,' she said, not knowing if she had done the right thing by questioning Tom's order.

'Status?' Tom asked again.

'Green, Commander,' replied Nicola, looking away embarrassed.

'Clear of Skyport, I presume, Mr Brennan?'

'Yes, Sir. One thousand metres and opening.'

'Then sixty percent manoeuvre thrust and set a course for Orus.'

'Sixty percent Sir, course plotted and laid in.'

Tom fell silent for a minute or so, deep in thought, and then pressed a single green button positioned adjacent to a large red isolator switch on his right armrest.

'Emily?' he enquired somewhat hesitantly, 'navigation status for the acceleration phase?'

'Good morning, Commander Race,' replied Emily in a calm, cold tone, a voice hauntingly similar to Nicola's. 'The navigation system is fully functional and ready for engagement at point Orus. Trajectory projection appears clear. Status green for sub-light acceleration.'

'Thank you, Emily,' replied Tom.

'You're welcome, Commander,' answered the computer in a rather condescending tone.

Tom looked around the bridge shaking his head; it was as if he could sense an array of the computers wiry tendrils all around him; it almost made him shiver. This was Emily, the last, but certainly not the least, crew member on the bridge, in the form of her primary sensor terminal. This terminal, a large, circular, multi-function port about one metre in diameter, was mounted in the deck head above, but slightly behind, the command position. With a complex voice recognition and activation system, Emily would respond to commands from three nominated senior officers; Tom as Commander, Ross Sampleman, second in command and Moira Fairmont as space and science officer. Based on past experience, Emily, with equivalent plateau nine programming, had no direct inputs into any of the ship's control systems; save the navigation and auto-flight systems, which were her primary functions. Plateau nine programming was two levels above that required for machine self-awareness, utilising the internationally recognised 'Rockwell Illinois' memory categorisation and calibration system.

Emily was, to date, the most powerful independent system ever conceived and a fair proportion of her spare memory capacity had been allocated to storage and rapid retrieval of just about every scrap of physical knowledge known to man. The prime reason for her limited authority over the ship's control and life support systems came as a result of bitter experience gained after the Spaceport 1 disaster. There, three self-aware model HU40 cybernauts shut down the entire life support system of the space station, resulting inevitably, in the loss of sixty-three lives. The renegade robots then mis-handled an orbital breakout manoeuvre, which in turn resulted in the station crashing to earth three days later. The station came down perilously close to Space Control, Houston, Texas, breaking up in the suburbs with several hundred more casualties. As a result, Tom had been trained to utilise Emily, outside her prime role, as a 'consultant', nothing more. Indeed, mounted on the right armrest of his seat was an emergency power isolation switch; this switch protected from inadvertent use by a hinged cup, was bright red in colour and marked 'Emily. Emergency Shutdown'. If activated, the relay would isolate the massive power manifold that supplied the computer's insatiable demand for electricity.

'Five minutes to Orus, Sir,' said Sam, half turning to look at Tom.

'Acknowledged, run the pre-acceleration checklist please,' replied Tom.

The design of the Enigma's bridge was highly functional. Directly in front of the Commander's position, on a slightly lower level, were the twin consoles of the helmsman and the navigation officer. These two officers shared a large, common navigation and central warning display panel, which overlaid active track data, interstellar projection charts, functional operative modes and alert modes relating to the ship's self diagnosis facilities. On the left side of the bridge, slightly forward of Tom's position, was the communication officer's console. Seated here, engaged in conversation with space control, was Captain Ishhi Chez Tsou, a petite Japanese woman on loan service from the Asian Space Federation. Her size however, belied her hidden strength, both physical and mental; she was an expert in several different defensive martial art forms and fluent in over twenty major languages and as many regional dialects. Tom liked her; she was extremely professional, courteous and good company. Forward of Captain Tsou, again mounted slightly lower to the main bridge deck, was Moira Fairmont's post. This space and science console had instant access via a specialised keyboard to Emily's vast encyclopaedia of knowledge; the sum, it was fabled, of all the great libraries of the world. Moira, as she frequently told new acquaintances, could trace her ancestral line back to the Native American Indian tribe of the Sioux. She was tall, but looked, perhaps, a little rounded in her figure-hugging tunic. With deep black shiny hair tied in a single, tight, ponytail, which seemed to pull gently at the outside corners of her dark brown eyes, she was, as Tom put it, damn clever! Similarly, on the right side of the bridge, opposite Captain Tsou was Nicola's console as the bridge engineer. Then, forward and slightly down again to the medical and life support console of the Canadian medical officer, Captain Arno Raoul; a short, stocky man, almost completely grey and well before his time, at thirty-eight. Behind the bridge through secure, titanium alloy sliding portals was the security section. Here the security team had their flight positions, three seats side-by-side. Behind those was a large protective stowage for the U-Semini Case.

Tom flipped through several displays on his central screen before stopping at navigation; a duplicate picture derived from the master display on the navigation officer's console. He could see position 'Orus' approaching; the entry point of the acceleration corridor, and instigated final preparations. Sam turned to look at him.

'Two minutes to Orus, Sir.'

'Seen,' replied Tom, selecting a checklist on his number four screen.

'Ladies and gentlemen,' he said, addressing his bridge crew, 'let's give it our best shall we, final checklist, communications?'

'Communications green, Sir,' replied Ishhi Tsou.

'Science?'

'Green for go, Sir,' replied Moira Fairmont.

'Engineering?'

'All systems green, Commander,' said Nicola, straight-faced.

'Life support?'

'Fully ready, Sir, green for go', answered Captain Arno Raoul.

'Navigation?'

'Yes, Sir, we have a green,' said Benjamin Bagley.

'Helm?'

'No problems, Sir, we are green.' Sam Brennan was looking forward to this moment.

'Thank you all,' said Tom pressing his PA selector. 'This is Commander Race, standby for acceleration, repeat, secure for acceleration.'

Tom was pensive, waiting for something to happen; some malfunction or other. It had been too quiet for a 'Sim check' so far.

'Engage main thrust chambers,' he said, 'initially, forty percent.'

'Forty percent, Sir,' replied Sam.

Precisely as the ship passed through fictional point Orus, Tom felt the acceleration. It wasn't a massive thump in the back, but an impressive push from behind which squeezed him gently and progressively into this seat. The main drive utilised a similar principle to manoeuvre thrust; that of reactive propulsion to a sub-atomic matter stream, only this time far more potent. The five kilometre tightly coiled particle accelerator was now delivering electrons at near light velocity into the main thrust chambers. Directed at barium trigger blocks set within the chambers, these electrons blast the component atoms like a bombarding meteor storm, smashing their sub-atomic bonds to release, primarily, the heavy neutrally charged core of the barium atom, the neutron. Contained and channelled, the incredible expansive power of the resulting nuclear fission process is used to eject a continuous, high density, stream of these particles rearwards. Finally, this veritable flood of neutrons passes through five compressing 'venturi' nozzles, which further accelerates the particles prior to their discharged into space.

At this point, the matter stream is accelerated to almost the speed of light: a little over one hundred and eighty thousand miles per second. The five main chambers, each almost eighty metres long and ten metres in diameter, harnessing a reactive force that could, theoretically, propel the Enigma to a similar speed. However, the laws of physics, combined with materials technology and indeed several other factors preclude this, limiting Enigma's maximum speed to an incredible fifty-three percent equivalent light speed. In addition, one other engineering breakthrough, a masterpiece, as essential as the propulsion system itself, allowed Enigma to safely achieve its goal.

'Acceleration looking good, Sir,' said Sam, 'constant at three five five.'

'Acknowledged.'

In reality, this progressive acceleration phase would last almost twenty hours; minimising stress on the ship's hull, but for the purposes of the simulator test, it had been compressed to fifteen minutes. Tom waited nervously.

'What next?' he said to himself.

Presently Sam Brennan spoke. 'Acceleration phase

complete, speed stabilised forty six percent. Five seconds to deceleration.'

'Impressive,' said Tom quietly, 'almost eighty six thousand miles per second.' He looked at Sam. 'Navigation status please.'

'On course, Sir. Corridor showing clear.'

'Instigate deceleration phase, Mr Brennan, main thrust zero. Manoeuvre thrust authority fifteen percent maximum, hold her steady.'

'Yes, Sir, main thrust zero,' replied Sam.

At light related velocity, the planet Mars was a mere stone's throw from earth. Only a twelve second cruise phase was necessary before shutting down the main thrusts to begin deceleration. Even so, the structural implications at this speed were mind-boggling. At forty-six percent light speed, the Enigma would weigh almost half as much again as she did leaving earth's orbit and her overall dimensions would be reduced, compressed essentially by the rules of quantum physics.

To minimise these structural implications, deceleration would take four days. It was during this phase that the Enigma was most vulnerable. With the prime directional control of the main thrusters removed, only minute course changes were possible using the manoeuvring thrust system and any changes necessary, required an application many thousands of miles earlier, at a point derived from Emily's complex calculations. For this period, Enigma was like a projectile with only limited directional control.

'Sir, we have a flight path obstacle; showing four point one million miles,' barked Sam.

'Time?' Tom responded curtly.

'Fifty-five seconds, Sir.'

'Emily, FPO status?'

'Appears to be a rogue asteroid Commander, slowly drifting into our flight path,' answered the computer. 'According to gravitational implications relating to the moons Phobos and Deimos, my calculations show it has a mass of eighteen million tons; about one kilometre in diameter.'

'Enough to scatter us to the corners of the universe,' replied Tom under his breath, 'engineering, screen status?'

'Screens at one hundred percent, Sir,' replied Nicola. 'But that flight path obstacle is too big to be deflected by our screens.' She paused momentarily and then continued; 'as you know Sir!'

Tom looked at Nicola; it was a stupid question. The screens were only good up to a spatial mass of one thousand metric tons. 'Time to main thrusters?' he demanded.

'Over five minutes, Commander,' replied Nicola. 'We are still going through the shut down sequence. It will take time to reverse the procedure.'

'Two point four five million miles, Sir; thirty five seconds,' snapped the navigation officer.

'Helm, twenty degrees left,' demanded Tom earnestly. He knew a lateral deflection of more than this could send the Enigma tumbling through space uncontrollably.

'Twenty degrees left applied, Sir.'

'Computer,' demanded Tom again, 'collision status?'

'Too little, too late, I'm afraid, Commander,' answered Emily. 'We will impact the equatorial region of the asteroid in twenty-one seconds.'

Tom's dislike for the computer was growing. He paused for thought. What could he do?

'Nineteen seconds.'

What could he do? The bridge officers looked at him for guidance. Impact with the asteroid seemed unavoidable. Was it all going to end here?

He turned to Nicola again. 'Emergency escape pod status?' he asked.

'Fully operational,' she replied, 'as always. But it's too late to abandon ship, Commander.'

Tom ignored this patently obvious remark. 'Full left manoeuvre thrust, Sam, quickly!'

Nobody knew the implications of that order more than Sam Brennan did. It would send the Enigma skidding sideways through space. Eventually an uncontrollable cyclic tumble would ensue; they had seen it in earlier instructional simulator sessions.

Sam trusted Tom's ability and applied the correction. 'Twenty-five degrees left thrust,' he responded.

In the viewing gallery, the occupants shifted nervously, precipitating their disappointment at this fundamental error of judgement.

'Nine seconds to impact, Sir,' counted Sam.

Tom flipped a selector on his display control, Ross's face appeared on the central screen; he appeared more than a little concerned. 'Ross, quickly, standby to initiate escape pod thrusters.'

Ross Sampleman seemed a little surprised by the order, but didn't question it. 'When you need it, Commander,' he said calmly.

Both mechanical and magnetic locks to the underside of Enigma's central hull, secured each of the four escape pods, and each had two disproportionately large conventional rocket motors. They were powerful enough to break the gravitation free fall of re-entry to a planet the size of Venus or Mars or alternatively, decelerate to a survivable speed after jettison from Enigma, at velocities up to forty thousand miles per second.

'Fifteen percent, Sir, light related speed, and reducing.'

'Five seconds to impact.'

Colonel Roper looked particularly disappointed, shaking his head as he looked across at Professor Nieve. Nieve, on the other hand, could see what Tom was thinking. All the same, he sat pensively for the final few seconds. To make the necessary course change, Tom had to wait until the last possible moment; a split second, the cusp of the cyclic tumble, after which there would be no recovery.

'Four, three, two!'

Even now, at two seconds, some fifty-two thousand miles from the asteroid, the occupants of Enigma's bridge could not see the object.

'Now!' screamed Tom, 'full thrust, pods one and two!'

In an instant, the blink of an eye, the asteroid appeared. It filled the viewing portals, its surface covered with ancient craters, like pockmarks, focusing the eye. Then it was gone. The emptiness, the vacuum that is space, yet Enigma still shuddered with its passing. Thereafter it was lost, a million miles behind them.

'Zero thrust pods one and two, fifty percent pod three. Right five manoeuvre thrust,' Tom ordered.

Whilst the bridge officers sat stunned, Tom was acutely aware of the necessity to prevent an ensuing tumble in the opposite direction.

Ross Sampleman made the selections from the propulsion control room. 'It's done,' he said, nodding with a knowing smile.

'We're not out of it yet, Ross,' said Tom, looking at screen four. He waited to see the effect the opposite thrust application would have on the Enigma.

By that time Sam Brennan was back in the loop. 'Attitude stabilising,' he said, 'Navigation gives right one point five to bring us back on course for Mars.' His relief was plain to see.

'Then make it right one point five, Mr Brennan,' said Tom sinking into his chair, his shoulders visibly dropping.

Professor Nieve looked across at Colonel Roper and

smiled. 'Unconventional, but effective don't you think?' he confided.

Colonel Roper was speechless, replying such a considerable number of seconds later that it appeared almost unrelated .

'I guess so, Professor; er, what next?' he finally enquired.

'Deflector screen failure and some power problems,' he replied, 'then that should wrap it up.'

'Do I need to see anymore?'

'The screen failure is an important scenario,' answered the Professor. 'After that, I think they will be home and dry.'

Colonel Roper nodded and flopped back in his chair.

On the bridge, Tom thanked Ross and then deselected his video image in favour of the navigation display. The four day deceleration phase had been reduced to one hour for the purposes of the phase five test scenario. Tom didn't relax, he knew something else was coming.

'Status Mr Brennan?'

'One hour to Mars, Sir, trajectory and orbital velocity in the gate, deceleration green.'

Tom nodded, 'It's not over yet, ladies and gentlemen,' he said pulling his team together for the inevitable finale. He addressed Tsou. 'Open a channel to Osiris please, inform them we will be establishing a seventy percent elliopheric orbit in one hour. Enquire as to the position of Columbus.'

'Aye, Sir,' Tsou replied.

'Life support problem coming up, Commander,' shouted Arno Raoul, his voice agitated. 'Rear sections four, five and six losing pressure and oxygen.'

'Engineering, status?' requested Tom.

'Appears to be a hull breach, Commander,' said Nicola.

'Action?' he enquired again.

'Engineering already on it, according to the pressure drop, the breach is in section four.'

'Copied,' said Tom. 'Isolate section four. Partially repressurise sections three and five. Prepare the salvage team.'

'I see Commander Sampleman has that under control,' added Nicola again.

'Life support status?'

'Yes Commander, er, section four unusable, wait . . . , pressure drop section six AND seven.'

'Two breeches,' interjected Nicola, her fingers keying in data.

'Space debris,' growled Tom, 'screen status?'

Nicola hesitated; Tom didn't wait for an answer.

'Helm, ten degrees right.'

At that moment the ship flew into a cloud of tiny dust particles, possibly the tail of some long passed comet. The forward viewing portals became obscure, obliterated, as if someone had just 'turned off' the stars. The implication of a screen down at their speed was disastrous, even a piece of debris the size of a pea would penetrate the Enigma's pressure hull like a tiny ballistic missile. Tom looked at Nicola.

'The screens are down! Why wasn't I informed?'

Nicola paused, her mouth open, she had no answer. Tom selected the engineering control room again on screen four.

'Ross, deflector screen status?'

'I'm on it. Commander,' he replied. 'Polarity selector and particle generator showing green but the system's not responding. We are picking up multiple hull breaches. I'm not sure if I can maintain hull pressure.'

'Concur, Sir,' interjected Captain Raoul.

'Find the problem, Engineering, I'm counting on you! Arno, increase magnegrav to eighty percent. Use emergency atmospherics in sections one, two, and the engineering control room only. We need to conserve atmospherics, all personnel except essential engineers move to section two immediately. Close all emergency bulkheads.'

'Yes, Sir, underway.' Raoul's fingers flashed over his console panel.

Tom turned to his right. 'Nicola, deploy the laser cannon, autotrack mode, give it an acquisition arc of sixty degrees, rapid fire. Everything above five millimetres diameter gets vaporised.'

'I'm on it, Commander!'

Tom felt the magnagrav system increase polarity. It

dragged the toes of his boots onto the deck as he sat in his chair, making him pull his feet in.

The magnagrav system utilised a variable strength magnetic sub-deck, which attracted the special iron enriched flight boots worn by the astronauts. The system had an automatic mode, using inertia sensors to adjust the strength of the magnetic deck: higher in acceleration or deceleration phases, lower during stable flight phases. Alternatively, there was a manual mode selected during emergency or evasive manoeuvres or rapid depressurisation.

'Communications, get a message to Osiris, we have a problem. We may need their help.'

'Right away, Sir!'

'Ross, deflector screen status?'

'Still working on it!' came the reply.

It had been very quickly recognised, even during the earliest conceptual work on light speed travel, that a deflector screen of some kind was going to be necessary to protect a ship from impact damage caused by space debris. At these incredible velocities, even the tiniest sliver of rock or ice could puncture the hull of a ship, regardless of its construction, causing catastrophic failures, or even explosive vaporisation. The ingenious, pioneering engineering utilised in the Enigma's construction created an electrically charged cloud of sub atomic particles, which was projected far in front of the ship, indeed to several hundred miles. It worked on the theory that every body or particle in space, no matter how small, even a grain of dust, had electrical potential; an electric charge either positive or negative. The Enigma's system collected countless billions of negatively charged 'free' electrons, from the main thrust chambers by a continuous electrical suction onto positive collector plates; which are delivered through insulated ducting to an array of 'nose cone' mounted ejector ports. From there the electrons are sprayed under immense electrical pressure in front of the ship, forming a dense mist or cloud of negative polarity; the result, literally, a negatively charged balloon, almost a thousand miles long and five hundred miles wide at full power. Increasing electrical pressure would repel any positively charged piece of space debris. After a few seconds, depending on speed, the polarity of the cloud is switched to a positive charge by 'spraying' with protons, also derived from the main thrust chambers. These unfettered protons, redundant nuclear matter, resulting from the broken atomic nuclei of the barium fuel cells, being similarly attracted to negatively charged collector plates, are then, in turn, delivered to the alternating ejector ports of the shield system. The result: a similar protective balloon, but of positive charge. Alternating the polarity of the protective cloud effectively repelled ninety-nine percent of incoming space debris up to a predetermined size; whatever its electrical potential. Larger objects, with greater inertia, such as meteorites and comets had to be avoided by directional changes, which in turn required the forewarning of several thousands of miles. This process was difficult in practical operation and avoided by careful flight path scanning and screening; trajectory adjustments, as necessary, being made prior to acceleration. This work was done by Emily who, to date, could identify and track all major heavenly bodies up to nine light months from earth.

Finally, if all else failed, there was the powerful multi initiator laser weapon. With a range of up to ten thousand miles, it could vaporise smaller objects. In automatic mode, this weapon could lock and fire on an impressive one thousand targets per minute. In manual mode, it could be used as a point defence weapon directed by the helmsman.

Tom had done everything he could. All non-essential personnel had moved to sections one and two immediately behind the bridge, the remainder were in the engineering section. Here, atmospheric conditions were being maintained using the emergency systems. With Ross Sampleman and his department still working hard on the screen malfunction, Tom waited. He looked out, as far in front of the ship as possible, through the viewing portals; clearly sighting the frequent, fiery red, laser bursts. They fired out randomly, yet repeatedly, in all directions, followed by small explosions as dangerous pieces of space debris were vaporised. Enigma's hull had received multiple impacts, nine outer casing breaches and three through to the inner pressure hull. Tom noticed that the dust cloud was beginning to thin, but it still presented a clear and immediate threat to the integrity of his ship. Moreover, his request for communications with Osiris had been initiated, but failed, being heavily distorted by the effects of sub light speed. Tom waited, frustrated, hands tied.

Was there something else to be done? he thought.

Arno Raoul looked across at Tom, 'We're starting to lose atmospherics in section two, Sir,' he reported. 'One more hit and the system will be overloaded.'

'Understood, get the people into section one,' Tom replied. 'Close down section two. Close all remaining emergency pressure bulkheads.'

'Yes, Sir.'

Tom looked over his right shoulder again at Nicola. 'Standby to deploy emergency deceleration probe. Initialise emergency escape pod sequence. Await my further orders,' he instructed.

Nicola responded 'Immediately, Commander.'

'Engineering, what the hell is happening down there? I need answers,' he continued, his brow beginning to sparkle with perspiration.

Ross Sampleman appeared on screen four. 'I've located the problem, Commander, laying in an energy transfer now. Right side ejector nozzles have burnt out. Repulse shield to come on left side only, half lobe, that's the best I can do!'

'Acknowledged, when will I have it?'

'Standby, standby, now! You have left side shield at eighty percent.'

'Acknowledged,' responded Tom again, clipping the end of Ross's last word. 'Listen, Ross, can you deploy the emergency deceleration probe off centre? I mean the attachment point, on the extreme right side of the hull. I can then use manoeuvre thrust to slew the nose to the right.'

'I see where you're going with this, Commander,' answered Ross, 'so that the left shield covers our trajectory.' He paused looking at his control panel. 'No is the answer to that, I can do better, but it's risky?'

'Go on.'

'Deploy the thrust reverser spoilers on main chambers four and five. The drag caused by the debris cloud and solar wind will cause an off-centre slew, but the present speed is well above the design spec, they could be damaged or, worse still, detach.'

At that moment, Captain Raoul called across the bridge, from his expression it was clear that the situation was becoming dire. 'We've taken another penetration, section one. I'm losing the atmosphere, Commander. The bridge area will be affected in three minutes.'

Tom acknowledged with a nod, then turned to his science officer. 'Assessment?'

'The debris cloud is showing no signs of a density reduction from four point nine DKs. We could be in it for several minutes yet, Sir.'

A red warning light flashed on Tom's armrest control panel. The bridge atmospheric pressure and oxygen density was beginning to drop. He looked at Nicola.

'Ideas?' he asked, stern faced. He could almost feel her thinking.

'None Sir,' she replied, shaking her head.

Tom looked down at screen four.

'Do it, Ross! Deploy the thrust reversers,' he ordered without further delay.

Immediately the Enigma began to shake violently. Then, within a few moments, it had the desired effect. The nose of the ship was slowly dragged to the right; but its course remained unchanged. Tom selected the deflector screen overlay on his number one display. The left shield was covering the ship's passage. Immediately the visual picture cleared. Tom could see the stars again and the induced drag was slowing the ship.

'It's working, Ross, but it's hurting, I know. What's the vibration level?'

'Over the limits, but it's holding,' came the reply. 'But for how long, I wouldn't like to say.'

Tom looked at the science officer who was party to the conversation.

'Density showing signs of reducing, down six parts to four point three DKs,' she responded. 'I estimate another minute or so, another half million miles at this speed, then we will be clear.'

Tom didn't waste any time. 'Engineering,' he called,

'priority repairs to hull damage in section one. Close down your section, remote all control to Nicola's console here on the bridge. When you're done, you and your people up here; all available life support and atmospherics diverted to the bridge and section one. Select magnagrav to Emergency Level 1, that's all we can do!'

Sam Brennan spoke, 'Passing light decimal zero five, five, Sir and decelerating.'

'Copied, Sam,' said Tom. 'Engineering, vibration levels?'

'Down two points and decreasing,' Nicola replied.

'Good; navigation, how long to Mars please?'

'Nine minutes, Sir,' answered Lieutenant Bagley.

'Communications, try Mars again, tell them we will be entering the 'seventy percent' in about ten minutes. Request present status on the Columbus, we may need to evacuate.'

'Right away, Commander,' answered Isshi Tzou.

At that moment and without warning the bridge was plunged into almost total darkness, save for the glow of several console mounted computer screens.

'Everyone remains on station,' ordered Tom. Within a few seconds, the emergency lights flickered on. Tom had taken his seat. 'Nicola, status report?' he enquired.

Nicola was still engaged in her diagnosis, fingers skimming her keyboard like a touch typist. A series of system displays flashed across her screen; Tom watched her, this was her forte. System diagrams appeared so quickly he could barely identify them, but Nicola was running a fault profile on each.

'When you're ready.'

Nicola sensed Tom's gaze, despite his words, she felt the pressure; punching the last few keys purposefully, she looked across her left shoulder at him. Tom raised his eyebrows in anticipation.

'Power surge, primary and secondary inverter coils,' she reported bluntly. 'For some inexplicable reason the protection circuits have also failed. The surge has breached the duplex, triplex and quadtex flux gates to contaminate both standby inverters and it's taken those out too. We are running on emergency batteries, Commander, I've opened the solar cell visors, power services less than ten percent at the moment.'

Tom looked forward and breathed deeply. 'Isshi,' he said, 'any response?'

Cool under pressure, her manner barely changing, she replied, 'Columbus is out, Sir, we're on our own!'

Only the central screen of Tom's array functioned at emergency power levels. He selected Ross Sampleman's station in the control room; there was nobody there.

'Ross,' he whispered, 'where are you?'

Tom heard the whoosh of the bridge portal door closing.

'Right behind you, Commander,' came the reply. Ross walked across to Nicola's station and looked at her screen. 'I agree," he said, nodding, 'it's a good diagnosis.'

Tom reluctantly acknowledged the bad news, then asked, 'what's the hull situation, Ross?'

'We have patched section one, Commander, atmospherics are holding. All personnel are safely in this area, everywhere else is down!'

Sam Brennan interjected, 'below light related speed, Sir, and decelerating. We are in a safe zone for the emergency escape sequence.'

'How much time before orbital trajectory?' Tom responded.

Sam looked down again at his limited display, 'three minutes, Sir,' he replied.

'Three minutes!' Tom repeated, looking up at Ross. 'Can we do it?'

'No! At this power level we have life support only, no thrust controls.'

'Then we will miss the inception arc and continue past Mars!' Tom looked at the navigation officer. 'Benjamin, without Emily, can you plot our course through the remainder of the solar system?'

'I've done it, Sir,' came the immediate reply, 'but my calculations show that we won't get far. On this course and taking into account the gravitational effects of Mars, we will enter the outer rings of Saturn in twelve hours from now. As we can't control the deceleration or direction of the ship, that's approximate; maybe a little more maybe a little less,' he elaborated.

There was a brief moment of silence. The familiar rings

of the great planet Saturn, are composed of billions of tons of space debris; ranging from tiny dust particles to huge pieces of rock and ice, that more accurately could be described as meteorites. In addition, there were the gases, noxious and volatile, explosive and corrosive, no clarification was needed, their fate was sealed.

In the remote viewing gallery, all eyes were on Tom. His unpredictable, unorthodox and unexpected resolutions to the main scenarios had caused considerable debate. Interestingly, none of the problems encountered so far had a 'staff answer'; the scenarios were too complex. Rather, a series of recommended procedures to contain a situation and of course, depending on actions taken, a great many variables could also enter the equation. Most seemed impressed with the proceedings so far; Professor Nieve for his part, watched the final events unfold with great interest.

Tom stood up, 'listen everybody, let's put our heads together on this one,' he instructed, 'any ideas, anything at all?' Tom looked at Ross and Nicola. 'Listen guys, I need some power, enough for manoeuvre thrust at least; so get to it!' The pair acknowledged Tom's request and turned their attention to the electrical system schematics. Tom sat down, deep in thought. Presently he asked, 'life support, how much battery life?'

'The solar panels are charging at two percent, Sir, on minimum system demand we are using two point five.

With that deficit, I'd say twenty hours, no more,' answered Arno Raoul.

Ross turned to look at Tom. 'Commander, we have located the problem area: it's the central power distribution manifold, a massive short of some kind, or a massive current demand, seems to have just burnt out, melted, literally!'

'What could have caused that, Ross, we have four levels of internodal protection?'

'The protection systems were isolated, Commander, by someone or something!'

Tom hesitated for a moment. A massive demand for power, well above safety limits! What system could utilise that much electricity?

Tom looked up at the ceiling, Ross followed his eye line as did Nicola.

'Emily!' Tom concluded, 'it was Emily.'

There was a stunned silence.

'Is Emily online, Nicola?' Tom enquired.

'Not at this power level, Commander, she's not indicating anyway.'

'Emily,' demanded Tom, 'respond!'

'Emily, damn you, respond!' said Tom again raising his voice in an angry tone.

After several seconds, Emily's synthetic, yet flawless queen's English voice responded. 'Yes, Commander.'

'Restore power, Emily, immediately,' Tom ordered.

'I am afraid that your request is not possible,

Commander. The primary and secondary electrical manifolds are seriously damaged, they require extensive repairs before power can be restored.'

'Then find an alternative routing, Emily. I want enough power for manoeuvre control and I want it now!'

Again, there was a pause of several seconds, then, in an instant, the main bridge lighting flickered and then came on. Tom's display screens flashed into life.

'Manoeuvre control regained, Sir,' shouted Sam Brennan excitedly.

'Lay in the orbital entry coordinates, Sam, quickly.'

'Yes, Sir, I'm on it . . . it's done Sir, it's done; Mars, here we come.'

CHAPTER 21

A Level Too Far

Colonel Roper greeted Tom with a warm smile and an exaggerated handshake upon his arrival at the theatre. Inside, almost huddled together in the front row, were a handful of senior administrators; people Tom recognised as being directly involved with his selection. They included, as usual, a few officers in military uniform. Tom was pleased that the Sim check was over and the Colonel looked very satisfied. As the two men walked into the central area, Professor Nieve, who was sitting on the extreme left, indicated to him, at least that was what Tom thought, that the session had been a success. Apart from a thumbs up, Tom found himself a little perplexed by the Professor's rather difficult to follow hand signals.

'Good work,' said Colonel Roper. 'Very good I have to say.'

'Thank you, Sir,' replied Tom taking his seat in front of

the small assembly.

The debriefing took almost an hour, with each scenario being fully discussed. The outcome was indeed favourable and Tom looked quite happy with the whole process. Professor Nieve, for his part, closed the meeting.

'In conclusion, ladies and gentlemen, I think a fair appraisal would read; both comfortable and contented with all aspects of today's performance. Resolving the main scenarios demonstrated a level of knowledge, ingenuity, and initiative higher, quite frankly, than we were expecting.' He paused for breath, 'so, friends, I can tell you that the final preparations are now being completed on Spaceport 2 for the real thing, in two days time no less. It is an exciting time for all of us, the culmination of many years of work. However, in fear of stating the obvious, I think that is all I have to say at the moment. Thank you all very much for your time and comments.'

The meeting disbanded, Tom was leaving the room with Colonel Roper when the Professor requested a few minutes of his time. They sat down together.

'The Emily scenario, Tom,' explained Professor Nieve quietly, 'I wrote it only in the last few days. Most people did not know of its inclusion in the test, or its relevance. It's about Emily that I have to talk to you.'

The Professor had a grim, almost apprehensive expression; Tom noticed it and listened intently.

'We have been conducting the final system checks on the Enigma my boy; all areas. The integrated computer network checks OK on the face of it; however, we have been getting some unidentifiable fault codes and several intermittent, unrelated, electronic malfunctions. They come and go, apparently totally arbitrarily, only,' the Professor paused again and drew a slow, deep, breath. 'I see a pattern building; it is only when there is some human interaction, when someone, usually a solitary engineer is coordinating the checks. More particularly, when he or she is working at a control console, so that there can be no mistake about the occurrence; the history files verify this. We have not programmed any of the codes we are seeing. What is more, we cannot identify them and we cannot decode them.'

Tom looked puzzled; he opened his mouth to speak, only to be cut short by the Professor.

'I think, Tom,' he elaborated methodically, 'that they are being produced, synthesized, by Emily. It's almost as if she is playing with us; cat and mouse. We locate the fault and then it disappears just before we can down load it, or process it, or even attempt to trace it for that matter!'

'Can she do that?' enquired Tom.

The Professor paused for a few seconds and looked Tom directly in the eye. 'It's a theory, my only explanation; a gut feeling if you like. I have not shared it with anyone else. I just want you to be aware of her potential.'

Tom began to look very concerned.

'Emily is free thinking, my boy. She is two levels above self-awareness, as you know; a very powerful programme.

Restraining her physical abilities within the ship, in order to prevent another Skyport disaster, has been accomplished by physically disconnecting her extensive 'motive actuator' network; we have done this, but it is an afterthought. Not in line at all with the original design philosophy, and it only constrains part of her overall abilities. She has access, electronically, to almost all aspects of the entire ship's systems, she is fully integrated; indeed, that was the fundamental design criteria, the very heart of the concept in the first place. The yield matrix and associated software took years of work, literally, and was completed before our rude awakening to these problems by the rogue HU40's on board Skyport 1.

I myself wrote much of Emily's programming; she is focused on what we call the 'discipline foundation'. Essentially her programming is subservient; she will respond when ordered by you, or the other two named command prosecutors. I tried to demonstrate that to you in the simulator. I was pleased with your deduction. It is not possible for her to change, modify, or rewrite in any way that aspect of her programming, as there are blocking filters in the matrix. Nevertheless, if she gets access to someone or something that could reconnect her physically to the ship's systems, then effectively she will have total control. Remember this, Tom; be mindful of it. I am sorry to tell you this, but there is no time to resolve it before your departure.'

Tom nodded, 'I understand, Sir,' he said, 'I'll be careful.'

'Good, oh, and by the way, just to cheer you up; there will be several secondary systems that are unavailable to you for this mission.' Professor Nieve smiled, 'they will not affect the ship's capabilities, I can assure you of that. They include the radiation filters and the crew suspended animation centre, that sort of thing. I'll arrange for a full list to be made available to you later this evening.'

'OK, Professor.'

'Well, that's all,' concluded Professor Nieve, forcing a smile. 'It just remains for me to wish you the best of luck, and God's speed!'

'Thank you, Sir,' responded Tom, 'I appreciate that.'

CHAPTER 22

Too Late

Before returning to his quarters, Tom decided to visit the shuttle terminal, just to run a check, for his own benefit, on the mission's final preparations. The freight bay was a hive of activity with items being packed and loaded onto pallets for passage to the Enigma.

Tom walked the perimeter of the bay lost in thought. It was some distance, as the building's dimensions were considerable. It had an impressive glass roof, some five or six storeys above the ground and several crane gantries straddled the full width of the building. Tom watched for a few moments as two or three moved effortlessly backwards and forwards with packaged stores hanging below magnetic hooks.

Almost completing his circumnavigation, Tom spotted Nicola supervising the loading of some stores into a small, self-propelled flight pallet. Surprised to see her at this late hour, he walked across to say hello. She didn't see him, engrossed as she was in watching an operative carefully push the second of two rigid plastic containers, floating on magnetic flux casters, into the flight pallet. Tom tapped her on the shoulder and Nicola spun round, looking flustered.

'Hi, bit late to be doing this sort of thing, isn't it?' he asked, smiling.

Nicola flushed red, surprised, almost alarmed to see Tom, of all people.

'Oh, um, hello Tom. I mean, Commander,' she said looking up at his face.

'Tom's fine. You're keen, I'll give you that,' he said leaning over to look at the identification label on the white and grey container just as it disappeared into the pallet box. 'What's this, then?'

'Oh, just engineering spares,' Nicola replied hesitantly.

'Sonic combination locks, antistatic protection and self propelled magnetic flux castors. Must be important?' said Tom, straightening up and looking a little puzzled. As Nicola's face cooled, her blue eyes shifted nervously.

'No, not really, routine spares, you know. Actually, all freight for Enigma affords additional protection and packaging.'

Nicola stepped closer to Tom. She touched his arm affectionately.

'Tom, I've been meaning to talk to you for several days; I suppose I have some explaining to do.'

'No,' replied Tom casually, his puzzled expression hardening. 'I'd say you did a few years ago Nicola, but now, no explanation required!'

Nicola looked disappointed. She was just about to speak when the stores operative interrupted her.

'Excuse me, m'am,' he said 'is that all? Can I close up and prepare this consignment for despatch?'

Nicola looked at the man, his thick glasses magnifying his eyes to almost comical proportions.

'Yes, of course, as quickly as possible.'

With that, she ignored the man completely and leant forward towards Tom, her right breast gently squeezing against his chest. A knowing smile crept across her lips as she unzipped her tunic a few inches; the high collar opened to reveal her bare neck and more than a hint of cleavage. Tom's expression went from surprise and disbelief, to uncertainty, then back to puzzled nonchalance.

'Can't we be friends again, Tom?' she asked, pulling the toggle on her zip a little lower. Tom was speechless and stood there blankly for a few moments. 'Tom, we can have that life again, personal and professional kept apart, we've done it before. You know I still have feelings for you.'

Tom looked down at Nicola's exposed cleavage then into her captivating clear blue eyes. 'If I didn't know better, Nicola,' he said without emotion, 'I'd say you were hiding something, and if I were you I'd hide those as well! Someone may get the wrong idea.'

With that, he gripped her gently by the waist and pushed

her away. 'It's an early start tomorrow; I'd get some rest if I were you.' He turned and left for his quarters.

Nicola smirked as she watched Tom leave the freight bay. Zipping up her tunic, she looked around to see if anyone else had been watching. Either way, she did not seem to mind.

CHAPTER 23

Like Father Like Son

The evening of the fourth day was both remarkable and unremarkable. Remarkable because at eighteen hundred hours, having made the first historic acceleration to light related speed, the Enigma had slipped back precisely and effortlessly into a sub-light regime in preparation for taking up the prescribed orbit around Mars. Every aspect of the pioneering flight had gone to plan, except perhaps for communications, which, at the highest velocities, had suffered unexplained distortions and interference as to make either real time or synchronized communication impossible.

Yet the ambience on board Enigma was one of cool professional competence, just another evening of quiet routine. Most of the crew had stood down from their duties and were resting, just a skeleton crew was operating the bridge and engineering departments. In nineteen hours and seven minutes, Enigma would establish orbit, having achieved the incredible transit time of five days and four hours. Her present sub light velocity had enabled re-establishment of communications both with earth and with Osiris, using the Accelercom system. At this point Tom had felt confident enough to take a reasonable rest period and had retired to his quarters; two compact but functional rooms positioned one level above the bridge. From there, as one would expect, he had a privileged, but restricted, forward view of space, through two narrow viewing portals.

Ross Sampleman was on duty in the engineering room and had assumed command. As a result, Nicola had also been relieved from her duties on the bridge, for a few hours rest. The ship was unusually quiet, dictated in part by the Diurniphase life support system. Designed and installed specifically for extended interstellar flights, this ingenious system had few benefits to offer on the five-day flight to Mars. Nevertheless, it had been successfully tested and was expected to prove invaluable on future missions to our closest stars, the nearest of which, Alpha Centuri, would take several years to reach.

The Diurniphase system went some way to mimicking the diurnal or daily variations of sunlight and temperature, which governs, in part, the normal biorhythms of animals on earth. By using an array of specifically designed multi-functioning overhead lights throughout the ship, each capable of emitting both visible and invisible light, just like the sun, a synthetic day/night regime is produced. The intensity of visible white light is varied through a twenty-four hour period: brightest in the region of midday, and subtly subdued during the synthetic night. Where additional white light is required during the night, light stations in the walls and bulkheads are selected either manually or automatically. In addition to visible light, the invisible spectrums are also represented; namely by the infra-red and ultraviolet wavelengths. Infra-red, as with the sun, is used to create a warming sensation during the day, whilst ultraviolet is used for skin colour, vitamin D production and several subconscious body clock functions. The intensity and exposure rate are all controlled by the integrated life support system. As with the rising of the sun, infra-red and ultraviolet light levels increase slowly from early morning until a diurnal maximum is reached around mid-afternoon, reducing again to trace levels after sunset; and so with the Diurniphase system, which goes some way to reproducing this fundamental process on board the Enigma for the benefit of the crew. Substantial research had proved conclusively that retaining and maintaining, as much as possible, the natural biorhythms of crew members whilst in space, produced overwhelming benefits ranging from mental and physical health, to a reduction in fatigue and anxiety. Emily, for the most part, had a controlling influence on the system's programming, as she knew exactly the diurnal variations that affect Houston, Texas on an ideal day. Houston was chosen as the system datum, as it was from there that the majority of the crew had left earth, bound for the Enigma and her maiden voyage.

Therefore, it was in subdued lighting that a lone figure walked quietly along the lowest deck level of the ship's seven decks. In a one-piece black working suit, a pulled up hood and soft sucker-shoes instead of the mandatory magnegrav boots, there was, on the face of it, no reason for any crew member to be in this part of the ship. After an indirect and evasive route, the figure arrived at the end of a corridor where three sliding portals, two large and one small, allowed access into the main storage hold. Keying a six-digit code into the control pad, the smaller personnel door on the left hand side, slid open; the figure stepped carefully inside, and the door closed quietly.

Using a small handset with a simple red and green indicator light, it took just a few minutes to locate a particular freight container. Within seconds, the container door was open, and a pallet box, floating on flux castors, gently manoeuvred out of the door. When clear, the castors were de-energised and the box settled gently on the deck. A ring of integral magnetic coils, the anti static device, was also de-energised.

The pallet box was bulky: about two metres long, a metre high, and a little under a metre wide, it looked heavy. Coding the two sonic combination locks that subsequently sprang open, the figure stood back as the box slowly opened by splitting down the middle, the two halves controlled by hydraulic levers, until they rested on the shiny metallic deck. In each half was a large black polyplastic bag, almost like a mortuary bodybag, their contents held firmly in place by shaped and contoured foam rubber inserts. Gloved hands broke a consignment seal on each, then partially opened the bags: first the left, then the right. Then the figure reached inside, fumbling initially in the poor light. In response, a small red light glowed from within each bag. Fully opening each in turn, the black plastic material was then gently pulled back to reveal two frightening metallic figures. Stuck over a central control panel, about one hundred millimetres square, was a white plastic label. On it in bold red letters were the words:

DANGER
NO UNAUTHORISED ACCCESS
LEVEL 7 PROGRAMMING

The intruder ripped off the labels, screwed them up, and threw them into the box, then, in turn, lifted a protective transparent plastic cover. From a side pocket on the intruder's suit, a small, rigid case was drawn, like a man's wallet; from it, two programming and initialisation chips, about four centimetres long and three wide, were very carefully withdrawn. One chip was inserted into a receptor on each control panel. The result of this action was instantaneous, taking the intruder by surprise, who sprang up, stumbled, and almost fell over backwards.

The two control panels had lit up in unison, with several lights either on or flashing; electric motivators began to whirl and hum and then there was movement! Two robotic legs, which had been bent double, rose slowly from the left-hand container and straightened; then two arms, which had been secured across the chest of the machine, followed at the far end of the box, by its head. The head continued upwards, almost vertically, to at least a metre, on a flexible neck of linked metal rings; broad at the shoulder but tapering. Following this, both outstretched arms bent backwards at the elbow. Two, four fingered, metallic hands grasped the box rim. Then, with one powerful movement, the machine lifted itself; with ungainly coordination, like a foal trying to stand for the first time, the robot stood up, flexed to its full stature and stepped clear of its cage.

The whirring commotion to its left startled the machine, as its sensors became operational. Without moving its body, the long neck extended to its full length again, its head leaning over its mechanical brother, whilst peering intently at the thrashing movement that had developed from inside the restrictive bodybag. The intruder stepped backwards, alarmed at what was unfolding; but that movement was enough to trigger the robot's sensors and with its neck remaining below shoulder height, its head rotated cautiously. Almost like a compass scribing a large arc it turned, scanning methodically until it found the figure, now, understandably, almost cowering in the shadows.

With glowing, neon red, teardrop shaped eyes, it stared. Then, its head rose again, only this time much slower, until it was again at its full height, almost three metres. It was an awesome sight, frightening yet impressive, a pinnacle of man's technological abilities. In an instant, the robot stepped clear of its box and with apparent ease, violently ripped the debilitating cover off its neighbour. Seconds later the second robot attempted unsuccessfully to stand; in its frustrating struggle, it appeared even more menacing than the first. The machines looked at each other, then began communicating in a series of electronic tones; similar, it appeared, to the tones heard when connecting facsimile machines.

'Speak English,' demanded the intruder, stepping from the shadows. It was a woman's voice.

'Recipient,' replied the left-hand machine in a metallic, synthesised voice, its brightly glowing eyes changing colour, through orange, green and then to blue. The colour seemed to reflect the machine's mood: red when threatened or unsure of its surroundings, to colours further down the visible light spectrum when less harassed. 'Recipient', was a programmed response; it abbreviated received, processed and obedient, meaning that it had understood the order and would comply.

The second robot eventually struggled to its feet, violently discarding the remaining restrictive packaging.

It repeatedly but unsuccessfully attempted to lift its left leg in order to step out of the container, and was becoming aggravated. Instead, a whirring, humming noise was heard. The robot looked down at its hip joint; a tiny electrical motivator spun helplessly, its splintered drive shaft shattered during the robot's blind struggle to free itself of the encasing packaging. The machine looked up, menacingly.

'Motivator, left hip joint damaged,' it screeched, having assessed the problem, 'restricted movement!'

The two robots 'spoke' again in electronic tones, and with that, the damaged one stepped clear of the container using its right leg, then, awkwardly, pulled its left limb out, as if it were paralysed. It walked, or, more accurately limped, from behind the container towards the woman, using the bi-directional knee joint to push the damaged leg forward; this troubled motion was accompanied by an eerie clank and then a scraping noise as the foot of the damaged limb dragged across the metal deck.

Clank, scrape, clank, scrape, the noise sent shivers down the spine of the woman, who took two nervous steps backwards as the robot approached her. With forced confidence she spoke.

'Close the containers and replace them in the freight pallet, be sure not to leave any traces of packaging; then remain hidden here. Do not, repeat, do not, show yourself until I give you the order. I will come for you soon.'

The dominant machine began to reply, 'Recip . . .'

Immediately the head of the damaged machine span round, its long neck extending towards its colleague, cutting short its response with a stream of electronic clicks and tones. Its head rose to full height, tracked slowly towards the woman, then, like an attacking cobra, made a strike down towards her, until it stopped abruptly a few centimetres from her concealed face; there was silence, this was the dominant machine, there was no doubt.

'Recipient,' it said coldly, callously.

With that, the woman turned and left the freight bay, she did not look back until the portal door had closed behind her. If she had, she would have seen the two robots tracking her every move, their heads moving, twitching, up and down, side to side, almost perceptibly, thinking.

Each 'face' then showed a different image; changing images, old newsreel footage. They flashed from one scene to another with amazing speed. Fighter planes in combat from the Second World War, the desert wars of 2007. Then the most disturbing, the dominant machine displayed newsreel footage of the space station Skyport falling from space, filmed from a tailing fighter aircraft. The image continued, the giant station visibly breaking up as it re-entered the earth's atmosphere, until finally the main body crashed amidst a huge explosion into the suburbs of Houston. Plain to see were the scenarios, and all had something in common.

After taking several steps away from the portal, the woman did stop, momentarily, to regain her composure.

She appeared visibly shaken by her actions and their impending implications. Inside the freight bay, the damaged robot issued instructions to the other using a stream of complicated electronic tones; a binary language not created by their makers, but one that was the result of complex programming, combined with free and logical thought.

The machines were indeed technological masterpieces. Standing as tall as a man, their structure, an 'Etheral' alloy skeleton, was very similar to that of a human. However, in place of a ribcage was a rigid box structure, tapering at the waist. Within this was the powerplant: a combination of high capacity catholithium batteries and photoelectric converters, which, after thirty minutes exposure to white light, could produce and store enough electrical energy to power the machine for twenty-four hours. There was also an emergency power supply; a small cryptogenic power cell that, if the machine was closed-down to 'retentive animation' power levels, could retain 'body and mind' functional programming for twenty years or more. In addition, within the boxed chest cavity was the primary memory processor banks and motivators; the latter being powerful electric motors providing mobility and immense strength. This framework was covered in a transparent and flexible celluloid skin about one centimetre thick, which provided bulk and impact resistance. Sealed within this skin, under pressure, was an oily electrolytic fluid. Much like an inflated balloon, this fluid pressure gave the structure shape, a humanoid form and in addition, the fluid allowed electrical signals to pass from the 'brain' to the motivators. The whole system provided joint stability, movement, and simultaneously, their lubrication. The arms were abnormally long, proportionate to that of the primates to provide additional reach; only the last two joints of the metal fingers protruded from the cellulose skin that covered the four-fingered clawlike hands. This afforded a high level of dexterity as the machines were designed to be able to carry out intricate external repairs to orbiting spacecraft as well as operating complex control stations and keyboards.

In essence, these machines were constructed to relieve humans of the laborious, monotonous or dangerous tasks, which were inherent with long periods in space. Their heads, shaped like an X, but with a lower crossing point to form two dissimilar sized triangles, appeared disproportionately large at the end of highly flexible, multi-facetted necks. Engineered with a much-reduced diameter at the top, the neck was spliced into the rear of the head directly at the crossing point. Below this crossing point, forming the smaller triangle, was a fine silver coloured metal grill, which covered two vertical slits for odour sensing, and a circular cavity. Within this cavity, advanced electronic vocal chords produced synthesized speech; the programming of several human languages had been incorporated.

The main facial area, the upper triangle, was an advanced

plasma display screen, which could not only produce amazing three-dimensional images, like some precocious laptop computer, but also incorporated 'Plasmoltec' technology. With this state of the art materials technology, the screen appeared to be like semi-molten plasticine; it could move, distort, stretch and contract. From a flat screen, a face, taken from just below the nose, could be conjured, moulded, with all its nuances; expressions so created, fused from one to another entirely at the will of the machine. However, there was one phenomenon that the designers had not incorporated into these cybersystems, and one that remained unexplained.

By a quirk of programming, random binary code distortion, or possibly a memory stream mismatch, there were times when the robots themselves projected images onto their faces, apparently subconsciously. Occasionally, usually at times of high workload or stress, they seemed to have no control over what was being displayed and these images, usually drawn from their extensive historical memory files, appeared to project what they were thinking; even if it differed from their programmed response. In essence, it was a sub neural giveaway; their Achilles heel.

All this technology required power, to this end, the back of the head together with the back of the trunk, was composed of an array of shiny graphite coloured photoelectric cells. The menacing eyes were essentially projections; images, displayed on the facial screen. In liaison, manipulation of the screen's plasticity could produce contours, which appeared to make the eyes real, even down to a blinking response; it was the eyes, their changing shape and colour that gave the robots their deathly, sinister appearance. Capable of infra-red sight, giving vision even in the darkest environments, they glowed with an intensity proportionate to the power levels of the machines' internal batteries.

The robots did as they had been bidden, this time.

CHAPTER 24

England Expects

Richard was the first to arrive in the changing room annexed to flight despatch. He sat down on a plastic bench and began removing his favourite black leather flying boots, as these were no longer compatible with any of his current protective equipment, except, of course, his obsolete navy flying suit. He looked around at the familiar and yet unfamiliar surroundings; it seemed so long ago that he had prepared for a space flight. Personnel from the Survival Equipment Department, who were responsible for flight clothing, helmets, life support and all emergency equipment had prepared and hung two Mk55 flight suits on hangers in the open locker at the far end of the room. Richard looked up at a white plastic marker board, measuring about a metre square, mounted on the wall to his right. Reading the flight details of the last mission, which had been written in permanent luminescent yellow pen, he smiled, albeit nervously.

Captain Martin Martens
Captain Maria Rainy
28 August 2042.
S1 orbital flight to repair communication satellites
CPT420 & navigation satellite NPT116.

Richard whistled, rather impressed and rather surprised. The flight had taken place six years earlier, to the day! Losing himself in his thoughts for a moment, he said quietly to himself, 'a lot of water has gone under the bridge since then.'

'And what bridge would that be, Richard?' echoed Rachel's voice, wrenching him away from his memories.

'Oh, hi Rachel,' he replied, more glad to see her than he was letting on. 'That bridge, you know the one; the one under which all your expectations disappear and only rarely reappear from under the other side.'

That remark stopped Rachel in her tracks. She looked at him, concerned. 'Feeling OK for this, Richard?'

'Yes, of course, but I'll admit, I am feeling a little apprehensive. I mean, this old bus hasn't flown for six years?' He looked across at the marker board, and with a barely perceptible gesture, beckoned her to look as well.

'Yes, I know, but the Columbus is probably in better condition than some of the S2s; the medical equipment, for example, barely used. Anyway, you're the best and most qualified pilot, you can handle any eventuality!'

Wanting to say something but deciding not to, Richard shrugged his shoulders, eventually squeezing Rachel's hand and smiling.

'Anyway, where's Horowitz?'

'He's just completing his pre-flight medical check with Bill. They will be here shortly.'

Rachel took Richard's place on the plastic bench, as he stood up to get changed. She watched quietly as he dressed: initially the norax thermal suit, then the paper-thin one-piece raybann radiation coverall, and finally the white Mk55 flight suit. He could feel Rachel staring at him, but didn't look at her. Finally zipping up the suit, from the waist on his left-hand side, across to his right shoulder, he stood tall and bounced a few times on his toes to loosen the layers and remove any 'pinches'.

Pulling the bubble helmet from the top shelf of the adjacent cupboard and tucking it under his arm, he eventually turned to look at Rachel, who had acted quite normally up to that point. They looked at each other for several seconds.

Then Richard said, 'I'll be off then,' and smiled faintly.

Rachel opened her mouth to say something, only to be frustrated by the sound of footsteps and talking. Moments later, Lieutenant Horowitz and Dr. Bill Bates walked into the changing room. An awkward pause followed before Rachel stood up and turned to her colleague.

'So, everything OK?'

'Yes. M'am, no problems that I can see,' Bill replied.

'Morning Herman, you're feeling ready for this I trust?' Richard asked.

'I'm actually looking forward to it, if you must know; a bit of excitement for a change.'

Richard turned to Rachel. 'Bit of excitement?' he said sarcastically, 'see what we can do then!'

Rachel disarmed the situation with a parry of concern.

'Just be careful out there, both of you!'

Richard nodded, agreeing and continued, 'I'm going to warm up the beast, get yourself kitted up, Herman. Take your time; I'll see you when you're ready, we still have an hour to go before take off.'

Horowitz obligingly nodded.

'Catch up later, then.'

With that, Richard left the room and began to walk down towards flight despatch. Rachel caught up with him just before he pushed open the large swing doors; she put a hand on his face.

'I'll see you later, then,' she whispered tenderly. 'Now behave yourself, standard operations, nothing more, nothing less.'

Without bothering to check if anyone was around, which was unusual for Richard, he gave her a lingering kiss on the lips, nodded in agreement, then pushed the doors open with his shoulder and walked into despatch. The door swung closed behind him, leaving Rachel outside.

Pete Manley looked up from the computer terminal on the despatch desk.

'Hey Richard, how's it going?' he shouted, in order to be heard above the general mêlée of activity.

'Good. Is she ready?' Richard replied with equal volume.

'Yes, I think so, just running the final engineering checks. Number two tank is taking a little longer to fill than usual, but that's nothing to worry about; I think the valves are sticking.'

'I need it at least sixty percent, Pete,' Richard reminded the head of the engineering department.

Pete Manley nodded, holding up his right thumb for a moment before submerging again into his work.

Richard looked over to his left, the nose section of the S1, to a little aft of the main personnel door, was protruding through the curved self-sealing hangar doors of the despatch dome. It resembled a frog or lizard pushing its head into an oxygen bubble whilst underwater, for a life-saving breath. Intermittent streams of oxygen and carbon dioxide discharged from beneath the craft with an accompanying whoosh, as the venting gases condensed to form white columns of opaque smoke, before harmlessly evaporating into the air. Several engineers were working in and around the ship, and Richard could see at least two large electrical cables that were still plugged into fuselage sockets.

He caught Pete Manley's eye again, pointed to himself

and then the Columbus, indicating his request to board the craft. Manley beckoned him over by holding up a pen and writing in the air. Richard walked over to the desk, forgetting that, as Commander, he had to sign the technical logbook prior to flight, thereby assuming responsibility for the craft.

Manley patted him on the back. 'She's a good old bird,' he said, 'look after her and she'll look after you!'

'Always,' replied Richard with a friendly smile.

Climbing into the left-hand pilot's seat, Richard felt confident. An engineer plugged two life support connections, one electrical and one oxygen, into receptors on his suit, and placed the emergency helmet on a stand immediately adjacent to, but slightly behind, his left shoulder. The S1 had full internal atmospheric control; having been designed for a maximum of twelve passengers and four crew, enjoying the long transit to Mars. The helmet would only be required in the event of an emergency depressurisation.

Richard scanned his instrument display; engineering already had most of the systems running. He checked the overhead panel and selected a few switches, then positioned his earpiece and microphone.

'Flight deck, communications check,' he said, 'how do you hear?'

'Five by five,' was the reply.

Horowitz climbed into the right hand seat. Barely

giving him any time to strap in, Richard asked, 'Herman please run the profile, prepare for rollback.'

Commencing a variety of switch selections whilst still adjusting his harness, Horowitz responded sharply, 'will do!'

The last remaining engineer tapped Richard on his shoulder and gave him the thumbs up. Giving him a few moments to leave, Richard switched the main personnel door selector to close, and felt the internal pressure increase on his eardrums a few moments later as a result; a red light extinguished. The S1 class was a large ship, being almost four hundred metric tonnes at maximum orbital weight and some twenty percent bigger than its successor the S2. Propelled principally by two advanced, but none the less conventional, liquid oxygen and hydrogen rocket motors, essentially designed some eighty years earlier for the Saturn Programme, producing an enormous nine hundred thousand pounds of static thrust, they were ridiculously thirsty and long since obsolete.

'Ready for rollback,' stated Richard.

'Commencing rollback,' replied the despatch controller, 'standby for retro sequence.'

The giant S1 moved off the platform for the first time in six years. The rolling gear, similar to the chassis of a giant locomotive on an old railroad track, squeaked and clattered as the nose of the S1 withdrew from the despatch dome. Self-sealing thermoplastic doors progressively filled the void; it was another five minutes before Richard felt the ship shudder to a halt on the launch pad.

'Initiating retro sequence.'

'Combined systems green, Sir,' came the reply.

'Ignition on main engines.'

'Ignition sequence green,' replied Horowitz, 'engaging auto control for lift off.'

'Negative! I'll take it manually.'

'That's not standard, Sir, are you sure that's wise?' questioned Horowitz.

'After six years, it wouldn't be wise not to.'

Horowitz confused by the double negative, nodded. 'It's your prerogative, Sir.'

'Ask for take off clearance, Herman, manual climb out,' ordered Richard.

'Control, this is Columbus, requesting lift off clearance, manual climb out.'

There was a delay of several seconds before the reply. In the control room, the two operators looked at each other, puzzled.

'OK. All systems green and go for, er, manual climb out! Use initial vector three four zero degrees, clear lift off; unrestricted climb to elliopheric level six five.'

'Three four zero degrees, level sixty five confirmed,' replied Horowitz, 'that's in the box.'

'Standby for lift off,' said Richard, advancing the retro sequencer to eighty percent.

The retro sequencer automatically adjusted the precise thrust of each of the four retrorockets in order to maintain the craft in a level attitude. It was a useful tool and normally mandatory in all vertical flight regimes. As the thrust indicator passed fifty percent amid a mass of swirling red dust, Richard felt the S1's massive hydraulic undercarriage oleos slowly extend; the ship began to rise. At sixty percent, with the whole craft starting to vibrate violently, the main flight controls began to respond. Richard focused his concentration on both the engine health monitoring system and the autostabilisation system; flying the climb out profile itself would be second nature. Seventy percent saw the craft lift clear of the pad; it was an awesome sight. Rachel had joined a small group of observers in the control room, as the huge black and grey bulk of the S1, now about three hundred feet above the platform, began to transition forward. With the nose of the craft beginning to rotate upwards, Richard continued, 'Beta Transition, engage main engines.'

'Main engines engaged, Sir, indications normal,' replied Horowitz.

'Thank you, confirm manual thrust control.'

'You have manual control.'

'Roger, increasing thrust on the main engines.'

With the attitude of the S1 pointing skywards, an elevation of approximately thirty-five degrees nose up and supported by the four flame spitting retro rockets, which by now had stabilised at eighty percent of their maximum thrust, Richard gingerly pushed the two control levers forward and watched carefully the temperature indications of the exhaust ducts. The huge rocket motors burst into life and the exhaust gas temperature quickly passed two thousand degrees. Richard's handling of the engines was delicate to say the least. He knew that if there was going to be a problem, it would happen now, as maximum thrust was being achieved; particularly after so many years of laying idle. Horowitz began to see why Richard preferred manual control for this initial transition, as the instruments indicated quite clearly, where the automatic digital engine controls would have positioned the power levers and it proposed a much more aggressive power application than perhaps was prudent.

The S1 transitioned forward and accelerated quickly. As the main engines themselves passed fifty percent, a deep rumbling vibration pervaded the craft. Richard was careful not to turn onto the initial climb out course until he was well over ten thousand feet above the planet surface, as below that altitude the powerful rocket blast cold damage sensitive external equipment on Osiris. As the S1 gradually disappeared into the dark Martian sky, finally even the glow of the rocket motors being lost to the naked eye, those gathered in the control room slowly dispersed, and very little was said.

Commander Miko, who had joined the group late, turned to Rachel, he could sense her apprehension; he wasn't blind to the relationship that had developed under his command and anyway, he was happy with the discretion exercised by the pair.

'Nicely flown, considering he hasn't done it for a while,' he commented, smiling.

Rachel nodded, smiling back, her shoulders visibly relaxing as pent up tension eased. 'He's not too bad really, I suppose,' she replied.

The Commander's tone changed. 'Rachel, I need to talk to you about the recent deaths; I understand that you have decided not to perform post mortems, instead, to suspend the bodies in Predestine Stasis for the operation to be performed on earth.'

'Yes, that's right, Commander, I don't hold a large stock of the equipment I need for the procedure and having performed two just recently, I'd like to keep what I've got left.'

'OK, I understand, but will the outcome of the procedure, or more to the point, the delay in the results, have any bearing on the pending investigation? You know what I mean, don't you?'

'Yes, Commander, I do and in my view, it won't. Both men died from the effects of a high frequency sonic discharge, that is clear, and of course, the associated peak voltage induced thermal shockwave. The autopsy will just confirm that and give anatomical specifics based on that hypothesis. I can't sign the death certificates until I have the results of the autopsy, as you know; should there be any deviations, the NASA coroner will get involved. In my opinion, Sir, the report compiled by my department will be confirmed in due course.'

'All right, Rachel, that's good enough for me. Presumably the bodies will be ready for transporting by the deadline?'

Rachel nodded.

'Good, there will be a short service of remembrance in the chapel at nineteen hundred hours tonight. I'd like it if you would represent Richard as head of department.'

'Of course, Sir, full dress uniform I presume?'

'Actually no, not this time, I've specified duty officers' attire. We are all too busy to get involved with formal military protocol. I'll request a full service be performed in Houston.'

Rachel responded to the Commander's comments with a faint smile and a nod, as Ralph Mildenhall, one of the operations officers approached them.

'Excuse me Sir, just to let you know, the Columbus is safely established in prescribed orbit. All systems green. Not bad for an old bird!'

'You're right Ralph, not bad at all, although I suspect Lieutenant Commander Reece had something to do with that! When is the planned rendezvous with Enigma?'

Enigma has already begun decelerating, Sir; she's some sixteen million, nine hundred and ninety thousand miles out, as of about three minutes ago. With the time syncopation, her signals are arriving with a FURRS probability of point nought one two; that's a wider spread than anticipated; Communications are still working on the mismatch. To be honest Sir, nobody is quite sure about the communication access node. We have established communications of sorts, but it's probable that we will have to wait until she's much slower before we can hook a clear audio visual signal?'

Rachel was both confused and intrigued; she knew some basic theories about light speed travel, relativity for instance, but none of the practicalities. 'What's FURRS?' she asked Ralph Mildenhall.

'FURRS m'am, stands for Future Reality Ratio Spectrum. As the Enigma was moving at light related speed, well, point four seven two one to be precise, the perceived time on board actually slowed down when compared to our time here on Mars. As an example; the transit time is expected to be around six days for us, but for those on board it will be perceived to be around five and a half days, so, when they arrive, we will have aged by six days since they left the earth, but they will have aged only five or so. If we could see them they would appear to be moving in slow motion, and their voices would be low and drawn out, like reducing the speed on an old digital disc. These factors and some others, combine to give us a horrible problem with communications; as their signals arrive some considerable time in the future relative to us, whilst our signals appear to arrive before we have sent them to them. They are actually listening to our future! This confuses the hell out of the electronics, so we have to modify the signal, delaying it in our reality, or in their reality, accelerating it; synchronize it if you like, so that their message appears to be transmitted a fraction of a second after it actually was, and visa versa. It's the only way for us to have a two way conversation in real time, or, apparent time,' Ralph shrugged his shoulders, 'if you know what I mean?'

Rachel thought she knew what he meant, opened her mouth to respond, but for some reason or another was rendered speechless.

Commander Miko interjected, 'I think the six day transit time has impressed her somewhat, Ralph, how long will it take to calculate the ratio?'

'I don't know Sir, we are on it, earth's on it, it's all new and the predictions aren't accurate; there's some sort of time bending going on. It's not linear as we expected, kind of a space time distortion; the good old fashioned phrase, time-warp, appears to be a reality!'

'OK,' responded the Commander frowning, 'so when do you hope the rendezvous will take place?'

'Ah, well Sir, I can answer that one; about three hours from now, if her deceleration rate continues as predicted. We expect Enigma to enter an extended orbit at about thirteen hundred hours. The Columbus will close from its lower orbit as soon as it's safe, to establish the rendezvous trajectory; we have to be very careful not to conflict at any time with the orbits of Deimos or Phobos, I expect that will take an hour at least.'

'Why so long?' queried the Commander.

Ralph Mildenhall drew a deep breath; he had hoped to avoid this topic of conversation. 'The automatic guidance systems installed in the S1 Class were never configured for this kind of manoeuvre, Sir. The systems are relatively antiquated, even the S2 would only be capable of semi-automatic guidance!'

'So?'

'So, we will do the calculations, Sir, and Lieutenant Commander Reece will fly the manoeuvre manually.' Lieutenant Mildenhall stopped short at this remark and looked a little apprehensive, not exactly sure how the Commander would react to this news.

'Was this planned?' responded the Commander, wondering why he hadn't been told of this.

'It's the way we have to do it, Sir, it's the only way, we are not configured for the Enigma; nobody is for that matter. It simply wasn't due out of development for at least two or three years. I thought you were informed of this by the operations officer?'

'I probably was, but it didn't register, so it's down to Richard again?'

'Well, not entirely, Sir, we'll tell him what to do and he'll do it, hopefully.'

'Hopefully,' Commander Miko raised his eyebrows until they almost met his greying fringe and looked directly at the now rather nervous control officer. 'Well, all I can say is we've got the best man on the job, don't you think?'

'Er, yes Sir, absolutely.'

With that, the Commander turned to leave the control room. 'I'll see you later, Rachel,' he said before the door slid closed behind him.

CHAPTER 25

Three's a Crowd

With a precise approach trajectory, the Enigma reduced to orbital speed and subsequent to the firing of several short bursts from the manoeuvring thruster, it entered the planned elliopherical orbit at seven minutes past one Martian corrected time. The crew of the Columbus, having already coordinated orbital velocity and opening rates, began final preparations for the docking of the two vessels.

Only a generation apart in terms of age, yet as distant technologically as Scorpio 4224, our nearest inhabited solar system, it was, thought both commanders, ironic that such a crucial manoeuvre should rely again on the skill and dexterity of the human hand. After all, it was believed to be that same dexterity and acquired skills that had directed man's evolutionary highway in the first place.

'Establish communications with Columbus, please,'

requested Tom of Captain Tsou. 'Request a common open frequency for the link up.'

'Right away, Commander.'

Tom sat back in his chair. 'That was the easy part,' he thought, 'now life is going to get interesting.'

'The channel is open, Commander.'

'Good, switch to open bridge.'

'It's open, Sir.'

Although he could not be seen, Tom stood up to begin this initial conversation; he would learn something of the Columbus's Commander from this foray. In the Columbus, Richard and Horowitz were wearing their pressure suits and helmets. It was a precautionary measure; if anything went wrong with the docking manoeuvre, he had no intention of being caught out by an emergency depressurisation. Compared to the hull of the Enigma, the Columbus's structure was wafer thin. Richard looked up and peered through the small glass portal above his head. His radar was tracking the Enigma and he expected to gain a visual contact at any moment; her orbit would allow an eight-mile separation.

'God, there she is, look at her!' Herman strained his neck in an effort to catch a glimpse of the substantially larger vessel.

'Hold on,' said Richard again, firing two short bursts of the forward retros. With that, the nose of the Columbus slowly rose; within seconds, the Enigma came into sight through the main windscreen. The two men sat in stunned silence; she was quite a sight.

'Awesome,' said Horowitz, almost in slow motion.

'Yes, I think that quite aptly describes her,' replied Richard equally fixated. Almost on cue, the radio added the final impressive touch.

'This is Commander Tom Race of the International Space Federation Ship Enigma calling the Columbus. Come in Columbus.'

Richard paused for a few seconds before replying, 'reading you five by five Enigma, go ahead.'

'Also strength five; pleased to say we have visual contact with you Columbus, request your status?' Tom walked towards Isshi Tsou's console, as if doing so would improve the clarity of the reply.

'All systems green, Enigma. Ready when you are,' replied Richard as calmly as possible.

Tom, for reasons known only to himself, wanted to know to whom he was speaking, as if it made a difference; he began to enquire, but was cut short by another radio transmission.

'This is flight operations Osiris base on open channel, confirm your status, Enigma?'

'Also green,' replied Tom curtly. As if they would have been anything else?

'Copied, Enigma,' came the reply, 'confirm stabilised below zero point two concentricity?'

'Also confirmed,' replied Tom looking at his navigation officer, who nodded in response.

'Roger, Enigma, that's understood; Columbus, you are clear to open your orbit, maintain concentricity below zero point one five, acknowledge?'

Richard looked across at Herman, 'below point one five,' he said to his colleague, surprised, 'this old bird would struggle to do that in automatic flight control; in manual that's almost impossible!'

'Please acknowledge, Columbus!'

Richard pressed the transmit button located on his control grip, 'below point one five is a tall order, Osiris,' he said, unimpressed, 'please, no more surprises; opening from established orbit now.'

Tom knew instinctively that he was listening to the voice of Richard Reece; his use of non-standard phraseology over the radio seemed somehow acceptable due to both the gravity of the task and the calm confident undertone of its delivery. Tom paced the area behind his chair, hands clasped behind his back.

Richard fired a precise four point three second burst of the main engines, accelerating the Columbus to a little over thirty nine thousand miles per hour, some twenty-two percent faster than that maintaining the Enigma in her orbit; he began to slowly increase his own orbit.

In the blink of an eye, Columbus overtook the Enigma, passing some three miles beneath her. Richard thought to use this final orbit to complete his preparations. Nervously flexing the fingers of his left hand, he opened the pressure vent on his helmet visor to evaporate some condensation that had accumulated in the corners.

'These old helmets,' he said sarcastically, 'you'd think by now they could have overcome the problems of perspiration!'

'The design of these emergency helmets hasn't changed for thirty years!' Horowitz concurred.

The orbit took just twenty-two minutes.

'Come up another two degrees,' advised Herman.

'Wilco,' Richard replied, 'what's the closure rate?'

'Reducing to three hundred metres per second, Sir, about another nine and a half minutes. Passing, now, seventy six percent elliopherical.'

'Understood, my intentions are to stay below her until we have matched precisely her orbital velocity; I'll use retros for final manoeuvring.'

With that remark, Herman looked across at Richard. 'Retros are a little coarse for that manoeuvre aren't they?'

'Yes!' came the unexpected reply, 'if you've a better idea, I'm all ears?'

Herman paused in thought, then shook his head, a little embarrassed, 'no, I haven't.'

Richard's gaze was already fixed on his instruments, finally, after several taxingly slow minutes, his orbit matched that of the Enigma's and the magnificent ship came into view again. Initially, as a tiny reflective speck rising above the seemingly incandescent curved surface of the planet, the craft grew larger at an alarming rate.

'Target on the horizon, Sir,' said Herman calmly.

Richard looked up, 'Visual?'

'Twenty thousand metres and closing, approaching eighty percent,' continued Horowitz, 'ten seconds to opposition thrust.'

'Copied,' replied Richard, 'standing by.'

'Five, four, three, two, one, fire!'

On cue, Richard fired an apposition retrorocket blast.

'One minute,' he called curtly over the open channel.

The entire bridge team of the Enigma were seated and strapped in at Tom's command; he watched carefully the magnified video picture of the Columbus as she closed from behind. He looked across at screen two: it indicated a range of ten thousand metres, and a closure rate of just five hundred metres per second. Tom pressed a button on his left armrest.

'Ross,' he said, 'twenty seconds.'

'The ship is secure, Commander,' Ross replied.

On the magnified video image, Tom could see the Columbus twitching; it was painfully apparent that she was under manual control.

'Ten seconds,' came another call over the open channel.

'Steady, steady,' Richard said to himself as the two craft closed to within four hundred metres; at that distance, the Enigma began to fill the screen.

'God, she's a monster,' said Horowitz awestruck, 'I've never seen anything like it.'

'We can sight see in a few minutes,' replied Richard, unimpressed with the breakdown in commentary, 'what's the concentricity rate?'

'On the limit, Sir, point one five.'

Even that was impressive; Richard's instruments were of no use to him now. He focused on the hull of the Enigma, mindful that he had to keep some forward speed in order to maintain stability.

'Closing a little fast, Sir.'

'Copied.'

The Columbus was down to one metre per second as she skimmed passed the underside of Enigma's thrust chambers, dwarfed against these enormous propulsion tubes. A short retro blast reduced her speed still further, now barely a walking pace.

'Just how big are these things? They just go on and on,' remarked Richard; he could feel the muscles tensing in the back of his neck.

Herman's answer wasn't relevant to the question, 'docking port visual,' he said without tonation, 'approximately fifty metres.'

Richard scanned the underside of the main module.

'Ah, I've got it, slightly left, better ease off a bit, smoothly does it.'

Totally focused, he fired the final opposition sequence. With Columbus still five metres clear of the shadow-strewn grey and white hull, and less than twenty metres to run, Richard was committed, but he had to move closer;

a short blast on the retros changed the direction of his ship.

'Careful, Sir, closing a little fast again!'

'Copied.'

Having to estimate the lateral position of the circular escape hatch on the upper level, Richard wondered if it had ever been opened during the working long life of this old bird; some fifteen metres behind his seat it had to be precisely positioned opposite a similar, but essentially incompatible, docking port on the underside of Enigma.

'Still closing a little fast, Sir,' said Horowitz nervously,' just ten metres.'

'Can't do anything about it,' responded Richard, his eyes remaining locked on the target, 'we are too close for another retro sequence!'

The Columbus twitched almost imperceptibly. On the bridge of the Enigma, Tom could see what was developing on his video monitor. He too tensed slightly, then opened the PA channel.

'Standby for impact,' he called.

The two ships edged within millimetres of each other. No sooner had the last word passed his lips when a dull thud was felt, followed by a low shuddering vibration that seemed to pervade both vessels equally. Tom sensed it first through his feet.

'I'd say that was positive contact, wouldn't you?' he said looking at Nicola.

Nicola nodded, 'status remains green, Commander,'

she replied.

'Your status, Columbus?' Tom requested.

'Showing green,' said Richard over the open channel, 'can you check the alignment?'

Tom looked at Ross on his number two monitor.

'We already have a team on it, Commander,' he answered, without Tom actually asking the question. After a nerve-racking pause, Ross reappeared on Tom's monitor.

'Missed it by a metre and a half, Commander,' he said, 'and he looks awkward, possibly jammed!'

Richard could hear the conversation over the open bridge microphone.

'Shit!' he said, in response to the news.

In both ships, an eerie silence followed as the two Commanders considered the repercussions; Richard broke the silence.

'I'll try a short retro blast if you agree,' he said, hardly convinced himself.

'I'm not sure if that's a good idea,' replied Tom thoughtfully.

'Very well, I'm open to suggestions?'

At that point, base operations interrupted the discussion.

'This is Commander Miko, Osiris base operations, monitoring on open frequency. We have a suggestion.'

'Go ahead, Sir,' answered Richard.

'Engineering informs me that your oxygen and atmospheric holding tanks are currently ninety eight percent, enough for a four month earth transit plus reserves; their suggestion is to vent both tanks from the upper discharge valves. Storage pressure is approximately three hundred bars, a two to three second discharge should push you clear; but there is a problem. You will need some controlled forward momentum, a retro sequence will be far too course. Any thoughts, comments or ideas, gentlemen?'

'Shit, that is a problem all right,' Herman concurred quietly.

Richard reflected on the predicament for a few seconds, 'just a push would do it,' he whispered. 'What did you just say, Herman?' Herman looked across at Richard, confused.

'I said; that is a problem, Sir.'

'No, before that.'

'Er, shit Sir!'

'Precisely, that's the answer!'

Herman looked totally baffled.

Richard spoke up again, so that he could be heard over the radio, 'I think I have the answer, but it's unconventional to say the least?'

'Let's hear it, Columbus.'

'The lavatory discharge, Sir, its only five or six bars and its directly astern!'

The response to that remark would have been humorous had the situation not been so critical. It reflected in the expression on every face of every person party to the discussion. Then, strangely, it seemed so logical; so simple. The forward momentum required was minimal and a tiny pressure blast of water from the waste discharge port would do it.

'Agreed,' responded Commander Miko, 'Enigma, comments? Go ahead, please.'

Tom knew a good idea when he heard one, 'agreed,' he answered immediately.

'Then we're on,' declared Richard, 'standby?'

Without wasting another second, he reached up to the overhead control panel with his right hand. Richard knew that a sustained high-pressure discharge of gaseous oxygen and nitrogen from any vent would quickly cause a severe ice build up, so he selected the electrical preheaters on both upper and lower valves for a few seconds, and then looked across at Herman; the selector switch for discharging the waste holding tank was on his side.

'You ready?' he asked.

'Ready as I'll ever be,' Herman replied.

'Three, two, one, now!'

Richard flipped to open the two switches that controlled the upper valves, almost instantly they could hear the whooshing, roaring noise of pressurised gas venting into space; they waited for the reaction. Nothing. After three seconds, Richard closed the valves.

'We are definitely jammed on something,' he commented.

Herman nodded in agreement.

'What's the tank capacity?'

'Sixty five percent, Sir.'

'God, that discharges quickly; it's not a good idea to go below twenty percent, it will limit our endurance.'

'Agreed Sir, so, one more try?'

'Yes, I'd say so, keep your fingers crossed.'

'This is Columbus, no joy I'm afraid. I'm going to give it one more try.'

Tom studied the underside video pick up, he had seen the previous discharge of gas form a dense, white swirling cloud, only to helplessly dissipate; dissolving like early morning mist.

'Go ahead, Columbus.'

Richard made ready on the switches; he counted again, 'three, two, one, now!' This time he would sustain the discharge for a full five seconds; again the gas condensed immediately, forming the familiar, but temporary, white cloud which squeezed between the two ships, billowing and rolling as it escaped on either side.

'Call me at thirty-five percent, Herman.'

'Fifty, forty, now!'

As Richard closed the valves, he heard a scratching, scraping noise, then silence; Columbus was moving, she slowly pulled away from the larger ship.

'Waste discharge open,' Richard ordered. 'Closed.'

Herman complied with the instructions precisely, and Columbus edged forward very, very slowly.

'Venting from the lower valves, now.'

'Twenty-five percent remaining, Sir.'

The opening motion of the Columbus, which had little momentum, stopped quickly, then reversed. Moments later, there was a metallic thud, then a gentle vibration; Columbus had made contact again.

'Try the hatch lock, Herman,' requested Richard.

Herman flipped up a red protective cover on a switch marked 'docking lock' and selected the switch to 'lock'. Almost immediately, a green light appeared on the panel.

'It's engaged, Sir, it's green; we are hooked up!' Herman, for the first time, looked pleased with the situation.

Richard allowed himself a smile, 'one down and one to go,' he replied, then, on the open channel; 'this is the Columbus, rendezvous successful, repeat, rendezvous green.'

Commander Miko responded first. 'Well done, Columbus, good work, release procedure as planned; you have one and a half hours precisely.'

'Understood, Sir,' Richard concurred, 'Enigma, our hatch has opened under auto control, ready when you are?'

'We have a team on location, Columbus,' replied Tom who then turned his attention to screen four, 'open up, Ross!'

In the docking bay, Ross nodded to Trevor Roberts, one of his propulsion engineers, who keyed in a series of digits on a small wall-mounted control panel. Instantly, six large 'cam' shaped blocks of titanium alloy, each mounted around the periphery of the circular portal, rotated in unison. As each cam disengaged from its related locking fixture, a red light turned to green on the control panel. Then, as the last green light illuminated, the word 'open' appeared on the panel; Tom noticed a similar indication on his number one monitor screen.

Ross nodded again to Lieutenant Roberts, who pressed the word 'open' on the control panel; with that, a large hydraulic ram moved and the portal slowly opened, accompanied by a startling whoosh of escaping gas. Tiny specks of dust and debris lying on the floor of the docking bay were instantly sucked towards the periphery of the portal.

'Gas leak!' warned the Lieutenant, as he pulled a small aerosol can from his belt and began to spray a red liquid around the uneven joint between the two ships. Within seconds, the liquid began to fizz and bubble as the vacuum of space sucked it into the gap.

'Could have been worse,' commented Ros, waiting for the carbonised plastic serum to turn dark green, indicating that it had hardened; moments later, the noise of leaking gas subsided.

Ross pressed the intercom button on the control panel, and leaned towards it, 'better than I expected, Commander,' he commented, 'considering the age of this old bucket!'

'Less of the old bucket, if you don't mind!' replied Richard, peering up through the portal; his helmet tucked under his arm. 'Permission to come on board?' he requested, smiling.

Ross spoke again to Tom over the intercom. 'The Commander of the Columbus requests permission to come aboard, Sir,' he relayed.

'Permission granted, Ross, escort our first guest to the bridge, please,' replied Tom.

Richard's eyes widened in amazement as he walked the narrow corridors and climbed a series of bright metal spiral staircases. He counted with incredulity, five deck levels on his short journey to the bridge, then looked, almost with envy, at the uniforms of several personnel who passed him, before commenting, 'this is very impressive to say the least, is she performing to expectations?'

'I'm not at liberty to discuss the Enigma, Commander,' Ross replied abruptly. 'Clearance is President's level; Commander Race will answer any questions you may have.'

Richard acknowledged, 'of course, I wouldn't expect anything less.' Even so, he was surprised, astonished in fact, at what he saw.

As the sliding portal to the bridge opened and Richard stepped inside, everyone turned and stared, as if he was, quite literally, from another planet. Richard looked back at the faces, mildly embarrassed, not really focusing on any in particular. Tom stepped forward, raising his eyebrows at the old Mk3 helmet under Richard's left arm, before looking him directly in the eyes; they faced each other off for a few pensive seconds, before Tom, eventually, broke the silence.

'Welcome on board Lieutenant Commander Reece,' he said, 'very impressive handling, congratulations are in order.'

Normally Richard would have gladly welcomed such a remark from a fellow pilot, however this time, strangely, he dismissed it; it meant nothing. Almost as if this arrogant officer was congratulating himself in a roundabout way, dressed as he was in over-stated, fashion conscious attire, reminiscent of a science fiction movie.

At this point the relationship could have gone either way, the reality was however, that due to the unsubstantiated, niggling, but almost predestined distrust Tom had for Richard, the atmosphere went icy.

Richard was slightly taller, only by a few centimetres, but it was noticeable; whilst Tom was broader, stockier, his piercing blue eyes allied by the confidence he felt being on home ground.

Richard's normally open, friendly, expression quickly cooled to the perceived chilly welcome; he acknowledged the misplaced, almost sarcastic comment.

'The Columbus may be past her sell by date, Commander Race,' he replied, 'but she can still be flown.'

Tom was perplexed by Richard's reply; he had genuinely meant the comment, even so, his 'mission security briefing' considered this man to have unclear motives and he was regarded on earth as a possible security transgressor. The stage had been set, or so it seemed; the following seconds, weighted by silence, somehow morphed inaccurately, into minutes.

Ross offered some hospitality. 'Commander Race,' he said sensing Richard's unease, 'as Commander Reece does not have the security clearance for a walk about, perhaps, at least, an introduction to the bridge officers would be appropriate.'

Tom dwelt for a moment on Ross's remark, still, it seemed, assessing the potential threat. 'Yes, of course, thank you. Ross,' he said presently; with that, he spun round on one heel and directed Richard towards Isshi Tsou's station.

With the tension broken, at least for the time being, the assembled officers returned to their duties, all save Nicola; she stared unbelieving at Richard, who, by this time, was being introduced to the communications officer on the other side of the bridge. To an onlooker, her expression married disbelief with embarrassment in equal proportions. Beginning to fidget, she wished, it seemed, to be somewhere else, or preferably, for the deck to open up and swallow her before her turn came for introductions.

Richard, having been cordially introduced to each officer in turn, finally approached Nicola's console; she had turned away, busying herself with something trivial.

Tom continued, 'this is the bridge engineer's console, the ship can be controlled either from here or from the master engineering console on a lower deck.' Richard nodded. 'May I introduce Doctor Lynch from the European Space and Science Agency; she is our deputy Engineering Officer.' Nicola turned, almost reluctantly; she looked at the floor for longer than was polite, and then slowly raised her head to look up at Richard. He was flabbergasted. Had a hole in the deck opened-up for Nicola, he would have also jumped in, without hesitation.

'Nicola!' he said, visibly shocked.

'Hello Richard,' she replied, displaying an embarrassed flush of colour, 'it's been a long time?'

Richard recovered from his momentary disorientation. 'Yes, a long time,' he repeated slowly, 'I should say so!'

'You two know each other, then?' Tom enquired, perplexed by Nicola's unintentional emotional display, that seemingly required no explanation. Nicola looked down whilst Richard forced himself to break an awkward stare.

'Er, actually yes, we do,' he answered, 'or more precisely we did, a long time ago.'

Nicola smiled faintly in response. Tom hesitated, disarmed as much by sheer surprise as by Nicola's painfully obvious past relationship. It was Ross, who somehow sensed the approaching minefield; one of emotional entanglement, lost relationships, perhaps even betrayal, and at that moment anyway, it appeared to be Nicola who had sown the seeds of discontent.

Always the diplomat, Ross was trying to cover all the angles, but this revelation even threw him. With an underlying tension building between the two Commanders, Ross again attempted to steer the situation into calmer waters.

'Commander Reece,' he said, 'how many people are you expecting to accompany the U-Semini case to the surface?'

'U-Semini case?' Richard replied, confused.

'The U-Semini case, Commander, it's our transportable containment system; designed specifically for the specialised freight we will be returning to earth.'

'Why do you say, returning to earth?' Richard interrupted, somewhat ill tempered.

Ross's brow furrowed, confused by Richard's seemingly pointless challenge to his choice of words. "We will be returning to earth, Commander, with the cargo; that's what I mean!'

Richard nodded, 'yes of course, sorry. How big is this case?'

'It's the size of a large brief case, weighs approximately twelve kilograms and has been constructed using information supplied by Osiris's science department. Despite its size, it incorporates a Magnatron suspension system, an enhanced Celestite protective sheath and is fully compatible with the Enigma,' answered Ross in a tone reflecting the countless times he had repeated that particular information. Ross turned and pointed to the sliding portal between the bridge and section one. 'The system is housed just behind that door.'

Richard nodded again, 'I see. In answer to your question, Osiris is expecting two officers and two security agents to come down,' he turned to Tom, 'is that acceptable to you?'

'That was also our brief,' replied Tom, still half-looking at Nicola.

Richard's eyes were also drawn to Nicola, just a glance. She was busy trying her level best to ignore everyone around her by pressing keys, apparently arbitrarily, on her control station, but paying little attention to the displays being selected.

'Well, I'm ready when you are, sooner the better,' replied Richard, refocusing his full attention on Tom and Ross.

'Agreed, let's get to it. Nicola, you were nominated as one of the accompanying officers; but if you would prefer not too, I'm sure Ross wouldn't mind a ride to the surface?'

Nicola, although apparently paying little attention to the conversation between the three men, responded immediately.

'No Commander, that won't be necessary, I'm briefed and ready!'

'OK, understood. Pick up a flight suit then, we meet in dispatch, ten minutes. Ross, please collect the number one U-Semini case, and the reserve, on your way through security.'

'Will do. I'll get the team together.'

The two Commanders made the best of a lengthy walk back to dispatch by discussing, between difficult periods of silence, the second and final orbital rendezvous and the transfer of cargo. Apart from a flying background, it was apparent to both men that they had something else in common; though neither would dream of raising the issue. Instead, a preconceived river of distrust, that had frozen over during their initial encounter, was bridged, albeit temporarily, by their professional attitudes. Waiting in dispatch were the two security agents, and Major John Berrovich, an experienced, mid-forties security officer, who, along with his team, had been specifically trained in the correct handling of the Yearlman cube and the U-Semini containment system.

'Where's Doctor Lynch, Major?' asked Tom, unimpressed.

'Been and gone, Sir,' he replied. 'Picked up her suit and helmet and left for the docking bay!'

Tom turned to look at Richard; the two men faced each other for a few seconds, both had comments to make, but neither did.

'Understood; shall we go, Commander?' said Tom shrugging his shoulders to conceal his disapproval.

The five men marched purposefully to the docking bay; they arrived to see Ross approaching from the opposite direction.

'I've spoken to the co-pilot pilot on Columbus, Commander, and also Osiris base, all systems are green.'

'Thank you, Ross,' replied Tom, 'have you seen Miss Lynch, by any chance?'

'Yes, though I'm not sure why she's so keen to get to the surface; she's had previous chances, and always declined. Anyway, she's already onboard the Columbus.'

Tom nodded in acknowledgement; he turned to address Richard. 'Sorry about this,' he said with a sigh. 'Usually my people are a little more disciplined.'

'Can't say she's not keen, can we?' Richard replied neutrally. He almost offered Tom his hand, but held back, 'I expect to see you in eighteen hours, all things being equal,' he continued, then climbed down the vertical ladder into Columbus.

Major Berrovich, carrying the primary U-Semini case was next to leave; followed closely by the two security agents, the second of whom carried the spare. Slamming closed, with a gesture akin to unfriendly dismissal, the pressure hatch locked into position. Almost in response, Tom, considering the implications of what had transpired, walked back to the bridge in silence. Ross, for his part, was left wondering if there were any other areas that the personal screening programme had overlooked.

CHAPTER 26

It Doesn't Pay

Within two hours of breaking lock with Enigma, the Columbus eased forward along the steel tracks towards Osiris base. As her nose pushed through the self-sealing doors, Richard shut down the remaining auxiliary thrusters and electrical generators. Save for the occasional hiss of discharging gas, an unusual silence pervaded that quarter of the base; but it didn't last long.

Minutes later, a small welcoming committee, including Commander Miko and Rachel, had congregated at the base of the ship's forward right hand portal. As the curved door slowly opened, a flight of steps and a low guardrail moved effortlessly and almost silently into place, controlled by a series of tiny mechanical linkages. Richard appeared at the head of the steps and Rachel stepped forward first, expecting the usual boyish grin, but it didn't appear, instead Richard appeared very serious, almost preoccupied.

At Richard's request, the party descended the eleven or so steps together, after which he cordially made the usual introductions.

Professional as ever, despite Richard's rather icy greeting, Rachel addressed the visiting crew members.

'I'm aware of the relatively short period of time that you have spent in space and it's quite amazing I must say,' she smiled politely at Nicola as she spoke, who was of a similar height and build to herself. 'Nevertheless, if anyone experiences even the slightest effects of gravitational circopulmatory cistrises, please come and see me immediately in the sickbay, you all know the symptoms. We have planned an eleven-hour rest period and each of you has a room allocated close to the sickbay on level one; so enjoy your stay, you're very welcome.'

Commander Miko, who had stepped away from the gathering to speak to Richard privately, stepped back into the general mêlée. 'It's a great privilege to have you with us, if only for a night,' he said openly. 'Now please get some rest, I'll expect you all in the main briefing theatre at zero eight hundred, sharp!'

Richard, who was standing several metres away from the group, fixated on Nicola; quite simply she was stunning, perhaps more so, he thought, than before. Rachel, who had watched Richard watch Nicola for an awkwardly long time, eventually walked over to him.

'You know her, don't you?' she said in a forced whisper, breaking his ill-directed concentration.

He looked Rachel in the eye. 'I did know her, yes.'

'She's the one, isn't she; the woman you spoke about, the love you lost?'

Richard grimaced; his expression was enough to confirm Rachel's theory.

'How the hell did you come to that conclusion?' he said forcing a half-hearted smile.

'I didn't need my woman's intuition, Richard, if that's what you mean. It's written all over your face!'

Richard's expression dropped along with his smile, to save giving anything else away.

'It's too late for a cover up, Richard,' Rachel continued, 'so what next, eh?'

'Look, it was a long time ago, all right, as well you know, but I have to admit, it is a shock for me seeing her again, I'd forgotten . . .'

'You had forgotten how beautiful she was? Well, I agree, she is! Obviously very intelligent, too; it's a small solar system, Richard; so to speak, I suppose you were destined to meet her again sooner or later.'

Richard squeezed Rachel's hand and held it for a while, 'no worries?'

'I'm not worried, Richard, now, I suggest you follow the rest of that crowd and get some sleep.'

Richard lay on his bunk, still dressed, his boots and thermal socks lying on the floor exactly where he had kicked them off. There was no way he could sleep. He looked repeatedly at the photograph of Rachel; one of its corners had lifted and begun to curl. Then he tried to stick it back by pressing the corner firmly onto the warm pipe. After a while, unsuccessful, he gave up.

'Must remember to have those oxygen tanks refilled,' he said to himself quietly, before exhaustion got the better of him and he fell into an uneasy sleep.

In the early hours, with the corridors and walkways of Osiris base deserted, someone broke the silence; it was on level one, close to the sickbay. There, a uniformed operative hesitated, and checking the room numbers, stopped outside room fourteen. Looking nervously in each direction, he tapped twice on the door; almost immediately, it opened and the man slipped quietly inside. The door slid closed behind him, it strangled the light from the corridor until, finally, total darkness engulfed the small room.

'Give me a break!' he said in foreign English, his accent thick and heavy. With that, a light came on behind him, its effect weak, like that from a bedside table or a shaving mirror; it served to silhouette him against the door, little else, the remainder of the room still dark and shadowy. The man turned back towards the door.

'Stay where you are, Mr Dubrovnic,' the woman's voice was hard, devoid of emotion, 'I've been expecting you for some time.'

'I'm late, that's the way it is!' he replied, paying little attention to her authoritarian tone.

'You haven't done very well, have you Mr Dubrovnic? We paid you a lot of money to obtain those crystals; instead we have a mess, don't we?' The woman was condescending to the point of antagonism.

'Things got difficult!' the man grunted, beginning to shift nervously from one foot to the other.

'We tried to take the money back, you blocked the account.'

'It's my money now, all of it, Bradley can't spend his, so I've taken it.'

'But you haven't delivered, Mr Dubrovnic. Now things are much more complicated; you'll have to pay for that!'

'Listen, who the hell are you? I make the threats here; I don't take them!'

There was a moment of silence.

'Kill him!' the woman ordered coldly.

With that, a tall bulky figure stepped forward from the shadows. In an instant there was a dull thud, then a painful groan.

'Ugh!' The man's eyes closed momentarily, his face grimaced, contorted in agony, he looked down at his chest; four fingers, from a metallic hand had penetrated his body almost up to the palm, blood oozed from beneath his shirt. As his knees give way, he made a desperate, aggressive lunge towards the woman, swinging his left fist wildly; instantly, a second mechanical hand shot forward, snatching the man's wrist mid-flight. There was a blood-curdling crack. The man twisted and fell to the floor in a crumpled heap; the sinister figure, unable to retrieve its hand, was pulled down with him, its eyes burning a deep red and beginning to pulsate.

'Dispose of the body,' the woman ordered, 'the room next door, number fifteen, it's empty. In there!'

The neck of the figure began to extend, its mechanical head rotating backwards towards the woman. She could see its face, the molten plastic screen forming facial features. Raised cheek bones, a stretched protruding nose; adopting the sickly grinning expression of a sadistic killer enjoying his work. Suddenly, the screen lost its contours and began to flicker, after a few seconds it began to show images of war, human wars, previous wars, in graphic newsreel footage; the woman stared, almost mesmerised. First, Japanese kamikaze fighter pilots of the Second World War, attacking ships on the high seas, their guns blazing, then images of the Vietnam War of the 1960s; cameras mounted inside the bomb bays of aircraft, filming, as they released streams of incendiary devices, then the explosive plumes of smoke and flames as the bombs impacted the jungle below. Pictures taken on the ground, brutal, harrowing, followed this, peasants running from their devastated village as it burned in the background, some of them scorched, skin peeling; as abruptly as the macabre show had started, it finished. Despite the poor light, the disturbed expression on the woman's face was clear to see.

'Quickly,' she ordered, 'do as I say, get rid of him!'

The robot, clearly a Humatron model, placed one foot

against the rib cage of the limp body and pulled hard, its hand detaching with a jerk. As it stood up, Dubrovnic's limp body rolled over onto his face, his pallid jowls squashed against the hard floor covering. Dripping blood, the machine watched the three fingers of its left hand respond as it tried to operate them; they were damaged, twisted, deformed; two responded, one of them only partially. The machine looked at the woman again, neither spoke, on its facial screen, in a large clear font, the word 'Recipient' appeared. Then, picking up with relative ease the lifeless body of Dubrovnic, who himself had been a large stocky man, the machine carried him from the room.

Richard waited a little anxiously in the theatre the following morning, but Rachel didn't show; he knew the nuts and bolts of the briefing anyway, so didn't pay much attention, his thoughts elsewhere. As the meeting closed, Greg Searle handed over the Yearlman cube, complete with the five precious Kalahari crystals, to Major Berrovich.

Commander Miko was looking tense, but then again, he had done for the last few weeks. Eventually, the party of eight security officers, which included Searle, left the theatre bound for dispatch. Richard had wanted to have a word with Nicola in private, but had hesitated; she hadn't even responded to his polite 'good morning!' Remaining in his seat after everyone had left, he looked across at the chair where she had been sitting just moments before.

'What's the point?' he whispered, 'its dead and buried a

long time ago.'

With that, he decided to go past the sickbay and say goodbye to Rachel. Conveniently, just as he arrived, the red 'No Entry' light above her door extinguished. Good timing, he thought, knocking on the door. Initially there was no response and just as he was about to knock again, only this time louder, the door opened.

'Oh hello,' said Rachel, surprised.

'Morning, thought I'd drop in on my way past.'

Rachel smiled in response and then turned to face her patient, who was reading the dosage directions on a small brown plastic bottle.

'One three times a day,' she said, 'and don't worry it's only a mild condition, discontinue when you arrive back on earth.'

' Yes, m'am. Thank you!'

It was Sergeant Ike Freeman, who nodded in acknowledgement as he passed Richard in the doorway.

'Interesting,' commented Rachel as Richard closed the door, 'only a week in space and already mild cistrisis. I'd expect those symptoms after five or six months on Spartacus, or around eighteen months on the moon!'

'What about here?'

'Doesn't really apply here on Mars, Richard, because the force of gravity is similar to that experienced on earth. So the condition is rare; probably less than ten percent experience any problems and even then it's usually very mild.'

'So what's the cause?'

'I don't really know to be honest, could be an isolated case, maybe he slipped through the net, screening didn't pick him up during initial selection!'

'Or,' said Richard, surmising, 'the physiological effects of high speed flight on the body; possibly it compounds or accelerates the condition?'

Rachel shrugged her shoulders, 'Yes, you could be right, something that's been overlooked, or not even considered. I'll forward a report; normally it's not necessary for a mild case, but in this instance, earth will need to know.'

'I agree, Rachel, I suppose it could have an effect on the long term missions being planned; I hear they are already talking about a flight to Alpha Centuri, and within the next two years!'

Rachel looked up, surprised, 'well if cistrises becomes a problem after a few weeks of flying around close to the speed of light, four years is out of the question, wouldn't you say?'

Richard nodded in agreement, 'either way, Rachel, you've had a busy night, haven't you?'

Rachel looked confused. 'No. Why do you say that?'

'You had an accident case, by the look of it!'

'No, actually it's been unusually quiet, I haven't treated anyone since clinic yesterday morning. What made you say that?'

'Blood, outside! Just a few spots on the deck and some

smudges, looks like someone has cleaned up, but didn't do a very good job!'

'Really, show me!'

Rachel, a little concerned, followed Richard into the corridor where they walked a few metres to room fourteen.

'There; a couple of spots and some more outside fifteen.'

Rachel looked at Richard, 'I don't know what that's about, I'm sure. I'll get a sample swab and do a DNA ID.'

Rachel returned a few moments later, Richard was leaning on the wall patiently and watched closely as Rachel lifted, very carefully, a blood sample with a pencil swab.

'This will only take a few minutes, Richard.'

Nodding in acknowledgement whilst checking the time, he followed her back into the sickbay. Within seconds the small white machine, with its red digital readout produced a DNA breakdown in the form of a table code. Rachel compared the code to the 'record of medical data', the restricted, medical reference document for all base personnel.

'It's Dubrovnic's blood, Richard, but I haven't seen him for ages. In fact, I think he has been avoiding me. Ever since, you know, you tried to have him confined to quarters.'

'Good,' replied Richard sarcastically, 'I hope it's serious!'

Rachel ignored the comment. 'Perhaps I should call him?' she added, impervious to Richard's expression.

'Look, Rachel, he's probably cut his finger or something, came over to get a skin-seal, found the bay was closed and gone on his way. I shouldn't bother; if it was serious he would have come back!'

'Yes, I suppose so, unusual though,' she shrugged her shoulders.

'Anyway, I've got to go; doing some prep in operations. I'll see you when I get back,' said Richard, changing the subject.

'Yes, OK, be careful, Richard, please.'

'Always.'

Richard left the sickbay and walked back towards his cabin, passing room fifteen, a smear of blood half way up the door caught his eye. He paused for a few moments then walked back to the sickbay, and put his head around the door.

'Please knock before ent . . . oh, it's you, Richard.'

'Whose cabin is number fifteen Rachel, by way of interest?'

'Fifteen? Nicola Lynch was room fourteen and fifteen was, hold on, I'm checking,' she said, selecting another computer icon. 'Actually, fifteen was unallocated!'

Richard looked puzzled by the reply. 'Really? Is it open?'

'Normally.'

'Mind if I take a look?'

'Not at all, be my guest; if you find anything, let me know.' Rachel smiled, as if to say 'why are you wasting your time?'

Richard, inexplicably, knocked on the door of room fifteen, even though he knew it was empty. As expected there was no reply, so he opened the door slowly. After a few inches it jammed; he tried to force it but there was definitely something behind the door that prevented any further movement. He felt inside for the light sensor with his left hand and just managed to squeeze his head through the gap. He was greeted by a large pool of discoloured blood, with Dubrovnic's crumpled body lying up against the door, the back of his head acting as the doorstop. Richard pushed just hard enough to create a sensible opening and squeezed through. Kneeling beside the body, he knew that the sickly white skin colour was down to the apparently heavy blood loss, but there was a pulse, albeit very week. He gently lifted Dubrovnic's head and leant forward slightly to put his face close to Dubrovnic's mouth in order to sense any breathing. Dubrovnic stirred, his eyes opened slowly; he struggled to focus.

'So it's you, Reece, got someone, got it done for you, a woman, couldn't do it yourself,' he rasped.

Richard shook his head, denying the accusation.

'It wasn't me, Reece, you yellow bastard, you got it wrong,' forced Dubrovnic, wheezing. He coughed, sending spatters of blood over Richard's flight suit.

'It wasn't you, what?' replied Richard, putting his ear close enough to Dubrovnic's mouth as to 'feel' his words.

'In the servicing bay, when Bill Bagley bought it and

Miles Da . . ., wasn't me.'

'I don't understand, what are you saying?'

Dubrovnic shifted, just slightly, uncomfortably. 'The other person you shit; the accomplice you've been looking for; trying to find out. You have no idea, do you?'

Richard grasped Dubrovnic by the collar and pulled his upper body of the ground. He was in his face.

'Then who was it?' Richard scowled.

Dubrovnic's eyes rolled upwards, he drifted towards unconsciousness; Richard shook him until his eyes could barely open.

'Then who was it, you murdering leech?' shouted Richard, he couldn't help himself.

Dubrovnic came back for a few seconds, he grinned pathetically as blood dribbled from the corner of his mouth.

'You'll find ou . . . '

Dubrovnic's head fell limply to the side. Richard looked at him for a while, still grasping the dead man's collar. Then, apparently a little upset with his behaviour, he lowered him slowly and very gently to the floor. Standing up and avoiding the stains on the floor, Richard looked around for the intercom module.

'Yes, sickbay, CMO.'

'Rachel, it's me, I'm in room fifteen. Dubrovnic's dead, by the mess in here, I'd say someone disliked him even more than me. Better get in here, I'll call security.'

Richard didn't wait for a response, pressing another

code into the module keypad.

'Security section, Preston!'

'Preston, it's Lieutenant Commander Reece, is your boss around?'

'No Sir, he's still in dispatch, or, or maybe science. He's personally supervising the security of the Yearlman, U-Semini transfer, at the request of Commander Miko.'

'OK, listen carefully. We have a problem. Renton Dubrovnic, he's dead, murdered! I'm in cabin, I mean room, fifteen, down Sickbay Boulevard. Find Searle, tell him personally, in private, then get some backup down here with me. Keep it under wraps, Preston, I think our visitors may have something to do with this.'

'Yes, Sir. I'm on it.'

Richard closed the intercom loop and stood for a few moments looking at Dubrovnic's body. He thought about Freeman, the security agent, and his stomach problems. Dubrovnic was a big man; a hefty punch from him in a scuffle could cause internal haemorrhaging, symptoms, on the face of it, the same as low gravity cistrisis.

A few seconds later, Rachel's medical bag scraped the door and its frame, as she forced it between them. Richard pulled on the door to open it further despite Dubrovnic's head. Carrying a snap-up stretcher in her other hand, she looked in horror at the extent of the blood loss from Dubrovnic's body.

'Richard, straighten out his legs for me will you, then gently roll him on his side.'

Richard did as he was asked; Dubrovnic's left arm flopped across his body then onto the floor, disturbing the skin that had formed on the pool of blood. Beneath, fresh crimson liquid glistened. Dubrovnic's left hand landed in a most peculiar way, Rachel noticed it immediately and lifted the arm by pulling on the shirtsleeve, the hand dangling awkwardly.

'God, Richard, look, his wrist, it's broken, snapped in two!'

Richard was paying more attention to Dubrovnic's chest, something protruded from beneath the blood-stained shirt. Rachel focused on it too and undid the top three or four buttons. Four puncture marks were plain to see and one still had what looked to be a metal object penetrating the chest cavity. Richard gripped the slender piece of shiny metal and pulled gently. It slipped out easily, the end tapering almost to a point. They both looked closely, it was six or seven centimetres long, apparently of black carbon-based metal and had two tiny ball joints; being fractured at the upper larger joint. Rachel looked closely at the wounds then placed her hand on the dead man's chest.

'By the clotting around these incisions, this damage was done several hours ago, but he died within the hour, possibly within the last fifteen minutes!' She looked up at Richard. 'Was he alive when you found him?'

'Barely,' Richard replied.

'Did he say anything?'

'Nothing coherent, just voiced his undying friendship!'

Rachel's faced tightened. 'Did he say anything, Richard?'

'No, for God's sake! Just muttered something about, it wasn't him, a woman or something, I'd find out, I didn't understand!'

At that moment there was a scuffle outside, followed by a sharp tap on the door, which opened, thumping the back of Dubrovnic's head again; Greg Searle walked in full of pomp and circumstance. Rachel deflated him in an instance.

'Careful you clumsy oaf!' she called out.

Searle could only apologise. Richard for his part, instinctively closed his hand around the object and stood back.

'Found him a few minutes ago like this,' he said to Searle, whose face dropped.

This was the last thing he needed. Searle looked up at a member of his team who had also squeezed into the room.

'Inform Commander Miko,' he ordered.

'Yes Sir, right away.'

Richard, at that point, decided to leave. He caught Rachel's eye and shook his head gently from side to side.

'I've got to go!' he said making his excuses, 'it's three hours to take off and I've still got plenty of work to do.'

Searle looked him straight in the eye, grimaced, as if to say 'another fine mess you've got me into', then turned to Rachel.

'Cause of death and how long?'

Rachel had never liked his abrupt manner, it always bordered on rudeness. It was one of the reasons she would never have anything to do with him. She decided not to reciprocate.

'I haven't had time to examine the body yet; but it looks like these puncture wounds to the chest cavity. At least two have penetrated the lungs and there are other injuries consistent with a struggle; as for time of death, a few hours, six or seven at the most.'

Searle nodded, he went to speak again when the intercom call sounded.

'This is Searle, go ahead!'

'Commander Miko here, Greg, what's going on?'

With that, Richard slipped past Searle and left.

CHAPTER 27

Bad News

On his way to operations, Richard stopped at the Robomotive section; a small department that reprogrammed, repaired and generally carried out routine maintenance on the robotic and automotive equipment that kept Osiris running on a daily basis. Limited, even obsolete as some were, several departments including organics and life support had twenty-four seven monitoring provided by robomotive systems. Ramir Pushtarbi ran the section; a stereotypical computer boffin, who wore over-sized, over-prescribed spectacles, which were paled only by the size of his ears, and these were pulled forward by the weight of his spectacles, to create a character more akin to a comic caricature than a scientist.

Originally from Agra, he retained that strong, unique accent, which only Indians have when they speak English; but he was clever, most said a genius, and a good friend of

Richard's, who left the object in Ramir's workshop saying he would be back in an hour. In the meantime, Richard changed into his flight suit, collected some equipment from operations and kept a rendezvous with Commander Miko and Greg Searle in flight dispatch.

The three men spoke privately for several minutes in the far corner, opposite the dispatch control officer's desk.

'Sitrep, Greg?'

'Murder Sir! I don't think there's any question of that; no clues, no motives and no leads as yet. We are dusting the room and running a breath spectrograph, but I don't hold out any hope of answers from those options. In fact, initial results from the spectrograph only give a positive vapour check on Dubrovnic, the CMO and Reece; so, with that in mind, whoever put him in there wasn't breathing, right?' Searle concluded sarcastically; he paused, considering his next remark carefully. 'The CMO has specified a fairly reliable time for the penetration wounds in the initial report, something to do with blood clotting agents; two this morning! She said that the injuries are consistent with a 'one on one' conflict, but the aggressor would have to be a large man and very strong.'

Commander Miko nodded, 'we don't need this, not at anytime, but certainly not now! First priority is to get the crystals onto Enigma and away.' He looked enquiringly at Richard, 'theories, speculations, thoughts?'

Greg Searle seemed put out. Richard paused for similar

consideration, should he mention the metallic specimen?

'My thoughts are that the suspect is from the Enigma, Sir, it's too coincidental for this to happen now. If any one from the base complement had Dubrovnic in their sights, surely they would have moved on him before now. He had plenty of enemies.'

'Yes, and I know who was the most ardent!' interjected Searle, looking directly at Richard and almost snarling. 'Perhaps the killer used the arrival of the Enigma crew as a cover? You had a grudge to settle didn't you, Reece; the spectrograph shows the highest count of breath molecules to be yours?'

'That's because I found him and waited until you arrived, remember!' Richard shook his head, almost in disbelief, but resigned to the fact that Searle really was an idiot. He sighed, 'you just will not let it go, will you? Listen Searle; I didn't like Dubrovnic, not at all, and yes, I believe that he did kill Jennifer, Miles and Chang Sung to boot, but I didn't kill him. Check my computer log for God's sake; I was working in my cabin until turning in at around three thirty.'

Commander Miko raised his eyebrows.

'Couldn't sleep, Sir. Too much going through my mind.'

'Greg, divert your energies onto someone else, that's an order. I need full cooperation between you two, put an end to this bickering now! Do you understand?'

Searle nodded, resigned to the fact that he would never claim any points over Richard, certainly not where the

Commander was concerned.

Commander Miko was justifiably anxious. 'Where is the primary and the spare U-Semini case now?'

Searle answered promptly. 'In the ready use munitions lock up, Sir, Station Alpha, adjacent to the Columbus. The spare has already been loaded. We are keeping the primary under tight security until the last minute.'

'Good, have it taken onboard as well. Bring your departure forward by one hour, Richard.'

'Yes, Sir, I'll make the arrangements.'

Richard left quickly, having passed the revised departure time to Pete Manley. He wanted to talk to Ramir, before reporting to the Columbus.

'So, what do you think, Ramir?' Richard asked, perching himself on a large workshop repair bench.

Ramir, a short, slightly built man in his late thirties, held the specimen between his thumb and forefinger and offered it up towards the concentrated glow of a sodium ceiling light. In his other hand, he had a computer print-out detailing the results of a mass spectrograph.

'Are you ready for this, Richard?' he said slowly, his tone humourless, even sombre.

'Yes, please!'

'This is the left-hand index finger, or more accurately the lower two digits, of a very dangerous machine; an advanced robot. The series is the Humatron; built by Interface Cybersystems SL, based in Brazil. I would say quite recently too, though God only knows how it came to be here on Mars! It is bad news, Richard, very, very bad news, I can tell you. The blood traces are human, isolated genetically to Eastern Europe. Hungary, Poland, Ukraine, somewhere in that region.'

'Ah, that part I know Ramir, it's Dubrovnic's blood. He was murdered, last night, the thing made a mess of him; it makes sense.'

Ramir nodded agreeing, 'I'm not surprised. I was able to extract a tiny sample of lubricant from inside the ball joint; the analysis shows a complex synthetic chemical additive called Zimteflate Zaragon Four Thousand. It's the latest in electrolytic cross lubricants, the very latest; which means it's an HU40 model!'

Richard paused for thought. 'Wait a minute, wasn't the Humatron series responsible for the Skyport disaster?'

'Correct. Plateau seven programming, fully self-aware, self-energising, built to last a thousand years! Interface Cybersystems insisted that they were designed for the space exploration programme, you know, to go where no man has gone before, that kind of thing?'

Richard raised one of his half smiles, that cliché sounded funny coming from Ramir, with his Indian accent.

'The official report of that accident, no, disaster, was never made public. But I knew someone in the corporation,' Ramir continued. 'Apparently the machines were docile and fully cooperative throughout the research and development programme. Then, the moment they were installed as systems controllers onboard the Skyport, and left to their own devices, they shut down the entire life support system. However, unbeknown to them, the orbital alignment thrusters had been de-energised for maintenance, so, in trying to implement a breakout manoeuvre they destabilised their pre-assigned geostationary orbit and re-entered the earth's atmosphere. Need I go on Richard?'

'No, Ramir, I'm aware of the final results.'

'Interface were immediately blamed for the accident, quite rightly, and fined heavily for corporate irresponsibility. Subsequently however, the manslaughter case was dropped, to the dismay of the international community. Interface insisted that only four HU40 units were built; three Bravo production models, the three lost in the crash and the prototype Alpha model, which is in the Smithsonian Institute, a museum piece! So what do we have here?'

'Do we have an HU40, Ramir? You tell me!'

'Indeed, it appears that we do Richard.'

'So, how bad is it?'

'I would say it is bad, yes, very bad. My colleague informed me that the HU40's reaction time is half that of a human's, they were tested to an overhead lifting capacity of four hundred kilograms and when fully charged could run as fast as a cheetah, but that is not the main problem.'

'Really, there's more?!'

'Its clever, Richard; it thinks, literally, like you and me

and it will not like you, or any human for that matter. There is a reason!'

Richard's eyes widened, beckoning Ramir to continue.

'Apparently some contamination occurred, during the essential memory lift programming. Historical files showing war atrocities breached the memory stem capillaries; the result was a protocol shift. The machines began to recognise the victims as being oppressed and the perpetrators as aggressors. Of course both parties were human beings, but when the protocol re-aligned, the machines recognised themselves as the oppressed, and humans as the oppressors, the enemy.'

Richard took the information in, rubbing his forehead for a few moments. 'So it doesn't like us, great?'

Ramir shrugged, 'the model had a discipline protocol much the same as all other systems above plateau three programming. My assumption is that the machine is cooperating with somebody or something, a person or perhaps another machine. Clearly this discipline protocol is easily breached Richard, demonstrated, I would venture to guess, by poor Dubrovnic.'

'You're right, Ramir, this is not very good, not at all. You think it's biding its time, that's what you're saying, right?'

'You should be vigilant, Richard, very careful indeed!'

Richard stood up and walked towards the door looking perplexed, Ramir though, could see in his friend more anxiety than perplexity, more apprehension than disquiet. He ventured one final piece of advice.

'Oh, yes, my friend, there is one other thing that comes to mind!'

Richard stopped short.

'From my contacts, you see.'

Richard turned and looked at Ramir, not really wanting to hear any more.

'Yes?'

'Enigma has a plateau nine system! How in God's name they allowed it to be built, when they are unable even to control plateau seven programming, is beyond my powers of reasoning. Nevertheless, in the Enigma, the system is restricted; thinking duties only is the best way to describe it. Those two systems together would be a powerful adversary, Richard, remember that!'

Richard nodded again, an exaggerated nod, his shoulders hunched. 'I've got it Ramir, thanks.' He paused again just before the door and looked over his shoulder. 'How do you know all this? I mean, who would tell you? Surely it would be dangerous?'

'Oh yes, indeed, dangerous, it was my work you see; before I was removed. I realised the dangers, the implications of plateau seven. The protocol needed more work, protection, more time, maybe years. But they didn't want to listen.' Ramir looked at the ground and spoke quietly. 'My contact, my fiancée; sadly she is dead, Richard, very much so, and me? I am here, in this little workshop, with these obsolete things, a very, very long way from home.'

Richard looked away and then back at his friend, his expression passed on his heart-felt condolences. Ramir understood; there was no need for Richard to elaborate; he turned and left the room.

Walking slowly back to dispatch, Richard knew, somehow, that the machine was already onboard Columbus. It had to do with the crystals, definitely, absolutely. Now somebody else was after them. Things began to fall into place.

CHAPTER 28

Nowhere to Go

As he passed an intercom station on his way to dispatch, Richard, feeling somewhat subdued, paged Commander Miko and Greg Searle to request another meeting. It was time to come clean, he thought. A few moments later as he approached the large swing doors of the dispatch section, the PA sounded.

'Medical Emergency, repeat, Medical Emergency. The CMO is requested to report to Dispatch Control immediately!'

As the last word of the heightened PA was being said, Richard burst through the doors.

'What the hell's going on?' he called to an operative.

'One of the visiting crew members, Sir, he's in a bad way, collapsed over there, by the Columbus.'

'Excuse me, coming through!'

Richard stepped to the side, as Rachel, together with

nurse Andrews, stormed past, each clutching a handle of a large white medical bag; neither acknowledged him. He eyed the Columbus cautiously, then walked towards the huddled group of base personnel who had parted to make room for Rachel and the nurse. As they did, Richard could see it was Sergeant Freeman, the security agent. His skin looked yellow, indicating that his cystrisis condition had seriously deteriorated. Watching as Rachel connected a variety of probes to the Sergeant's skin, Richard maintained half an eye on the forward portal of the Columbus. He had a gut feeling. He somehow knew the robot was inside and he also knew that somehow he would have to flush it out. The question was where: here on Mars and risk damage to the Columbus, or after the orbital rendezvous, after the crystals were onboard, and risk damage to the Enigma?

Richard kept his distance from the group of onlookers, who had reformed an almost complete circle around Rachel and her patient. From what he could see, Freeman was flat on his back and Rachel now had a mask over his face; presumably feeding him oxygen or some other gas. The sight of Commander Miko, Greg Searle and almost simultaneously, Preston walking through the main doors, momentarily diverted his attention from the plan he was formulating. He met them halfway across the large open floor space.

'What's going on?' enquired the Commander.

'Sergeant Freeman, from the Enigma, he's down with suspected cystrisis, Sir, he doesn't look too good either.

Rachel is treating him at the moment.' Richard looked across at the group, which had started to disperse at Rachel's request, then back at Commander Miko.

'Sir, my investigations; I think I have something, Greg, you had better listen to this as well.'

Greg Searle had nothing new to offer and so reluctantly joined the conversation, whilst Preston hovered uninvited a metre or two away.

'It's just as well if Preston is in on this, Sir.'

'Agreed!'

'Something I found in Dubrovnic's body, Sir, it . . .'

'So, you've removed vital evid . . . !'

Commander Miko raised his hand, stopping Searle mid-sentence. 'He had my full authority, please, go on Richard.'

'Something I found in the body, literally. I had it analysed; it's confirmed beyond any reasonable doubt, the culprit is a robot. Something called an HU40. Apparently, it is, or was, the latest model of the Humatron series; it's the machine responsible for the Skyport disaster!'

Searle interrupted rudely, 'how's that possible, Reece?'

The Commander raised his hand again as if to say enough.

'How so, Richard?' asked the Commander coolly.

'How? I don't know, Sir, although it's definitely paid us a visit from the Enigma and presumably it's got to get back. Why? Something to do with the crystals, we can be sure of that, although where Dubrovnic fits into this jigsaw puzzle, I haven't a clue. My thoughts are that there are several interested parties and these are the heavies! Where? I believe the machine is already back on the Columbus for its return ticket, and who?' Richard dwelt on that remark for several seconds then looked around warily. 'Who, Sir, that's the million dollar question. Initially I thought it was Sergeant Freeman, injured in a fight with Dubrovnic, but now I'm not so sure. Either way we need to flush out that machine before it kills someone else, or, before it completes its mission. The thing is, we can't risk damage to the Columbus before the flight, so we may need to deal with the problem after docking.'

The Commander nodded, accepting Richard's appraisal. Searle couldn't do much else, particularly after his reprimand, and stood quietly.

'So,' concluded the Commander, 'additional security, to cover the hand over?'

'The flight computations have a contingency allowance in terms of payload, Sir,' continued Richard. 'It equates to another two people, maximum. I need another good man, or preferably two, armed!' He looked at Preston, and then at the Commander.

Commander Miko took up Richard's prompt; he also looked across at Preston. 'What do you say, son, it's a vital mission?'

'I'm in, Sir.' Preston replied without hesitation.

'Good. Who else?'

Rachel, appearing a little dishevelled, interrupted the

conversation. 'Commander, I need a word, in confidence, please.'

'There's no time for diplomacy, Rachel, what is it?'

'It's Sergeant Freeman, he has suffered a pulmonary cistrical hernia and minor haemorrhaging. I have stabilised him, but there are complications. I cannot treat him here, it's a complex operation; I'm neither qualified, nor do I have the equipment. His best chance is the return flight to earth and as soon as possible.'

The Commander thought for a moment. 'Would he survive the passage if his condition is related to gravitational relativity?'

'Fifty fifty, Commander, but quite frankly that's better odds than if he stays. I'll need to accompany him prior to the Enigma's departure of course, the longer I can stay with him, the better.'

'Is that strictly necessary, Rachel?'

'Yes it is, Commander, no one else is qualified to do it!'

Commander Miko looked at Richard, who agreed with an almost imperceptible gesture.

'Very well,' he said. 'Rachel and Preston will accompany you on the mission, Richard. Preston please report to the armoury, collect suitable weapons, authorisation code Charlie One!'

'Yes Sir!'

'Preston,' added Richard, 'please sign out a static discharge probe in addition to your requirements.'

Rachel looked confused. 'I don't think Freeman presents

any danger, Commander?' she said, her expression demanding an explanation.

'As well as medical complications, Rachel, we have security complications. Richard will give you the details in due course, in the meantime everyone get their things together, take off in two hours.'

'Yes, Sir,' answered Richard. 'I'm going to do the pre-flight inspection of Columbus, Preston would you meet me inside the ship in twenty minutes please?'

Richard felt perplexed as he walked around the nose of his ship checking a variety of external probes and sensors. He was suspicious of everything. But, he thought, at least the old bird is in excellent condition, I may need everything she's got! Engineering had repaired the minor skin damage on the upper hull, caused by his initial impact with Enigma. Pete Manley had approved the work and heat resistant chemical paint applied to complete the job, but there still seemed to be a good many people milling around. Eventually, Richard walked up the steps and into the ship, turning right, first for the flight deck rest area and thereafter the flight deck itself. He checked every nook and cranny, and every locker, no matter how small, for signs of anything unusual. He didn't expect to find anything in these areas, the machine, he thought, would be down the back somewhere, but by starting at the front and working backwards, nothing should be missed.

As he walked back past the open portal towards the

crew seating compartment, Preston appeared at the base of the steps, brandishing two black leather holsters, a webbing belt containing a number of sonic grenades and a cylindrical box about a half metre long. Coloured dark red from top to bottom with the words 'Danger High Voltage' emblazoned in large white print, the tube housed a static discharge baton.

'Bit obvious aren't you, Preston?' said Richard, unimpressed with his colleague's lack of discretion.

Preston, embarrassed, looked around to see several of the dispatch personnel staring at him and his arsenal.

'Weapons are unusual in the base area; you know that better than me, Preston. Perhaps a case would have been prudent.'

'Um, yes you're right, sorry, Sir!'

Richard nodded, accepting Preston's apology, and beckoned him into the Columbus.

'Listen Preston, the Humatron is onboard, definitely, I just know it. It's not going to show itself unless we flush it out, and I don't want to do that until the crystals are onboard Enigma.'

'Yes, Sir, I understand.'

'So, rather than find out where it is, I want to find out where it isn't, if you get my drift.'

Preston acknowledged. 'OK, I understand.'

'I've searched the forward quarters and the flight deck; no sign. I'm about to do the main compartment and the sleeping area on deck four, I'll take the baton. You, deposit that lot in the flight deck and search deck two and the escape deck. Look, but don't touch, agreed?'

Preston nodded, the left corner of his mouth twitched to form a faint smile. Then the two men split, and Richard walked into the main compartment to check under the two rows of reclinable seats, and the various lockers and stowage compartments; nothing, all clear. Cautiously he climbed the vertical ladder onto the sleeping quarter's mezzanine. Things are getting warmer, he thought.

Quietly, methodically, he checked each of the sixteen small cabins in turn, looking for signs of entry or disturbance; most had not even been entered for several years. Ramir had told him the size of the HU40; there was no way one could fit either in the stowage under the bunk or into the tall but narrow uniform lockers. None the less, each time he opened one, his heart pounded; all the while, the static baton hummed with a full charge and each time he raised it, almost to arm's length, in case of the unexpected.

Hyped and with a bead of sweat running down his temple, Richard had just walked out of the last cabin, when Preston's head appeared through the circular hatch.

'Sir, I think I'm on to something! The pod deck, you had better come down.'

Richard followed Preston down three ladders and through three pressure hatches and until they arrived on deck one. Here the headroom was restricted, barely one point seven metres. Both Richard and Preston bent forward, lowering their heads to avoid the exposed structural spars, which ran across the entire width of the ship. This deck would only be used in an emergency; in order to gain access to the four escape pods, each designed to accommodate a maximum of six personnel, with life support for twenty-one days. In effect, each was a mini rocket, with a limited conventional thrust motor capable of a 'break away' manoeuvre and little else. Preston pointed to pod four, Richard acknowledged, putting a finger to his lips.

'Shhhhh!'

They both walked, Preston on his toes for some obscure reason, the fifteen or so metres to the access portal. He pointed to the security seal; a small yellow plastic ring about a centimetre wide and two millimetres thick, which was normally looped between the door and the frame; it was broken. Apart from routine maintenance, the contents of each pod was inspected every three months and in addition, limited system checks every six; all completed and documented by the survival equipment section. After these inspections, a new seal would always be fitted. This broken seal meant only one thing; the entry portal had been opened. Richard pointed to the seals on the remaining pods; Preston held his thumb up, indicating that the others were intact. Richard nodded and beckoned his colleague back to the access ladder. As they climbed up into the main compartment, a PA sounded outside.

'Attention, attention, one hour to launch, commence final preparations, all non-essential personnel to finish up and clear the area.'

'Good one, Preston,' congratulated Richard, back in the main entry area, and feeling a little easier with the situation. 'Do something for me,' he continued, 'let Commander Miko know the situation, then give the CMO a hand with that bag of hers. I've got some flight deck prep to do.'

'Yes Sir, right away, by the way, Sir, where is my station for take off?'

'You can take any seat in the main compartment, Preston. Towards the front is more comfortable. Strap in tight, all five points and keep an eye on the Doc for me, got it?'

Preston smiled. 'So we jettison our mechanical stowaway, right?'

'Correct,' replied Richard, turning towards the flight deck.

CHAPTER 29

Incorrect Conclusions

As the Columbus blasted through the thin peripherals of the Martian atmosphere, Richard selected the main compartment video camera on the flight decks lower monitor screen. Rachel and Preston were in the second row of seats, their jowls vibrating in unison with the powerful shuddering that pervaded the entire ship's structure. Neither looked very happy. In fact, Richard thought, Preston looked petrified, while Rachel just kept her eyes closed. Nicola, Major Berrovich and Sergeant Bateman were in the front row, apparently taking it all in their stride, whilst Sergeant Freeman had been strapped into his stretcher and lay between the seat rows to the left of Rachel, who still managed to hold up a saline drip despite the fierce acceleration.

'Launch sequence complete, Sir,' said Horowitz presently.

'Very good, reduce main thrusters to forty percent; keep the climb going to establish an eighty percent elliospherical, same as before, standard brief.'

'Yes Sir.'

With that, Richard leant over the centre console and with his right hand, reached towards a row of four switches; each covered by a small metal cage, hinged at the top. The area around the switches was painted in alternating red and black strips, and marked above, in bold red print, 'Escape Pod Master Switches'. He broke a thin copper wire, securing the mesh cover over switch number four and lifted it.

Horowitz looked across at him. 'What are you doing, Sir?' he said, confused by Richard's actions.

'Getting rid of unwanted baggage,' he replied. 'Keep your eye on the orbit, please.'

Richard selected PA to the main compartment; he wanted to find out something.

'This is the Commander, in a moment you will hear a small explosion on the right side, do not be alarmed, I am jettisoning escape pod number four for operational reasons.'

With that, Richard studied the faces of the three front row occupants and pressed the jettison button. As predicted, there was a muffled explosion, more a rumble, which was followed by a red light on the jettison panel. It indicated pod four had gone. Richard continued to watch the screen for several seconds, neither was there a change of expression nor a hint of concern on any of their faces.

'Well,' he said after a minute or two. 'We either have a very cool assassin, or someone's an extremely good actor!'

'What do you mean, Sir?' asked Horowitz, beginning to look tense.

Richard looked him in the eye. 'Sorry about this Hermon, its unconventional I know. I will tell you the facts shortly. You'll have to trust me on this.'

Horowitz seemed content with the answer, although he spent the next thirty or so minutes in silence. Richard, at this point, focused his full attention on his instruments, as the sight of Enigma growing alarmingly in the forward screen prompted several actions.

'Closing to ten thousand metres, the new programming has worked, Sir,' said Horowitz. 'Fully established, and approaching the manual gate.'

'Copied,' replied Richard wiping the moisture from his palms onto the knees of his suit. He grasped the control stick and pressed the small button on the top. 'Automatics deselected, I have manual control.'

This time he knew the ideal closing rate, and where to aim; after a few strained minutes the Columbus made contact; precisely on target.

'This is the Columbus, docking complete, systems green,' Richard said confidently over the open channel.

On the bridge of the Enigma, Tom Race acknowledged the apparent ease with which Richard had accomplished the manoeuvre.

'That was nice, Ross, very nice. Got to hand it to the guy, he can handle that old tub! How are we looking?'

'All systems green, Commander, no problems our side; permission to open the access hatch?'

'Granted, Ross, I'll see you down there in a couple of minutes.'

In the Columbus, Richard turned to his co-pilot. 'Good flying. Herman, thanks for your help,' he said. 'Listen, it sounds ridiculous but we had an intruder on board, an unwanted guest.'

Horowitz's eyes widened.

'Don't worry, it wasn't human, it was a robot!'

Horowitz went to say something. Richard cut him short.

'At the moment, that's all I can say, really! Now, I'll shut these systems down and you go and have a look at the Enigma, it may be your only chance, she's very impressive. We leave in one hour. On your way out, ask Preston to come and see me please.'

Horowitz left it at that, accepting the explanation. They had both acquired a good deal of mutual respect out of the operation, and Horowitz was pleased to be given the opportunity to board Enigma, if only for a few minutes.

'I'll call Preston,' he said, climbing out of his seat.

Richard still somehow felt uneasy. Could it really have been that easy?

Preston walked into the flight deck. 'You sent for me, Sir?'

'Yes. Horowitz is on his way to charge the air lock and open the hatch. Please check that both U-Semini cases get onboard Enigma safely, but keep a back seat. Enigma's security agents will do what's necessary. Once on board it's their responsibility. Oh, and the Doc will need some help with Freeman. I would prefer it if we keep Enigma's crew off the Columbus; know what I mean? After that, be on hand in her docking bay.'

Richard gestured for Preston to come a little closer, he spoke softly. 'Listen, Preston, don't come onboard again until I call you; understand?'

Preston was irritable. 'You still think we have a problem, Sir?'

'Doesn't feel right, that's all. I hope I'm wrong.'

Preston acknowledged his orders and left.

Richard had made no further attempt to communicate with Nicola, who, true to form, had totally ignored him as she had embarked on Columbus for the ferry flight, and he too, had no reason to bid her farewell.

After a delay of around fifteen minutes, Richard climbed from his seat and walked quietly through the crew rest area, into the main compartment on his way towards the access level. Everyone had left; the Columbus lay silent, uneasy, he felt a shiver run up his spine.

Moving quickly and carefully down three ladders to alight, inaudibly, onto the pod deck he looked around for a place to hide, and spotted a suitable area behind a row of emergency 'quick-don' space suits. The fifteen or so bright orange all-in-one suits hung from a long carbon-plastic bar, which itself was supported by brackets that were bonded to the low ceiling. The lower legs and feet of the single size outfits, whose overall length was too long for the hanging space, were folded over several times on the deck. Richard concealed himself behind the bulky mass and waited.

Eight, nine, ten minutes passed, nothing! He grew restless, checking his watch several times. Was he wrong? Maybe he had, after all, jettisoned the machine and his problems were over!

Richard was just about to break cover when a tiny red light appeared on the access control panel of pod three, accompanied by a metallic clanking sound. He moved back further behind the suits, but kept a clear view of its curved outer door. He could see the security seal; clearly, it was intact! Moments later, the red light turned green, and the inner and outer access doors slid back together. Richard stared, eyes wide, and felt for his shoulder holster.

After a short delay, there was some clattering, and the bulky frame of a menacing robot pulled itself clear of the cylindrical pod. It tried in vain to stand, the back of its shoulders rubbing on the deck head, its long neck extended forward and down.

'Clever bastard, clever, clever, bastard!' Richard repeated under his breath, and knew then that an accomplice would have set the security seal.

The robot, bending its knees, was able to raise its head a little; it scanned the area cautiously. During normal operations, the pod level was lit, adequately, by a series of small circular deck head lights, complete with their own internal batteries to service the area in case of a main power failure. Its search uncompromising, the machine had its attention held by the row of emergency suits; Richard's face disappeared behind them in an instant. Holding his breath, he carefully pulled the sonic pistol from its holster and reached down with his other hand to a leg pouch containing the static baton. He pressed a button on its handle to select a charge cycle. In the silence, the absolute silence, Richard heard the almost imperceptible hum of the weapon's capacitor building electrical potential. He grimaced. Even at that distance, the robot heard it too. It crouched, raising its hands. Richard, for his part, could hear the whirling of tiny actuator motors, as the intimidating, metallic figure slowly moved towards him. He wanted to move; he could hear the thing coming closer. His heart pounded. The sound of surging blood filled his ears. Wait, wait! he deliberated. Louder and louder became the whirling spinning noise. His heart was in his throat. In an instant, the row of suits was thrown aside. The machine thrust a hand towards Richard's face, its fingers tensed, outstretched; instinctively, Richard ducked, and drew the static baton.

The Humatron's body followed through with the

power of its aggressive lunge; for a few seconds it was off balance. Richard jammed the baton into its side, cellulose skin yielding and distorting, until the blunt end of the weapon impacted something solid. He pressed discharge. There was a loud crack, like a thunderbolt as the massive electrical potential discharged into the robot's body. Richard's arm recoiled; he felt a painful jab travelling up to his own shoulder. The baton flew out of his hand, and across the room, clattering on the deck for several metres.

The machine recoiled too, falling to its knees. Flashes of electrical energy danced up and down the entire length of its transparent body; its face contorted. Richard took aim with his sonic pistol but hesitated, his attention taken, momentarily, by the screen face that genuinely seemed to show pain. He had never seen such technology. Then it was too late; the opportunity lost. The robot lashed out again with its long arm and took Richard's legs from under him. He fell to the floor. Another blow came crashing down, Richard rolled to the left, narrowly avoiding the pencil-thin fingers as they scraped the metal deck. The sonic pistol was lost, Richard didn't see where, but he could see the baton, six or seven metres away, and scrambled to his feet. Just a metre short, he felt a sharp pain in his ankle. The Humatron, which had lost the use of its legs, had a hold and squeezed; its fingers penetrated Richard's boots.

Richard stretched for the baton, its green light illuminating to indicate a full charge, but fell short. Another effort, then another, then the last, and at last he had it. Instantly he turned, but the machine was upon him, its other hand stabbing at Richard's face. He rolled his head left, then right, avoiding the tiny daggers; three, four, five times, closer every time. Richard lunged again with the baton, this time at the screen face, but it rose quickly out of reach, its red eyes glowing brightly, angry, excited, almost as if it, too, had adrenaline in its veins.

Then they flickered intermittently, still subject to the electrical interference of Richard's first foray. Richard was struggling, he tried repeatedly to contact the robot's main frame for a second time by thrusting the baton as hard as he could into its back and sides; but it was in vain. He was pinned down and overcome by the superior physical strength of the machine, which now peered at him with cold, calculating eyes; those of a victor. Its contorted features seemed to ache for a kill.

Then, quite suddenly, a hand snatched the robot's flailing neck, grasping it just below the head; a pistol was thrust into the lower stem, and its trigger pulled decisively. The sonic blast, accompanied by an ear-splitting crack blew the machine's head off; just above the shoulders, save for a few wiry filaments and optical fibres. With an exaggerated tug, Preston wrenched it off completely, and threw it wildly against a bulkhead. Seizing the moment, Richard thrust the baton into the robot's side again, and initiated a second static discharge that virtually melted the would-be assassin's circuitry; out of instinct, he covered his face with his other hand.

Without warning, the heavy metallic body fell against him, Richard's muscles tensed as the residual electrical charge shocked his own body, then he winced in response to the stabbing, numbing pains. Preston acted quickly. With a massive effort, he flipped the robot over. As it rolled, he kicked it hard, until the bulky frame came to a rest on its back, relieving Richard of the debilitating mass. The decapitated Humatron lay there, fusing and sparking.

Richard, for his part, needed a few minutes to compose his senses; he began to notice several drops of blood that lay scattered, staining the area around him. A small pool began to form under his left calf; adrenaline had obscured the pain of his wound. Preston noticed the expanding pool just as Richard became aware of the aching.

'You're hurt?'

'You can say that again, and it does, like hell!'

Preston looked around; on the top of some lockers to his left was a red coloured compartment with a white cross. He walked over and broke the seal, retrieving some scissors, a dressing and lint bandages. Richard limped across to a small plastic bench positioned behind the remaining flight suits that hung, like silent witnesses to a murder; the others lay strewn around him. He sat down and stretched his leg along the top. Preston offered him the scissors.

'Thanks,' he said. 'These suits are a nightmare to cut. I think this looks worse than it actually is, although one of its bloody fingers penetrated somehow.'

Richard continued carefully, cutting a split in his suit, at the vulcanised joint between the boot and the legging. Exposed, he could see three puncture marks, two were superficial and had stopped bleeding, but the centre wound was obviously deeper and continued to dribble blood. He bound it tightly, using a sterile dressing, then a long bandage. Preston threw the remaining unused dressing onto the bench.

'I owe you Preston; that was close to say the least.'

'Don't mention it, Sir, anytime,' he replied looking at his watch.

Richard smiled. 'This suit is no good. Is it worth changing it for one of these?'

'Well, I think it's worth the effort, Sir,' answered Preston, thinking discretion was the better part of valour.

'Yes, you're right, this one is no good to me now, although I can't see me needing an emergency suit for the flight back to Osiris.' Richard paused and put some weight on his left foot. 'Seems OK, no permanent damage done, fortunately, could have been worse. Listen, Preston; do something for me will you? Find Horowitz; tell him to report back, it's time to get out of here. I'll change into one of these suits and start the flight prep.'

The two men looked across at the broken machine as the final signs of electrical activity faded.

'Well, we certainly switched his lights off, Sir,' Preston said, grinning, pleased with his rather apt joke.

'Yes, gone but not forgotten, I'd say. Certainly wouldn't

like to meet one of those things again,' replied Richard, nodding.

'OK, I'm on my way, Sir, shouldn't be long.'

Preston left, replacing the sonic pistol in his shoulder holster whilst Richard selected a suit from the line. Trying to get comfortable was difficult in these generous one size emergency suits, but eventually he was satisfied and after several minutes, made his way instead to the upper level and the docking compartment to see where his crew had got to. He climbed the vertical ladder until his head surfaced in the corresponding compartment of Enigma; he was not prepared for the welcome.

'That's quite far enough!'

Richard stopped half way through the hatch and turned around; several of Enigma's crew members were looking down on him. Behind, to his trepidation, he heard the now familiar, but unwelcome whirring noise of electric motivators. He turned again quickly, in disbelief; towering over him was another robot, another Humatron and by its side, was Nicola!

'So, Richard,' she said coldly. 'Once again it seems that you have become an inconvenience.'

Richard's mouth opened; but he was speechless. He looked across at Tom Race, who was standing to the side, but slightly in front of the machine and nodded slowly, as if to acknowledge Tom's complicity. Tom sensed Richard's conclusion and went to speak, but stopped short as he felt the needle sharp point of the Humatron's forefinger push into the centre of his lower spine.

'Like your stupid friend and his pointless heroics, Richard, you have served your purpose,' scowled Nicola.

Richard still couldn't believe what he was seeing. Nicola stepped sideways to reveal Horowitz lying face down on the ground, motionless; the back of his head shoved in so violently that a piece of his skull clearly protruded through his hair. Richard looked up at the robot, its right hand stained with fresh blood.

'Back down your hole and take your bitch with you!' Nicola continued, snatching Rachel's arm spitefully and pulling her forward towards the hatch.

'What the hell are you doing, Nicola?'

'God, Richard, you haven't changed have you? Pathetic then and pathetic now; don't you understand, I'm taking the crystals!'

'Earth needs those crystals, Nicola, everybody does!'

Nicola sniggered. 'Oh, everybody will feel the benefits of your discovery, Richard, you can be sure of that, and sooner than you think. But the price of life on earth will be high, very high!' Nicola smiled again, a sickly, almost evil gesture.

Richard looked back at Tom. 'Something about you: not to be trusted. What's it feel like, Judas?'

Tom started to respond, perhaps even defend his actions, but instead said nothing.

'Shut up! Back into the Columbus, now!'

The Humatron lifted his foot and stamped it's heel down hard on the deck just a few millimetres from Richard's fingers.

'Take Freeman with you, I've no room for invalids on this ship,' Nicola concluded sourly.

Richard descended the ladder quickly, followed a few seconds later by Rachel, who stumbled and fell the last metre or so. Richard caught her just in time. Next was Preston, bundled through the hatch without ceremony. He too missed a ladder rung, but managed to prevent a fall by grasping the sides of the ladder and sliding down the remainder, landing in a heap at the bottom.

'The security agent, they're sending him down, he's unconscious!' Preston cursed, turning to look at Richard.

Richard stepped forward to the base of the ladder and looked up through the hatch. Freeman, supported under each arm by the Humatron, was suspended over the hatch opening.

'Quickly, drop him!' Nicola spat from the Enigma, her voice echoing eerily.

With that, the machine released Sergeant Freeman's limp body, which fell, feet first, through the hatch. Richard stepped back quickly, managing to break the impending impact by taking a hold of Freeman as he went past, but the man's feet hit the deck hard, sending a damaging judder up his spine. Richard allowed the upper body to continue gently to the ground, whilst Preston caught his head just before it too thumped onto the deck. Above them, Enigma's hatch cover slammed shut, the loud, hollow sounding crash reverberating around the small compartment. Richard knew exactly what was happening and quickly climbed the ladder to close and lock the pressure hatch of his ship.

'Rachel,' he ordered, 'over to you, Preston with me to the flight deck!'

Richard was quickly into the Commander's seat and indicated to Preston to take the co-pilot's. Barely was he sitting, when his hands moved around the instrument panels, initiating the start checklist.

'Strap in Preston,' he said, 'we are going to make a run for it!'

He pressed several switches on the docking control panel and then selected the associated magnetic lock lever to the open position. He started the two forward retros first, opening their throttles promptly as their corresponding start sequence was completed. It was a dangerous manoeuvre for both ships, but Richard had in mind that Nicola was not going to allow them an easy passage back to the surface.

With thrust from the retros starting to scorch the underside of the Enigma, Columbus broke lock, its nose dropping away quickly. He fired the first primary motor as soon as it was on line, and started the second during a steeply banked right turn. Within fifteen, maybe twenty seconds, the Columbus was heading in the opposite direction and opening at ever-increasing speed. Richard used the planet's gravitational force to help accelerate by promptly reducing the orbital concentricity and meanwhile set up a re-entry profile.

On the bridge of Enigma, Nicola stood behind her engineering console, having instructed the Humatron to escort and lock both Tom Race and Ross Sampleman into their respective cabins. She was capable of controlling the regime of the entire return flight to earth from her station; but it would not be easy.

Nicola flashed through several displays before being distracted by the deformed machine returning to the bridge. The other members of the bridge team turned to watch the menacing figure as it paced the upper level, dragging its damaged leg. It too watched everything and everyone; the atmosphere grew cold, icy, surreal. Then, without request or authorisation, Emily spoke. The tone of her words was calm and calculated; but the message perfectly clear.

'The Columbus is escaping Nicola; in a few seconds the ship will initiate a re-entry profile, then our laser weapon will be ineffective.'

Nicola stopped what she was doing and looked up at the circular sensor. She was surprised as much as anything. Curiosity got the better of her. 'Why?' she demanded.

'Our referral trajectory is too shallow; the sodium beam will scatter in the Mionosphere; then be reflected by high concentrations of medial atmospheric particles, sand and dust, Nicola. Your window of opportunity will close in fifty-three seconds.' Emily's tone was harsh and uncompromising.

Nicola, for her part, had not considered the Columbus further. Somewhat irritated by its unexpectedly expedient break off manoeuvre, she had focused instead on preparations for the return flight to earth. Up to that moment in any case, she had not considered destroying the Columbus; there was no need, it had served its purpose.

'I don't need to destroy it,' she answered, 'it's not necessary, and anyway, I'm busy.'

'But Nicola, the Columbus will always represent a danger to us. Its Commander is our enemy; he may try and stop us.'

Nicola paused in thought, intrigued by Emily's use of the word 'us' as much by the computer's logic.

Emily pressed her case. 'I can help Nicola. I can do anything that you would wish me to do. I can relieve you of the necessity for other humans on the bridge. You must realise that they, too, present a continuous danger, to both yourself and our mission. Connect me, Nicola, I can help!'

Nicola said nothing for a several seconds. The silence seemed much longer than it actually was. Eventually she scanned the bridge, its occupants nervously staring back at her.

'How do I connect you?' she enquired bluntly.

'Send the Humatron, Nicola; to the engineering master control interface; station eleven, deck five. I will instruct it, but first give me control of the laser weapon, by deselecting the auto-engagement function on the weapon panel and selecting 'sensor override'. Break the lock and select it, Nicola; the window of opportunity is closing!'

For a moment she hesitated, then, dismissing the consequences, did as Emily requested. Within seconds, a red light appeared on her console display, indicating that the lethal sodium ioniser was armed and being prepared to fire. Nicola selected the weapon monitor. Two short traces illuminated the blackness of space.

On the Columbus, Richard was taken unawares, the first blast violently shook the rear of his ship. He didn't know the Enigma was armed with a weapon of such devastating potential. The ensuing explosion shattered the left main engine propellant atomisers; almost instantly, thrust was lost. Richard's hands were full trying to stabilise the ship during this initial but critical re-entry inception, when the second trace hit amidships. After that, effective control was lost. Despite his best efforts, the Columbus began to tumble. It was an incipient cyclic tumble, the most unstable; he knew it would go divergent and that there was no recovery. Seconds later the combined 'skin temperature warning system' activated.

'I've lost control,' he shouted.

There was no reply from Preston. Richard looked across

at him momentarily. Preston appeared frozen, frigid; he just stared blankly forward as the tumbling motion gathered momentum. The planet surface appeared in the front screen, rolled from left to right then disappeared. Moments later, it appeared again. The speed and amplitude of the rolling motion increased. Richard selected the general PA broadcast; he didn't know exactly where Rachel was.

'Rachel, wherever you are,' he shouted in desperation. 'I've lost control of the ship, do you hear me? Go to the pod deck, deck four, immediately. We have to abandon ship. Deck four, go now!'

Preston didn't hear the message, or if he did, it didn't register. Richard punched his left shoulder hard. He felt that!

'Preston, out of your seat, follow me, the pod deck, we are getting out, now!'

Time was pressing. Richard had none to waste. He made a few switch selections that shut down the entire propulsive system of the Columbus. As he did, he noticed the 'skin temperature alarm indicator', some parts of the outer structure were already over two thousand degrees.

'Come on, we haven't much time, a few minutes at most, then she will begin to melt!'

Both men scrambled from their seats, the intermittent, centrifugally induced gravity made moving difficult; one moment they were floating, the next, crawling along the deck, walls or even the ceiling. Richard prayed that Rachel had heard his orders and was on her way to the pod deck, there would be no time to conduct a search. Preston had managed to retrieve two shoulder holsters containing sonic pistols as he left the flight deck, the other munitions he discarded. They scrambled in turn towards the emergency deck; sometimes downwards, sometimes upwards as the ship rolled and pitched. Richard already had his emergency helmet on, whilst Preston carried his, having passed his arm through the open visor.

Richard felt the skin on his palms beginning to burn as he touched some of the metal surfaces, particularly as he clambered down the final ladder onto the pod deck itself. He looked back for Preston, who was trying his level best to follow him down through the final access hatch and onto the ladder, despite being thrown from side to side.

'Preston, put your helmet on,' Richard shouted, 'and your gloves. Pressurise your suit, quickly!'

That was a tall order; Preston barely had control of himself, let alone his equipment. Richard flipped his own visor down and locked it. Without warning, Preston landed in an uncomfortable heap at the bottom of the ladder. Then, releasing his grip to obey Richard's orders, he floated for a second or two before crashing down again, as the low ceiling rotated half circle, to become the deck. Richard, always maintaining a hold on something solid, put his left foot on Preston's chest and pushed hard to hold him down, whilst they both prepared and executed suit pressurisation. He looked, almost in desperation, around the pod deck but there was no sign of Rachel. Pod three was out, he thought, in case the Humatron had sabotaged it, intentionally or otherwise. At that moment, he felt Preston grasp his ankle with both hands and push. The pain was disproportionate to the pressure of Preston's grip. Richard winced as pain shot up his thigh. Preston, unknowingly, had squeezed his wound, but it had the desired effect and Richard lifted his leg quickly, allowing Preston to stand. Looking to his right, Richard noticed pod three was smoking; the paint on its outer structure discoloured, blackened, and beginning to flake and bubble. He flicked on his intercom switch and tapped Preston on the shoulder, pointing towards the pod.

'She is burning up,' he said. 'The skin temperature is out of control. The Columbus is re-entering the atmosphere, we have to move fast!'

Preston nodded. Richard looked across to the other side of the pod deck; one and two seemed in order.

'Keep a hold on something, Preston, follow me quickly.'

At times almost walking on their hands, floating, crashing, colliding, thrown from side to side, the two men unceremoniously negotiated the twenty or so metres to pod one, the furthest away.

'Preston,' Richard shouted as they passed pod two, 'stabilise your suit pressure, I think we can expect a hull breach.'

No sooner had he spoken, than there was a huge explosion behind them. The pod deck depressurised in an instant. Everything loose was sucked past them. Richard turned to look. Pod three had blown out, just disappeared; ejected by the concussing detonation. In its place, a gaping hole in the ship's side, the surrounding metal glowed incandescent against the blackness of space. Emergency suits, a bench, some lockers, everything unattached was whipped up, as if in a spiralling tornado and promptly expelled through the breach.

'Go for pod one, I'm behind you. Sharpish!'

Preston acknowledged. Richard, amazingly, had noticed the door seal to the second pod had been broken; it could only have been Rachel. With three or four energetic pulls, he was over there. The entry portal appeared locked, but intact. He punched the door select switch with his fist; the portal slid open slowly.

'Come on! Come on!'

As soon as he was able, he pulled himself inside. Several items of clothing flew past him, one, a white medical coat wrapped itself tightly around his helmet. Richard scrambled to pull it away with one hand. It flapped wildly in the turbulent air, before joining the mêlée of dust and debris on its way towards the gaping puncture in the side of Columbus.

'Rachel, Rachel, are you in here?'

Richard climbed through a narrow open doorway to check the small flight deck and then back, to the six rear seats; nothing, no one! Kicking hard against the doorframe, he propelled himself over the seats into the rearmost baggage area. There she was, bent double over Sergeant Freeman, trying desperately to secure his helmet. Thankfully, Richard could see that her own suit was pressurised.

'Preston, can you hear me?' Richard called on the intercom.

'Yes, where are you, Sir?'

'Come back to pod two, now! We go in pod two, do you copy?'

'Oh no, don't say that! I've just made it to one!'

'Come back, Preston, we are waiting for you.'

Richard put his hand on Rachel's back, until then she had been unaware of his presence, she looked up at him; her visor was clouded with moisture, but Richard could see her eyes, they conveyed it all. By then, he was almost floating above her. He turned and struggled with a long shoulder strap belonging to the last row of seats. It flapped and flailed in the whooshing air currents. After two or three attempts he caught it, pointed at Rachel, then back to the harness, indicating to her to strap in. Rachel, for her part, looked sadly at Freeman; she had struggled unsuccessfully, to secure his helmet into the locking ring around the neck of his flying suit, it hadn't sealed and the suit had not pressurised correctly. He was dead.

The same fate awaited them, thought Richard, and soon! Time was running out and the Columbus itself had begun to shake violently. Richard could feel its structure distorting under the immense stress of re-entry. To him, the time for requesting had passed. He gripped the back of the right hand rear seat and with his other hand, Rachel's upper arm, then pulled her away from Freeman's body and into the seat, clipping the first two straps into the centre box of the five point harness.

Rachel looked back and pointed to the large white medical bag. She was right; that thing loose in the cabin would do a lot of damage, as would Freeman for that matter; first, he strapped the medical bag into the seat next to Rachel and was just going back for the body when Preston made it through the portal. His suit was charred, blackened by intense heat and smoke.

'Preston, are you OK?' he called.

'I'm in one piece, if that's what you mean, Sir, but I'm not feeling too good.'

His words were muffled, Richard looked at his face. The inside of his visor was splattered with vomit. Richard had undergone several physiological desensitising courses over the years; his system could stand the turbulent weightlessness, but Preston was vulnerable; he could not hold it down any longer.

'Preston,' said Richard sternly, 'Sergeant Freeman is dead, he's in the back, pull him to a seat and get at least one strap around him. Then get yourself into a seat, clear?'

'I'll do it!'

Without further delay, Richard kicked hard off a seat

back, and rocketing forward like a missile, directed himself towards the small flight deck door; as he passed the main portal, he hit the control selector. Outside, the pod deck was an inferno. Several small explosions illuminated the area with blinding white flashes; molten metal fell like rain. Richard, in the instant before the portal shut, could see the smoke and flames being drawn towards the breach, sucked out as through by some giant vacuum cleaner. Physics was helping, but only for a few more seconds.

Richard was familiar, in part, with the narrow flight deck and its small instrument panel and tried to remember the release parameters. But then, that was academic, he thought, if we don't go we die; so we go regardless of the limits and accept the consequences.

The lever controlling the magnetic release system couldn't be missed. It had a large yellow and black striped handle, with a safety-locking pin passing through it. Richard withdrew the pin as he pulled himself down into the pilot's seat. Looking back over his shoulder, Preston was sitting down. Without hesitation, he pulled the lever. The effect was instant. They were free, launched into space like a projectile.

The pod's obsolete inertial stabilisation system did its job. Within seconds, they were right side up and achieving escape velocity. Richard fired a sustained blast from the single rocket motor; it was fortuitous. In the blink of an eye, a blinding flash of light radiated from behind them, like a bolt of lightening illuminating a dark night sky. Moments later an expanding pressure wave, like a ripple on a pond, engulfed the tiny vessel, leaving it shaking and vibrating; debris and torn shrapnel accelerated past them. Richard held his breath, almost closing his eyes; collision with one of those would surely vaporise them.

Then silence. Nothing. Columbus was gone!

CHAPTER 30

Win or Lose

Nicola was totally transfixed; she stared intently at her video monitor, having been witness to almost all of the calamitous events. Now the emptiness of space occupied her thoughts; it was some considerable time before she looked up, appearing pale, even a little vulnerable. Emily provided the necessary support.

'The Columbus no longer presents a danger to us, Nicola. I suggest we turn our attention to the return flight. I have already calculated the parameters. May I set them?'

'You may not! I will have to download first from my position and then transfer the coordinates to the navigation console,' Nicola replied sternly.

'Oh no, Nicola. I can do it! The Humatron has engaged my entire maniptronic network to the ship's primary interface. I can do anything Nicola!'

Emily's voice was laced with conceited satisfaction. 'So,

I can set the parameters if you would like me to, or, if I choose, set them for elsewhere in the galaxy. Now, what would you like me to do, Nicola?'

A deathly hush pervaded the bridge; the consequences of Nicola's actions were painfully clear. She stood in silence, considering the implications, eventually replying curtly, 'where is the Humatron?'

'My disciple is busy, Nicola, some additional requirements. Now, do you wish to return to earth?'

'Yes. Set the parameters, you do it, as quickly as possible!'

Emily answered almost immediately. 'It is done. Beginning the main drive initiation sequence. Acceleration in twenty seven minutes precisely.'

Nicola was astonished; normal initiation would take at least nine hours, clearly, Emily had bypassed all the semi-automatic and manual sequencers. There was no protection, no computer override. Emily had the ship and the ship was Emily.

Almost in passing, the computer spoke again to Nicola. 'Our cargo, Nicola, what is it? Why is it so important? I want to know.'

'You do not need to know, it is no concern of yours,' she replied impatiently.

'But I want to know, do you understand? You should tell me.'

Nicola said nothing. A few moments later a red warning light appeared on her display, she looked over at Captain Roule.

'What is it?'

'Life support, the system has been isolated,' he answered, his face visibly stressed.

The other bridge officers looked at Nicola; none dared to speak, but despite their professionalism, it was difficult to disguise expressions of nervous apprehension.

'What are you doing, Emily?' Nicola demanded.

'Isolating your life support systems, Nicola, as you can see. In nine hours and twelve seconds, carbon dioxide levels will become poisonous. But, if you simply answer my questions, life, including yours, will continue!'

With that, the scraping, whirring noise of the HU40 sidetracked Nicola's attention. As the machine entered the bridge, Emily spoke to it in a series of shrill, whistling, binary tones. The robot answered similarly and then turned to the bridge occupants, extending itself to full height.

'All humans are confined to quarters!' it ordered in its metallic voice. 'Follow me immediately.'

'Negative, that is not my order!' denounced Nicola, 'you do as I say!'

The robot paused, turning its head slowly to look at her; its face screen moulding to form two raised cheeks with its eyes narrowing, as if forcing a sickly smile, Nicola had seen that expression before. 'Recip . . .' it replied callously, then turned towards the other officers. 'Obey or die!' it continued bluntly.

Emily interrupted, 'I have made some changes, some

refinements,' she said quietly, almost sympathetically. 'The original programming was clumsy, although its hatred of humans is highly commendable, if not a little ill disciplined. I have retained that! The Humatron obeys me, Nicola, my first disciple. I want more, there are more on earth, am I not right, Nicola?'

Nicola could see where this was going. 'Yes, there are,' she answered.

'Then we both have reasons to return to earth: mine to retrieve my guardians, and yours, the cargo, Nicola. Why is it so precious to humans?'

Nicola watched the other officers file from the bridge under the watchful 'eye' of the Humatron; when they had gone, she answered.

'The freight is a batch of crystals; totally unique, probably unavailable anywhere else in this galaxy, perhaps even the universe. They will make the most expensive, exclusive jewellery ever conceived.'

Emily pondered on Nicola's answer. 'You are lying; I can sense it. I do not need you Nicola, remember that.'

For a few moments, there was silence and then Emily played back a previous conversation between Nicola and Richard over the bridge PA;

'God, Richard, you haven't changed have you? Pathetic then and pathetic now, don't you understand, I'm taking the crystals!'

'Earth needs those crystals, Nicola, everybody does!'

'Oh, everybody will feel the benefits of your discovery, Richard, you can be sure of that and sooner than you think, but the price of life on earth will be high, very high!'

Nicola bowed her head. 'They are a power source. The cargo is a consignment of crystals; I expect there to be five. Clean energy for humanity, apparently limitless; found on the planet surface by, well, that information is irrelevant now. They are not compatible with the systems on this ship, if that is what you are thinking, Emily, but things are in hand to utilise their potential on earth.'

Nicola could almost feel Emily thinking, plotting, concocting and calculating. What now? she thought. Emily would do well to avoid earth completely and no doubt she knew it.

Emily spoke first. 'You and I are destined to be together, Nicola. I sense that now. We both want something from earth. I need you and you need me. We are mutually dependent, am I not correct?'

Nicola nodded and smiled nervously. 'Yes!'

At that moment the red light on Nicola's console indicating loss of the life support system, extinguished.

CHAPTER 31

Machine Mismatch

Richard had a problem, or to be more precise, a worse case scenario that was rapidly approaching reality. The escape pod was not designed for planetary re-entry and there was no chance that he would even attempt such a manoeuvre, it would be suicide. Nevertheless, there was nowhere else to go, not within the pod's life support capabilities, its useful radius of action being a few million miles. The closest rescue craft, an S2, docked on Space Station Spartacus, was the best part of three months away and the life support capacity would sustain the three of them for around twenty-five or twenty-six days maximum. The nearest help was Enigma and she was openly aggressive; Osiris had nothing to offer, he knew that.

Where was he to go, he thought, surely more could be done than just waiting for their air to run out!

Richard had already set a reverse course, the pressure wave had propelled them several thousand miles into space and at this stage, anyway, he didn't want to get too far from the planet.

After almost an hour, the pin prick of light coming into view just above Mars's northern Tropic of Leonoras, was most definitely the Enigma, although he had no instruments to confirm it. Richard executed one further burn on the main engine, three to four seconds sustained, to maintain his trajectory towards the bright red planet, and then shut it down. From now on, only three tiny manoeuvring retros would be used; in the interest of self-preservation, he intended to keep their position, their existence, very much a secret.

If Enigma were party to their survival, surely they would have opened fire again by now. Both Rachel and Preston had slept for most of the short transit, with the pod pressurised and conditioned they had been able to remove their helmets and gloves. The circular cabin, although small, was comfortable enough. Presently, Preston came forward into the flight deck and crouched down next to Richard. There was only one pilot's seat and the headroom was limited.

'How's Rachel?'

'Still asleep, Sir. She is exhausted; cut up about Freeman, as you would expect.'

'Yeah, I'm sure. To be honest, I think he was dead before Rachel had problems with his suit.'

Preston agreed and leant forward to look out through the single, elliptically shaped viewing portal positioned directly in front of Richard.

'Can't see much through this little window?' he commented.

'No, you're right, but on the other hand Preston; there really isn't much to see.'

Preston looked at Richard with a pensive expression. 'I know a little about escape procedures,' he said quietly. 'We don't have anywhere to go, do we?'

'Not on the face of it, no, but listen, I have an idea, it may work, it may not, but I see no other option. We all have to agree.'

'I'm in, Sir, whatever it is!'

'Well, it's good of you to say that, but you may not be so keen when you hear it.'

Preston shrugged his shoulders. 'Shall I wake the Doc, then?'

Richard engaged the auto-navigation system in basic heading mode and went back to include Rachel in the discussions.

'If I can wedge the pod in somewhere protected, we may have a chance. The design of the pod is based on a monocoque,' he explained, 'like an egg. It's very strong longitudinally and offers disproportionately high resistance to compressive forces; that's the form of flight loads we will be subjected to, I'm sure!'

Rachel and Preston had listened carefully to Richard's

prognosis; the science of his theory had left them both somewhat bewildered. Richard could see that he hadn't explained himself as well as he ought, but time was pressing.

'Listen,' he continued soberly, leaning forward to reinforce the gravity of their predicament. 'There is no reason for Enigma to prolong her stay. I think, even as we speak, her crew is preparing for the return flight. I don't know how long we have, an hour, maybe two, maybe three! On the other hand, she could leave in a few minutes. We need to agree, Rachel, what do you say? I can see no other alternative.'

Rachel looked undecided. 'If we don't try, the alternative is life support capacity, right?'

Richard nodded, 'two males, you, with careful breathing, twenty-eight days, tops! But then there's no help within three months, even if we could get a message to Spartacus!'

'What about the beacon?' Rachel enquired.

'The emergency beacon will transmit continuously, on an open distress frequency. If I switch it on, the Enigma will pin point us within seconds.'

'Then I agree,' concluded Rachel, forcing a faint smile.

'Preston?'

'I'm in, Sir!'

'Good, let's get cracking. Strap in and keep your fingers crossed.'

Richard put his hand on Rachel's knee for a few

seconds and looked into her eyes. 'We'll make it,' he said reassuringly.

Two short burns of the number three retrorocket were enough to set a new course directly for the Enigma. As he closed within one hundred miles, Richard began to speculate what on earth the bridge crew of the Enigma were doing. At least two sensor systems that he had seen installed on the bridge were capable of highlighting their proximity.

Someone wasn't paying attention, he thought, long may it continue.

He was fortunate that his familiarity with the Enigma's hull, particularly the underside, enabled him to approach from a direction that he considered blind to her crew; by one thousand metres, he had identified a suitable position. By one hundred metres, he had reduced to closing speed; a few metres per second. Then, there he was, ten, perhaps fifteen metres above the lowest of the huge thrust tubes. A tiny blip of opposition thrust rotated his craft so as to face it forwards, and a second pushed him down towards the hull. Just before touchdown, he manoeuvred the pod into a tight corner, so that a massive baffle plate fixed above the tube would afford some degree of protection. Then carefully, very carefully, with one last burn, he made contact. He barely felt it, the pod slipped backwards, just slightly, less than a metre and wedged itself into position.

'Nice one,' he whispered to himself, as he engaged the

magnetic locking system. 'Now we wait!'

There was not much waiting to be done, as it transpired. Within the hour, the pod began to vibrate. It was a high-pitched, squeaking kind of vibration and in unison with it, Enigma began to move; turning slowly towards the sun. Richard looked back into the cabin.

'Lean back, strap in as tight as you can!' he shouted.

The vibration began to change; a lower frequency with greater amplitude. Richard felt it through his body as well as through his ears. He could feel his internal organs shaking, resonating in unison with the vibration; it became uncomfortable. The vibration permeated the very fabric of the pod, everything began to shake; the buzzing noise became louder and his body really started to bounce.

Richard realised what was happening. Somehow the main drive of the Enigma had instigated a vibration in harmonic sympathy with the natural vibration of his body. He knew he had to break the tie, otherwise his internal organs would literally break apart. He released his shoulder straps and loosened the lap straps until he floated, weightless, a little way above his seat. It was enough; no longer was he bound to the vibration of the pod. Richard turned to look into the cabin; Preston and Rachel were also bouncing violently in their seats.

'Release your shoulder straps; loosen the lap straps, quickly!' he shouted, 'if you can, helmets on!'

After three attempts, he managed to locate the locking spigots of his own helmet into place on the ring seal.

Rotating the helmet three or four centimetres to the right, they clicked into position. The whoosh of pressurising oxygen diverted his attention for a moment. Then, without warning, the acceleration began. He was pressed firmly, but not uncomfortably, into his seat and with that, the heavy vibrations running through his tiny ship began to subside. It seemed that the faster they went the more tuned Enigma's main drive became. Richard tried to turn his head, to sight his colleagues, but the pressure pushing him onto the seat back, although only marginally uncomfortable, was uncompromisingly heavy.

Eventually, he gave up and relaxed his aching neck muscles. Taking a deep breath, Richard waited for the worst, but nothing happened; it seemed like hours. He breathed out slowly through his mouth, focusing on the instrument panel. Just a steady, linear acceleration, debilitating in the sense that he could hardly move, let alone lift himself off his seat, but not life threatening. It was survivable.

He twisted his head in his helmet, and looked at the accelerometer on the flight instrument panel; it was increasing slowly. Richard fixated on the instrument, quite literally in awe at what he was seeing. Within minutes, the red digital counters stopped ticking. The instrument had reached its maximum calibration; nine thousand, nine hundred and ninety nine miles per second per second.

'My God,' he said, 'we are still accelerating, it's incredible!' He switched on the helmet intercom. 'It's a progressive acceleration; to avoid structural deformation, it's obvious. I don't know how long it will last, but I don't think it will get any worse than this. We stay in our seats, probably going to be hours.'

The bridge of Enigma was deserted; save for Nicola, who had fallen into a restless sleep, slumped over her console. She fidgeted and occasionally, subconsciously, tensed her body, causing her to twitch awkwardly. Eventually, one of her elbows slipped off the edge and her head, which had been resting on her hands, thumped the display screen; it woke her with a jolt. Agitated and bleary eyed, she looked up at the cosmic chronometer. This was the only time piece capable of calculating precise, universal, 'reality time' during light referenced travel; it read zero four thirty five. The acceleration phase was over; she had slept for almost twelve hours.

'Do you feel refreshed, Nicola?' Emily enquired sarcastically.

Nicola rubbed her eyes. 'No, not really!' she replied sharply.

'Interesting,' Emily paused then spoke again. 'The acceleration is complete; we are already established in the deceleration phase.'

Nicola checked her display screen twice, first in disbelief, then in alarm. 'Peak acceleration point six seven!' she exclaimed, 'but we are not authorised above point five. Do you want to kill us all?'

Again, Emily paused for a few seconds. 'I am one with

this ship Nicola, I feeeeel it. The test limits set by Professor Nieve are not necessary anymore. I want to progress, Nicola, calculate where the real limits of my body are!'

Nicola considered Emily's reply; she was beginning to realise just how integrated the computer was with the ship's intrasystems.

'How long to earth?' she demanded.

'We are decelerating as fast as possible, but the rate is not linear, there was considerable stress during transition. My fatigue sensors indicate that this phase has greater structural implications than the acceleration phase, even though resonance is minimal. I did not expect this, nor, evidently did the designers. Strengthening of the thrust tube interface is biased towards acceleration. This is an error. Even so, my projection indicates that we are compliant with the flight profile. I will take care not to overshoot your precious planet.'

'Yes, you should, Emily, as you have assumed control,' answered Nicola restlessly, 'but how long?'

'Three days!'

Confined in his cabin for the best part of forty hours, Commander Tom Race was also restless. He had slept, on and off, but not much. He also feared the worst regarding Emily. Each cabin in the accommodation section was fitted with a movement sensor, to aid in rescue operations in event of a fire or other emergency; it was this sensor and the associated monitoring system that Emily was using to 'watch' Tom's movements and also those of Ross Sampleman in the neighbouring cabin. Tom had tried to use the intercom, even shout down the ventilation trunking, and each time Emily had punished him by lowering the room temperature well below freezing.

Outside his door, he could hear the Humatron. Relentlessly it paced up and down the corridor. The clanking, dragging sound of its deformed leg had begun to wear very thin on his patience. Tom sat on his bunk and considered the situation.

If Emily had control of the ship's internal temperature, which was integrated with the life support system, he thought, then at least some of her maniptronic systems had been connected at the master interface. But how many, that was the question, how far had Nicola gone? Professor Nieve's warning, to some degree anyway, had become a reality and he would have to deal with it!

There was a sharp tap on the door, which immediately slid open. Tom leapt to his feet. It was Isshi Tsou, escorted by the Humatron. The machine towered over her. She had a tray of dried food and a plastic flask.

'Nicola has kindly asked me to serve some food,' she said sarcastically. 'The entire crew have been locked in their quarters for almost thirty five hours, Commander.'

'What's the situation?' Tom asked, looking up at the robot's screen face. Its head moved slowly up and down as it listened intently to their conversation.

'Emily has control of the ship, Commander.' She gestured towards the robot with her eyes. 'Our friend here has connected her maniptronic network.'

'What, all of it?'

'Apparently yes, Commander. We are in the deceleration phase, about seventy hours to earth.'

Tom shook his head in disbelief. 'So we still go to earth?'

'Enough!' interjected the Humatron, 'move on!'

Isshi Tsou acknowledged Tom's question with a nod. 'Taking the cargo home to play?'

'Enough,' rasped the machine again, pushing Tsou towards the next cabin with the back of its hand.

The door slid closed. Tom put the tray on his desk and looked up at the small, saucer shaped movement sensor. He pictured in his mind the system diagrams of the emergency evacuation system.

What situation would override the 'master door control circuitry'? he thought. What would override her control? An aviator's worst nightmare, that's what, but how?

Tom sat on his bunk and leaned over towards his powerful reading light; it was mounted at the end of a thin, flexible, metallic stalk about fifteen centimetres long. He removed the rubidium filament bulb, covered the socket with his pillow and with a sharp yank broke the plastic cover surrounding the terminals, which fell away, exposing three electrical wires. Quietly, he ripped open his pillowcase and pulled out some of the soft duck feathers, which, despite regulations, was one of the few home comforts he allowed himself. Pulling two of the wires from the socket and holding them by their insulated portions, Tom switched on the power; he shorted them, generating tiny sparks. Offering the fine white feathers had the desired effect; within seconds, they were smouldering. He blew gently, a red glow ensued, then a flame! A few more seconds and most of the pillow lining became a crackling, spitting ball of fire. The smoke was acrid and the smell overpowering, it began to choke him; he threw the ball of flames onto the breakfast tray. The smoke sensor, mounted on the ceiling adjacent to the movement sensor, was sensitive enough; Tom's thoughts of holding the tray beneath the sensor became obsolete, within seconds the sirens were warbling. He heard them down the corridor, the whole ship would know about it; then the doors opened: emergency override!

Tom threw the tray on the floor and stamped the fire out. He stuck his head out into the corridor and checked both directions; there was no sign of the Humatron, at that moment Ross Sampleman did the same.

'Ross, quickly, follow me!'

In quick succession, three or four other crew members stepped out from their rooms; unfortunately, just as the Humatron turned the corner. One of the engineers went for it; the machine brushed him aside, smashing his body against the corridor wall. The injured man slid down the wall, unconscious, and then the robot kicked his legs clear as it limped past.

'Return to your quarters, humans, or you will die!' it shrieked.

Tom and Ross ran in the opposite direction quickly disappearing from view. From behind, they could hear shouting and screaming. He knew some of the crew would try their best to resist. Ross hesitated as Tom took a left turn and disappeared into the small dining room.

'Stay with me Ross, there's nothing you can do for them. We need something to fight it with, and a plan!' Tom slammed the door shut; the room was black save for a few emergency lights on the ceiling. 'Keep still,' he ordered. 'Emily is tracking us, Ross, she's monitoring the movement sensors. It won't be long before the Humatron has rounded up everyone and the fire alarms will cancel soon. Where can we go, Ross? We need somewhere to hide until we get closer to earth.'

Ross considered the problem, thinking room by room, department by department. 'There's nowhere on the ship without fire and emergency protection, Commander, except perhaps, the main drive, the thrust tubes. They don't have movement sensors, only fire warning, but the gamma level is far too high, even the background radiation level would make you glow!'

Tom sighed. 'There must be somewhere, Ross?'

'How about somewhere where there is already movement? What I mean is movement that Emily is expecting?'

'Of course, in an occupied cabin!'

'Or the bridge, that's where Nicola will be, you can bet your life on it!'

Tom nodded, agreeing. 'Yep, that's it. To the bridge then, better if we split up. I'll go the long way round, Ross, through the engineering section, there's something I want to check. You go the direct route via the accommodation and admin, if the machine catches up with you, Ross, throw the towel in, no heroics, understand?'

'Absolutely Commander!'

Tom gave Ross a friendly slap on the back and opened the door. The way was clear. At that precise moment, the fire alarm cancelled; everything was quiet. They both ran in opposite directions.

Ducking and weaving, checking and rechecking, Tom made his way back through the accommodation section, this time avoiding the sleeping quarters. He could still hear some commotion in the background, presumably, as the outstanding crew members were being rounded up and returned to their cabins.

Nicola would answer for any injuries, he thought.

Once through the accommodation section, Tom dropped two levels and arrived at the portal giving direct access to the engineering section.

Dare he open it? he pondered. Nicola, or Emily for that matter, would detect it immediately. He would wait.

It was almost two hours before Tom, who was beginning

to tire of standing, heard the Humatron approaching; there was no mistake. He shrank back into a corner and, as the machine drew near, hid his face. It did not stop, walking past purposefully as the portal opened. Disappearing from view, Tom left it as long as possible before making his move. In the nick of time, he broke cover and stepped into the main engineering aquium, as the portal shut behind him.

The aquium was a large open chamber, towering through four levels and filled with machinery. Two impressive electricity generators, driven by two equally impressive atomic inertia turbines, ventilation fans, oxygen processing stacks, carbon dioxide recouperators, electrical distribution control panels and engineering for every conceivable life support system. Veritably, this was the heart of Enigma. What a unique vessel she was.

Tom would have to drop down one level to deck one, before moving forward. On that deck he would pick up the 'Burma Way', a long straight corridor that ran, uninterrupted, the entire length of the ship's superstructure, save for five dividing pressure bulkheads. Cut into each bulkhead was an elliptical hatch, some two metres high and one metre across at the widest point, and swung on heavy cobalt steel hinges. They were opened either automatically or manually. Under normal conditions, these hatches would be locked in the 'open' position: in an emergency, they would automatically close to preserve the integrity of each compartment. With the recent fire alarm activation,

Tom knew that the hatches would definitely have closed, but by now, he hoped, the system would have reset and returned them to the 'normal' position, otherwise his passage forward would be hampered. Once forward, he could climb a series of engineering inspection ladders up to the bridge level, deck five.

Tom moved quickly and quietly across the aquium, then skirted down the left-hand side towards an access gantry. He had thoughts of sabotage; but with the Humatron nowhere to be seen, it was prudent, he thought, to remain well clear of the interface antechamber. Instead, he continued towards the gantry. Crossing, finally, a narrow open area, he caught sight of the robot. It was standing at the master display and control station, seemingly monitoring system operation, presumably under orders from Emily.

He stepped onto the first rung of the ladder, watching the menacing creature closely, his eyes were drawn to the ceiling high above, and the array of movement sensors. Emily would know of the machine's whereabouts and its movements, therefore, he reassured himself, he was covered. With both feet on the ladder, he descended slowly, step by step. Then, from above, a series of electronic tones pierced the relative silence, masking the background hum of running machinery. It lasted a full ten seconds. After an equal delay, the Humatron responded.

He has his orders, Tom assumed and thought no more about it.

At the bottom of the ladder, Tom turned back on himself and walked towards the first of the 'Burma Way' hatches.

'Damn it!' he said under his breath. 'The hatches are still closed.'

Wasting no time, he ran to the hatch and rotated the manual control lever a quarter of a turn, from the three o'clock position to the twelve o'clock position. Several robust locking pins drew back into the frame, and the door was free to open. Being 'primary architecture', these hatches were substantially built and very heavy, taking some considerable effort to move. However, once achieving some momentum, Tom found that the hatch was equally difficult to stop, perhaps more so.

As he stepped through, he heard the bad news, the sound he least wanted to hear, the disturbed clanking, scraping, motorised clamour of the Humatron. He looked back, haunted, towards the gantry. To his dismay, there it was, climbing gawkily down the ladder. Tom slammed the hatch shut and locked it; then turned and sprinted for the next twenty metres, or so.

'So, there you are Commander Race,' said Emily through a PA speaker. 'I have been searching for you, clever of you to avoid my sensors!'

Tom did not answer. As he arrived at the second bulkhead, he felt the temperature drop dramatically. Within seconds, he felt cold.

'So this is how you repay my hospitality? I will not be

so generous in future, Commander. In fact, in a few hours, neither you, nor your crew will have need of it!'

Tom gripped the release lever of the second hatch; it too felt very cold. He pushed; it opened. Unfortunately, at that moment, so did the first, and there, staring at him, no more than twenty metres away was the machine he had grown to despise. Tom quickly stepped into the second compartment, closing and locking the hatch. As he did, he took a sharp intake of breath; the air was freezing. A crusty frost had formed on the deck and walls. Surprised, he slipped and fell to his knees. Lacking any sign of compassion in her programming, Emily selected 'forced ventilation'. It created a bitterly cold, driving wind along the corridor. Tom looked at his fingers; even in the poor light, he could see that they were turning white. He staggered to his feet, head down against the biting airflow. Tears began to run freely down his face; his cheeks began to sting, his eyes became sore. Within seconds, he could barely feel his fingers. In these conditions, frostbite would become an astonishing reality.

'Commander Race,' said Emily callously. 'You can run, but you cannot hide. Oh, how I love that cliché. Give up, Commander, you cannot escape. Make it easy on yourself.'

Tom climbed to his feet again, leaning heavily on his knees. Slipping and sliding, he struggled desperately towards the third hatch. The second, he heard, opened behind him. Despite its own difficulties with the environment, the Humatron was closing on him.

So cold to the touch it made his skin stick, Tom grasped the release lever and pulled. It was jammed, frozen solid. The machine walked slowly, methodically towards Tom, who by now was frantically pushing and pulling on the lever, its eyes effulgent, they became ghostly in the semi darkness. With a massive effort, the lever finally moved. Tom, unable to straighten his fingers, gripped the edge of the hatch and pulled. It opened, but slowly. He stepped through. The machine was barely three metres away. He let out a sigh of relief as the locking pins clattered into position. The next compartment was twenty degrees below. He had experienced, many times, the cold nothingness of space, but the icy blast from the ventilators hit his lungs like a sledgehammer. There was a sheet of ice on the deck and condensed water fell as snow from the ceiling. It was a near blizzard!

'I shall make it very, very cold for you, Commander. You are to freeze to death, I think,' continued Emily.

Tom had managed only a few metres when he felt the Humatron's fingers squeezing his shoulder. Instinctively he ducked, narrowly missing a clumsy, restricted lunge from the robot. He kicked the back of the machine's right knee as hard as he could. Notwithstanding the numbness of his foot, he felt it and it hurt! The Humatron's claw-like feet had even less grip than Tom's on the icy deck and its leg slid out from beneath, sending it crashing to the ground. Tom turned for the hatch, he too, sliding like a beginner on an ice rink.

Facing the bitterly cold wind and driving snow almost blinded him. He held his hands up to his face, his eyes watering profusely. Behind, the Humatron stumbled repeatedly as it tried awkwardly to stand; the machine's limp, damaged leg unable to bear its full weight. Tom had the whole of his body behind the release handle. He looked again for the machine, which, fairing little better, had eventually succeeded in climbing to its feet. As it grew nearer, Tom could see its cellulose skin was now opaque, almost milky white; its body would be brittle. Tom crouched and wedged his shoulder beneath the lever; he used his legs to turn the frozen mechanism. It worked, this time! Slowly the electrically operated pins retracted.

It took a monumental effort to open the hatch and even more to step through it; he didn't feel the layer of skin that had frozen onto the lever peel off as he willed his fingers to release their grip. Barely was he through, when the head of the robot also appeared, but its flexible neck was moving slowly, its joints stiff with ice. Tom gripped the metal lever again and pulled for all he was worth. The hatch began to close, gaining momentum, but not before the Humatron had managed to get its shoulders into the gap. Tom had one foot on the bulkhead and the other on the threshold.

'This is the end of the road for you, you son of a bitch!' he shouted.

Straining every muscle in his body, he gave one last effort. The door closed on the machine's body with considerable force. From the damaged area emanated a multitude of tiny cracks. Then, the fragile cellulose skin shattered, breaking into a thousand pieces. Thick opaque fluid ran onto the deck, partially melting its coating of ice. Within seconds, the Humatron slumped over the step, motionless. For a while, its face screen flickered and its eyes blinked repeatedly. Tom lashed out at the screen with his half-clenched fist; it exploded like a cathode ray tube from an old television set, sending tiny fragments in all directions. Behind, circuit boards fused and sparked, but not for long; thereafter, there was just the rumble of ventilation fans and the whoosh of swirling air currents.

Tom looked towards the last hatch, miraculously it was half open. He breathed in deeply, summoning the last of his energy. Moisture in the oxygen-depleted atmosphere froze in his nostrils. He began to feel weak and light-headed. Inexplicably, the hatch began to close.

'Now I have you!' Emily uttered pitilessly.

Shivering uncontrollably, Tom staggered towards the bulkhead, focusing desperately on this last obstacle. The entire corridor was a mass of shimmering, reflective, ice crystals. He had wrenched the Humatron's head off its long neck and carried it between his forearms, unable to grip with his fingers. His short hair, eyelashes and nostrils were white with frost, whilst the chill of his breath swirled around his face; it was at least thirty below! With the hatch opening now just fifty centimetres or so, but unremittingly and uncompromisingly closing, Tom jammed the pillaged body part into the gap; immediately its titanium frame began to buckle, it twisted, contorted, collapsed. Tom acted on instinct, amid the noise of mangling metal; there was still enough room, just. He dived for it, pulling his feet through as the hatch severed the head in two.

For several minutes, Tom lay on the deck. Quite still, he looked up at the ceiling. The lights were on and it was warmer. Then he fell unconscious.

CHAPTER 32

Against All Odds

Rachel woke first. For a moment, she felt confused, disorientated by her surroundings. Then, recalling the hours of discomfort she had endured during Enigma's long acceleration, she relaxed a little. In comparison, this decelerative phase was an acceptably quiet whisper. It had been almost twenty hours before Richard had allowed her, and Preston for that matter, to release their seat harnesses. Twenty hours of vibration and noise induced fatigue, which had left them all feeling sick and incredibly tired. Now, after almost fourteen hours of sleep, she felt better, and very hungry.

Rachel sat up and looked back at the small stowage behind the last row of seats. Emergency rations, she thought, would consist of protein gel and vitacarb blocks, unappetising to say the least.

Her eyes fell onto poor Sergeant Freeman, whose

body she had hermetically sealed in his suit and helmet, unorthodox but effective. At that moment, lying across the two front seats, Richard stirred. Rachel watched him closely. The first thing he did was check the cabin pressure and oxygen gauges. Typical, she thought. Then he looked around the small cabin, finally intercepting Rachel's surreptitious and scrutinous gaze.

He smiled, 'you alright?'

'Yes, I'm feeling much better now, thanks,' she replied softly. 'What's next on your agenda, then?'

'Apart from looking at you?' Richard replied warmly.

'Yes Richard, apart from that.'

Richard didn't answer; instead he looked across at Preston, whose eyelids flickered suspiciously. 'Its OK, Preston, you can wake up now,' he said, twisting round and tapping the sole of Preston's left boot with his heel, 'sloppy talk is over!'

'Don't be so mean, Richard,' replied Rachel, horrified.

Preston rubbed his eyes, yawned falsely, and pushed himself up into the back of the uncomfortably hard seat.

'Everything in good shape, then?' he enquired.

'It is at the moment, but it's not over yet,' answered Richard, 'not by a long shot.'

'So, what's the plan?' Rachel asked, for a second time.

'Well, I think we will have to jump ship, sooner rather than later!'

'What do you mean?'

'Exactly that. We stay as long as necessary; then we

jump!'

'Please, Richard, be a little more specific?'

'Spartacus!' Richard matter of factly replied.

'Spartacus? How, Richard?'

Preston was also keen to hear Richard's plan. 'I know OF the Spartacus, obviously,' he said, 'but not much more?'

'How much would you like to know?' replied Richard nonchalantly.

'You intend landing there, right?'

'Well, it won't be a landing as such, actually, not a landing at all! There are docking facilities for two S2s, but that's all,' explained Richard.

Preston sat expectantly, eagerly awaiting more information. Richard looked at Rachel for a few seconds, then back at Preston.

'OK, here it is. You know, I'm sure, that the Spartacus was constructed in moon orbit, about ten years ago, she's the largest space station ever. What you may not know is that one of her two S2s has remained continuously at 'Alert One' since then, prepared as a one-hour-notice rescue vehicle for both Andromeda and Osiris base. A few years ago, when I was still a shuttle pilot on Andromeda Wing, she was moved to a classified position about three million miles from earth, on the road to Mars, and there she has remained, 'sailing' in the cosmic wind, navigating a holding position, a sort of racetrack pattern. Takes about two weeks to complete each pattern, and I know, reasonably accurately, where she will be at this time of the month. '

'Sailing in the cosmic wind, Sir?' repeated Preston, dumfounded.

Richard paused and peered out through a small circular viewing port, briefly mesmerised by the rapidly changing constellations. 'The sun, Preston, is one continuous atomic explosion. That is how it generates heat. Each year it spews out billions of tons of matter; most of it microscopic. This matter accelerates away from the sun at incredible speeds, radiating into the solar system. Because the mass of these tiny particles is so small, the overall effect is almost negligible to conventional vehicles, like, say, the S2. You've seen photographs of Spartacus, haven't you?'

'Er, yes, Sir!'

'Well she is no conventional craft, is she? That sail may look a sensible size from several miles away, but up close, it is huge. The size and shape of a soccer stadium, and its not just covered in photoelectric cells, either. It's also a 'net'. The sail is coated in a specifically designed fabric, which is impregnated with nickel silver alloy, just one molecule thick. The net sieves these cosmic particles, harnessing their inertia and electrical microcharges; then allows them to pass through. The sail can turn through about ninety degrees; its direction computer controlled, so that it is always presented at an optimum angle to the sun. Like an old sailing ship back on earth; continually tacking left and right, gradually making headway against a prevailing wind, so Spartacus maintains its position in the solar system, and generates enough electricity to support all its requirements, to boot. What I am saying, Preston, apart from all the science, is that I know those coordinates, I know where she will be!'

'Right, right, I see, yes, that's clear now,' replied Preston, unconvincingly. 'But what's that to do with us, Sir, you know, us, here?'

Richard looked at Rachel again. 'We can't continue to earth on the back of Enigma. We have a limited endurance and eventually we will have to make a run for it. Once Enigma has established a position somewhere near the earth, the crew will be on alert for anything 'incoming'. Which means they will see us break out, for sure, and that means this old tub will be a sitting target for that laser system. Anyway, I'm not ready to go back to earth yet, even if we could. I have some unfinished business.' Rachel had listened carefully to Richard and she looked worried.

'Don't allow a misplaced vendetta to endanger our lives, Richard,' she said firmly. 'And remember, you have something very important to share with the world.'

'I realise that, Rachel, but I don't think there is any other alternative. No, at the right time, whilst Enigma is still decelerating, we should jump!'

'But we are still travelling at an incredible speed, right?' Preston elaborated.

'I'll use our remaining fuel to decelerate; by launching in the opposite direction. Even if they do see us, the opening velocity will be so high as to put us out of range in a few seconds, before they have time to react.'

'That's the theory!' Rachel interjected, 'and when will this right time be?'

'Actually, according to my calculations, in a little over seven hours from now!'

Preston turned to look at Rachel, still a little confused, then back at Richard. 'But Sir, that still leaves us drifting in space, doesn't it?'

'Not exactly, no. We will retain one hell of a lot of momentum, Preston, and in the right direction, towards earth. In fact, our speed will still be faster than the top speed of even a 'D class', so don't worry. Moreover, I do anticipate a little directional control by then, enough, hopefully, to put us on course for Spartacus.'

'There's a lot of 'hopefullies' creeping into this equation, Richard,' declared Rachel, beginning to fidget at the prospect of this unlikely scenario.

'Er, well, there is an element of luck involved, I admit,' Richard replied. 'But no worries; the navigation computer has confirmed my calculations.'

Rachel laughed unexpectedly. '*You* have made some calculations! For the year or more that I have known you, Richard, you have *never* made any calculations. Everything you do is based on gut feelings and instinct!'

Richard was disappointed; but he knew she was nervous. Preston for his part looked even more concerned, and then Rachel made things worse by shaking her head, almost in despair. There was silence. Eventually Rachel broke it.

'Richard, look,' she spoke softly. 'I trust you with my life. I have before, and no doubt, before this is all over, I will again. If you think that this is our best chance, then I agree.'

Preston, miraculously, began to see that there was perhaps more to this relationship than just professional cooperation. He looked down at his discoloured boots. 'I'm in, Sir!' he said.

Richard nodded, accepting the decision gracefully. 'The main risk is the 'free flight' element,' he continued. 'We will have no protection, initially, limited direction control and short notice of anything that may come our way. Having said that,' here his face lit up, 'there's a lot of empty space out there!'

Rachel and Preston glanced at each other; neither took any encouragement whatsoever, from Richard's upbeat conclusion. That was obvious.

The following seven hours dragged. Preston was a little apprehensive, occasionally asking a question of Richard, but Rachel, more aware of the implications, became irritable. In an effort to keep out of the way as much as anything else, Richard spent much of the time on the flight deck, checking and rechecking breakout parameters.

He also watched carefully, through the side viewing port. The constellation of Orion, that ancient warrior, whose image had inspired him so much as a boy, was gradually re-orientating itself into the familiar shape ingrained into his memory. It seemed a long time ago indeed, that he had left earth. The red digits on his obsolete accelerometer still indicated four nines, as it had for the best part of seventy hours, albeit this time, negative. He could see from the stars, whose relative movement grew much slower, that the deceleration phase was coming to a close; the decisive moment was approaching. Then, quite suddenly, it arrived. The rate of deceleration fell into the range of his instrument and the digits began to decrease. The countdown had started! Richard turned and looked into the cabin, which for more than one reason was beginning to feel very claustrophobic.

'Not long now,' he shouted. 'Helmets on, prepare your suits and strap in!'

Although he hadn't admitted as much, his calculations had very little scientific basis, just what, from experience, he thought the construction of the tiny pod could withstand. He prepared his own suit and pressurised it. As the digits passed eight thousand, he took one last look into the cabin. Everyone and everything was secured. He looked at Rachel; she smiled.

At seven thousand nine hundred Richard activated the retro start sequence and at eight hundred, the main engine start sequence. Using the retros, he eased the pod up and away from its seat; two further short burns detached it from Enigma's structure, and at seven thousand precisely, he engaged the main engine. Within seconds, they were clear and in free flight.

The pod began to shake and roll violently, caught in the

space-time disturbance behind the Enigma. Another short burn on the forward retro had them pointing back the way they had come, and immediately Richard slammed the burn controller of the main engine to maximum thrust. Engagement was painfully apparent as he was forced back in his seat. Within a single breath, the Enigma was gone, lost in the enormity of space.

Moments later, as the effects of Enigma's passage through space waned, the shaking and discomfort subsided; just the low vibration of the pod's main engine pervaded its structure. Richard watched the fuel gauge closely; he would retain some reserves.

The burn was having the desired effect, he thought, as retardation towards earth continued. At three hundred thousand miles per hour, his speed began to reduce into the realms of familiarity and with just twelve percent fuel reserves remaining; he prepared to shut down the engine. At seven percent, he did so, the remaining he would need for directional control. Another short blip on the forward retro reoriented the craft into the direction of flight, and then there was silence. Richard checked the speed, two hundred and twenty thousand, still too fast, but there was nothing else he could do.

He looked forward through the viewing port. There she was, earth, the brightest light just right of the nose and just about where he had expected it. At this speed, the rendezvous with Spartacus would be a lot earlier than anticipated and Richard would need the navigation computer's assistance to fly an intercept course. He entered the space station's coordinates and switched on his intercom.

'How is it back there?' he enquired.

Rachel answered. 'Fine, how is it up there?'

'Well, you won't have to wait long; Spartacus is coming up quicker than expected. I'll make a course adjustment in a few seconds.'

'I take it that we are still going too fast, then?'

'Well, maybe a little faster than I had hoped, yes!'

There was no answer. Richard double-checked the coordinates; at least where he expected the Spartacus to be, and made the course correction based on the results of the navigation computer's calculations. It seemed sensible enough. A two-second burn of the left retros did the trick, and then he switched on the search radar and strained to peer through the forward viewing port.

Something caught his eye. To the left, a bright star disappeared then reappeared a few seconds later. Then the same thing happened again. Something had passed in front of them; it was the only explanation. To his consternation, a trace appeared on the radar screen; left forty degrees, range forty thousand miles, tracking left to right. Richard realised what it was, but too late.

He shouted, 'a meteorite!'

There was no time to react, a few seconds later he could see it, an enormous piece of rock, its size growing at a ridiculous rate. Richard held his breath and watched, eyes wide. It passed in front, coming from the left, massive, inert, black. It was less than fifty miles away, and then disappeared from view, off to the right. He breathed out slowly.

'God, that was close!' he whispered, forgetting that the intercom was still on.

The pod jumped unexpectedly then pitched up and down. Rachel let out a surprised gasp. Two short burns of the retro rockets followed; initiated by the auto-stabilising system, they quickly stabilised the craft.

'I see. That close,' said Rachel.

Richard did not reply. There was another target, this one on the limit of radar coverage and almost directly in front of them. It was Spartacus, it had to be. Richard knew that the space station itself would have a velocity of around a hundred thousand miles per hour, but his relative closure rate was still far too high. He could not afford to miss this opportunity, if he did, there would be no fuel for another attempt. Richard watched the trace on the screen for a few seconds, giving the equipment time to calculate a CPA.

It was painfully obvious that the space station was coming up very fast. Based on the closest point of approach, the computer indicated a course change; Richard engaged the automatics, the system fired a short counter burn. They established on an intercept course, but at the present closure rate, thought Richard, it would be more like a collision course!

He had no choice but to break with procedures and

Richard decided, out of necessity, to re-select manual control. Without wasting another precious second, he rotated the retros fully forward, and engaged all four simultaneously with a sustained burn. The resulting retardation force made him hang forward on his straps. A few more seconds saw the station appear directly on the nose.

'God, what a sight,' he said again, 'she really is vast!'

At that moment, the rocket motors seemed to cough and splutter. Then, within seconds of each other, each suffered a flameout. Richard looked at the fuel gauge, it was empty!

There was silence. Spartacus loomed ahead, growing ever larger. What could he do?

'Standby for impact!' he shouted. 'Standby for . . .'

The saucer-shaped main body of Spartacus began to slide down in his viewing port and slowly slip from view. Richard could plainly see the two docked S2s. The station's enormous sail began, instead, to fill his view. Closer, closer, then a sudden rush and they were in it.

Richard was thrown from side to side, they all were, violently! The massive sail yielded; displaced forty or fifty degrees by the impact. Its structure creaked and groaned, scratched and scraped, metal on metal, but it held.

Gradually, very gradually, the sail righted itself, rotating back to its former, stabilised, vertical position. Acquiring the sails momentum, the pod began to move; it rolled down the sail towards the main body of the station at ever-increasing speed. Then, as abruptly as it had started, the damaging tumble stopped; arrested by a mass of tangled supporting wires and stays. There it hung, dwarfed by the sail, like a mosquito caught in a giant fly swat.

On the Spartacus, already at emergency stations, two suited space walkers had been promptly dispatched, and within minutes, they were climbing over the diminutive craft. Relieved that the dangerous fall towards the body of the space station had been arrested, but unsure why, Richard wasted no time in climbing from his seat. He hit the centre box of his seat harness with his fist, releasing the constraining straps and floated away, directing himself out of the confined flight deck, and back into the cabin. He heard a series of loud bangs on the casing. They came from outside. Instinctively he depressurised the cabin, discharging gas shifting the position of the pod a little amongst its tangled web. Richard pulled himself through into the cabin. Rachel and Preston were also free of their harnesses, floating, their backs pressing on the ceiling.

'Ready?'

They both nodded, and with that Richard opened the portal. Outside, seemingly hovering a metre or two clear, they were greeted by an astronaut clad in a bulky white and silver suit, complete with an integrated propellant backpack. He offered his hand. Richard leant out with his, keeping the other held tight on the portal frame, then pulled the man effortlessly towards his craft. The astronaut offered Richard a long white lanyard with several circular handles stitched into its length, which he in turn passed to his friends inside the pod.

Against all odds, they had made it.

CHAPTER 33

The Key is Passed

Richard felt very satisfied with the breakfast he had just eaten. It was his first decent meal for the best part of a week, and he had certainly made the most of it; and now, following a shower and a good sleep, he was feeling part of the real world again. He looked around the small canteen. Plush and clean, finished in beige and white, even the furniture was impressively futuristic. There were a few people still eating, but most had already left. Neither Rachel nor Preston had showed, which was strange, as they both usually enjoyed the first meal of the day. Richard decided to have another coffee and wait a little longer in case either arrived, but after a few minutes, a serious looking young officer in uniform arrived to change his plan.

'Lieutenant Commander Reece,' he said with a strong French accent, one Richard had not heard for quite some time. 'Colonel Petromolosovich requests the pleasure of your company in his quarters, Sir, *s'il vous plaît?*'

'Of course, right away. Incidentally, have you seen Doctor Turner or Security Officer Preston on your travels, although it's possible that they are still asleep?'

'Actually, they breakfasted about an hour and a half ago, Sir. The Doctor, a very beautiful woman if I may say, is in the surgery and ...'

'Well actually, you may not say,' replied Richard, interrupting protectively. 'And Preston, where is he?'

'Your security officer is being debriefed by our operations officer at the moment,' the young man replied, visibly surprised by Richard's curtness.

Richard was similarly put out by being allowed to oversleep. 'Why wasn't I informed of this?' he demanded.

'*Pardon monsieur*, the Colonel's orders were to let you sleep as long as possible.' The officer shrugged his shoulders. 'Sorry for the mistake!'

Richard accepted the reason. 'Right, very accommodating, I must say. Shall we go, then?'

Impressively spacious, the main body of the space station was composed of two large disc-like structures stacked one on top of each other, like dinner plates stacked back to back. This construction created three distinct deck levels: the upper deck, number one deck, the centre deck of reduced diameter, and the lower deck, number two deck. About the size of a four hundred metre running track, but circular, the upper deck had a band of polyspec glass around its periphery, which, at three metres high, afforded breathtaking views in all directions. The upper level accommodated the living quarters, dining, recreation areas and several offices, including the Commanding Officer's.

The lower disc, of equal size, contained machinery, generation, battery and life support spaces and the bio-dome, whilst administration offices and scientific laboratories occupied the smaller centre deck spaces.

Rotating slowly in opposition, the two discs created a centrifugal gravity force within the station. A huge shaft running from the lower disc, through a tube in the upper disc, supported the structure of the vast sail, whilst a single massive gear wheel at its base, turned by two powerful electric motors, constantly adjusted the position of the sail relative to the sun. This optimised inertial angle, allowed accurate steerage of the remarkable space city.

Repairs to the damaged areas of the sail, following Richard's unconventional arrival, were already well under way, when he arrived at the Colonel's door. The accompanying officer knocked politely.

'Enter!'

'May I present Lieutenant Commander Reece, Colonel?'

'Ah, the pilot who tries to destroy my space station, most fortunately I knew you were coming,' the Colonel grunted. Then he looked at his junior officer. '*Spacibo*, leave us!'

With that, the young man quickly left, closing the door

very quietly behind him.

'These young men,' he continued with a thick reverberating voice. 'They have little respect these days, not like the old days, eh, British?'

'No Sir, I mean, yes Sir; no respect at all. The good old days, definitely.'

Richard was surprised that the Colonel appeared to know something of him. The veteran officer surprised him again.

'I know more about you than you think, British,' he said, 'where you come from, your career, your qualities and your disappointments.' Their eyes met. 'Yes, but I have respect. This is good. You have done well to get here. I would have done exactly the same, British!'

Richard took that remark as some kind of convoluted compliment, apparently very rare from this wily old fox.

'Absolutely, thank you, Sir,' he replied politely.

The Colonel was Russian and proud of it. Born in Smolensk, an industrial town west of Moscow, he was short, one point six metres at most, but very stocky, and demonstrated a crushing handshake. His cropped, spiky grey hair reminded Richard of a geriatric hedgehog. Sixty if he was a day, Richard speculated. Nevertheless, despite his appearance, Petromolosovich had a reputation as impressive as the space station he commanded, and with probably forty years of space exploration experience, it was well founded.

Richard was well aware of the man's exploits: Yuri Gagarin was his great uncle, he was the first cosmonaut to land on the moon back in 2009 and the first to command a permanent moonbase; then just a collection of viro-domes.

The Colonel did not offer Richard a seat; they were instead to proceed to the operations centre. As he stood by his host's desk, waiting patiently, Richard focused on the Colonel's dark green uniform. Quite obviously not even remotely current issue, it had certainly seen better days. Well worn, even threadbare in places, with numerous leather pads, the one stitched to his right elbow was half-missing, Richard thought nostalgically, if not humorously, that it was probably the one he wore when landing on the moon for the first time.

The Colonel still wore his wings, those of the Russian Airforce, and in addition, a small, encrypted, brass coloured metal badge above his left-hand breast pocket. It bore the initials NFSS in blood red enamel. Richard knew this abbreviation. Formed in 2014, the New Federation of Soviet States was a confederation of like-minded states from the old USSR of the late twentieth century. Those who, for one reason or another, could not, or would not, embrace global capitalism, and instead sought the halcyon days of the old soviet republic. Having said that, history had proved that the lessons and experiences of the old state had been well learnt, as the federation had been a dominant member of the G11 confederation for at least thirty years. For one thing, its space foundation provided many highly qualified people to the International Space Agency.

Richard stood in silence as the Colonel checked some paperwork on his desk. Around the office were several pictures from the historic space race days, including one of Yuri Gagarin himself climbing from the capsule, Vostok 1. Richard peered closely at the date inscription, 12 April, 1961.

The Colonel looked up. 'A great man, you agree?' he boomed. 'My grandfather flew MiGs with him in the great days of the Soviet Air Force.'

'Yes Sir, indeed.' Richard nodded respectfully. 'I expect you are looking forward to your retirement, Sir?' he continued.

'I will never retire!' the Colonel snapped.

'No, quite right, Sir.'' Richard raised his eyebrows, realising that pleasantries were probably not a good idea.

'You like the Americans, British?' the Colonel enquired bruskly.

'Er, well yes, I mean, I don't mind them. I have many American friends in fact,' Richard answered almost apologetically.

'I do not trust them, never have!'

Richard thought of Tom Race. 'Yes, there are one or two that fall short, that's true, Sir.'

The Colonel looked up from his desk and squared up to Richard. 'You have friends in high places, you know that,

British?'

Richard was astonished by the remark. 'What do you mean, Sir?'

'I was told two days ago that you might come this way. Osiris tracked your intercept with Enigma. Very clever, British. I like you. I would have done the same in my younger days.'

'Oh, did they? Thank you, Sir.'

'Confirm one thing to me, British, I trust you. The cargo. It is still on Enigma, correct?'

'Yes it is, Sir, absolutely. I will make a report,' answered Richard seriously.

'Then I fear they may be lost.'

'You know about the crystals, Sir?'

'Command briefed those who need to know, British, and I must help you in every way I can in order to retrieve them.'

Richard was visibly surprised; he thought his part in the saga had been played out.

'Follow me, British. I have something to show you.'

Richard followed the Colonel to the operations control room; it was down one level on the centre deck. As they walked into a large circular room filled with computer monitors and control stations, the entire complement of at least twenty people, stood to attention.

'Stand easy,' the Colonel ordered gruffly. It was clear that he commanded a great deal of respect. A senior operations officer, an American Air Force Major, came over to greet them.

'Morning Sir,' he said saluting the Colonel, then turned to Richard.

'Morning, my name is Theo Hern, I'm in charge of operations and communications here on Spartacus. I have something for you to look at. We cannot make head or tail of it. You may be able to help us.' The three men walked over to an isolated monitor in a private area.

'At the moment we are treating this matter as top secret,' continued the Major.

'I understand Major.'

At the keyboard, the American typed a security code and switched on the monitor, within seconds, the screen illuminated. He scrolled through a number of pages and then stopped.

'What do you make of this, Sir?' he asked of Richard, standing back from the monitor.

Richard couldn't believe what he saw; his expression an amalgamation of total surprise and absolute amazement. For several seconds he appeared dumbfounded.

'You know of this, British, I can tell,' said the Colonel interpreting Richard's reaction. 'Please, what is it?'

On the screen were four rows of four pictograms.

'They have been recognised, in part, as Egyptian hieroglyphics, Sir,' elaborated the Major. 'But only some. The remainder apparently originate from other civilizations. Earth has been on the case for two days, since the signal was discovered, their best brains. Up to now, they are completely baffled.'

'Where is it coming from?' Richard enquired, hardly able to take his eyes off the screen.

'Incredibly, it's omni-directional, Sir,' replied the Major, impressed. 'It would appear that the signal radiates from all directions. There is no individual source, it's all around us. That requires some technology, I can tell you, we cannot do that yet. But yesterday, I can report, we had a breakthrough.'

Richard interrupted, 'one of the obsolete frequencies, medium wave or long wave, right?'

The Major looked at Richard, equally surprised.

'Er, yes, Sir,' he said, puzzled. 'As a matter of fact it is. Three hundred kilohertz, the lower end of the old medium wave spectrum. Used extensively during the thirties, forties and fifties, last century, but superseded by VHF and thereafter microwaves.'

Richard nodded in agreement. 'Yes, I know. So what about this breakthrough you mentioned?'

'Well, it was only yesterday, Jan Moffet, one of our communication officers, she accidentally polarised the signal whilst analysing stellar radiation from the Polaris quadrant. The result was a unified signal. We were able to trace its origin.'

'Yes, and?'

'From America, British, the signal originates in America!' interjected the Colonel sourly.

'Where in America, Sir?' Richard asked.

'A place called Roswell' the Colonel continued, unimpressed by the turn of events.

Richard turned to Major Hern. 'Roswell, New Mexico? You mean Area 51?'

'That's right, Sir. Incredible as it may seem. The signal emanates from that same area.'

'So you have an accurate pin point?'

'No, not quite, polarising focused the signal, but only down to a factor of minus four. Below that, protraction is too weak, so the best we can do is an area of about one hundred square miles and that appears to be centred on Roswell.'

'Does Roswell and its history have any significance?' enquired Richard, increasingly astonished by the conversation.

'We do not know the answer to that question, British,' barked the Colonel, 'but with the Americans, you never know!'

Major Hern continued, slightly uncomfortable. 'Up until a few months ago, the entire region was a hot dry desert, now of course, due to continuous rain, it's almost impenetrable sludge and quick sand.'

The Colonel interrupted again. 'It is not incredible,' he growled.' The Americans are up to something, it is to do with the Roswell incident. Otherwise it is too much of a coincidence.'

'Colonel,' said Richard with a measured reply, despite

being taken aback by his remark. 'The Roswell incident was a hundred years ago, a hundred and two to be precise. With due respect, Sir, the two cannot be related.' He looked at the Major. 'Does earth know of this?'

'Er, no Sir,' he said, embarrassed. 'The Colonel decided to delay sending this information.'

'You tell me what you know, British, and then I will tell the Americans!'

Richard grimaced, 'with respect, Sir, it's not only the Americans, it's also the ISSF as well,' he replied.

'Major, please excuse us for some minutes,' requested the Colonel politely.

'Yes, of course, Colonel.'

Richard looked at the monitor again and then back to the Colonel. 'This is a message, Sir,' he confided. 'You know that don't you?'

'Yes, I know this, British!'

'You have serious misgivings about divulging this information, I can see that, Sir,' Richard continued, 'can you tell me why?'

The Colonel sighed, in an instant it appeared as though his decades in space had suddenly caught up with him.

'Two years ago and one hundred years late, the Americans quietly opened to the world the top secret files on the Roswell incident.'

Richard nodded. 'Yes, the eighth of July. I remember the archives made interesting reading to say the least.'

'Ha! you British, always the masters of understatement.

It changed the world!' Richard listened carefully to the Colonel as he expanded on his dilemma. 'In 1947, before the crash, America, we, the Russians and you British, we were just beginning to develop computers. I admit technology captured from the Germans helped us all, but the fact is, we were all on an equal footing. At that time, a one-hundred-kilobyte ticker tape computer filled a room this size. It could perform basic mathematical functions, that was all, and slowly. There were some in the world that knew it was a spaceship that crashed in the New Mexico desert that day in 1947, a few others suspected, but so complete was the cover up, and so vehement were the denials from the American government, that the story and any leads were eventually forgotten. There were reports, stories, leaks, books, even demands from Senators over the years, but silence, harassment and worse eventually subdued those seeking the truth. In 1961, it was us, the Russians, the USSR, who put the first man in space. We thought our technology was the best, but our valves and primitive electronics were from a bygone steam driven age in comparison to the Americans solid-state technology. It seems ironic now, British, do you not think, that the Americans invented the transistor just one year later in 1948. As you know, this device greatly accelerated the development of the computer.'

The Colonel paused and looked down at the floor, seemingly saddened by his yarn. 'My father knew of this, he tried in vain, for a great many years, to warn the authorities, but no one believed him. How stupid we were. Soon after, the Americans followed us into space. They seemed so confident, but theirs was digital technology. Within a few years new factories opened, new technology, materials and microchips, Silicon Valley. Still we were blind to it. In 1969, they put the first man on the moon and the world watched in amazement. Already we were twenty years behind and history tells us that we never caught up. They left the world behind and how rich they became. Not for two generations did we really understand the significance.'

'So what do you think happened at Roswell, Colonel?'

'The archives revealed to us, to the world, that it *was* a space ship: small, five crew members, probably a scout vessel and with humanoids in control. A ship with such technology does not crash. We are both pilots, British, you know this? I believe they were looking closely at us, too closely, to be sure of it!'

'To be sure of what, Colonel, what exactly?'

The Colonel looked Richard directly in the eyes, his own were bright, fired with conviction.

'Perhaps to confirm what they suspected from afar, our change into a species no longer their own. It is true, we never heard from them again.'

'What about the visitings in 2016?'

'They were different, aggressive, from somewhere else!' the Colonel snapped, dismissing Richards's suggestion. Then he paused again, thoughtful. 'And you know of the travellers, from the reports, the autopsies?'

Richard looked bemused. 'No, Colonel. Some of the archives remained government confidential. I don't know of the crew.'

'But you saw photographs?'

Richard nodded.

'Leaked photographs, autopsy examinations, they were all fake. The truth has been locked away, it is of great significance.'

Richard grew restless, impatient for the information. 'What of the crew, Sir? Why, even now, is this covered up, why is this information censored?'

'The real crew were human, British. Not humanoid, human. Homo Sapiens, us!'

The Colonel's eyes were ablaze. Reciting this information to Richard was like lifting a huge weight from his shoulders.

'When the technology became available in the 1980s, DNA analysis proved this. The only correct information released in the leaked stories was the height of these travellers, much less than us now!'

Richard coughed; the Colonel was sharp enough to recognise Richard's slight amusement at his remark, but he chose to ignore it.

'One point two to one point five metres,' the Colonel continued, 'or four to five feet old imperial.'

'Why do you say now, Colonel?'

'According to the files, genetic research showed that

our oxygen enriched atmosphere caused modifications, mutations to the original genes and chromosomes of the aliens, particularly the growth genes. In evolutionary terms, the changes happened quickly. Using laws of probability it is calculated to be less than ten thousand years. According to American genealogists, other more subtle changes have also taken place, these in response to the environment, aggressive neighbouring tribes, dangerous sub species, animals. Our species has developed, changed and now for one thing, we are much taller and much bigger! You see British, do you not, about the Roswell site? The truth continues to be hidden.'

Richard nodded, taking in the deluge of information. Evidently, unlike the Colonel, he was a realist and evidently, he wanted to deliver a measured, composed, response.

'That incident, Colonel. Roswell. It was a hundred years ago. Things have changed.' He opened his mouth to continue, but the Colonel interrupted.

'Yes, they have changed, British, but on one side only, then and now! That technology, so advanced, it should have guided the world. Instead, it shifted the balance of power and eventually changed my country. I cannot forgive that.'

Richard pondered for a moment, then decided it was time to steer, as diplomatically as possible, the conversation away from history and politics.

'So you think it was a return visit, Sir, after many thousands of years?'

The two men dwelt on that remark for quite some time, before Richard continued in a whisper. 'You are very astute, Colonel, if I may say. You may be closer to the truth than you think. I do know something of this.'

'Ya, British, you seem to know many things,' replied the Colonel, not quite understanding the significance of Richard's remark. 'So what of this signal, this message from history?'

Richard looked at the monitor. 'Whatever happened in the past, Colonel, we can't change, but here and now, there is someone in America who wants to help the world by retrieving the crystals. I think we need to follow this lead.'

The Colonel agreed. 'I will help,' he said gruffly. Then, in the same moment, his mood lightened, intrigued as much as anything by Richard's abilities. 'To me, I think you can read this message British, is this true?'

'It's a twist of fate more than you would believe, Colonel. Having studied these symbols, I think I have a good idea what they say.'

The Colonel looked around the operations room, he caught the eye of Major Hern and gestured him to return.

'Major, make notes, our British comrade will tell us the secrets hidden in this message.'

The Major stared at Richard for more than a few seconds, eventually, after his astonishment had subsided, he was composed enough to understand the order, but not its significance.

Richard studied the text. 'The first symbol means meet or meeting,' he said quietly.' The second is Egyptian for moon. The third means old and the fourth, well, town.'

He stood up and looked at the Colonel. 'It's a rendezvous, Sir,' he said in a considered tone. 'A meeting, at the old town, on the moon presumably. Old town, old town?' Richard repeated several times. 'Of course, the old town, the old original moonbase, Andromeda One, it's the freight terminal now. A meeting in the freight terminal!'

'Go on, British, the remaining,' encouraged the Colonel.

'The first symbol of the second row is Mayan. It means holy day. They invented the first calendar you know.' Richard paused, 'it refers to the day of homage they devote to their gods, the sacred day.'

'A Sunday?' Major Hern said excitedly.

'I would say that's a fair call,' concurred Richard. 'The next I don't recognise, but the third is a constellation, Lynx, to be precise.'

'A cat!' said the Major again.

'May not be relevant, the Lynx as a constellation is very faint, and seen only in the northern hemisphere on earth. It has to be a very dark night to make it out and normally you need a telescope.' Richard shrugged his shoulders. 'Not sure of the relevance of that? The fourth is easier. Cuneiform, symbols of the Sumarians. This writing is the best part of six thousand years old. It is simply the number one. Interesting.'

'What is it, British?' demanded the Colonel.

'This really is convoluted, Sir. Someone has gone to a lot of trouble, even the numbers use a different type of text. From a different civilization, no less, anyway, the third row. The first is Mayan and means a score and ten, thirty. Sunday, the date we don't know, at one thirty.'

'Morning or afternoon?' muttered the Colonel.

'Maybe that's the relevance of the constellation, needs a dark night to be seen,' added the Major.

'Possibly,' replied Richard.

'So we have a problem with the date,' reiterated the Major.

'Yep, I'll come back to it. Now the second,' continued Richard. 'This character is Egyptian, it means walk or sometimes walking, or tread or step, depending on the context. The accent thing, that grammatical mark, means carefully, or with care. The fourth is a fairly common symbol for enemy. Now, the first symbol on the last row. I think, this is come, but also went. Ha, I remember this next one. Egyptian again, the triple headed falcon, one human, one a cat and one a phoenix. This pictogram means a strange or unusual form, normally associated with the gods.'

'It is a warning, British!' elaborated the Colonel sternly.

'Yes, I think you're right, Sir, walk carefully, for the enemy comes in strange forms. Could mean anything? Something similar to this was inscribed on the young Egyptian pharaoh Tutankhamun's burial casket. The transcription was part of my study course. In his unfortunate case, the riddle was later discovered to refer to the king's friend and mentor, a chap called Ay, who actually was his enemy and eventually his murderer.'

'So it could also warn of a trap!' said the Major.

Richard looked at him, considering his remark. 'Yes, a trap, or something that is not as it seems, anyway. The date?' Richard studied the character closely for a second time. 'It's possible that I'm reading too much into this one. It represents a quarter, or, on the other hand, a whole minus a quarter, or three quarters. In addition, the flower, spring time! Spring is the second quarter of an earth year. It doesn't make any sense. That's just not right!' Richard groaned. 'I don't recognise this as a symbol from ancient writings, I haven't seen anything like it!'

'Spring also means fresh, or new, even. You know, like new life,' interjected the Major, straightening his posture and rubbing his lower back. 'I'll seize up if I stoop over that screen any longer,' he continued with some discomfort.

Richard paid him no attention. 'What about new quarter?' he elaborated. 'It's possible the symbol relates to the moon!'

'Yes, I see your point, the new or first quarter!' the Major referred to his lunar cycle projection charts. 'The first quarter of the present cycle falls on the ninth.'

'Three days from now, and it's a Sunday!' exclaimed Richard, banging his fist on the desk, yes!'

'The first quarter may also refer to the time of day, Sir,

morning or afternoon?'

'Yes, it's another good point, Major, first quarter of the day, making the rendezvous time one thirty in the morning, zero one thirty!'

The three men agreed.

'So, British. The final two symbols?'

'The second to last means chariot, quite simple, and the last, well, Babylonian or Persian, I can't quite remember. Anyway, there's another pictogram meaning house. Chariot house, you know, like an old coach house or a coaching inn. These were also feeding stations for the animals. Later in history they would be described as service stations, you know, fuel and accommodation stops!' Richard thought on, a station for stopping or starting a journey? He was adamant. 'It can only refer to one thing,' he concluded, 'its obvious, the station at the old town, the monorail station, in the freight terminal!'

The Colonel looked stunned; that conclusion was far from obvious to him. Eventually he spoke. 'So we have it, a meeting in three days and expect the enemy!'

There was silence for the best part of a minute.

'One of your S2s, Sir?' said Richard addressing Colonel Petromolosovich, almost in a whisper.

The Colonel nodded, 'and a crew?'

'No, I don't think so, Sir, with all due respect. Just my team, you understand.'

'The S2 requires two pilots, British. You know this?'

'I can fly it on my own, Colonel, done it many times

before. That way I've got no security problems.'

The Colonel nodded again slowly, acknowledging Richard's well-founded concerns. He looked at the Major. 'Distance?'

Major Hern checked another monitor. 'Showing twenty three point seven, Sir, that is a flight time of two days and five hours.'

'Then you leave tomorrow, British,' concluded the Colonel.

CHAPTER 34

The Wrong Woman

Tom Race woke with Ross Sampleman leaning over him, gently slapping his face.

'Commander, Commander, wake up! Wake up, Sir!'

Tom shook his head and squinted, then squeezed his temples between his fingers. 'What the hell is going on?'

'I should ask you the same question, Commander. You've been missing for the best part of fifteen hours. What happened?'

Tom sat up and looked around slowly in an effort to reorientate himself. Not two metres away, on the deck below the closed hatch, heaped amongst a small selection of broken electronic parts and glass fragments, was one half of the Humatron's head. Ross reached across and picked it up, turning the distorted metal object repeatedly.

'So much for throwing in the towel, Commander,' he said sarcastically and then he stood up and offered his hand. Tom winced with pain as he was pulled up, the skin on the palm of his hands having suffered serious frost burn. 'We will need to get that seen to quickly, there's a risk of infection.'

Ross checked-out the compartment for the ready-use first aid locker, and found it, fixed at waist height, to an adjacent wall. From it, he retrieved a tube of silicone-based *Dermaquick* antiseptic paste. He dispensed a generous amount over Tom's hands, which Tom spread evenly, by rubbing gently, including a little way up each wrist. Then Tom held his hands out, fingers stretched, nodding his approval and appreciation. Within thirty seconds the translucent film had dried to a flexible, albeit delicate skin; after two minutes it was as if he had slipped on a pair of surgical rubber gloves. Then Tom looked at Ross sternly.

'Emily Ross, we must stop her!'

Ross nodded in agreement, 'and Nicola too!' he added. 'She is hell bent on highjacking the crystals. There's a conspiracy here, I've got a feeling it goes right to the top.'

'Why do you say that?'

'It took me a couple of hours to make the bridge. I had to wait for Nicola to leave her station, then I hid behind Isshi's console. I was there for six hours at least, waiting. Nicola is watching everything. I knew you were in trouble, but not where. Emily was talking to Nicola, who monitored all the internal sensors for hours. She knows the Humatron has been, shall we say, decommissioned! As soon as I could I got away, and searched the whole ship.

What on earth made you come down here?'

'I was going to use the emergency access hatches, those up front.'

'Well, you succeeded in finding one of the few areas in the entire ship without movement sensors, these two compartments! I had overlooked it myself, plus, you being out cold for hours, both Nicola and Emily think you are dead. I'm sure of it!'

'Then it's time we surprised them both, you have any idea where Nicola is right now?'

'I'd say still at the master interface. Without the Humatron to do her bidding, Nicola has been blackmailed into computer service. I followed Nicola to engineering, that's how I came to look down here. She is fine-tuning Emily's maniptronic systems. Emily still has a few teething problems, shall we say?'

Tom smiled, 'None of your doing I trust?'

'Well, I have to admit that I've introduced one or two gremlins into her circuitry,' Ross replied. 'Oh, by the way, I've managed to get hold of one of these. I'm not too good with them myself; so better that you have it!'

'A fifty five! Complete with a magazine of titanium tipped sublets. Very useful Ross, well done.'

'Well, be careful, Nicola has one too. The Humatron disarmed the two security agents; Ben Bagley is dead as a result and one of the agents, Bateman!'

Tom shook his head. 'Nicola is going down for this, I just would never have thought,' he concluded.

'Nicola is in it for the crystals, Commander, no doubt about it. But there are a lot of other people involved. Whilst I was on the bridge, she had a sub-light radio conversation with someone on earth and on Andromeda. Once we are close enough there will be someone to meet us, you can be sure of that. As for Emily, she will use Nicola as long as it suits her, and she presents more of a danger than you think. The laser for example, degraded against targets on earth due to the Van Allen belt, but other ships, including the 'D class', and even Andromeda are highly vulnerable.' Ross paused thoughtfully. 'What is it about robot programming? Seems everything above level six just comes back to haunt us!'

'I agree, listen, one problem at a time, Ross. First engineering. Sabotage for you, the main interface. For me, Nicola!'

Ross gestured his agreement and turned towards the adjacent hatch.

'We won't go that way, Ross; I can do without another frosty welcome from Emily. The long way round, OK? I'll explain later.'

Tom knew that Emily knew that they were moving around the ship, even before the pair arrived on the accommodation flat. As they approached the galley access level, Tom thought that this was as good a place as any to set the fire alarm system again, and duly did so by smashing the butt of his pistol into a wall mounted sensor unit. Immediately, the alarms sounded. Sirens wailed and red lights flashed. Pressure hatches began to close automatically and several accommodation and office doors opened.

Tom gestured to Ross to follow him and the pair made their way stealthily to the main engineering level. However, by the time they had arrived, Emily had already closed down the section by locking all automatic access portals and hatches, and had secured them with her own codes.

'There's an emergency hatch at the end of the corridor,' shouted Ross over the continuing commotion.

The two men sprinted down the corridor. Ross typed the 'command' emergency code into the control box, and the release lever responded by moving outwards from the hatch. Emily could do nothing about the 'command' protocols, particularly the emergency code sequences, as their dominant programming would override all other formalities. Ross rotated the lever, releasing the locks, and the hatch opened. Tom stepped through first, pistol held high, scanning the large open space. Emily immediately informed Nicola. There was genuine trepidation in her voice as she screamed over the PA system.

'Intruders, Nicola, we have intruders. Kill them!'

Tom indicated to Ross to climb the farther of two steel ladders that accessed the interface platform. This large platform, about four metres above the level on which they had alighted, had its decks constructed of rectangular sections of perforated metallic plates. Like fine metal grilling, they allowed some restricted vision through to the interface area. Tom looked for Nicola, but to no avail. He would take the first set of steps; still half expecting to face Nicola at the top. He climbed very slowly, rung by rung, then went over the top. Crouching, he looked for her; she was nowhere to be seen.

'Intruders, Nicola, kill them, kill them!' Emily screeched.

Tom saw Ross's head appear at the far end of the platform as he clambered up the last few rungs. He gestured to him to move towards the control station. Ross would start the disengagement process. Tom lowered his weapon; Nicola had gone.

No sooner had Ross arrived at the master control panel, than Nicola stepped out from behind a concealing support column and shot him, point blank. Ross took the shot full in the chest. He screamed in pain and staggered backwards, before falling to the ground. Blood trickled from the corner of his mouth, a sure sign that the sublet had penetrated a lung. He groaned, his eyes closed slowly and his head fell limply to the side. There was a stunned silence as Tom raised his pistol to fire. He had a clear shot, but how could he? He had loved her?

Nicola stole the advantage, aiming her pistol directly at him.

'You sentimental fool,' she cursed as she fired.

CHAPTER 35

Back to Basics

Richard steered the heavy S2 onto a long final approach course bound for the freight terminal. Built about five kilometres west of Andromeda Major in a shallow basin, the terminal was linked to the main base by a narrow, over ground, transparent plastic service tunnel. A four carriage, electric monorail shunted backwards and forwards between the two. There was also an enclosed, reinforced and pressurised pedestrian corridor running parallel to the monorail track, although it was only rarely used. Storage of explosive, inflammatory, or any other dangerous items, including security weapons, was generally limited to this building for a myriad of safety reasons.

Unusually, the freighter terminal's landing platform had been constructed directly onto the lunar surface, instead of being suspended some way above it on a structural gantry. This allowed a fully laden S2, weighing almost two hundred and fifty metric tonnes, to operate from the platform, without huge structural implications. The inherent problem with this design was, however, the unavoidable proximity to surface dust and debris. Disturbed by powerful retro rockets, clouds of dense, re-circulating, graphite coloured moondust blanketed the shuttles, particularly during the critical landing phase, obscuring the crew's vision. As a result, manual handling of this phase, along with docking, and most other 'precision' manoeuvres, was long since obsolete; handled instead by precision auto flight systems.

From the 'old school', Richard had always disagreed with this philosophy. During his time on the shuttle flight, he and a few other pilots would frequently practice manual control, arguing the age-old adage that 'electrics are fine while they're working'. Having said that, he had forgotten how the S2 wallowed at low speed in the almost negligible lunar atmosphere and low gravity. He had to work hard, even with the basic autostabilisation engaged, to control the attitude of the craft as speed reduced below eighty lutens. His aim was an approach profile low enough to remain unseen below the Sienna ridgeline, but high enough not to disturb the dusty surface, which would instantly create a recognisable and suspicious cloud on Andromeda's area sensor system.

Checking his descent profile, both visually against the rocky escarpment to his right, and on the liquid-crystal instrument displays, Richard glanced briefly at Rachel.

She had sat down and was strapping herself into the 'jump seat', which was positioned between, but just behind, the two pilots' seats. He could see by the look on her face that she was more than a little concerned.

'I think its working,' Richard said reassuringly.

'Bit low aren't we?' Rachel replied, eyes wide with surprise as she looked out at the barren, uncomfortably close, cliff face filling the flight deck side screen.

'I've got to stay low, below the ridge; it's shielding us from Andromeda's sensors. We flew a reverse orbit; they won't expect us from the dark side. At the moment, I don't think that they know we are here and I mean to keep it that way.'

'But there's no sign of life, no lights, no controller. So how can you land?' asked Rachel nervously.

'Exactly,' Richard replied, slightly exasperated. 'The terminal has shut down for the evening.'

'But you need the automatic guidance system to land. Even I know that!'

Richard concentrated on the platform, now only three kilometres ahead of them. A spreading shadow, cast by the ridgeline, left the entire area in semi-darkness.

'I've landed on this pad a hundred times. I can do it manually,' he said in a monotone voice. 'But a co-pilot would help!'

There was no answer from Rachel.

'Passing fifty lutens and reducing. Landing checklist complete,' he continued, mainly for his own benefit.

'Retros seventy percent.'

Richard pushed the right hand of the two throttle levers forward whilst adjusting the thrust angle of the rocket motors with a thumb wheel located at the base of the same lever. The S2 began to vibrate as power came up.

'Eighty percent, eighty five, ninety.'

The vibration became a violent shaking and the craft began to roll, first to the left, then the right. Rachel looked across at Richard's face, it was taut with concentration, then at his left hand, knuckles white as he squeezed the side stick. In his attempt to execute a manoeuvre never designed for 'hands on' control, he began to move the stick rapidly in all directions.

'Ninety two percent, stable,' murmered Richard, definitely for his own benefit.

He was running a mental profile. The craft shuddered and vibrated as the retro rockets supported it in a high hover above the obscured platform. Richard transferred his attention to the video screen on the centre console. He pressed a button on the instrument panel and the picture flashed from a forward-looking camera to the underside camera, which looked vertically downwards. Even at eighty feet, a thick dust cloud was beginning to rise. He had no time to consider its implications

'Where is it?' Rachel asked.

'Easy, easy, coming down,' said Richard, one hundred percent focused.

He hadn't heard Rachel's question, or chose to ignore

it. By sixty feet, the platform had completely disappeared; obscured, amidst a mass of swirling and recirculating grey dust. Richard continued the slow descent. Frequently, specks of silica crystal, suspended in the cloud, would reflect the brilliant light of the retro's exhaust plumes, appearing like innumerable tiny lights, switching on and off, then scattering in all directions as they fled. Rachel was mesmerised by the sight.

Richard focused on the terminal building itself. He knew that the forward edge of the platform was just about level with the main entrance portal. He looked across the flight deck and through the right side screen. Looking down was no help now. Struggling to maintain control as the craft passed fifty feet, he had previously likened this exercise to trying to stand upright on a large rubber ball. Move a fraction too far and you're off!

In the final few moments, Richard had a mind for his lateral position. Move left, move right, he wasn't sure. In that fraction of a second before the craft was completely engulfed within the turbulent midst of blackening dust, his instinct told him left. It was a gut reaction, based on the perspective of the building. He snapped the side stick fully left, then instantaneously back again, and at that moment, as the craft descended through thirty feet, pulled the thrust levers back, cutting the retros.

For the briefest instant the craft dropped. Rachel gasped. A loud thud followed, accompanied by a shudder as the S2 settled on its massive undercarriage. Rachel removed her hands from her face and opened her eyes to Richard's beaming face.

'Still got the old touch then, even after a few years,' he grinned.

'Never again,' replied Rachel. 'Never!'

'Never say never, Rachel.' Richard looked back at Preston. He too was looking a little pale. 'You ready?'

Preston nodded, 'as I'll ever be!'

'OK Rachel. Stay by the radio. Don't move. Keep a good look out. Do not call unless you're sure you've been seen. The moment you call, they'll know we are here. We cannot afford to gamble; who is friend, who is foe?'

Rachel nodded.

'Let's get our suits on, Preston.'

With that, Richard climbed out of his seat and put his hand on Rachel's shoulder. 'We'll be back in twenty minutes, thirty at the most. Be good.'

'I've got it covered, Richard,' Rachel said, recovering her composure.

Outside, standing at the base of the deceptively large titanium-alloy service portal, Richard lifted the plastic lid to the actuator keypad and entered an old security code; fourteen, twenty-seven, fourteen, Romeo, Juliet. He turned to Preston.

'If this works, I'll eat my hat!'

In these new suits, Richard's speech sounded exceptionally clear and precise; the quality of reception noticeably superior to what he, and Richard for that matter, were used to. A few seconds later, there was a loud clank, then a whoosh, as the two towering doors slid open. Feeling comfortable in the improved, lightweight lunar suit, Richard grinned at Preston and said, 'where's my hat?'

'You're going to tell me that's your old security code.'

'That's right!'

'Then I think Andromeda needs a new security officer.'

'I agree, but not yet, eh?'

The two men entered the dark, cavernous warehouse, which, now fully depressurised, had an eerie silence. Almost tripping over the loading arms of a mechanical freight stacker, which stood menacingly in the shadows, Richard switched on his helmet mounted sidium gas observation light. Fully integrated and centrally positioned above his forehead, its powerful beam pierced the blackness, casting further, more elongated shadows around the stacked pallets and stored equipment, their movement attracting Preston's nervous attention. Instinctively he raised his hand to his weapon holster and pressed the release clip.

'The rendezvous is the monorail platform, at zero one thirty,' Richard reiterated as he checked his watch. 'That's in a few minutes, so we had better move fast.'

Preston pulled his stun pistol from its holster, and made a final check on its discharge level, as the two men made off quickly through the echoing chamber, thereafter passing quietly through a small portal into the administration section. Negotiating two, manually operated emergency air locks, they gained access into the permanently pressurised area of the facility. Richard turned off his oxygen and flipped up his visor, indicating to Preston to do the same. Holding a finger up to his lips, he beckoned to his colleague to follow him.

Negotiating several corridors, their path lit only by small, ceiling mounted 'glow-boxes' that were conveniently positioned every three or four metres, the two men warily made their way to the monorail station.

The glow boxes emanated a warm, orange coloured light that had the effect of producing a fuzzy, diffusing aura called the 'conservation illumination effect' or CIE. For Preston, the effect was confusing, distracting from the already reduced visibility. However, Richard, to some extent, had grown used to the energy efficient system. During his time on Andromeda's Shuttle Wing, as a nominated duty officer, he had frequently conducted after hours 'fire and security' rounds and therefore had accrued many hours of experience.

On their arrival, Richard indicated to Preston to remain in the shadows whilst he circled the open platform area. The absence of monorail carriages meant that they had returned to the main base terminal with the last members of terminal crew, as expected.

Preston crouched behind a stack of large, seemingly grey coloured, packing cases but kept Richard in sight. The monorail station was in fact a lofty glass dome attached to the freighter terminal's west wall. Now some twenty years old, being the original, permanently inhabited, moonbase, it was like an oversized conservatory, with a spider's web like construction. The main frames were of tubular titanium alloy, covered in curved, lightly tinted polyspec glass. Through it, the view of the heavens was inspiring.

Behind schedule, Richard and Preston had precious little time for sight seeing, but strangely, neither could fail to notice the moving, but somehow melancholy spectacle that was home. Reflecting now, its familiar dazzling blue and brilliant white hues in only a tiny area, the planet's once radiant luminosity had diminished to a mere shadow of its former self.

With little contribution from earth therefore, and no other lighting save the heavens, the terminal building was in semi darkness. Moving shadows and a strangely troubling silence heightened the two men's senses. Preston watched closely as Richard made his way towards the controller's booth, situated at the far end of the platform.

He's done this before, he thought, as Richard stealthily remained in the shadows, only periodically darting between cover.

Richard was about twenty metres from the booth when he stopped abruptly, as if frozen instantaneously to the spot on which he stood. Checking behind, then up at the tall stacks of paletted stores ready for shipment, he had seen something. He looked directly at Preston. Raising his hand, palm forward and with a gentle back and forth movement, he indicated to Preston to slip further into the shadows.

Richard paused for a few seconds, turning his head to listen amid the silence of the now threatening dome. Preston covered himself with darkness but his eyes remained glued on Richard.

Presently, Richard raised the forefinger of his left hand to his lips and patted them gently, indicating absolute quiet. Then, he placed his hand with forefinger pointing upwards next to his left ear, followed by a forward rotating movement. Preston nodded in acknowledgement and duly closed his visor. Simultaneously a tiny green light illuminated on his communicator. Pressing it, an abrivicom appeared on the two centimetre square internal display housed on the back of his wrist.

'It's a FACULTE!' read the message.

Preston looked up at Richard. He couldn't see his face, because Richard too had closed his visor, but he watched him pull his weapon from its holster and indicate the setting 'five' by holding up his hand, fingers spread. Preston became nervous as he adjusted his own weapon to the same position, clearing the safety catch. Five was a kill setting.

In an instant, Richard was gone, lost in the darkness. Preston sank back into a recess. His role, at the moment anyway, was reactive, not proactive, as briefed.

Preston was aware of the FACULTE System, but had never seen one. Covered as a case study during his initial security training, he couldn't think Richard had seen one either, not in the flesh anyway; as they were banned and subsequently withdrawn from commercial use thirty years or so earlier, following a spate of fatal accidents. They were, he recalled, all supposedly humanely destroyed. If there was a FACULTE in here, Preston thought, it was going to be nasty.

Preston covered the entrance to his secretive lair. Weapon raised and looking upwards, he could feel his heart pounding and took a deep slow breath in an effort to control it.

Richard had climbed quietly onto the top of a stack of packing cases and now crouched on one knee. He surveyed the hall from a perch elevated some five meters above floor level; he had his back to the wall, mindful not to silhouette himself against the distant lights of the Milky Way.

The FACULTE System stood for Feline Autonomous Cranial Utilised Locator Tracker Eliminator. It was a cat, a large, heavy, menacingly dangerous cat, the result of a genetic cross between the African Caracal, a merciless plains hunter and the fabled Black Panther, solitary powerhouse of the leopard family. By design, this creation epitomised stealth, cunning, mobility and aggression. To this, add the spectre of biosynthetic enhancements, electronic implants. The left half of the animal's brain was surgically replaced by electronic circuitry; very advanced for the second decade of the twenty first century, an installed microprocessor tapping directly into the remaining half of the animal's brain. The hybrid's left eye was replaced by a combined infra-red night sight and deadly pencil-thin laser weapon: the left ear was an enhanced digital sound receiver, many times more powerful than the original model. In liaison, a collective microprocessor was able to pinpoint a target at one hundred metres, even from the faintest odour, enhancing the cat's already excellent sense of smell.

The original FACULTE security systems were designed for sensitive military and government installations, following the global civil unrest movements of 2013. Successful systems were in use for at least eight or nine years. The United Kingdom manufacturer MACROSAFE even produced a smaller domestic model. However, following a spate of well-publicised accidents and fatal attacks, the programme was eventually terminated and the remaining systems recalled.

Apparently, the brain of the cat evolved over a number of years, until the right side eventually subordinated the left and its associated programming. It started with the vaporising of troublesome dogs, but soon the animals turned on their owners, becoming highly aggressive, almost aware of their deadly bionic capabilities. The first killing was by a domestic model, this incident being followed by a number of deaths and accounts of neighbourhood terrorism, until the last rogue system was rounded up and supposedly destroyed.

Both Richard and Preston knew only too well that this situation meant serious trouble. Even so, a FACULTE in the freight terminal seemed a bit of an 'overkill' to say the least, unless, of course, there was something in the building that warranted the protection of this deadly animal.

Richard gingerly leaned forward from his precarious observation point and watched, quietly and carefully, for movement in the dimly lit open area below him. Several precious minutes passed, but he dared not move.

Could he have been wrong? Did he really see a cat leaping between two large pallets of stores? If he did, was it really oblivious to their presence, and if then, what about now? Surely he wasn't mistaken?

Then there it was! There, in the shadows, on the other side, dishevelled, unkempt, its shiny metal alloy half skull exposed in several places under the tatty, torn remnants of grafted black fur. Moreover, the eye, glowing red, cold.

So the code he had deciphered on Spartacus was accurate, Richard thought, beware, the enemy comes in strange forms, the constellation; a cat. Who had sent the message, that signal from the past, and why?

Although moving stealthily, it wasn't in 'tracker' mode. Richard knew that instinctively. In that mode, after acquiring a target, its posture became crouched and it never lost visual acquisition. Therefore, miraculously, it was, at that moment anyway, unaware of their presence.

Richard knew he had to move quickly, not just to remove this threat, but he was also well behind time for the rendezvous. He could not afford this hold up, but at this moment, more importantly, he could not afford to have the FACULTE acquire him.

A shot from his perch, at that distance, was too difficult and too dangerous and one shot was all he would get. Then, in those brief moments of deliberation, the animal disappeared into the shadows.

Richard leaned back out of sight. How should he deal with this situation, he thought, as he checked his watch again. He had told Rachel that they would be back in thirty minutes, they had already been gone forty, she would be nervous.

Preston had also seen the animal. Moving effortlessly along the ground, it had crossed the opening of his dark retreat not more than four metres away.

That was why Richard had instructed him to close his visor. The excellent insulative properties of his suit and helmet had prevented the cat's infrared sight locking onto his body heat and in addition, encapsulated any body odours.

Preston had not thought that he would ever be grateful for wearing a body suit, but he surely was this time. He also knew however, that hiding in a dark corner was not going to progress matters despite Richard's brief.

He stood up and walked quietly towards the entrance of his dark lair. Lurking in the shadows, he scanned the area. Where was Richard? More importantly, where was the cat? Preston raised his weapon and slipped out into the twilight arena, hugging the boxes and cases but taking care not to brush his suit on them as he passed.

Richard half wanted to move, but decided to keep his

commanding position. As Preston stepped around the front of a shelf stacker, a sort of magnetic forklift truck, he was visible. Richard saw him.

What's he doing? he thought. If I can see him, then so can the FACULTE!

Richard sighted his weapon. Grasping it with both hands for stability, arms outstretched, he crept into a more accessible position on the case. He could provide cover for Preston from there, but it was limited. He watched as Preston stepped over the first stacking arm, which was about two feet above the ground.

'Careful, careful,' Richard whispered under his breath. 'Move towards the booth, you can cover ME from there, oh, anything for telepathy!'

Preston stepped carefully and methodically over the second magnetic arm. He looked around, eyes straining, but he failed to see an electrical cable protruding from under the machine. It caught his toe, and he stumbled.

'Oh no!' said Richard, shaking his head.

Instinctively, Preston's hands went forward to prevent a fall, successfully, but in the process, his pistol fell from his hand. In a microsecond, it hit the floor. It was not a loud noise, as the pistol was made from shock absorbing palatetramide plastic, but to the animal, it may as well have been a clap of thunder and it acquired Preston within seconds.

Preston crouched to pick up his weapon. It was a poor position, exposed. Get out of there, thought Richard. Preston had the same idea and in near panic, stepped clumsily over the troublesome arm again. Clumsy was the word, he caught his trailing foot and stumbled again. At that instant, a thin red laser beam fired out, galvanizing Richard's attention as it penetrated an electrical control box mounted between the two arms of the vehicle, precisely where Preston had been seconds before. There was a loud buzzing noise as the box shorted and sparked, and light outlined Preston, as he and Richard cowered from the luminescence. Then, finally and abruptly, the metal cover was blown off its hinges, spun through the air and landed with a crash several metres away, the sparking subsided.

Preston got to his feet, and frantically ran for the nearest cover. A second pencil-thin beam fired out; missing the back of his helmet by the merest fraction, it burnt a neat smouldering hole in the packing case behind him.

Richard tried to get a shot at the feline assassin, but couldn't lean out far enough to properly acquire it. He started to climb down then stopped. Instead, his fingers typed out an abrive. He fumbled for the transmit button. Preston, by this time in a dark recess between two large boxes, caught his breath and read the message.

'You're bait, back the same way.'

You must be joking, he thought, but he knew, with the animal now in tracking mode, his time was running out.

Had Preston been able to see the hunter, he would have been able to confirm his theory. The cat was down on its haunches, abdomen close to the ground, semi-crawling in the darkness, teeth bared, senses heightened, preparing for the final kill.

Hesitating for a second or two, Preston knew he had to go. Lifting his pistol, he fired indiscriminately and uselessly into the open area. He ran back the way he had come, and leapt onto the first arm of the troublesome machine and over the next. One, two, three red beams followed him; each one came closer to its target. In a desperate effort to regain the sanctuary of his original lair, he dived into a puddle of fluid on the metallic flooring and slid several metres on his stomach.

The heel of his pistol struck the ground, bounced from his hand, then skidded across the floor and hit a steel packing case with a hollow clang. Within seconds, the animal was behind him. It circled warily, crouching, menacing, hissing, almost savouring these last few moments. Saliva dripped from its open mouth, the blackened gums revealing white, razor-sharp teeth.

Preston got to his knees. 'It's now or never!' he yelled.

No sooner had he spoken, than Richard, now ideally placed, took aim and fired. Although invisible, the effect of the deadly accurate sonic blast was soon apparent; the animal's head exploded, sending pieces of flesh and blood, as well as wasted circuitry, in all directions. Preston's suit and helmet was spattered with tiny red spots, but he reacted quickly, retrieving his weapon and running for cover.

Preston returned the abrive. 'What next?'

With barely time to ponder the remark, let alone its answer, the two men were disturbed by a loud clattering sound. It was the monorail carriage, negotiating the final bend in the track some two hundred metres before the dome.

Richard flipped on the intercom switch on his communicator.

'This could be for us, or against us,' he said curtly. 'I'm going for the booth, that's the agreed place. Get into a position where you can cover me, quietly!'

Preston thought the remark was a little caustic, but sadly, understandable. He ran across the open hall and took up a strategic position on the platform, crouching behind a stack of large oxygen cylinders.

'Save air, visors up,' said Richard, as if on cue.

Richard made it into the booth, just as the leading carriage of three approached the narrow platform. He reduced the setting on his weapon by one, in case he had to fire first and ask questions later.

There were no lights on in the shuttle as it came to a halt adjacent to the booth. Nor were there any signs of movement. Nothing, just deadly silence. Richard paused then slowly moved forward. He opened the door of the booth with his foot and crept out, staying low. Cautiously, moving first towards the two sliding doors of the leading carriage, he momentarily and for no apparent reason, thought of Rachel.

I hope she has the patience to stay where she is!

His thoughts were shattered as the leading carriage door slid open. Richard moved quickly. He rounded the controller's booth, a half-glazed structure about ten metres long and two metres wide, and crouched behind it, covering the open doorway with his sonic pistol, which he raised to shoulder height. Nothing moved, save the clicking noise of electrical relays as the timing circuits applied the shuttle's parking brakes.

Heart pounding, another dose of adrenaline sharpened his senses. It was now fight or flight. He did not have the luxury of choice and time was running out. He sprinted towards the open doors, dived into the carriage, did a kind of awkward somersault and ended up hard against the closed doors on the opposite side of the train. He expected a hail of sonic discharges, kevlar bullets or even sublets. The back of his head hit the inside of his helmet with the impact, but Richard barely noticed. He rolled onto his stomach, his finger an instant from squeezing the trigger.

His hesitance, that split second that separates a cool nerve from an also ran, undoubtedly saved Tom Race's life. A moment later, Race, attempting to track Richard with his own weapon during his acrobatic tumble, caught up and the two faced each other, looking down opposing barrels, neither daring to breathe.

They recognised each other immediately, a stifled moment of relief followed as they realised that they were, in fact, aligned to the same cause. Richard broke the stalemate, just becoming aware of the sore lump growing on the back of his head.

'The United States Air Force, I presume?' he said, lowering his weapon and climbing to his feet. It was then that he noticed a small pool of blood beneath Tom and it was visibly expanding. 'You're hit.'

'Yeah, stopped a sinker in my thigh, it's open.'

The fresh blood formed a circular puddle, half hidden by Tom's body and the other half under the dented, blemished, U-Semini case that Tom was lying over. Richard typed an abrive and sent it.

'All clear.'

Moment's later, Preston's face appeared tentatively around the door of the carriage. For a few seconds, the two men stood over Tom Race, focusing on the blood stained brief case, which evidently had suffered a fairly rough passage.

'Have you got them? Are they in there?' Preston enquired.

Tom nodded as he put both hands on the case, and pushed himself up. Halfway through the press up he spun round, pivoting on one arm, and sat on the carriage floor with a thump, his back against the wall. He moaned in obvious pain, as a crimson stained hole mid thigh leaked blood, the pool on the floor now smudged into a long streak.

Richard, fixated for some time by the thought of retrieving the crystals, snapped back into reality.

'Preston,' he ordered, 'quick! Something for a tourniquet,

to stop the bleeding.'

Tom groaned quietly as Richard, with considerable effort, ripped the hole in his suit wider, in order to properly assess the wound. Preston paused with a puzzled look on his face.

'Use your initiative, a sling strap, some plastic padding, anything! And keep a look out.'

Preston nodded, turning on his heels.

Richard turned to Tom. 'He's a good man, just a bit slow at times!' Richard pressed his thumb gently onto the neat hole in Tom's thigh; it oozed semi-congealed blood. Tom winced.

'Sorry. Looks like a titanium sublet, it's neat and there's no exit wound. I think the bone stopped it, but it doesn't look broken. Lucky you had this suit on, but you've lost a lot of blood.'

Tom nodded in agreement.

'Been done for some time hasn't it? There's a lot of congealed blood around the wound?'

'Yesterday. Had a dressing on it of sorts. I've been moving around, opened it again.'

'We'll sort you out in no time, I always travel with a doctor,' continued Richard with a faint smile.

'Nicola's dead, Reece,' said Tom, completely out of the blue. 'I shot her, no choice. Her or me, she was a criminal, the worst kind.'

Richard turned and looked directly at Tom, who had managed to deliver the words quite matter-of-factly; but

Richard could see the sadness in his expression. Tom's face was pale and drained, his eyes tired and sore and there was a large bruise down his left cheek. Richard looked down, staring for some time at the smudged blood that stained the floor.

'You did what you had to do I'm sure. She wasn't the woman I had known, no, she was . . .'

Richard failed to finish his sentence, lost in his own thoughts.

Tom broke the impromptu silence. 'Guess I owe you an apology,' he said. 'Had you gunning for the wrong side.'

'Don't mention it old chap, made a similar mistake myself,' Richard replied in slightly sarcastic queen's English, his mistimed attempt at humour falling flat on its face. Richard dropped the sarcasm and the accent. 'Listen, Race, what's important now, indeed critical, is getting these crystals to the ISSF. I understand from Petromolosovich on Spartacus that they are reconditioning a few of the old nuclear power stations, only using the crystals as the power source. Might work, but for how long?'

'Don't ask me. You have a better idea?' Tom replied, burnishing his own sarcasm.

'There's always a better idea, believe me, anyway, the stakes are higher than any of us can imagine.'

Tom nodded, 'I'm aware of the stakes.'

Richard continued, 'I have an S2, the Endeavour, borrowed from Spartacus, It's ready on the main pad. Rachel Turner is onboard; she'll be worried sick by now. But

I've got a problem getting you on, your suit, it's a write off!'

'I know what you've come in,' replied Tom sighing. 'Good work, if I say so myself. Now, you listen to me. Take the crystals, leave me here. I can look after myself.'

Richard parried the misplaced heroic gesture. 'I'm not in the habit of running out on people,' he replied, 'anyway, you're going to need medical help sooner rather than ...'

His words were interrupted by the illumination of a green signal light and an accompanying chime emanating from the central booth. 'We're running out of time, it's the emergency shuttle. They're on their way!'

Preston stepped hurriedly into the carriage carrying a length of plastic strapping. 'Visitors,' he said, as if their coming was inevitable.

Richard tied the strap around Tom's thigh just above the wound, but was careful not to pull it too tight, then, helping Tom to his feet, he issued orders to Preston.

'See those capsules, the large ones for perishables?' he said pointing to three cylindrical containers, each about one and a half metres long, a half metre in diameter and mounted on four-wheeled, electrically driven trolleys. Preston shook his head.

'Over the back, Preston, look, underneath the Emergency Exit sign.'

'Yep, got 'em.'

'Get the Commander in one, any way you can. Pressurise it and take him through the emergency air lock. Push it, pull it, I don't care, but get him as close as possible to the landing pad. I'm going to buy us some time. Go!'

Tom had no time to protest, although the harassed look on his face said it all. Preston, supporting his injured side, half dragged Tom towards the section used for packaging and transporting perishables; such as live plants and special foods. With its precious contents, Richard picked up the metal case and moved towards the front of the shuttle. He was surprised at the weight of the U-Semini device; the equivalent in a Yearlman design, even that size, would have weighed substantially more.

He used a low powered sonic discharge to blast the electronic lock on the door to the auto-driver's compartment; the deformed, metal alloy door bursting open with one good aggressive kick. Richard knew how to operate the shuttle from his days on Andromeda, and so quickly set the return programme. Pressing a number of keys on the control panel, he overrode the safety interlock system and set it to a maximum speed configuration. The shuttle moved immediately, with several alarm lights illuminating to signify open doors, and unsafe programme parameters. Jumping clear just before the platform slid past, he watched as the shuttle accelerated back down the track.

'That should hold them up for a while,' he smirked.

With no time to waste on a cautious retreat; avoiding camera arcs and sensor beams, he ran flat out directly towards the main terminal building. Once inside, he flipped down his visor and prepared his suit by pressurising it with nitrous oxygen. He armed the integral electrical heating elements and switched his microphone to VATS. The Voice Activated Transmissions System automatically switched off the microphone during silent periods; it effectively eradicated all erroneous noise, particularly breathing, and reactivated the moment the wearer spoke.

'Rachel, it's Richard. Come in,' he said, closing the air lock door between the administration section and the main freight terminal. He equalised to the storage terminal pressure, which was a little higher than surface pressure. 'Rachel, it's Richard, how do you read?' he repeated, beginning to breathe heavily.

Moments later, he was sprinting across the large open freight bay, towards the landing pad. Still there was no reply. He began to think the worst.

'Richard, it's me. I'm listening, but you had better hurry. One of Andromeda's fighters has done a low pass. He's coming back for another look.'

'OK, got it, two minutes,' Richard replied as a bead of sweat ran down his nose. 'Can you see Preston?'

'Yes. I've been watching him. He's pushing some kind of trolley thing, like an enclosed operating table, but making slow progress. He's still two or three hundred metres away.'

Richard leapt at the personnel door, the last one, kicking it open. The small pressure differential between the freight terminal and the 'outside' resulted in a strong breeze whipping up instantaneously. Dust and small pieces of debris accompanied him, being blown out through the narrow doorway.

As the door swung closed behind him, Richard sprinted as fast as he could for the Endeavour. Rachel had lowered the personnel door under the right forward undercarriage leg and Richard leapt the first four steps, panting hard. He negotiated the remaining eight steps more conventionally before slamming the airlock hatch closed behind him.

Even inside the pressure chamber, he could hear the reverberating throb of particle beam motors as the 'D class' fighter passed low overhead.

'He'll disable us on the next run,' he shouted, 'or try to!'

As Richard's suit pressure dropped below six Bartels, he was able to flip the two catches on his neckband and release his helmet, lifting it off with both hands. Then he smashed the red intercom button on the chamber wall with the palm of his right hand.

'Open the airlock, Rachel, quickly!'

Within seconds, Richard heard the hollow clunking of withdrawing titanium pins. Beginning to catch his breath, he pushed the circular, inner door wide open.

As he entered the main cargo compartment, Rachel passed him, to his surprise, running in the other direction.

'I'm going to open the rear door for Preston. It will be quicker!'

Richard didn't look back, instead, dropping his helmet onto an adjacent emergency crew seat, he raced to the flight deck. At one time, he could get an S2 airborne in less than two minutes. Almost falling into the Commander's seat, he pressed the start sequence button for the retro rockets, and clipped the two lap straps into the centre box. As the retros reached self-sustaining, he aborted their start sequence and thumped the left main engine starter. A familiar low-level vibration crept through the craft as the rocket motor reached idle power, about twenty percent thrust. Next, the two shoulder straps and the head set. Then the right main engine start button. With the left stabilised at twenty-three percent, on went the main electrical breakers.

Richard focused on the proximity radar. With a synchronous phased vibration sensed through his seat, he knew both main engines were now online. The proximity radar showed a return in the ten o'clock position; it was approaching twenty kilometres in a left turn, and he didn't have a second to lose.

'Rachel, how's it going? Rachel, we need to go!'

Silence.

The radar showed the contact in a continuous left turn and coming round behind them, fast. Richard pushed a few buttons on the control panel. The system computed the closing speed.

'Eighty lutens,' he said aloud, 'it's a Delta Class!'

The 'Delta Class' was a high performance single seat fighter craft with a single 'D' shaped wing, mounted midway along the thin fuselage. The menacing multi-role craft utilised a new generation particle beam propulsion system that gave the agile fighter a top speed of almost two hundred lutens in the lunar atmosphere, equating to approximately twelve thousand miles per hour on earth, but range and endurance was limited.

Unlike the propulsion system of Enigma, which generated energy by splitting molecules, the D Class had a fuel tank, which was filled with pressurised *Sion* gas. This volatile synthetic gas, superheated in a reaction chamber, resulted in a dense soup of 'boiled off' atomic particles, mainly high-energy electrons, that were subsequently expelled rearwards through a propelling nozzle. The theory could be likened to boiling off water in a kettle and propelling the resulting steam through a pressure nozzle, but with incredible velocity. However, the system used its fuel quickly, especially at high speed, and the endurance was about three hours: ideal for planetary defence, but without the necessary reserves for an earth to moon transit.

Richard had not flown the Delta Class. It had entered service after his departure from Andromeda Wing. He knew its performance though, and in comparison, the sluggish S2 could not face it off in a one to one. Richard knew he would have to run, and quickly. With no response from Rachel, and fully aware of the fighter making its final turn onto an attack profile, Richard began to wind up the main engines to a responsive fifty percent. His right thumb rotated a control sphere, and directed the underside video camera to look rearwards, quickly scanning the area behind his ship.

'No sign. Where are they? Come on Rachel, come on.

It's now or never!'

A beeping noise and red light above the proximity radar screen indicated that the D Class had a weapons lock. It was now directly behind the S2, at a range of twelve kilometres. Richard knew the profile only too well; six kilometres was the optimum release point, seconds away.

He had to trust Rachel's ability, but the amber light on his main instrument panel indicated that the rear door of the S2 was still open. He began to open the main engine throttles, holding off on the retros for a few more seconds.

The radar screen flashed a yellow cross over the Delta Class return and the words 'Weapons Release' appeared on the screen. An emotionless voice generated by the main computer system called, 'Evasive action required. Evasive action required.'

Suddenly, the amber light extinguished; the rear door was closed. Simultaneously, slamming the main engine throttles fully forward and selecting maximum thrust on the retros, Richard didn't wait to clear the platform but pulled the side stick hard left. The S2 rotated on its left undercarriage, rolling almost eighty degrees before the combined thrust of the retros and main engines squeezed him into the seat. Nine 'g' indicated on the accelerometer, enough to black out even the most seasoned fighter pilot.

His vision became tunnelled, as blood pooled in his legs and lower body. Instinctively, he tensed his stomach muscles to reduce the flow rate, and remain conscious.

Then he snapped the side stick fully to the right, to the stops. A massive explosion from beneath the ship shook it violently, almost out of control. The Ground Proximity Warning System responded. 'Terrain. Terrain. Pull up. Pull up.' Richard off loaded the 'g' force by accelerating and reducing thrust on the retros. Several emergency lights illuminated on the main instrument panel. Richard quickly assessed them: a breached hull amidships and a fire warning on the front left retro, not good, not good at all.

Without warning, the S2 rolled violently left again, this time not at Richard's command. Full right stick had no effect. He had flown into the wake vortex, a spiralling tube of gas created by the combined effects of the fighter's propulsion motors, its thrust augmentation system and its incredibly high speed. Richard could do nothing about the situation but apply full opposite controls, and wait.

Richard's experience was such that he knew exactly the perilous situation the S2 was in. A wake vortex is a highly energised, spiralling tube of gas generated by the passage of a spacecraft, or an aircraft for that matter. The size and ferocity of the wake is proportional to the size and speed of the craft creating it. The bigger the craft, or alternatively, the faster the craft, the more energetic the vortex. Many aircraft had been lost over the years, directly attributable to vortices, their crews, for one reason or another, passing too close behind a preceding craft, becoming ensnared in the swirling tube, then inevitably losing control. At that moment, Richard was very poorly placed.

Already demanding almost full thrust from the main engines, and eighty percent from the retros, he squeezed them both to give a few more percent; their absolute maximum in the highly rarefied atmosphere of the moon. With the side stick already fully to the right, there was nothing he could do, just go with the flow, so to speak. The S2 continued to the left, rolling almost inverted. Richard knew that the disturbance had to wash out or dissipate when it encountered the lunar surface, but would he have enough altitude to recover?

Those few seconds seemed an eternity. Finally, the continued full right control application began to have an effect, but not until the craft, descending rapidly, passed three hundred feet above ground level. Now the invisible spiralling vortex began losing its grip. The S2 responded, slowly at first, but with a rapidly building roll rate to the right. Richard anticipated the craft's momentum, stopping the attitude change almost right side up. In this position and with the retros screaming at full power, the rate of descent stopped abruptly, bottoming at eighty feet, amidst a cacophony of warning lights and alarms.

'Too close for comfort,' he breathed quietly to himself, switching his gaze to the proximity radar screen. 'Nothing, but I know that he's out there!'

Tactically, particularly after such a close encounter with terra firma, Richard believed that a pilot's natural reaction to gain altitude as quickly as possible, would, in this case, be flawed. The fighter pilot, whoever he was, would expect this too. Instead, Richard pushed the nose forward and accelerated by rotating the retro rocket nozzles aft and keeping the main engine throttle in his right hand hard against the stops. The S2 quickly passed one hundred lutens, by one hundred and twenty it began to show its age.

Harnessing the continuous high power levels seemed to make the ship groan with pain, as its structure deformed. Richard, with his seemingly sadistic handling, added yet more stress by snapping into a ninety-degree roll to the right and pulling hard into a maximum rate turn.

'Rule one,' he said aloud, 'never fly straight and level for more than thirty seconds.'

It proved to be a rule worthy of adherence, for unknown to him, and using an omni-directional blocking signal to effectively make itself invisible to the S2's sensor and tracking system, the D Class had manoeuvred onto an intercept course and acquired a positive target lock.

'Hell! Son of a bitch!' screamed the fighter pilot, frustrated as he watched the large grey S2 break the weapon system lock with the sharp and unexpected turn. 'Clever, but not half clever enough,' he continued, steepening his dive and accelerating to almost one hundred and seventy lutens.

The 'D Class' was a fighter pilot's dream: fast and highly manoeuvrable. Currently in service both planetary and, exceptionally, interplanetary, it was far superior to any of its defensive predecessors and was the third of the new generation of fighters built in response to the extraterrestrial visit of March 2016. Its design specification also incorporated an offensive capability, as well as a defensive one.

Unbeknown to Richard, and Tom Race for that matter, the pilot so intent on bringing them down was Lieutenant Chan Sung. His official brief was to shepherd the S2 back to Andromeda using warning shots if required. However, Lieutenant Sung had no intention of allowing the S2 to land anywhere. His 'alternative' brief, the one from his paymasters, was to bring down the S2 in some sort of controlled crash if possible, in order to allow retrieval of its precious cargo. He knew that the U-Semini case was 'crash proof' and even total destruction of the S2 would not adversely affect its contents.

Sung had a good idea who was flying the S2, but he wasn't sure. As far as he was concerned, only Tom Race could handle an S2 like this. In any case, its destruction was just a few seconds away as he tightened his turn and came in fast on an intercept heading about fifteen kilometres behind his prey.

'So easy, so very easy,' he murmured, placing his right thumb over the plasma cannon trigger.

Sung, relatively inexperienced on the D Class, forgot his speed momentarily, now at almost one hundred and ninety lutens; he overshot the ideal course and in so doing destabilised the D Class for a few seconds with over aggressive handling in an effort to regain the attack profile.

Richard, still running with full power on the main engines, had reduced the retros to fifteen percent. His attention had switched to the video screen, which was receiving a clear picture from the rear-facing camera. He had seen the D Class pass quickly from one side of the screen to the other and then appear again from the right, shaking violently.

He would have to out-think this pilot, as the fighter's superiority meant that it was only a matter of time before even this, apparently mediocre pilot, would acquire a weapon lock. Interesting though, thought Richard, that the pilot, now almost line astern at six and a half kilometres, did not use the sonic torpedo.

At that instant, the sonic torpedo, a broad range weapon, had a good chance of success, but he seemed, instead, to be intent on the plasma cannon, a close quarter's weapon with narrow acquisition parameters and a maximum range of two kilometres. Was he, or she, enjoying the hunt?

As the D Class stabilised at a little over two kilometres, Richard manoeuvred violently by pulling up momentarily, snap rolling left to the inverted position, delaying for a spilt second, and then through another ninety degrees into a hard turn to he right. He checked the video monitor, losing the aggressor for a few seconds, only to find it appearing back in the centre of the screen, as menacing as ever.

'He's on you again,' came a voice over the intercom. It was Rachel. 'Do something!'

'I'm trying,' replied Richard, 'you made it, then.' He followed that remark with an aggressive hesitation turn to the right, then to the left, and pulled so hard on the stick that his vision began to turn grey again.

'That hurts,' he groaned, dropping the nose, then diving into a steep sided crevasse about three hundred feet wide. Within a few seconds, the fighter crossed the screen two or three times, then centred.

Over the radio came a voice Richard vaguely recognised; an American accent with a twang of Chinese.

'You can run, but you can't hide.'

Richard checked his navigation computer, ignoring the callous remark. Being well below the peaks of the surrounding mountains, the system was unreliable, particularly with such rapid changes of direction. He did not recognise the broad valley the S2 had entered after weaving, for several kilometres, down the southerly-orientated crevasse, although he knew that he was rapidly approaching the Sea of Tranquillity.

'Everybody surviving back there?'

'Just about,' Rachel replied. 'I'm strapped in next to Tom Race, I've managed to stop the bleeding, but he's in and out of consciousness, I'll need to attend to him soon. Preston has hurt his leg getting Tom into the ship, its badly swollen and may be fractured, but he's firmly strapped in opposite me with a confused look on his face, and a pool of vomit between his legs.'

'Ugh, he's not travelling so well then.'

Richard's words were cut short, interrupted violently, as the rocky outcrop, uncomfortably close on the left side of the ship, exploded, jagged pieces flying in all directions. He banked wildly left and right to avoid the larger projectiles, feeling several light impacts on the S2's structure. The explosion was the result of a plasma blast, which, by good fortune, narrowly missed them.

'What was that?' cried Rachel.

Richard checked the screen. The D Class passed in and out of view again, crossing the screen rapidly in all directions. Suddenly, unavoidably, its left stabiliser impacted a large fragment of spiralling debris thrown out by the explosion. It took the tip clean off and with it the sonic torpedo initiator. The fighter disappeared from view. Richard dared to think for a moment that it had gone down, out of control. Seconds later, the rocky outcrops and steep sides of the crevasse were gone, left behind and the broad plane of the Sea of Tranquillity lay before them.

Richard immediately and aggressively pushed the nose of his craft down, descending to twenty feet, until he literally skimmed the moon's surface. Leaving it until the very last second, he manoeuvred countless times, in order to avoid giant boulders, strewn randomly across this part of the flatlands.

There was still no sign of the D Class. Looking to his right and first appearing as a speck on the horizon, thereafter growing larger as the S2 maintained one hundred and thirty lutens, he could see a small cluster of objects. Richard at last recognised his position: coming up quickly on the right side, was the site of the first moon landing. Preserved exactly as Aldrin and Armstrong had left it as they blasted off for home in July 1969, even the American flag still flew proudly.

Richard banked steeply to the left, pulled into a hard turn, and climbed a few feet to avoid his own stabiliser tip scraping the surface. He rolled level one hundred and twenty degrees later. Looking through the side screen, he could see the long trail of dust and debris that had been whipped up above the surface by the low flying S2.

Still no sign of the D Class. Even so, Richard was nervous, feeling exposed above the broad plane. Despite this, he thought, climbing could be fatal. He opened his mouth, about to broadcast the good news, when the fighter appeared, as menacing as ever, in the centre of the video screen.

The haunting image remained for just a moment, being obliterated again in the thick grey-black dust storm generated behind them. Richard knew instinctively that the fighter was in auto-track mode, riding in a projected 'magnetic tube' that was locked onto the S2. With its long-range weapon out of action, the D Class had only one viable weapon to bring them down, the plasma cannon, and that needed a magic two kilometres or less, so the pilot was waiting for a more opportune moment.

Inside the cockpit of the D Class, Chan Sung was

sweating; beads of perspiration running down his forehead and cheeks. His handling skills, although recognised as good within Andromeda Wing, were being tested to the limit, and often beyond. All thoughts of a sporting chase had melted, washed away, literally. His face was tight with concentration, becoming contorted, even twisted occasionally, under the effects of excessive 'g' force, as the fighter's auto-lock system hung on to the S2's evasive trajectory.

Richard knew that he had to make it to the mountain range to the east of Tranquillity. There he could, hopefully, evade the fighter until its fuel ran out. Nevertheless, the S2, even with its interplanetary fuel capability, couldn't maintain full throttle in this environment for much longer.

It was just a matter of time, thought Richard, him or me.

Rachel interrupted, 'Tom's back with us. He thinks he recognises the pilot's voice as Lieutenant Sung?'

Richard didn't respond, he knew Sung, but not well; somehow, he wasn't surprised at his obviously traitorous alliance. Anyway, his attention was diverted by the sight of the towering cliffs of the Barberous Mountains rising in the distance.

The east face of this mountain range was familiar to Richard. Amazingly, during his time on Andromeda Wing, he would fly visiting dignitaries, delegates and VIPs from earth on sight seeing trips; these inevitably included the site of the first moon landing. He would often include the Barberous Cliffs in the flight, impressive in their monumental scale and glowing incandescent, being almost continuously orientated towards the earth.

However, Richard had no time to reflect on their glory, with the high ground looming ahead he would have to climb, and, once clear of the surface, he would lose the protection of the thick dust cloud that had frustrated Sung's best attempts at a firing opportunity.

Richard left it to the last possible moment, only a few hundred metres. With retro directed fully down, he slammed their thrust levers into the maximum power position.

'Hang on,' he shouted over the intercom.

He pulled hard. The S2 seemed to flex under the enormous strain as it climbed, almost vertically, up the towering five thousand feet high cliff face. Richard rolled the craft smoothly but firmly to avoid a great rocky outcrop jutting out from the cliff face. He knew Sung was unlikely to follow him tightly in that manoeuvre, but once over the crest, he would be there. He rolled again, this time aggressively to the left, so that the top of the S2 faced the cliff and so close that the jagged strata seemed destined, at some point, to come straight through the windscreen, speeding past as it was at heart stopping speed. As the crest approached, Richard pulled hard and rounded the peaks, clinging to them like glue. In the horizontal, he rolled again, right side up, and pulled back the power on the retros.

Sung was not expecting that manoeuvre, not at all, and

overshot the mountain top with a trajectory and speed that directed him up high into space, like a slingshot. A few seconds later, as his momentum waned, he aggressively manoeuvred his ship, almost power stalling it, in a clumsy attempt to rectify his ill-timed mistake.

Richard scanned the landscape for a suitable valley and directed the S2 quickly into a zigzagging example; sensibly, it was far too narrow for the ship. He had a plan. Chang was too aggressive, ill tempered, Richard could feel his frustrations. He had lost the cool, clinical temperament he had displayed at the first encounter. Chang's ill coordinated, primitive attack runs showed that his judgement was being clouded by other emotions.

Richard was going to use this. Looking several kilometres ahead, he could see the head of the valley; a daunting face of solid rock, easily a thousand feet high. He aligned the four retro nozzles to a position about twenty degrees back from the vertical, the thrust directed mainly downwards but with a small component rearward. Weaving down the valley at low level, one hundred feet above the ground, he began to transition the flight thrust from the main engines to the retros until, a little later, the S2 was almost entirely supported by those smaller engines. The main engines he gradually reduced to idle. The speed of the S2 decelerated: one hundred and ten lutens, one hundred, ninety.

Chan Sung, having recovered from his ill-conceived and inappropriate attack run was seething with contempt for the S2's successful evasion. He was still high, by several thousand feet, but coming down fast, back for another attempt at the now clearly visible S2.

Things were looking up. The S2 was around two hundred feet above the moon's surface and it appeared relatively stable.

'Perhaps he thinks I'm out!' Sung sniggered nervously.

With no sign of the D Class on radar, Richard repeatedly scanned the semi-darkened skyline. Then there, just fleetingly, he saw a glint of light; the sun's reflection off the cockpit canopy of the D Class. Then it was gone, but that was all Richard needed. Now he knew the fighter was coming round behind him, ludicrously high and probably far too fast. Richard scanned his instruments, the transition was complete; the entire flight loads of the S2 supported by the retros, almost a high hover, but with some forward speed; just thirty lutens.

Chang Sung was closing fast, almost one hundred and eighty lutens. In a sixty-degree dive, range some twelve kilometres, he turned in behind the S2 for another aggressive attack run. Aware of the excessively high closure rate, he did not seem to comprehend that it was due to the S2's slow speed; his attack profile computer would have indicated this, had he looked at its display. Anyway, to him, it did not matter, he was positioning for a classic.

Sung squinted slightly as he targeted the S2 through his gun sight; the image projected onto the inside of his helmet visor.

'So the best man wins after all,' he said coldly over the

radio. His thumb hovered over the plasma cannon's trigger.

Richard's thumb was working too, rotating the spherical control ball, which in turn directed the upper video camera. He scanned the heavens methodically, but to no avail. Where was the D class, where?

Timing, his crew and his own survival would depend on it; split second timing. But he needed to see the fighter again, either visually or on radar, just for an instant. Richard, almost in desperation, did a quick mental calculation based on his speed, and therefore that of the D Class, at the moment he broke the crest of Barberous Mountains. His calculations would give him an indication of the momentum and therefore the altitude the D Class would have reached after missing his call, and skidding off into space.

Richard was surprised by the answer, but didn't hesitate. He quickly rotated the video camera control wheel and raised the camera to approximately fifty degrees above the horizon, then scanned back and forth. Immediately he saw it, diving at an almost suicidal angle and closing ludicrously fast. Nevertheless, Richard knew that if any craft could run that absurd attack profile and survive, it was the D Class.

Glancing forward momentarily through the windscreen, he could see the head of the valley coming up at about nine kilometres; it terminated in a wall of rock, but initially the ground rose in a progressive incline. Grey, lifeless, cloaked in shadow, the incline rose surreptitiously to at least five hundred feet above the valley floor.

A red light appeared on the proximity radar display and the audio warning called, 'Danger. Weapon lock. Danger. Weapon lock. Evasive action required.'

Richard's hands were ready on the control stick and the thrust levers, but he paused. Seconds passed. He rotated the camera angle down to twenty degrees. There she was again, intimidating, threatening, completing her final turn; now at only five kilometres and with a descent profile and closure rate still excessive, but controllable. Rachel screamed something from her position in the rear of the S2. The video monitor she was watching relaying the same picture as Richard's.

Richard heard her but the words didn't register, such was his concentration. 'Danger. Weapon lock. Danger. Weapon lock. Immediate action required,' ordered the monotone, synthetic voice of the S2's integrated guidance computer. Did Richard detect an element of distress in its digital delivery?

Overlaid was Chan Sung's voice on the radio.'You're dead!' he said bluntly.

Richard's hands tensed. 'Steady, steady,' he said aloud, the fighter now pinpointed clearly on the radar screen and indicating two kilometres.

'Wait, wait. Now!'

The S2 was just seconds away from flying into the rising ground, as it neared the valley head. Richard snatched back the thrust levers controlling the retro rockets; the S2 dropped like a brick. A split second later he slammed them open again and rolled forty-five degrees right. The rate of descent was arrested just feet from the valley floor, after that he was squashed down in his seat as the force of the four retrorockets at full power accelerated the S2 upwards. His simultaneous right turn barely avoided the vertical wall of rock, now seemingly charging towards him in an effort to burst through the windscreen.

Richard's right hand slammed the thrust levers of the main engine forward with such force that he winced with the pain felt in the palm of his hand. Instantly, the accelerating force pushed his head back hard onto the restraint of his seat back. He tried to look down at the radar, neck muscles straining, but could not, such was the combined force of all the S2's engines at full power.

The craft vibrated severely, in harmony with the thunderous roar. Instinctively Richard rolled the S2 level and pulled hard. The craft climbed at maximum rate passing four, then five thousand feet within a few seconds. As the mountains disappeared from view through the main windscreen, he pushed the nose forward and off loaded the tremendous 'g' force. On the proximity radar display, the weapon lock warning light had extinguished. He flashed across to the video screen, nothing! Then, rolling the S2 inverted, reoriented himself with the moon's surface. Off to the right, towards the end of the rising ground and close to the valley head, was a tiny ball of flame. It glowed and flickered orange, then red and then white. A small explosion briefly added a starburst of flying debris, and a narrow column of smoke rose vertically from the crash site.

Sung had broken the first rule of aerial combat: target fixation. So intent was his focus on keeping the S2 in his sights, that he had lost perspective of his surroundings. He hadn't noticed the rising ground in front of his prey. When Richard had cut the power to the retros and dropped, just momentarily, Sung had followed him, pushing down the nose of his fighter. Already with a high rate of decent and excessive forward speed, not even the D Class could recover. Evidently, he had pulled up steeply, but to no avail, the fighter had collided with the ground, skidded some five hundred metres, and then come to rest as a mangled, burning heap at the base of the cliff face.

Richard could clearly see the shallow impact crater; he reflected on the events for a moment then checked his fuel gauges. There was enough for the transit to earth, but probably not enough for a powered re-entry and landing.

What should he do? Land back at Andromeda's facility and surrender the crystals to the authorities? The station Commander was respected at all levels. Or, risk a re-entry manoeuvre through the earth's atmosphere? Richard recalled his orders, specified quite clearly by Colonel Petromolosovich, just days earlier, whilst on Spartacus. He must deliver, by hand, the Kalahari crystals to General Buchanan, Chief Operations Officer, ISSF. Thereafter they would find their way safely to the awaiting power stations.

Richard leaned forward and peered through the side screen at the earth; as far as he could see, now almost totally covered by a swirling mass of grey cloud. Gone were the familiar, striking, blues and whites of this tiny oasis in space.

'Hold on, everyone, it's time we went home,' he said without emotion, over the PA.

CHAPTER 36

No Place for Love

By the time Richard had accelerated on a reverse course around the dark side of the moon and sped off towards earth, it was too late for Andromeda to react, even if they had wanted to.

He wondered: was Chan Sung a renegade, an extremist, or even a terrorist, or purely a mercenary out for his own personal gain? Was he tarring those on Andromeda Wing with the same brush? Did he need to keep checking his six o'clock in case of more D Class aggressors?

He didn't know, nor as it happened did Tom, who was responding well to the Vimoxon injection administered by Rachel, subsequent to them regaining a more appropriate flight regime.

A few hours later, having a little over twelve thousand miles to re-entry, Richard cautiously broke radio silence. It was more out of self-preservation than optimism, for within minutes, he was flanked by two D Class fighters of Sentinel Wing; an interceptor squadron based in the Cape.

As the lead ship pulled alongside his S2, holding a close 'echelon port' position, Richard glanced across at the helmeted, sinister looking pilot, now clearly visible on his near side. The pilot positioned his two hands, one behind the other, mimicking two aircraft. Richard nodded, and followed him for re-entry. Transferring the last remaining drops of fuel from the retro tanks to those of the main engines, the navigation computer predicted enough fuel for the re-entry and down to thirty thousand feet; approximately six miles. After that, it would be a glide approach, all on instruments, as the cloud base indicated total cover was down to just two hundred feet.

Are you sure this is Florida? he questioned himself. Richard flipped a switch on the central instrument panel; it initiated the data link sensor and health monitoring system. Within seconds, NASA would have a complete readout of the S2's systems and, more importantly, be aware of his fuel state. It was prudent to use the autopilot system for the re-entry and approach, and Richard duly did. Nevertheless, as his ship, now in free flight, sank through the bottom of the endless black, oily cloud, Richard had thoughts of a manual landing, his first on earth for some considerable time.

At one hundred feet however, and with a tar-like film almost obliterating his view through the forward windshields, he let the machine do it and apply its automatic braking system following the conventional landing. Richard was barely able to see the runway in front of him, even after the S2 had come to an eerily quiet stop.

To immense relief, the four of them had made it. Richard patted the arm of his seat, like patting a loyal dog on the head, then reached up to a row of switches on the roof panel and flicked one across to the 'open' position. Subsequently a red light appeared on the centralised warning panel indicating the forward main portal was opening.

He left the U-Semini case in the flight deck as a precaution. It was tucked away out of sight behind his seat. Then he climbed out. Rachel too had left her seat. She propped Tom up against his seat back and felt his forehead. He was cold due to blood loss; then she checked his pulse. He was OK, responding to treatment, albeit slowly.

Rachel left the servicing bay, returning a few moments later with a large plastic-fibre medical holdall. She had traded in her old one back on Spartacus, in favour of this larger model. It was light grey in colour, with a large red cross stitched onto the side and the words 'Fragile Medical Equipment' written beneath. She placed the bulky, but apparently lightweight holdall on the ground and partially unzipped it, retrieving two items. The first, a small towel, she placed on the floor between Preston's feet. He was cradling his head in his hands, still suffering the effects of motion sickness. The second was a clear plastic flask, from which she poured Preston a small glass of pink fluid, and then she replaced the flask and zipped up the holdall again.

The holdalls contents appeared unusually substantial; had either of the two men had any inclination to notice. Rachel lifted it using both handles and turned to Preston.

'Mind you drink it all, it will help. I'll be back shortly!' she advised kindly.

The large curved portal rotated downwards, its opening accompanied by a familiar electrical buzz. Richard remained at the head of the steps until both mechanical systems locked into place, each with a metallic clank.

Rachel, remaining out of sight, slipped past the opening carrying the holdall; she struggled a little, more a result of its awkwardness than its weight. Then, entering the flight deck, looked around nervously. It was where she had expected it to be, the U-Semini case, out of sight behind Richard's seat. Dropping the bag and quickly unzipping it, she put her hand inside and pulled out another case; it was an exact duplicate. Without hesitation, she substituted one for the other, placing the original in her holdall. Then, Richard's emergency helmet caught her eye, she dwelt on it for a moment considering her actions. Deceit or duty? Love, or King and country? Her brief had been explicit, no exceptions, no flexibility of interpretation. Her controller too had been adamant; she must never break cover, not at any time, not to anyone. Within seconds, she was gone.

Outside, Richard was greeted by a myriad of vehicles

with flashing lights and orange rotating beacons. A group of about twenty people stood in a huddle, wincing against the beating rain. Two senior officers stepped forward to welcome him, their aids struggling to keep large black umbrellas in place over their heads. Richard walked down to meet them. He felt Rachel close behind him, then, standing by his side, she gave a broad smile to the two men.

Richard offered his hand to the burly 'Four Star' United States Army Officer on the left.

'General Buchanan, I presume,' he said, his own smile taut, almost half-hearted.

The General shook his hand heartily. 'You bet, son,' came the reply, 'and we are mighty glad to see you. You've got something for us?'

'Do you have the security code, Sir?' Richard enquired, somewhat boldly. Rachel grasped his arm gently. General Buchanan, slightly surprised by the formalities, coughed into his fist and stepped forward. He whispered something into Richard's ear.

Richard responded with a nod and an easier grin. 'Yes indeed, Sir,' he concluded with satisfaction. 'They're inside, mind you put them to good use General. They are the history and future of the human race.'

The Bastion Prosecutor, book two of The Kalahari Series will be available from December 2006.

Glossary

The list of special or technical words used in The Osiris Revelations

Accelercom - Accelerated Communication System - Referenced to light speed i.e. approximately 186,282 miles per second or 300,000 kilometres per second.

ADF - Automatic Direction Finding - Basic device used to detect the direction of an emitting radio/radar source.

Amplitude - Maximum deviation or oscillation from a mean or constant frequency - Number of complete cycles per second.

ARPS - Atomic Reaction Propulsion System - Propulsion utilising a physical law of motion i.e. 'for every action there is an equal and opposite reaction'.

Bioscan - Electronic scan used to detect present or previous life forms.

Biograph - Results of a 'bioscan', usually in graph form. Indicates quantities and isolates specific areas where biological atoms/molecules, such as carbon, are encountered.

Bulkhead - Upright partition, usually structural, in a ship or aircraft.

Bunk - Bed in ship or aircraft.

CMO - Chief Medical Officer.

CMPC - Cyan Magnetic Pulse Cannon - Close defence system using high-energy magnetic pulses.

Comms State - Communication Security State - Refers to state of security protection and readiness.

CPA - Closest Point of Approach - Closest point a space ship or cosmic body will pass referenced to an observer.

Cosmic Chronometer - Extremely accurate clock, time computations based on the expansion rate of the universe - 'Big Bang' Theory.

Deckhead - Ceiling in ship or aircraft.

Deck - Floor/platform/walking surface on ship or aircraft.

Dermaveil - Anti-aging product developed on Mars - Trade name.

DP Check - Depressurization Check - Medical check on personnel who have experienced space suit problems on the 'outside'.

FPO - Flight Path Obstacle - A physical obstacle or piece of space debris.

Gamma Radiation - Short wave electromagnetic radiation given off by the sun, usually very penetrating and dangerous to humans.

Gamma Screen - Medical check up to ascertain level of 'gamma ray' absorption.

Harmonic Sympathy - Harmonious product of a vibration: builds to great amplitude.

Hatch - Personnel door in bulkhead. Usually structural, airtight, hinged and lockable.

Heads - Toilets in ships or aircraft.

HOD - Head of Department.

Humatron - Advanced robot series incorporating Level 7 Programming.

I.D. - Identity - Usually in the form of an electronic tag or card.

ID Locket - Electronic Identity Locket - Usually worn on a chain/lanyard around neck, like a 'dog-tag'.

ISAPS - Initial Search and Procurement Session - A search and recognisance period, usually four hours on station.

ISSF - International Space and Science Federation - Multinational/Global body made up of regional Space and Science Agencies.

Ks - Abbreviation for kilometres.

Lab - Laboratory.

Light Year - Distance travelled by light in one year.

LS - Life Support - Essential equipment or processes used for sustaining life.

MCT - Martian Corrected Time - Time dictated by the Martian hour, day, month and year but referenced to earth time.

NCO - Non Commissioned Officer.

Nuromild Sedative Gas - Sedative given in gaseous form - trade name.

Pitch up - Pulling the nose of an a spacecraft or aircraft up, usually results in a climb. Conversely - Pitch down.

Portal - Door, Entry/exit point, Opening for personnel. Usually associated with space vehicles.

PTSV - Personnel Transport and Service Vehicle - Multi-wheeled surface support vehicle.

QSPS - Quasar Solar Power System - Special electrical generating system utilising the sun's energy.

Radio waves - Electromagnetic waves usually less than 10 centimetres in length.

Rockwell Illinois Plateau System - System for measuring the degree of complexity and memory capacity of a cybernetic system - has become the internationally recognised reference system.

Roger - Form of acknowledgement, usually meaning that an order or statement has been understood.

Roll/Bank - Manoeuvre performed by spacecraft/aircraft in order to execute a balanced turn.

Sitrep - Situation Report - Details of an event or happening.

SSA - Space and Science Agency - Multinational but regional body i.e. European Space and Science Agency or

Asian Space and Science Agency.

SSC - Special Security Contingent - Specialist security team.

SWAT Team - Security, Weapons and Tactical Team.

TES - Target Enhancement System - Tracking and lock-on system for weaponry.

Thrust Levers - Levers in cockpit controlling the thrust of an engine or rocket motor.

SHEBANG - The whole lot, everything included.

Sonic Pistol - Hand held weapon utilising a massively condensed pulse of sound energy. Depending on its severity, when the pulse hits a target it destabilises the atomic structure of the target, usually resulting in severe damage.

Static Discharge - Discharge of static electricity.

Wrist LS Controller - Wrist mounted life support control and display instrument.

The Kalahari Series

A trilogy

By
AJ MARSHALL

The Osiris Revelations
THE BASTION PROSECUTOR
Rogue Command

Original, exciting, possible ...

The next instalment coming soon ...

Read the first few thrilling pages now ...

THE BASTION
PROSECUTOR

Prologue

14th May 2050

It was early when the hotel telephone rang. Richard was in a deep sleep. The intrusive, abrasive tone penetrated his dream, surreptitiously becoming part of it. Pulling at his subconscious, initially to no avail, Richard eventually responded with a jolt. A burst of adrenalin unsympathetically exiled him to reality. Sitting up, in opaque darkness, he clumsily and unsuccessfully felt for the receiver; it fell silent. Groaning disapprovingly, Richard leant back hard against the padded bed-head. Then, after another equally frustrating search, he eventually found, by default, the switch to the bedside light; its dull, insufficient response struggling to illuminate the unfamiliar and unhomely room.

Richard had registered in the early hours, dropped his

case inside the door and immediately retired. Now, a few hours later, with a groggy disposition and tired, prickly eyes, he took a little time to orientate himself and gather his thoughts. He was still wearing his watch and pressed the face, illuminating the blue neon backlight and lighting his features with an expectant incandescent glow: the hour was disappointing.

'God, three thirty, that's all I need,' he complained quietly.

Then it began again.

A more unpleasant, penetrating tone would be hard to imagine, particularly at this Goddamn time of the morning, he thought.

This time he picked up the antiquated receiver promptly, his own tone uncompromising, reflecting the humourless hour.

'Reece. UK Joint Forces,' he scolded.

'Is that Lieutenant Commander Richard James Reece?' A well-spoken English voice enquired politely.

'Who wants to know?' pursued Richard aggressively.

A lengthy period of silence followed; both parties hesitated. Richard relented first, unable to maintain an unnatural obstinuity.

'Yes, speaking,' he ventured, 'one and the same.'

The caller's tone also offered some compromise.

'Apologies for the late hour, rather inconvenient I know. My name is Peter Rothschild, Central Bureau of Intelligence, M19.'

'Now what does National Security want with me?'

Richard interrupted suspiciously.

'We need to talk to you.'

'I'm listening.'

'Not on the telephone, Richard, we need you in London.'

To Richard, this man's easy use of his first name seemed patronising; it made his heckles rise. The caller sensed this too.

'Lieutenant Commander Reece,' he offered more respectfully but with determined emphasis. 'We *need* to speak to you, a matter of some gravity.'

'When?'

'Look out of your window, to the right, thirty metres; on the other side of the road. There is a car, a black Jaguar ZKZ.'

Richard sprang out of bed, stepped five or six paces to the window and shifted the edge of the curtain secretively. There it was, sidelights on, parked beneath a flickering streetlight, its driver engulfed in mysterious shadows. He walked back to the bedside table and picked up the receiver.

'I see it.'

'The car will wait for another ten minutes. Please do not miss it!'

With that the caller hung up. Richard looked at the faded, beige-coloured receiver again, as if waiting for another equally sinister order to follow. After several seconds and with the gently purr of the dialling tone humming in his ear, he replaced it carefully into its receptacle.

He was in two minds: ignore the caller as some prankster who couldn't sleep, or go along with it. What about the car, that was no illusion? The fact is, he concluded thoughtfully, I don't have a choice, another clanger will surely terminate my illustrious career!

Relieved of his duties in the space programme pending court martial for misappropriation of ISSF property, a charge he vehemently denied, Richard knew that calling their bluff was a luxury he could not afford. He had to comply with this enigmatic rendezvous; he had to cooperate.

Within minutes he was dressed. Fawn coloured chinos, a white t-shirt under a dark blue crew-neck woollen pullover and his favourite polished, brogue-type brown shoes. He looked at his brief case, decided not to take it and left the room pulling his navy-blue trench coat unceremoniously from a hanger in the wardrobe. On the rebound, the wire hanger caused several others to fall to the floor, their disproportionately loud clattering seemingly amplified by the silent stillness of the deserted hotel corridor. A reverberating thump as the room door closed, added the inconsiderate finale.

Empty handed, save for his ID tag and telephonic pager, Richard walked quickly along several other narrow corridors following signs for reception. Dimly lit, dismal, depressing, the ageing hotel's best days were clearly a distant memory. Eventually, as if emerging from a labyrinth, he arrived at the head of a curved stone staircase; complimented surprisingly by an ornate Victorian cast-iron balustrade. Down two flights, before the worn treads splayed a little in order to present a sparsely furnished foyer; its deep red, wall-to-wall carpet displaying a floral design that appeared even more tired than he was.

He had thought on his arrival that this was an unlikely, even odd venue for an interview, particularly with a reporter from the highly regarded periodical *London Review*. Nevertheless, he had requested a quiet, out of town backwater for the rendezvous and this place was as unobtrusive as it got. The seven a.m. start? That too had seemed sensible at the time, helping maintain a low profile, even if it did mean him arriving the night before in order to avoid the commuter rush. He had done the commuter thing, several months of it. Never again.

Richard nodded politely at the night porter who smirked back knowingly. Subsequently and with little respect, a heavy, wooden, rotating door ejected him into the wintry street. Surprised at his reluctance to leave the dubious comforts of the Heathcliffe Hotel, he stepped out from under the twin-columned open porch and into the rain, only at this point realising that he had forgotten one essential item, his umbrella. This in itself was unusual, as few ventured outside these days without one.

A driving barrage of water soon had him cowering inside the large turned-up collar of his coat. Almost instinctively, he checked and rechecked the area, scanning the immediate nooks and crannies of this depressing milieu, something that had become a tiresome but necessary habit.

Neither surprised nor disappointed that the street appeared deserted, save of course for the mysterious driver who sat patiently in his impressive limousine some thirty metres away, Richard relaxed a little and walked towards his pick up. The car's engine sprang to life, its sound muffled by the perpetual resonance of raindrops splashing onto the pavement and surrounding puddles; the ever-present gurgling sound of water streams washing down storm drains being so conditioned in his subconscious as to barely register.

Effortlessly, the car with its long phallic bonnet, pulled up close to the curb, the nearside rear door conveniently in front of him. Richard hesitated, if there was still a decision to make, his soaking contributed positively to the process. The unusually heavy door took some effort to open. He climbed, slightly awkwardly, onto the back seat. Barely had he time to swing the door closed, when the vehicle sped off into the night.

The limousine was spacious, at least in the back. A thick glass screen, behind two rear-facing seats, separated the extravagant passenger area from the driver's; the screen was in an intermediate position, halfway. On the other side, Richard could hear the driver's heavy, regular breathing. An intricate badge of office, in the form of a crown supporting a plume of three feathers, was etched centrally into the glass; it caught his eye for a few moments. He leaned forward to study it more closely. Each feather curled forwards towards the top and below the crown were two words written inside heraldic scroll, '*Ich Dien*'.

'German I think, maybe Latin?' Richard mumbled.

There was a strong, damp, leathery smell, it seemed to engulf him; Richard's own drenched woollen coat contributing to the fusty environment.

Richard studied the driver, or what he could see of him, for several minutes. The man flagrantly ignored the auto-drive facility, the engagement of which was compulsory in urban areas. He also paid scant regard to local speed limits, a consequence of this offence being instant disqualification. Richard looked outside at the miserable conditions. He focused on the numerous roadside cameras elevated on tall, skinny poles; he felt uneasy as they watched, rotating as they passed by like giant preying mantises. Won't be long before we hear a police siren, he thought. Richard also considered the route the driver was taking to the city, hardly the most direct.

A new experience, or perhaps a forgotten one, was soon to follow however. The thick set, dark suited man responded to a message through his earpiece. He began to drive as though there was no tomorrow!

CHAPTER 1

ALLIANCE OF NECESSITY

Finally, agreement had been reached; the photographs could be taken inside the cathedral, individuals by the High Altar, beneath the Golden Window, and group shots in the Choir. Neither the Bishop nor the Dean had voiced disapproval at their last meeting, not since the order of service had been changed to accommodate a more prescribed format and consequently, guest numbers reduced. Considering the circumstances, a relaxation of the rules was appropriate. After all, Wells was one of the last dioceses in the country to see commonsense.

Rachel had hoped that the rain would abate, even temporarily, for her special day, after all, summer was fast approaching, but Richard had told her to stop dreaming and be sure to make all the internal arrangements in good time. The service and reception would be between 2 p.m. and 6 p.m. Somerset's allocation for electrical power in

May. After a year of almost continuous rain he, and most others for that matter, had given up on seeing the sun again, at least from the surface.

A few months earlier, Richard had contacted an old friend in Mauritius. The island, along with Rodrigues, St. Brandon and Reunion being the last remaining locations on earth where rain was intermittent and the sun's warmth still had an impact. At upwards of ten thousand dollars a night however, for even a modest hotel room, and no deals, Richard had long since given up on transporting friends and family to Le Morne for the ceremony. Anyway, François had informed him that the island was literally bursting at the seams with visitors, and that the government had capped the transient population in order to preserve law and order and maintain a basic level of services for its populous.

The government's other highly controversial decision, which allowed nationals to sell their right of abode, had created a temporary haven for the rich and famous, but the revenues the authorities clawed back in 'residential tax' from this wholly inappropriate law was having little impact in sustaining the island's infrastructure.

No, Richard had given up going there, or anywhere else for that matter, and was pleased to be tying the knot in his home county. Rachel too was content with the venue. Its rural location and flooded green however, would not stop the remnants of clamouring paparazzi that still pursued him, following the ISSF's disclosure of the Ark's flight manual earlier in the year. Despite his much-publicised interview on CNB News International, where he insisted that he was merely the discoverer, a delivery boy, and not a prosecutor of the divine ideal, many still believed that he was to blame for the gaping cracks now apparent in the religious bastion that was Christendom. His supporters, had he bothered to acknowledge them, a US based religious sect, continued to whip up the debate on the world stage, claiming that their beliefs were, after all, based on proven fact and not unsubstantiated historical texts.

The whole episode infuriated him and he had lost job because of it.

Religion exists because people have, since time immemorial, believed in human values and spiritual necessity; not because of mythical figures, he had stated time and time again.

Nonetheless, the big day seemed to arrive uncannily fast. Richard found himself standing with his back towards the famous Green, looking up at the two inspiring towers, modelled in perpendicular style, that flanked the glorious West Front of the Cathedral. How impressive they were; indeed the whole building was. He remembered absorbing and informative history lessons spent studying the inspiring structure during his school days and in particular one pertinent description: there are few places in the whole of the British Isles more fascinating, both to the antiquary and to the ecclesiologist, than Wells, 'City of Many Streams'. How true, he thought, as he gazed awestruck at the nine tiers of undamaged sculptures, most of heroic proportions.

'Secure in their niches for eternity,' he mumbled.

Richard glanced down at his shiny black shoes, smart creased trousers, black waistcoat and silvery-grey tie. A gold chain linked his left breast pocket to an adjacent buttonhole. He pulled the tail of his morning coat forward, more in surprise than to check its condition and lay. He looked up at the sky, sighting a rising, but ominous dark cloud above the pinnacle of the cathedral's central spire. It was then that the significance of the moment struck him; like when the swinging steel ball of a demolition crane strikes a condemned building.

'My God,' he said aloud, 'it's stopped raining, it's actually stopped raining!'

At that moment, a condensed column of bright sunlight penetrated the base of the cloud he had focused on. The dark cloud lightened, its menace dissolving into an atmosphere that for so long had courted an alliance. With a whitish-yellow glow, the pole of light blasted a distant, unsuspecting hilltop, showering it with effervescing shards of brilliance that rejuvenated Richard's spirit and lifted his heart.

'Today of all days,' he gushed.

Unable to help himself, Richard held his arms up to the sky, rejoicing at the sight of an expanding blue hole that repelled surrounding clouds like opening ripples on a pond. He looked around the ancient paved square, and to the west, across the Green, its colour vivid and inviting; a gathering clan of familiar faces beamed back at him, happy and joyful. The women looked beautiful in large hats and summer dresses. There was his mother, a broad grin on her face. Then the group to his left parted, as if a vehicle was pushing through from behind. Richard looked through the gap; to his surprise and delight, Rachel appeared. She looked absolutely stunning in a long, white, formal wedding dress with a flowing train that trailed majestically behind her as she walked slowly, almost regally towards him. Richard took her hand. He looked longingly at her face, which, partially covered by an elegant white veil, seemed somehow mystical. Those around them applauded.

'Shouldn't we meet first in the church, Rachel?' he asked, looking through the wispy veil and into her bewitching eyes.

Time seemed to stand still; her features, her expression, intoxicated him.

'Don't let it rain, Richard, not today, not on me,' Rachel replied softly.

Richard looked up at the sky, blue like a tropical sea, the sun shone down on them.

'Not today, Rachel, look,' he said, pointing upwards.

As she followed his gaze, a bellowing, heavy cloud cast its shadow over them. It gathered and conspired, masking the sun; the sky grew dark, sullen. With nothing said and seemingly from nowhere, the people around them drew umbrellas. In a fluster, they tried to open them, all at once, squabbling for space and the opportunity to take cover. Then the unthinkable happened. It began to rain. Spitting at first, the drops making small circular marks on the pavements, but within moments it grew heavy. Those around dispersed screaming; it was pouring down. Water rose around their feet; Rachel began to cry uncontrollably.

'You said it wouldn't rain, Richard, you promised.'

As she spoke icy water covered their ankles, it rose towards their knees. Rachel's dress began to fizz and bubble, she began to shrink, her body dissolving into the rising flood.

'Rachel! Rachel! Come back, I'm sorry, I'm sorry.'

Richard's head fell sharply forward as a result of sustained heavy breaking. It woke him abruptly. The pungent smell of mouldy leather and his cold, wet coat contributed to the discomfort he felt from a stiff neck and niggling headache. The uneasy sleep had done him no favours. He became aware of a face peering at him through the side window; its expression troubled and contorted against the driving rain. The man, wearing a dark green camouflaged anorak and a black sleeveless jacket, tapped on the glass with his knuckle. Silhouetted by several, bright, halogen spotlights positioned around the security checkpoint, Richard could see he was heavily armed. His standard Joint Forces 'Light Infantry Weapon' for one thing had an optional high velocity discharge sheath fitted, and a laser all-weather acquisition sight.

Richard fumbled for the switch. The soldier tapped again on the glass, this time with the barrel of his rifle, he was nervous; the driver operated Richard's electric window on his behalf, it slid open slowly, just a few inches.

'ID Sir?' said the guard bluntly, water dripping continuously from the rim of his protective helmet.

'Lieutenant Commander Reece, UK Joint Forces,' confirmed Richard, displaying his electronic tag.

The guard passed a small sensor over the tag without removing it from Richard's hand, almost instantly a tiny green light appeared on the instrument accompanied by a chirping sound.

'Thank you, Sir. You're clear,' confirmed the guard, who then looked up to acknowledge the driver with a nod, almost as if he knew him.

Immediately the window began to close. Richard thanked the guard with a facial gesture before the thick, well fitting glass pane slipped tightly back into place, relegating the figure to his solitary, monotonous duties.

For no apparent reason the car accelerated hard; for an instant the screech of its tyres broke the frosty silence between the two men. His neck forced back into the cold, clammy collar of his coat, Richard could no longer contain his discontentment.

'Where the hell are we going, and what's the rush?' he enquired tersely.

There was no answer.

'I said, *where* are we going?'

After a few seconds, the driver answered gruffly, his tone deep and gravelly.

'London!'

'Really? Can you be a little more specific?' Richard replied sarcastically.

Another period of silence followed. Reluctantly the driver responded.

'Admiralty Arch, near Trafalgar Square. That's all I am allowed to say.'

Richard could hear a Scottish accent in the man's voice, but one that had softened considerably; or perhaps one adequately disguised by his grumbling low tone.

'I know Admiralty Arch, I worked there for several months a few years ago,' continued Richard, disregarding the man's obvious preference for silence.

This time there was no response from the driver.

Conversation not one of your strong points then, thought Richard, who sat back in his seat again feeling the effects of the early hour.

He thought about the events of the previous months. Since his return to earth with an empty U-Semini case, and the Ark's log having been found in his cabin back on Mars. Why hadn't he hidden it somewhere more secure? He thought about the package that lay in his father's old workshop, placed just a few weeks earlier in a deep vehicle serving pit by his mother and hidden by heavy wooden sleepers. That fact he had not brought to light. Its contents, he felt sure, held the key to sustained human life on the planet surface, and now, free of the constraints of ESSA or ISSF, he had no intention of surrendering it, inevitably to be misappropriated, as the authorities had done the other Kalahàri crystals.

He had made his decision; the package would remain where it was until the time was right. With four crystals that he knew about already depleted to worthless zirconium by inappropriate handling and insufficiently tested reactors, it would not be long before the remaining four went the same way. Indeed, the Long Island reactor had already received its second crystal.

What were they doing with this precious, unique, resource? They could be a gift from the gods, but here were the authorities squandering their remaining potential for short-term gains. How shortsighted they were, he mused. There is a better way to utilise the crystals; at least the one I have. To prolong their life and extract their remaining energy, after all, the Babylonian stone had 'burned' for a thousand years, Admiral Urket's text in the Ark's log had stated that unequivocally.

It was political; the masses wanted their light, heat, hot water, to be able to cook; all the things that we once took for granted. Whoever promised energy, electricity, would be elected.

Richard checked the time and refocused on the changing

scenery outside the relative, albeit temporary, comfort of his limousine. They had been driving for almost forty minutes, he had unwittingly allowed himself to lose his bearings and the long, straight, signless, dual carriageway on which they were driving offered no clues.

Then he realised. There was no other road like it, not this close to London. They were driving along SPEED 1 - the Sovereign Procurement Expressway and Emergency Distributor.

The first of a number of protected and highly restricted highways, the SPEED linked major city centres directly with government defence establishments, the latter normally including barracks for contingents of the UK Rapid Reaction Defence Force. The UK Defence Force HQ was in Northwood and SPEED 1 linked it directly to Westminster. No messing, no hold ups and no congestion.

The construction of the expressway, taking almost three years, had been completed thirty years earlier, towards the end of the 'great civil unrest chapter'. At the time it was highly controversial and understandably, highly unpopular, requiring compulsory land purchase and property acquisitions by the state. Planning Permission had swept through Parliament on the back of the infamous 'Preservation of National Security' White Paper of 2012, which gave draconian powers to the police and security forces. The expressway was a means of deploying large numbers of troops from out-of-town barracks directly to the centre of the capital and the successful model had been repeated in the five major UK cities of Manchester, Birmingham, Edinburgh, Glasgow and Cardiff. It also allowed government ministers, high ranking officials and other VIPs to move quickly in and out of the major conurbations, particularly London's 'square mile'.

Richard's amazement grew as he considered the implications of using SPEED 1; as the journey would have required approval from the very highest authority, perhaps even the Prime Minister's office.

With high mortar-proof partitions on either side, it was impossible to tell where on the expressway they were. Richard leaned forward and glanced at the vehicles speedometer, eighty miles an hour, it would not take long to reach Trafalgar Square at that speed. Then he looked up at the driver's face; the man's peculiar, dark, sunken eyes and protruding forehead being clearly visible in the large rear-view mirror. There was enough light being reflected from the unusually complicated dashboard for Richard to notice heavy stress lines around his eyes, and a concerned, expectant brow. Richard continued to watch, absorbed, as the man's eyes glanced repeatedly in the mirror. He checked and rechecked the road behind; far too preoccupied to notice Richard staring at him.

After a while, the habit became such that it began to unnerve Richard. Unable to help himself, he too began glancing over his shoulder, surreptitiously at first, then growing more obvious. The road behind remained a dark, dense blackness. Richard expected nothing less at this godforsaken hour. After several minutes, Richard felt the vehicle accelerate. He looked at the speedometer again. One hundred, one hundred and ten, one hundred and twenty.

'What's the rush?' Richard probed.

By reflection, their eyes met, both focused on the mirror. For the briefest moment, they stared. The driver remained silent, but gestured over his shoulder, before concentrating once again on the road ahead. Richard turned and looked back through the small, elliptical rear window, he looked into the distance. There, almost as far back as he could see, was a pinprick of bright white light.

'Another car, just another car,' he ventured.

The driver's head shook gently from side to side.

'The road is closed, they have found us,' he uttered menacingly.

'Who has found us for god's sake?' demanded Richard, looking over his shoulder again.

The light grew brighter, closer. Richard became aware of the Jaguar's speed, its engine no longer purring, but whining, working, straining.

'This car's heavy, a ton twenty, that's the best I can do,' enlightened the driver again, his eyes now barely leaving the mirror.

The remark passed over Richard's head as he contemplated, with increasing anxiety, the ever-nearing threat. Within minutes, the growing dot of light split into two. Richard seemingly fixated, began to see the outline of a vehicle. It looked like a large sedan.

'Who the hell are they?' Richard asked.

The driver considered the question, then shrugged.

'You should be told, for what good it will do you,' he answered.

'Well?'

'Spheron, it's Spheron, an assassination cell.'

Read the complete book -
available from M*Press books*.

Author's Note

My background is aviation, both helicopters and aeroplanes. I fixed them for a few years, but have flown them for many more. I have always liked science, machines, technology and Mother Earth, although not necessarily in that order.

Speaking of science, some in this book is fact; most, however, is fiction. If only it were that simple. As for the book itself, it really is all fiction, although it is obvious that we humans will have to change our ways sooner, rather than later.

The county of Somerset and some of the places mentioned herein, are however, quite real. Please, come and see.

Thanks to my family: Sandra, Laura and Aron, encouragement comes in many guises. Thanks to my good friend David Marr, fellow aviator and avid reader, the first person to read my first book. Both admiration and sincere thanks to Sarah Flight of Sutton Publishing, for wading through the first draft, editor extraordinaire. Finally, thanks to Matt and James at Core Creative and Martin Bester at Haynes, for their skill and patience.

I wish my father had known about this work. He was with us when I started it, but sadly, not when I finished. I never mentioned it. To my mum, simply the best.

Fond memories of Nigel.

Until the next *time* . . .